England's Perfect Hero

Also by Suzanne Enoch
in Large Print:

London's Perfect Scoundrel
The Rake

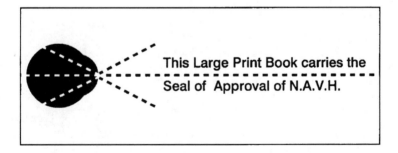

This Large Print Book carries the
Seal of Approval of N.A.V.H.

England's Perfect Hero

Lessons in Love

SUZANNE ENOCH

Thorndike Press • Waterville, Maine

Published in 2004 by arrangement with Avon Books, an imprint of HarperCollins Publishers, Inc.

Thorndike Press® Large Print Core.

The tree indicium is a trademark of Thorndike Press.

The text of this Large Print edition is unabridged.
Other aspects of the book may vary from the original edition.

Set in 16 pt. Plantin by Al Chase.

Printed in the United States on permanent paper.

Library of Congress Cataloging-in-Publication Data

Enoch, Suzanne.
    England's perfect hero / Suzanne Enoch.
        p. cm.
    ISBN 0-7862-7004-7 (lg. print : hc : alk. paper)
    1. Aristocracy (Social class) — Fiction.   2. England —
Fiction.   3. Large type books.   I. Title.
PS3555.N655E54 2004
    813′.6—dc22   2004057990

For Nancy Bailey, Sheryl Law,
Sally Wulf, and Sharon Lyon —
the best lunch support group ever.
Thanks, guys.

As the Founder/CEO of NAVH, the only national health agency solely devoted to those who, although not totally blind, have an eye disease which could lead to serious visual impairment, I am pleased to recognize Thorndike Press* as one of the leading publishers in the large print field.

Founded in 1954 in San Francisco to prepare large print textbooks for partially seeing children, NAVH became the pioneer and standard setting agency in the preparation of large type.

Today, those publishers who meet our standards carry the prestigious "Seal of Approval" indicating high quality large print. We are delighted that Thorndike Press is one of the publishers whose titles meet these standards. We are also pleased to recognize the significant contribution Thorndike Press is making in this important and growing field.

Lorraine H. Marchi, L.H.D.
Founder/CEO
NAVH

* Thorndike Press encompasses the following imprints: Thorndike, Wheeler, Walker and Large Print Press.

Prologue

Rain began tapping harder against the window, as if trying to be heard over the argument inside Lucinda Barrett's drawing room.

"We should write these down," Lucinda said, raising her voice to be heard both over the summer shower and the debate. She and her rather vocal friends all agreed that most men had no idea how to act as gentlemen, but realizing that fact obviously caused nothing but frustration and a great deal of annoyance. Time, then, to take action.

She pulled several sheets of paper from a drawer and returned to the table, handing one blank page to Georgiana, another to Evelyn, and keeping one for herself. "The three of us wield a great deal of influence, particularly with the so-called gentlemen to whom these rules would apply," she continued.

"And we would be doing other ladies a service," Georgiana Halley said, her annoyed expression growing more thoughtful.

"But a list won't do anything for anyone but ourselves," Evie Ruddick countered, though she took the pencil Lucinda handed her anyway. "If that."

"Oh, yes, it will — when we put our rules into practice," Georgiana returned. "I propose that we each choose some man and teach him what he needs to know to properly impress a lady."

Now, that made sense. "Yes, by God," Lucinda agreed, thumping her fist on the table.

Georgiana chuckled as she began writing. "We could get our rules published. 'Lessons in Love,' by Three Ladies of Distinction."

Lucinda's List

1. *When speaking to a lady, a man should be attentive and not gaze about the room while he's conversing, as if looking for someone more interesting to come along.*

2. *At a dance, a gentleman should dance and interact. Attending an event for the sole purpose of staring or of being*

seen — especially when some ladies are left lacking partners — is rude.

3. *A gentleman should look for interests in more than just the latest popular trend. A fine mind is more interesting than a well-tied cravat.*

4. *Simply because a gentleman is courting a lady doesn't mean he has to agree with everything her father says — though he should still be respectful, even behind her father's back.*

"This is fun," Evelyn said, blowing on her page to remove the excess pencil lead.

"I do have a question, though," Lucinda said, examining what she'd written. "If we create three perfect men, are we doing Society a favor, or harming every other man's chances of finding a mate?"

Georgie chuckled. "Oh, Luce. The question is whether or not any man can be taught to behave for the sake of gaining a lady's admiration and respect."

"Yes, but if we do train these hypothetical men, we should at least have an idea about what we are going to do with them afterward," Lucinda countered. "After all, I have to assume that we'll succeed."

"You have more confidence than I do, Luce, but then Georgie and I have brothers." Evie smiled. "Which isn't necessarily something to boast about."

"And I have a general for a father."

"I declare us all equally fit for the challenge." Georgiana slid her paper clockwise, taking Lucinda's in turn. "These are good." They all took turns reading each other's lists, and Lucinda, at least, was struck by how . . . personal they were. And how like their authors.

"So who goes first?" Evelyn asked.

All three ladies looked at one another, then burst out laughing. "Well, I know one thing," Lucinda said. "We won't have a shortage of potential students from which to choose."

Chapter 1

I never saw a man in so
wretched a condition.

— Robert Walton, *Frankenstein*

Fourteen months later

"No, I don't think you cheated, Evie, and I wish you'd stop saying it." Lucinda Barrett sent her friend an exasperated look as she settled deeper into the window seat.

"I know," Evie replied, "but I only intended on delivering lessons to a scoundrel. And now I've ended up married to him." With a scowl she rose, striding toward Lucinda's refuge and back again. "I mean, for heaven's sake, less than two months ago I was plain old dull Evie Ruddick, and now I'm the Marchioness of St. Aubyn. I can't even believe —"

11

"You were never plain or dull, Evie," Georgiana interrupted as she glided into the drawing room and signaled her butler to close the door behind her. "And as for apologizing, firstly I'm late for my own tea, and secondly I seem to have married the object of *my* lesson as well."

Lucinda grinned. "Neither of which is an offense for which you need to apologize, Georgie."

Smiling, Georgiana motioned Evie to a seat on the couch and sank carefully down beside her. "Perhaps, but a little over a year ago I would have shot anyone who even suggested I would marry Tristan Carroway. And now here I sit, Lady Dare — and two months away from bringing yet another Carroway into the world."

Evelyn chuckled. "Perhaps it'll be a girl."

"That would only begin to even the odds against me." Georgie shifted, plainly uncomfortable. "I'll never understand how Tristan's mother could be brave enough to produce four more boys after the example he set. If not for his aunts, I should be completely outnumbered — and they've abandoned me to take the waters at Bath."

"Speaking of the Carroway brothers," Lucinda said, knowing she was deliberately stalling, now that she'd finally decided to tell her friends about her own plans, "did I hear you say that Lieutenant Carroway is due back in London?"

"Yes. Bradshaw's ship should be in Brighton by the end of the week. He's hoping for a new assignment to the West Indies, of all places." Georgie narrowed her eyes. "Why do you want to know about Shaw? You've decided on him for your lesson, haven't you?"

"Good heavens, no." Lucinda's cheeks warmed. "Can you imagine my father's re- action if I began paying attention to a Navy man? Not that delivering a lesson means im- minent marriage, of course."

Evie snorted. "The odds do seem fixed in that direction."

Georgie's gaze was more speculative. "Nor is that possibility something you should ignore." She sipped her tea, gazing at Lucinda over the rim of the cup like some all-seeing blonde-haired gypsy girl. "You have decided on a student."

"Oh, I knew it!" Evie seconded, ap- plauding. "Who is the villain?"

Hesitating, Lucinda looked from one suc- cessful lesson deliverer and happily married friend to the other. What would they say if they knew she'd watched their maneuverings with a combination of interest and growing jealousy? Did they realize that since Evie had married St. Aubyn she'd been on the lookout for a student of her own? And not so much one in need of a lesson as one she wanted to marry. She sighed. Of course they realized it. They were her closest friends.

"Well, I have narrowed down the search," she hedged.

Yes, she'd narrowed it down — to one.

"Tell us," Georgiana pressed. "This whole lesson thing was mostly your idea, anyway. No more delays, my dear."

"I know, I know. It's just —"

"And no excuses," Evie interrupted.

"Fine." Lucinda took a deep breath. "It's Lord Geoffrey Newcombe." She closed her mouth to wait and to watch.

Lord Geoffrey, the Duke of Fenley's fourth son, was quite possibly the most beautiful man she'd ever seen. Other ladies of the same opinion referred to him simply as "the Adonis." Curling golden hair, light green eyes, broad shoulders, and a smile that could charm a cobra — it was no wonder that women threw themselves at him with nearly calculated regularity.

And that was the problem. The choice was so obviously directed more toward matrimony than lesson giving. Dozens of more poorly behaved single gentlemen practically littered Mayfair, after all. John Talbott, for example. What did it matter if he only had one eyebrow that ran almost ear to ear? Or there was Phillip R —

"Lord Geoffrey," Georgiana said slowly. "He's a splendid choice."

"Yes," Evie seconded with her pixie smile. "I agree."

Relief made Lucinda's shoulders sag. "Thank you. I really have given this a great deal of thought. I mean, he's a war hero — a fact of which my father would certainly approve — and he's quite handsome, but at the same time he could definitely use a few lessons. He's arrogant and insensitive. . . ." She trailed off. "I'm being terribly obvious about why I chose him, I'm afraid."

"No, you're not," Evelyn countered. "You're being brilliant, as usual. I mean, how can you ignore the fact that Georgie and I both fell in love with and married our students? You *have* to take that into consideration."

Georgie was nodding. "Nor can you ignore the fact that you and your father are quite close, and that General Barrett would have to have some fondness for whomever you decided to take on as a student, whether you thought anything beyond your lessons

15

might occur, or not."

"Exactly," Lucinda said, smiling at the effort her friends were willing to go through to justify her choice. "As far as I can tell, the general thinks highly of Lord Geoffrey socially, and I know he worries that I'll be left all alone when he hops the twig, as he puts it."

Rising awkwardly to bring the teapot to Lucinda, Georgiana chuckled. "I've never seen you make a false step, Luce. How can we help?"

"Oh, I think I can man—" Tea overflowed her cup and splashed onto the saucer and the front of her gown. "Georgie!"

The viscountess jumped, righting the teapot and tearing her gaze from the window. "Oh! I'm so sorry! It's just — look!"

Out on the front drive Georgiana's youngest brother-in-law, ten-year-old Edward, was climbing onto the seat of a high-perch racing phaeton. Helping him was Evie's new husband, the Marquis of St. Aubyn.

"Saint," Evie gasped, sprinting for the door. "That blasted team will pull Edward's arms off! Saint!"

Georgie was close on her heels. "Edward! Don't you dare —"

Chuckling, Lucinda carefully set aside her overflowing tea cup. "Don't mind me,"

16

she muttered, standing. "I've only a gallon of hot tea spilled down my front."

Over the last year she'd come to know Carroway House almost as well as her own, and with a last glance to make certain no one was killing anyone on the front drive, she made her way upstairs to one of the spare bedchambers.

She didn't know how Georgiana coped with Dare, his four younger brothers, and his two aunts, but her friend seemed to thrive on the chaos — as did Evie in the face of Saint's continuing devilry. Of course, since Lucinda had been five, Barrett House had meant just her and her father, General Augustus Barrett. She was far more used to quiet than to the continual uproar Georgie faced.

Dipping a cloth in a washbowl, she dabbed at the tea stain running down her front. "Blast, blast, blast," she muttered, frowning into the mirror at the darkening splotch across the bosom of her green muslin walking dress.

A slight movement in the mirror's reflection caught her attention. Blue eyes, as deep as the bottomless northern lakes in summertime, gazed at her. With a start she turned around.

"Oh, my goodness! I'm so sorry. I didn't mean to . . ."

He was a Carroway brother, of course. *The* Carroway, as far as the rumormongers were concerned. He sat in a chair by the window, an open book in one hand.

Robert. The middle brother. The one who'd been wounded at Waterloo. The one the wags said wasn't quite "right." She could count on one hand the number of times she'd seen him in public since he'd returned from the war. And she'd barely spoken a word to him since then, even at Georgie and Tristan's wedding.

Slowly he closed the book and stood. "My fault," he said in a low, ill-used voice. "Excuse me."

"Don't go," she said, blushing as she belatedly lowered the cloth from her bosom. "I'm just making repairs. I'm afraid your brother Edward is determined to learn to drive a racing phaeton, despite Georgiana's objections."

He paused halfway to the door. "He threw tea on you?"

"Oh, heavens no. Georgie saw him through the window conspiring with St. Aubyn and spilled on me." Chuckling, she made another dab in a more dignified spot. "Apparently I should have ducked."

How had he known it was tea? She remembered the whispers that said those blue eyes could see right through you. *Nonsense.* He'd smelled it, or something.

Dark azure assessed her for another moment. The gauntness in his face had faded in the three years he'd been home, but he was still lean and wary — like a wolf, she thought abruptly. And rumor or not, that gaze was most . . . unsettling.

His jaw clenched, then with a visible effort he lowered the straight line of his shoulders. "Have you chosen yet?"

She looked at him blankly. "Chosen what?"

With what looked like a wince, the cobalt gaze broke from hers. "Nothing. Good afternoon." With a few steps of his long, slightly limping stride he was gone out the door.

Lucinda looked at the empty doorway for a moment, then glanced at the book he'd left on the windowsill. *Frankenstein, or the Modern Prometheus,* by Mary Shelley. The edges of the pages were worn, and the back broken as though he — or someone — had read it almost completely into ruin.

"Luce?"

"I'm in here," she returned.

A moment later Georgie entered the room. "Did I drown you? Is the tea coming out?"

She shook herself and went back to dabbing. "No, you didn't drown me. How's Edward?"

Lady Dare sighed. "Careening down the street with St. Aubyn holding the reins. I'm so sorry I spilled on you."

"No harm done." Lucinda hesitated. "Georgie, have you told anyone about our lessons?"

The viscountess frowned. "Just Tristan, and only about me. Why?"

Why, indeed? Was that what Robert Carroway had been asking her about? Hm. Not unless he truly *could* read minds. "No reason. I was just wondering. There. That's about as good as it'll get."

Lucinda followed Georgiana back down the hallway. As they started downstairs she glanced behind her — just in time to see a pair of broad shoulders vanish back into the bedchamber.

"Georgiana," she continued in a low voice as they reached the bottom of the stairs, "how is Tristan's brother these days? Robert, I mean."

"Bit?" The viscountess shrugged. "He seems to be feeling well. His limp's nearly gone. Why?"

"Oh, nothing. I just . . . spotted him upstairs. He —"

"He makes an impression, I know," Lady Dare said softly. "I hope he didn't fright—"

"No! Of course not. He just surprised me." Still, as they entered the drawing room again, she couldn't help looking back up the stairs. What had he asked her? And if it was regarding what she suspected, then how had he known?

Robert Carroway moved to the head of the stairs as Georgiana and Miss Barrett returned to their friend Evelyn and the drawing room. Georgie made excuses for him. He'd heard her do it before, but that was the closest he'd heard her come to apologizing. He knew Tristan, Georgie, Shaw, Andrew, the aunties — they all had an answer ready if someone happened to inquire about him, or more likely, about his absence.

At least Tristan had asked whether he wanted to go to Tattersall's this morning; Tristan always asked if he wanted to join them, and if he didn't, Georgiana did. He wondered how long it would be before his continued refusals discouraged them from asking at all. Sometimes he only agreed so they wouldn't give up completely.

His own family might not understand, but they let him sit quietly when he wanted to, and they let him leave when he felt the walls closing in. Guests, though, or crowds, meant polite conversation about the weather and fashion and any other meaningless idiocy they could conjure to waste time with. He shuddered just thinking about it.

Gripping his book, he limped back down the hallway to the guest bedchamber. His own room left him more comfortable, but he liked the cool afternoon breeze. And besides, he could hear the three ladies down in the drawing room when they laughed. He could hear Lucinda when she laughed. He wondered what she would say if she realized he made a point of being close by whenever she came to call on Georgiana.

"And what the hell does that matter?" he muttered aloud, automatically glancing toward the open door as he spoke. *Stop it.* He was home, in England. In London. No one was going to withhold food and water or beat him bloody for daring to speak. No one had done that for three years. He was free; he was safe.

"Stop it," he said, forcing his gaze to remain on the book, refusing to acknowledge that he was glad it was still light outside, or that he desperately wanted to disappear into his own room and lock the door. "Stop it. Stop —"

"Have I chosen what?"

He flinched, whipping his head up and around to face the doorway again. Just as quickly he lurched to his feet, before his mind even registered that he was going to do so. "Miss Barrett."

He'd always thought her hair brown, until she walked forward into the late afternoon sunlight pouring across the floor. Red highlights glinted through the swooping riot of curls piled atop her head. A curling strand had escaped to caress a high-boned cheek. Her skin looked smooth and soft as cream.

"I'm sorry," she said, her fair skin darkening to rose as she blushed. "I didn't mean to startle you."

Several seconds passed before Robert realized both that he was staring again and that she expected him to respond. "I should have heard you coming."

Soft hazel eyes studied him, while he waited for the inevitable comment on the weather. Usually this far into a conversation — if he stayed for this long — he saw discomfort, or contempt, or fear, or worst of all, pity. Lucinda Guinevere Barrett, though, gave a small smile.

"For the past week the general's been reading a study on the tactics of American

Indians — the Iroquois, specifically. He greatly admires their stealth, so I've been practicing sneaking up on him. Apparently I'm better at it than I realized."

General Augustus Barrett — another of the reasons Robert rarely attended social events. With an effort, he wrenched his mind away from the abrupt haze of blazing muskets and smoke and screaming, back to the tall, slender woman who still stood in the doorway and had the misfortune to be Barrett's daughter. *Say something.* "Your student," he blurted, then clenched his teeth together just too late to stop his idiocy from escaping into the air.

She blinked. "Beg pardon?"

Clarify, he shouted at himself. *For God's sake, you know how to put a sentence together.* "I meant, have you chosen your student yet?"

Her fine blush paled. "How — what — how did you know about that?"

Lucinda's aghast expression actually left him feeling a little more at ease. It was a look he'd become familiar with over the past three years — though usually it also signaled the moment he'd said something rude and direct and then turned on his heel and vanished. This afternoon she blocked the doorway, and he seemed to be staying. Part of him actually wanted to stay, so long as she remained. Robert shrugged. "I pay attention. Georgiana chose Tristan, and your friend Miss Ruddick decided on St. Aubyn — which worried you and my sister-in-law."

"We . . . we weren't that obvious, were we?"

He liked that she didn't try to deny their scheme. "No. You weren't."

"You . . ." She cleared her throat. "You haven't said anything about this to anyone else, have you?"

Robert felt his mouth curve upward in a motion that felt stiff and not quite natural. "I generally don't say anything to anyone, Miss Barrett."

Her expression softened into another smile that must have far surpassed his in elegance and attractiveness. "Thank you. It would be . . . embarrassing for all of us if the gossips were to find out that we've been making lists and taking on students."

Lists. He hadn't known about lists. Robert wondered what hers said. With the ease of long practice he hid a frown. She probably required a good conversationalist — or at least someone who could put two sentences end to end. "Your secret is safe." He waited a beat. "But have you?"

"Have I?" she repeated, then ducked her

head in obvious chagrin. "Oh. Chosen a student, you mean. Yes, I have."

He hesitated again. Did he sound as inept, as distant and desperate as he felt, trying to carry on a civil conversation? This used to be so easy. "May I ask who it is?"

Even as he was congratulating himself on being polite and proper and grammatically correct, Lucinda's face shuttered and she backed away a step. *Damnation.* After three years back in England he should have realized that he had no idea how to behave in a civilized manner, any more than he had an inclination to do so. Usually. Until this afternoon — when Lucinda Barrett had sought him out to continue a conversation.

"I'm sorr—"

"Lord Geoffrey Newcombe," she said, over his apology.

"You want to marry Geoffrey Newcombe?" he returned, surprised at her choice. "Why, in God's name?"

She flushed again, not quite as prettily. "We decided on lessons in order to teach a man to be a gentleman. The idea is to see whether I can convince or persuade him to conform to the items on my list. That's all."

"So the ultimate outcome isn't supposed to be marri—"

"No! I hope you don't think I would ever

26

attempt to trick someone into marrying me."

"I —"

"I have no need to stoop to such a low level, sir. And I do not appreciate the implication." Turning on her heel, she stalked out. A moment later her feet clomped down the stairs. Evidently she wasn't trying to be stealthy any longer.

Robert stood where he was for a moment, then squatted to retrieve the book he hadn't even realized he'd dropped. Bloody hell. Obviously he wasn't any more ready to make a return to Society than he'd been three years ago. And until five minutes ago, except for a few fleeting daydreams which had involved the woman he'd just insulted, he wouldn't have cared.

Robert reopened his book, gazing sightlessly at the page. He'd felt almost . . . human when Lucinda had smiled. It was a sensation he could grow used to. Sitting back, he lifted his gaze to the window. Logically, if he ever expected her to smile in his presence again, he needed to apologize. And soon, when it would still make a difference.

Chapter 2

He must have been a noble creature
in his better days, being even now
in wreck so attractive and amiable.

— Robert Walton, *Frankenstein*

Lucinda arrived at the Wellcrist soiree in the
company of her father. A year and a half ago,
General Barrett would have pronounced the
festivities a bore and elected to go instead to a
club with some of his political friends. A year
and a half ago, however, his daughter had
had other people with whom to attend the
Season's events.

Then, she and Georgiana and Evelyn had
been practically inseparable — the Three
Sisters, as a great many members of the *ton*
had called them. Now, though, fond as they
all remained of one another, Georgie and
Evie had found love — and with that, obli-

gations elsewhere. The general had realized that almost before Lucinda had, and like any good military strategist, he'd altered his tactics to fit the new situation. He obviously worried about her; she knew that, simply by his presence tonight. And the fact that he was worried, worried her.

Hence Lord Geoffrey Newcombe.

The lessons gave her an excuse, if only in her own mind, a justification for approaching Geoffrey. Even so, she knew full well why she'd chosen him. The general wanted to see her happy and well cared for, and she wanted to remain in the position of both easing his mind and of being able to look after him. That had been her self-appointed duty to an increasing degree — interrupted only when he went off to war — since she'd been five.

After careful consideration, she'd decided that marriage to the Duke of Fenley's fourth and youngest son was a nearly perfect solution. She liked him, her father liked him, and her dowry together with his stipend would see them settled quite comfortably. In addition, he didn't seem to be weighted down with any particularly bad habits or gambling debts. Safe and steady, amiable and uncomplicated — and not likely to add another burden to her busy life or to resent her duties to or affection for her father.

"Ah, there's Admiral Hunt with that up-start Carroway," the general said, a marshal gleam coming into his steel gray eyes. "Time to go sink the Navy."

Bradshaw Carroway had managed to make it back to London early, not that his resourcefulness surprised her. In fact, if not for his naval career, the charming lieutenant might have made it to the top of her candidates' list. Marrying a Navy man, though, would give her father an apoplexy. "Be nice to the admiral, Papa," she warned, only half joking. "No brawls."

"Of course not. Verbal abuse only, my dear." He hesitated. "Unless you'd rather —"

She waved him off, not waiting for him to offer to stand about with her all evening. "Go."

Delivering a swift kiss to her cheek, he strode away to confront his oldest friend and greatest rival. Poor Lieutenant Bradshaw Carroway was about to be caught in the crossfire. Smiling, Lucinda looked toward the refreshment table, and her grin deepened. She started forward to greet Evelyn, only to slow when Lord St. Aubyn appeared beside his bride, two glasses of Madeira in his hands. Lucinda sighed.

Three had used to be company. Now, though —

"Miss Barrett," a male voice said from behind her.

With a start she turned around, looking into the round, smiling face of her most determined suitor. "Mister Henning," she returned, nodding. Abruptly she couldn't decide which was worse — being the third member of a happy pair, or being the second member in an unwilling pair.

"Please call me Francis. No need for formality between us, eh?" He glanced at the dance card in her hand before she could conceal it. "Ah, I see you still have a waltz free. Splendid. Will you do me the honor? My grandmama's in attendance — you'll have to come by and say hello. The old gal dotes on me, you know, and seeing me with a chit as lovely as you, well, she's bound to be pleased."

The last thing Lucinda wanted to do tonight was be roped into conversation with tyrannical Agnes Henning, but she nodded anyway. "Let me sort myself out, and I'll certainly come by and say hello," she returned, favoring Francis with a dazzling smile and then slipping away before he could remind her about the waltz.

"That was close," a deep, less familiar

voice said at her shoulder.

Mm. The evening abruptly began to look up. "Lord Geoffrey," she said, curtsying, and pleased by the faint tremor that ran down her spine.

Much-admired eyes of dazzling emerald swept down the front of her low-cut maroon gown and back up again to her face. "Lucinda Barrett. Allow me to compliment you on that brilliant bit of strategy against Henning. Here I was about to rescue you from him, and all on your own you managed to avoid putting him on your dance card."

She blushed, wishing that for his own sake Henning had picked a less conspicuous place to accost her. She certainly hadn't wanted to embarrass him. "Oh, I didn't —"

"Which means, if I'm not mistaken, that you have a waltz left open. May I?" Reaching out, he lifted the card and pencil from her hand and wrote in his name. "That's our goal for tonight," he continued, nodding at the group of young men surrounding debutante Elizabeth Fairchild, "to keep Henning off the dance floor. The man's a danger to everything on two legs."

"Well, Mr. Henning may step on a toe or two," she returned, hiding a frown as she noticed Georgie smiling at her from the far side of the room, "but he's hardly the only —"

"One buffoon at a time, Lucinda. Once he learns his lesson, we'll move on to the next." Lord Geoffrey bowed over her hand, a lock of golden hair obscuring one twinkling eye. "Until the waltz."

As he left, the rest of his friends mobbed her, until she managed to save only one spot for poor Francis Henning. Little as she enjoyed dancing with Mr. Henning, she disliked the idea of someone being blackballed from the festivities even more — especially with his grandmother here from Yorkshire.

She glanced at Lord Geoffrey's broad shoulders as he maneuvered his way onto yet another young lady's dance card. Hm. Poor behavior from the man she'd chosen to teach a lesson. At least now she could cite a legitimate reason for deciding on him.

"Luce," Georgiana said, dragging her husband, Lord Dare, up beside her. "A good beginning, yes?" she whispered, kissing Lucinda on the cheek.

"Hush."

"Very well." The viscountess straightened. "I saw the general over talking with Admiral Hunt. Do we need to intervene?"

"Nonsense," Dare interjected. "Shaw looks petrified. A little terror will be good for my dear brother."

Lucinda chuckled. "Papa promised no bloodshed." She looked more closely at Georgiana, taking in her friend's rosy cheeks and the pronounced roundness of her hips. "And I thought you were going to stay in tonight," she chastised. "It's far too cold outside."

"That's what I told her," Dare returned, lifting his wife's hand to kiss her fingers. "She insists on spending every possible moment dancing with me."

"My poor, deluded Tristan," Georgiana said with an amused smile, drawing her hand around his arm. "I'm here for the desserts."

His expression warmed. "Desserts, eh? As a matter of fact, I know of a very tasty . . ." He trailed off as he glanced past his wife's shoulder. "What in the world is *he* doing here?"

Lucinda turned to follow his surprised, serious expression. Just inside the ballroom doorway, clothed in fashionable dark gray and with a cold, haunted look on his lean face, stood Robert Carroway.

"My goodness," Georgiana whispered. "Do you think something's wrong at home?"

"I'll find out."

Before Dare could move, though, Robert

saw them and disappeared back into the crowd with such ease that it startled Lucinda. Even as she wondered why the middle Carroway brother would bother to make an appearance only to vanish again without a word, he slipped between Lord Northrum and Lady Bryce and was there beside them.

"Bit?" Dare said in a low voice, obviously not as surprised by his brother's stealth as Lucinda was. "Is everything all right?"

Robert nodded. "I was invited, you know."

"I know that," his brother retorted. "But —"

"Bit!" Bradshaw shoved through the sea of guests. "Snap my anchor — what the devil are you doing here?"

" 'Snap my anchor?' " Dare repeated, more humor touching his voice. "My, aren't you nautical."

"I —"

"I wanted a word with Miss Barrett," Robert interrupted.

Lucinda took in Dare's lifted eyebrow and the blatantly surprised expressions on Bradshaw and Georgiana's faces. At the same time, the bleak desperation in Robert's gaze made her answer. "Of course, Mr. Carroway."

"Bit, if you —"

"Later," he said shortly, gesturing for Lucinda to join him.

"No wonder people say you're a phantom," she offered. "That was quite impressive, stealthwise."

He didn't answer, nor did he offer his arm, but the omission didn't bother her. Being near him unsettled her quite enough. Touching him would probably scorch her skin.

Gazes from a number of their more curious peers followed them until Robert slowed and shot a glare over his shoulder. Abruptly, then, they found themselves alone at the base of the main staircase. He faced her, looking at her for a long moment, dark blue eyes glinting beneath the faded chandelier light. "I came to apologize," he said finally. "For yesterday."

Her first impulse, to tell him an apology wasn't necessary and that she'd scarcely given their brief conversation a second thought, never passed her lips. It had lingered with him, obviously, or he would never have come to find her. "Thank you," she said slowly. "You were direct, but given how much you know about our lesson challenge, your conclusion was completely logical."

"I was rude."

She couldn't help her slight smile at this tall, magnificent, unsettling man insisting upon deprecating himself before her. "You caught me off guard, as any good soldier would do."

His body gave a slight shudder. "I am *not* a good soldier." With a curt nod he finally glanced again at the muttering crowd in the doorway. "Good evening."

"I have a quadrille left on my dance card," she said to his back as he turned away, "if you'd care to join me."

He stopped. "Give it to Henning," he murmured over his shoulder. "They're blackballing him."

"I know, and I was going to. I just thought you might want . . ." Before she could finish speaking he was gone, out of sight again, though for all she knew he might be standing directly behind her. Lucinda glanced over her shoulder. No one. "Hm."

When she'd had her London debut six years ago, twenty-one-year-old Robert Carroway had danced a quadrille with her. She wondered if he remembered. He'd only been an occasional visitor to London that Season, when he'd come down from school at Cambridge. She remembered him as a fine dancer, a devastatingly handsome, popular young man with a great deal of wit and a promising future. Then, however, he'd joined the army to go to war against Bonaparte.

"Lucinda?" Georgiana said, reaching her side. "Is everything well?"

"Yes, perfectly." She shook herself. "He thought he'd offended me yesterday, and wanted to apologize."

"Had he? Offended you, I mean."

"Heavens, no. Just a difference of opinion."

" 'Opinion,' " Georgiana repeated.

Lucinda took her arm, smiling. "Yes. And now I would like a glass of Madeira. I've conversed with Robert Carroway twice in one week, and we should make as much a mystery of it as possible." She chuckled, steeling herself for the noise and crowd of the ballroom, when she really just wanted a few quiet moments. "Maybe it will even make Lord Geoffrey jealous."

"Speaking of," her friend muttered, gesturing with her chin.

The golden Adonis emerged from the crowd and separated her from Georgie. "Our waltz is beginning," he said, all charm and good humor.

"Oh! I'm sorry. I hadn't realized."

"Understandable, considering."

His arm slid around her waist, and she hid

her slight smile. She'd only been joking with Georgiana about making anyone jealous — though Robert Carroway *was* a sight to please any woman's eyes. "Considering what?"

"Well, first the mute's appearance, and then the fact that he spoke — and to you," he clarified, bending his fingers around hers as they swung into the dance. "I half thought he'd died, and Dare had buried him in the cellar or something."

"That's nonsense," she said, annoyed until she realized his insensitivity — shared by most of the *ton* as it was — merely provided her with a further example of his need for her lessons. "He's simply a wounded soldier."

"I took a ball in the arm myself, at Waterloo," he countered, then offered her a jaunty smile. "Stung like the devil. Shall I tell you about my heroic actions?"

Lucinda knew he'd been shot; everyone did. She'd even heard the tale before. Still, as he smiled his dazzling smile at her, she decided that having him regale her with one of his amusing, heroic stories would be a good way for her to judge her starting strategy — and to forget the haunting gaze of a quite different soldier. "Please do," she said.

★ ★ ★

Robert detoured on his way back to Carroway House, stopping for a long moment at the edge of Hyde Park. At past midnight no one reputable would be on the grounds, and with a slight exhalation of breath that fogged the cold night air, he loosed the reins of his gelding and tapped him in the ribs. Muscles bunched beneath the sleek bay hide, and with a leap they were off.

Tolley charged at a dead run along the dim moonlit foot path, and Robert leaned forward along his withers, half closing his eyes at the wind on his face. Everything around them felt still and silent — the creak of leather and the pounding of hooves and the grunt of Tolley's breath seemed the only sounds in the world.

On nights like this, when he rode out from the dark, silent house to the dark, deserted park, he could forget. He could be nothing but a solitary rider on a fast horse, wind in his face and the world open around him. No walls, no bars, no quiet weeping or screams or death. None of that could catch him. On a night like this, none of it could find him.

Finally, when he felt Tolley's breathing become more labored and his stride shorten, he slowed and turned for home.

The grooms were asleep, but he preferred that, anyway. In silence he rubbed down the bay, gave him an apple, and returned him to his stall. The front door would be unlocked, awaiting Tristan, Georgiana, and Shaw, and he slipped through noiselessly.

"Where the devil have you been?"

He flinched, forcing tensed muscles to relax again as he recognized the young voice. "What the devil are you doing out of bed?" he returned, facing the stairs and the slim figure straightening from his seat on the bottommost step.

"I asked first," Edward stated, with every ounce of authority his ten years could command. "I'll have you know I've been sitting here for over an hour, while you were off who knows where, doing who knows what."

If it had been Tristan or Bradshaw or even Andrew standing there interrogating him, Robert would already have been upstairs with his door locked behind him. But Edward, shivering in his nightshirt and clutching a metal soldier almost hidden in one fist, was a different story.

"I had an errand, Runt," he said, sweeping the boy into a hug and steeling himself against the tightness of the thin arms that wrapped around his neck.

"Well, I was worried about you. I'm really

41

not old enough to be the man of the house, you know, but everyone else is gone."

Robert slung his brother over his shoulder and climbed the stairs, refusing to wince at the additional strain on his bad knee. One brother still saw him as undamaged, and he'd be damned before he let that change. Deeper down he knew he'd be damned *if* that changed. "What woke you up?"

"I dreamed that Shaw's ship sank."

"Shaw's dancing at the Wellcrist ball right now. Yell at him tomorrow for not waking you up when he got home early."

"I will yell at him," Edward returned sleepily as they reached his bedchamber. "You're not going out again?"

Robert set him on the bed and pulled up the covers as the boy snuggled against the pillows. "No. Good night, Runt."

"Good night, Bit."

As he closed Edward's door and went down the hall to his own bedchamber, Robert wondered why the Runt had settled on him, of all people, to rely on for comfort. Yes, he was there most of the time, but he'd hardly characterize himself as reliable. Still, the other brothers teased Edward for his fear of being alone in the house — after all, how could he think himself alone in a building full of servants, plus the aunties when they were in town?

Five years ago, Robert wasn't certain he would have been able to answer that question, either. But then five years ago he'd never heard of Chateau Pagnon — or of *le comte* General Jean-Paul Barrere.

As he shed his jacket he paced to the window and shoved it open. The nearly dead fire glowed deeper red behind the stone hearth and then faded again in the rush of cold air, but he ignored the sudden chill. Unless it was snowing he needed the fresh air to sleep — even what passed for fresh air in London.

A short time later he lay back in his soft bed, arms crossed behind his head. So Lucinda Barrett had been serious about setting her sights on Lord Geoffrey Newcombe. He'd stayed to watch, and the two of them had looked good, waltzing together at the Wellcrist soiree. *She'd* looked good, smiling and chatting with her many friends, a diamond among gemstones.

Robert sighed. He shouldn't have ridiculed her choice of student, talking as though he had any grasp on what made someone acceptable, any longer. She'd been kind and had accepted his apology, and she'd even asked him to stay. Just the fact that he'd been able to force himself to attend the soiree and talk to her with some measure of decorum surprised him.

He turned on his side, facing the window. A day ago he wouldn't have been able to imagine himself voluntarily attending a meaningless, crowded waste of time like that. It had been difficult, very difficult, but he'd managed it. And he knew why.

He hadn't been thinking of the close walls and the crowd and the heat and the blathering nonsense. He'd been thinking about Miss Barrett. And now he was thinking about talking to her again. He'd watched her from behind the gates of his private hell for three years, but now they'd spoken. She hadn't realized it, of course, but she'd drawn him a little toward the light. And now everything felt . . . different.

For the first time in three years he fell asleep thinking of calm and serenity and a quiet smile, rather than of terror and death and whether he would live to see daylight.

Chapter 3

You have hope, and the world before you,
and have no cause for despair.
But I — I have lost everything
and cannot begin life anew.

— Victor Frankenstein, *Frankenstein*

Lucinda leaned into the doorway of her father's office. "No, Papa, I don't think Lord Milburne is an anarchist. Why?"

General Augustus Barrett glanced over his shoulder at her, his expression stern but his gray eyes lighting with amusement rather than with the fire and thunder that had terrified many a green recruit into reconsidering his choice of career. "Look at him, Lucinda," he returned, gesturing her to join him at the window. "Red jacket, white waistcoat, and green trousers. He's either an anarchist or the flag of Spain."

45

Chuckling, Lucinda stopped at his elbow to gaze down at the street. "Good heavens. At least Spain is an ally."

"They wouldn't be if they saw an Englishman making such a mockery of their colors." His scowl deepened. "Good God, now he's waving at us. He's not a suitor, is he? If he approaches the house I'm going to have to shoot him."

Stepping back from the window, Lucinda shook her head. "No, he's not a suitor. I'm not going to marry anyone's flag. Now, do you have another chapter for me?" She motioned at the dark mahogany desk, crowded with haphazard piles of notes and stacks of heavily inked pages.

"Not yet. The notes I took at Salamanca are a bit worse for wear, I'm afraid. But don't change the subject."

"Which subject?"

He tapped a hand against the back of the chair facing his formidable desk. "Suitors."

Wonderful. "Papa, do not begin inviting your officer friends over again. You, me, and thirty men in red and white. *I* felt like the flag of France, under siege. I prefer peacetime negotiations. And you owe me a chapter. Stop stalling."

The general sank back into his own chair. "The notes are . . . much more of a mess

46

than I'd realized. It's a damned nuisance." He hesitated. "And my memory's not what it used to be."

"Hm. Considering the responsibilities the Horse Guards and the War Office keep heaping on you, I don't think they believe your incapacity any more than I do."

"A little sympathy would be a nice gesture, daughter."

"Yes, General." She didn't believe that his memory was fading, but the claim could very well provide her an opportunity for lesson giving. A low buzz of excitement ran down her spine. "You know, I believe Lord Geoffrey Newcombe fought at Salamanca. He'll be at Almack's tonight. Perhaps I might ask him to stop by and see whether he can assist you in deciphering your journal."

"Ah, Lord Geoffrey. Brash young lad, full of vinegar. Took a ball in the arm at Waterloo. You waltzed with him last night."

His gaze slid over to her, but she pretended to be occupied with straightening reference books. "I danced with at least a dozen gentlemen," she returned. "As I usually do. Lord Geoffrey mentioned the war, and I just thought he might be of some help to you."

"You know, you may just have something there, Lucinda," he said after a moment of silence. "In fact, I think I'll send a note over to him, and ask for his assistance."

"Splendid."

For the first time he seemed to notice the old blue muslin gown and straw hat she wore. "We have a gardener, you know."

"I know. I like tending the roses. And yes, I'll wear gloves so I don't get pricked."

The general dug into a drawer. "Just like your mother," he muttered, abruptly occupied with sharpening a quill. "Marie and her roses."

Lucinda smiled. "I'll make you up a bouquet for the office."

Retrieving her heavy gloves and pruners, she waited while the butler pulled open the front door. "I'll be in the garden, Ballow," she said.

"Very good, Miss Lucinda."

Worley, the gardener, had already set out a weed bucket for her, and humming last night's waltz, Lucinda strolled around the side of the house to the small garden. Her mother had planted one new rose per year after Lucinda's birth, and since her death from pneumonia, Lucinda had tried to keep up the tradition. The twenty-fourth rose, a lovely double-petaled yellow with a scent like cinnamon, had arrived from Turkey last week.

"How are you?" she asked it, kneeling on her skirts to check the soil. "You need some water, don't you?"

She hummed as she clipped a few bedraggled leaves that hadn't survived the plant's long journey. Using her father's memoirs as an excuse to have Lord Geoffrey come calling — it was genius, if she did say so, herself.

A watering can appeared beside her. "Thank you, Worley. You're a mind reader."

In mid-reach to pick up the can, she paused. Worley wasn't wearing his heavy work boots. Rather, he had on a very nice pair of Hessians. Lucinda looked up, and up, past tanned doeskin trousers, a black jacket, brown waistcoat, snow-white cravat, lean jaw, and a straight-set mouth, to a pair of azure blue eyes beneath over-long, black, unruly hair.

"Mister Carroway," she exclaimed, lurching to her feet. In her haste to rise she stood on her skirt, and toppled toward the rosebush. "Oh!"

Robert stepped forward, catching her beneath the arms. As soon as she regained her balance he released her, moving back and sweeping his arms behind himself, as though touching her bothered him.

"I don't bite, for heaven's sake," she muttered, brushing at her skirt as much to give herself a moment as him.

"I know."

Be nice, she reminded herself. If he'd come to see her, he had to have a good reason. Georgiana had spoken little of him, but both her friend and his public absence over the past three years had made it quite clear how difficult venturing out of doors was for him. "I didn't mean to snap at you," she said. "It's just that you startled me."

"I was practicing being stealthy," he returned in his low voice. "You seemed to appreciate the skill."

She looked at him sharply. His expression remained quiet, but the azure of his eyes held the veriest hint of a twinkle. So he still had a sense of humor. "Well, you're obviously much better at it than I am. I think we need to make a pact that we won't do any more sneaking up on each other, before we do permanent damage."

"Agreed." He shifted, his gaze moving beyond her toward the house. "I had a thought last evening," he said, the words coming slowly, as if with great reluctance.

"And?" she prompted.

He drew a breath. "You're wasting your time with Geoffrey Newcombe."

Lucinda lifted an eyebrow. "Really? In what way?"

He paused, studying her face. "I've offended you."

Well, if he could be direct, then so could she. "Yes, you have. But please explain."

"He's arrogant and spoiled."

Lucinda couldn't decide whether she felt annoyed or intrigued. "Hence the necessity of teaching him a lesson. I couldn't very well select a student known for his perfection of manner, now could I?"

He didn't look terribly impressed by her logic. "I —"

"Besides, I thought gentlemen didn't speak ill of one another in a lady's presence."

Robert nodded. "No, they don't. I'm not a gentleman, though, and you're Georgiana's friend. I just thought you should keep in mind that while Tristan and St. Aubyn might have been arrogant and misguided, neither of them was spoiled. Whatever lessons you plan to impart, I doubt he'll listen unless it's to his benefit to do so. He thinks the world should bend to his whim."

"For someone who shuns his fellows, you seem to think you know a great deal about them," she snapped, making a definite slide from understanding to annoyance. "Which conclusions have you drawn about me, pray tell?"

That stopped him. "You?"

"Yes, me. Surely if you've analyzed the character of Lord Geoffrey and St. Aubyn and your own brother, you can tell me about myself."

She bent down to retrieve her dropped pruner, surprised to realize that she was curious to hear what Robert Carroway had to say about her. Perhaps she was being a bit too direct with him, but she hadn't asked him to come over and pronounce his opinion of her possible, potential, future spouse.

"You deserve better than Newcombe," his quiet voice came. "I know that about you."

"Well, I thank you for your concern," she said, straightening, "but we'll have to agree to disa . . ."

He was gone. Lucinda turned a circle. He'd completely vanished, as though he'd been nothing more than a specter conjured by her imagination.

"For goodness' sake," she muttered, snipping off an errant leaf. "I could tell you a little something about *your* character, you rude man."

"Talking to yourself?" Her father turned the corner of the house to join her amid the rows of roses.

Sneaking was evil, she decided. "No. I was . . . just conversing with the new rose-bush," she stammered, feeling her cheeks warm.

"Ah. And did it answer?"

"I believe it to be shy."

"If it ever *does* answer, you will inform me, won't you?"

"Very amusing."

The general held out his hand, a letter gripped in his fingers. "This just came for you by messenger."

She took the note from him. "And you decided you must bring it to me yourself because all of the servants have broken their legs, I suppose? I know it couldn't be because you're procrastinating and don't know how to end chapter three."

"No, I don't know how I'm going to middle chapter three, thank you very much." The corners of his mouth turned up. "I'm discovering that campaigning was easy. Writing — like politics — is hard."

Lucinda chuckled, brushing Robert Carroway's troubling visit out of her thoughts — or trying to do so. After his three years of near solitude, something had brought them together thrice in three days. She shook herself. "You seem to be doing well with both. You may help me prune, however, if you wish."

"No, my dear. I think I'll bow to your superior skill and go back to my scribbling."

"Very wise strategy, General."

When he'd gone she took a last look around to see whether anyone else might be sneaking up on her, then opened the note. She'd already recognized the handwriting, and wasn't surprised to see that Evelyn asked whether she and the general wished to attend the small dinner party Lord and Lady St. Aubyn planned for Saturday evening. Lucinda began to smile, until she read the postscript in parentheses at the bottom of the page. According to Evie's neat hand, Lord Geoffrey Newcombe was being sent the same letter of invitation.

Lucinda shoved the missive into her pelisse pocket. Obviously her friends wanted to help her, but she couldn't help thinking the lesson scheme — which she'd begun, for heaven's sake — had become a complete sham. At least Georgie and Evelyn had chosen their students with the genuine idea of teaching them a lesson. Now when it came her turn, all three of them — and even a recluse like Robert Carroway — knew the lessons were only a very thin excuse. And even worse, her friends seemed perfectly willing to serve up Lord Geoffrey to her on a silver platter without even making a pretense that they were doing anything but matchmaking.

"Damnation," she said under her breath, using one of the less-colorful curses she'd learned from her father and his army friends. Scowling, she doused the ground around the rose with the water Robert had provided her. That wasn't how she'd wanted it, though obviously if she pretended otherwise she'd be fooling no one but herself — and perhaps Lord Geoffrey.

Well, she'd laid out her silverware, and there was nothing to do now but serve up the meal. And if Robert Carroway thought she needed advice, he was very much mistaken. Nor did she need to explain herself — and especially not to a near hermit who couldn't be bothered to excuse himself from a conversation before fleeing. Ha. He was just lucky she'd decided to concentrate on Lord Geoffrey, because Mr. Carroway seemed rather in need of a lesson or two, himself.

Robert slowed Tolley to a walk as they neared the boundary of Carroway House.

Edward and Bradshaw stood outside the stable, inspecting the new saddle the youngest brother had acquired on his birthday. Taking a breath, he started up the drive. After the way he'd botched his conversation with Miss Barrett, things couldn't get much worse today, anyway.

"Bit!" Edward called, running forward to clasp Robert's boot, "did Shaw tell you?"

"Runt, don't —"

"He's getting his own ship," Edward continued, ignoring Bradshaw. "He's a captain now!"

"Almost a captain," Bradshaw amended, his light blue gaze meeting Robert's. "Month after next, unless Bonaparte gets loose again."

Suppressing a shudder, Robert nodded. "Congratulations." He swung down from Tolley, reluctantly turning the reins over to a waiting stable boy. There were times when he preferred Carroway House the way it had been before Georgiana and her income had rescued them; back then he could tend Tolley himself, and he didn't have to wait until after midnight to slip out unnoticed.

"Where did you go?" the youngest Carroway asked.

"Errand," he answered, giving his usual reply.

A useless errand, at that. He wasn't even certain why he'd gone now, except that he liked the way Lucinda Barrett simply talked to him. Not many people did that any longer, even when he provided them with the rare opportunity to do so. At some point, though, he'd meant to offer her his assistance. Ha. As if he could assist himself, much less anyone else.

"Will you come riding with Shaw and me?" the Runt continued.

"I have some correspondence," he said. Correspondence and a keen dislike of the huge crowds filling Hyde Park at this time of day. With another nod he turned on his heel, heading for the house.

"Bit, hold up," Shaw said, handing the reins of Edward's pony back to the boy. "I'll be right back, Runt."

"Well, hurry — I want to get a lemon ice."

Robert slowed as Bradshaw drew even with him. Without either of them saying a thing, he could practically recite their conversation word for word; it was the same one he had with all of his family members every time one of them returned after an absence. "I'm fine," he said, trying to shorten the interrogation process.

"I just wanted to mention that I'll have a post for a third mate open under my command," Shaw said, his gaze on the butler pulling open the front door for them. "There's no reason you couldn't —"

"No," Robert interrupted, his voice sharp. He tried to stop the thought process, but Shaw had caught him by surprise. Already his mind was conjuring himself trapped in a crowded, minuscule cabin on a lone ship in the middle of the ocean, stranded for a year or more.

"Just because you've left the army doesn't mean you can't do something else useful."

Robert stopped short, facing his older brother. "As if floating around in a boat halfway across the globe is useful."

Shaw's face closed down. "You have no —"

"Leave me alone, Shaw. I don't want your life."

"Why not? You don't have one of your own any longer."

Shoving past Dawkins at the door, Robert limped for the stairs. "I know that, Bradshaw," he growled, striding for his bed-chamber.

"It doesn't have to be that way!" his brother yelled after him.

"Yes, it does," he muttered, his breath shuddering deep in his chest. Quiet. He just needed quiet and solitude for a few minutes.

Calm, and no more thinking about being trapped in a small, crowded space with no way out.

Inside his bedchamber, though, behind the closed, latched door, the walls seemed to come closer and closer around him as he strode to the window and back, over and over. His hands began shaking, and he clenched them into hard fists. Now that it had begun, he knew he wouldn't be able to stop it — the black, blind panic at nothing and for no good reason. Damn Bradshaw.

Eyes closed, he dropped onto the floor beneath the window. He'd overdone it, was all. Two trips into public in two days, trying to face those damned stares and whispers and at the same time carry on a civil conversation after three years of near solitude and silence.

Calm. Be calm. He wasn't going anywhere. Nothing was going to happen to him. He was safe. Safe. Quiet. Calm. He repeated the words to himself over and over until they blurred together into an incoherent chant, low at the back of his mind.

"Bit? Robert?"

Tristan knocked at his door. When Robert opened his eyes, light no longer reflected from the window, and he sat huddled on the floor in darkness. Slowly he straightened his cramped fingers and climbed to his feet, wincing at the stiffness in his muscles.

"Bit? Are you all right?"

He felt vaguely ill as he reached the door, but that meant the worst of it was over. His skin seemed too tight across his bones, and he felt a hundred years old. Taking a deep breath, he pulled open the door. "I'm fine," he grunted, gazing into his oldest brother's concerned face.

"May I come in?"

"No."

"You look like hell."

"I'm aware of that."

Tristan's lips tightened. "Shaw told me about his offer."

Dread welled through him. God, he couldn't go through it again. Not so soon. "And you think I should go?" he forced out.

"No, I think Shaw's an idiot, and that's what I told him."

"Good."

The viscount stood silent for a moment. "I wish you would talk to me," he finally said in a low voice. "I want to do . . . something, to help you."

Robert backed up half a step, his hand clenching the door. "I'm trying, you know," he whispered, not trusting his voice to remain steady if he spoke aloud.

"I know. Anything you need, anything or anyone you want, and I'll get it for you."

"I don't need —"

"You know what I've been thinking?" Tristan cut in.

"What?" he asked, mostly because he wasn't quite ready to face either the dark, empty room or the rest of his family downstairs.

"I think you need a hobby. No, I know you read, and I . . . know Tolley seems fairly well exercised. I'm not talking about embroidery or anything. In fact, I don't know what. Just something small, to start with. Something to —"

"To occupy me," Robert finished.

"Don't be angry. I'm —"

"I'm not angry." He took another breath. "You may be right."

"I . . . I am? I almost never hear that, you know. Make sure you tell Georgie. She'll be amazed."

The surprise and relief on Tristan's face made Robert feel guilty, and he forced a smile. With another glance behind him, he shoved the door open and emerged into the hallway. "I don't suppose you've held dinner for me?"

"That's why I'm up here. The Runt's

61

threatening to eat his utensils."

Robert lifted an eyebrow. "You didn't have to wait."

"Yes, we did. But don't worry about it."

Downstairs in the dining room he kept his eyes lowered as he took his seat. They'd all be looking at his face, worrying about him and trying to think of something to say that would be encouraging. Shaw would be angry, both at himself and at Robert, because after all, he hadn't done anything but offer his younger brother a chance at a second career.

"Evie and Saint have invited all of us to dinner on Saturday," Georgiana said into the silence.

"Do you mean *all* of us, or all of the grown-ups?" Edward asked.

"*All* of us, my dear. Just us, and Luce and the general, and Lord Geoffrey Newcombe."

"Oh, I like Lord Geoffrey," the Runt said. "He tells very good stories. And he knows Wellington."

"So does Saint," Bradshaw countered.

Robert could feel the various glances in his direction, waiting to see whether he meant to participate. He kept his head down and ate. He didn't have to say anything; in a moment someone would change the subject on his behalf, and they'd go on chatting without him. That was the procedure, and everyone knew it.

"Bit, do you know Wellington?"

Everyone knew it, that was, except for Edward. Robert wanted to ignore the question, but that would mean ignoring the Runt, and then soon Edward would stop talking to him, and then the last ounce of sanity would be gone from his life.

"I saw him riding about," he said, "and we shared a whiskey once, but not much more than that."

"Why did you share a whiskey?" the youngest Carroway pursued, bouncing in his seat.

"Because I had a bottle, and it was snowing, and he asked for a drink before he froze off his balls."

"Wellington said 'balls'?"

"Edward!" Georgiana squeaked.

"Bit said it first!"

Shaw began coughing into his napkin, while Dawkins, the butler, abruptly spied something interesting to look at out the window. Robert glanced at Tristan and Georgie, who both looked amused.

Robert wanted to close his eyes; after three hours of black horror and muscles drawn so tight he could scarcely move, he felt as tired as if he'd run to Newcastle and back. Sleep, though, was a prospect that filled him with further unease. He'd never been too tired, it seemed, to dream. Perhaps Tristan was right. Perhaps he needed something — a small, unthreatening something — to distract him.

"Garden," he muttered, not even certain he'd spoken aloud until he caught the puzzled look on his oldest brother's face.

"Beg pardon?" Tristan asked.

Flowers, plants, growing things. Things that didn't scream or bleed when they died. Things that wouldn't look at you oddly if you didn't know what the hell you were doing. By God, it actually made sense. "I'd like to make a garden," he elaborated.

"What kind of garden?" Bradshaw asked, his voice thin with hesitation.

Don't scare off the mute, Robert thought, working to turn his mind away from that, away from the careful looks and careful silences. Lucinda had a garden, he remembered. What had she been tending when he'd found her kneeling in the dirt, when she'd actually disagreed with him, argued with him, as though he was a perfectly normal person? "Roses," he grunted.

"Roses," Georgiana repeated, her thoughtful gaze touching his. "It's about time one of the Carroway men decided to cultivate something other than their poor reputations."

"I don't have a poor reputation," Edward stated, his expression a little baffled as he pushed sweet potatoes around his plate and looked at Robert. "Roses? Why don't you go riding with me?"

God, was he really being that stupid and useless? Flowers? He could see himself, some shuffling old halfwit blathering to his fistful of dying posies. But if he couldn't manage that one step forward, it meant he'd end up some shuffling old halfwit locked in a room and blathering to himself.

Choking on air, Robert pushed to his feet. "Excuse me."

"Just promise me you'll plant white roses," Georgie said as he strode from the room. "I love white roses."

Chapter 4

You may deem me romantic,
my dear sister,
but I bitterly feel the want of a friend.

— Robert Walton, *Frankenstein*

"Georgiana," Lucinda said, hurrying down-stairs to greet her friend, "am I being an idiot? I thought we were going shopping to-morrow."

"We are, and you're not," the viscountess returned, taking her proffered hands. "This is not a social call."

Georgie didn't look alarmed at anything, but Lucinda couldn't help recalling the rather abrupt ending to her conversation with Robert yesterday. *Wonderful.* All she needed was for her dearest friend to yell at her for verbally abusing her invalid brother-in-law. "What can I do for you, then?" she asked as she led the way into the morning room.

"Well, this is going to sound a little odd, but please bear with me, Luce."

"Of course."

Georgiana cleared her throat. "Tristan's been trying to find something for Bit — Robert — to do that will help him . . . find a little peace. I know it sounds strange, but —"

"No, it doesn't," Lucinda interrupted, concealing her jump at the mention of Robert's name. "Go on."

"Thank you. Last night Bit mentioned that he would like to grow roses. I —"

Lucinda blinked, an abrupt suspicion tickling at her. "Roses?"

"Yes. I don't know where the idea came from, but he wouldn't have mentioned it for no reason. I wanted to offer to help him get started, but I think that might make him back away." Lady Dare scowled, twining and untwining her fingers. "I shouldn't be talking about him to anyone, but I consider you my family, Luce."

"And I, you." Lucinda sat forward, pushing back her own reservations at becoming entangled in what looked to be a very complicated enterprise. Georgie needed her help — and perhaps so did

Robert. That fact intrigued her more than she cared to admit. "I can make some cuttings, and I have a few books on growing roses. Perhaps I'll just drop by with them and ambush Mr. Carroway."

" 'Ambush?' " Georgiana repeated. "I don't know if that's such a good idea."

"It'll make it more difficult for him to refuse," Lucinda returned, smiling. "Or to change his mind about this project of his."

"I . . . All right. I'll risk making him angry with me. I . . . I want him to get better. I want to hear him laugh."

With a small smile, Lucinda moved over to the couch and hugged her friend. "Being shot — what, five times — at Waterloo and seeing all of the horror there, Georgie. How could it not affect him?"

Georgiana's expression faltered, then recovered again. "Of course," she said, averting her face from Lucinda's curious gaze. "I will appreciate anything you can provide that might help him."

Her friend's reaction to her comment had been interesting. Now, though, wasn't the time to hesitate. She could try to figure out what Georgie wasn't telling her later. "I'll be by before luncheon."

Only a moment after Georgiana left, the general entered the morning room. "It

68

seems your idea may save my Salamanca chapter, my dear," he said, pocketing a letter. "Lord Geoffrey writes that he would be delighted to go over my journal with me and see what we can reconstruct."

"That's splendid."

"He'll be coming to call after luncheon. I would appreciate if you could be here to take notes."

At least some things were working as they should be. "I'd be happy to help." She stood, kissing him on the cheek as she passed by. "I should be home by then."

"Where are you off to?"

"I'm going to take some rose cuttings to Robert Carroway. He wants to start a garden."

The general clamped firm fingers over her shoulder, drawing her to a surprised halt. "Robert Carroway? He's not a suitor, is he?"

"No. Just a friend." She frowned at the serious expression in his eyes. "Why?"

"He's not my sort of soldier. Or my sort of man."

"Papa, y—"

"I know he's your Georgie's brother-in-law now, but keep as much distance as you can. Don't be too much of a 'friend' — his reputation will reflect on you. And on me."

"What reputation? He's barely been seen in public for three years, and he was shot at Waterloo. He's a hero."

Her father kept silent for a short moment. "So some say. Others were wounded there, however, and you don't see them hiding from their own shadows. Lord Geoffrey, for instance. Carroway's damaged goods, Luce. Keep that in mind, and keep your distance."

She really didn't think either request would be much of a problem, but she nodded anyway. "I'll be cautious."

"Thank you. You'll help an old man rest easier."

Lucinda grinned, tucking her hands around his arm. "Which old man would that be? You'll have to introduce me."

The Carroway family rarely breakfasted together. They all had their own schedules, meetings, planned excursions, and in Edward's case, lessons. Robert had none of those things, and a definite appreciation of solitude. At half past nine, when he entered the breakfast room, it didn't surprise him that he was alone but for a pair of footmen. He'd planned it that way.

He liked mornings; the rising of the sun had come to seem like a daily miracle. A freshly ironed copy of *The London Times* lay beside the place setting at the head of the table waiting for Tristan, but he ignored it. He didn't care what happened in the rest of the world — or in London. At the sideboard he shoveled ham and toast onto his plate, then sat at the far end of the table. He sliced a piece of ham and brought it to his mouth just as the butler stepped into the breakfast room.

"Master Robert, you have a caller," Dawkins said, looking uncomfortable. None of the servants liked to talk to him, though most of the time he made sure they didn't have a reason to do so.

Ignoring the thud of his heart, Robert finished his bite. "I'm not here."

The butler nodded. "Very good, sir."

As Dawkins left, Robert went back to eating. No one called on him any longer; it must have been a miscommunication, someone looking for Shaw. The butler would straighten it out.

Dawkins leaned into the breakfast room again. "Sir, Miss Barrett wishes to know whether she should leave the box here, or return with it later."

Miss Barrett? "What box?"

"I don't know, sir. Shall I inq—"

Robert pushed to his feet. "I'll see to it."

Lucinda Barrett stood in the foyer, a small wooden crate at her feet. He lifted his gaze from it to her, taking in the fashionable yellow bonnet over her auburn hair and a green and yellow gown to match. Unless he was very much mistaken, the expression in her hazel eyes was amused.

Robert shook himself. Invited or not, she was the guest, so he was supposed to say something first. "What are you doing here?"

She flipped him a pair of heavy work gloves, which he caught by reflex. "Pick that up," she said, gesturing at the box, "and follow me."

He almost did it, catching himself just as he started to stoop. "No," he returned, straightening.

Miss Barrett folded her arms across her pert bosom. "Were you, or were you not, rude to me yesterday?"

"Your point being?"

"I'm getting my revenge on you." With an easy, confident smile, she toed the box. "So come along. It's just a few feet, and I promise there's nothing in there that'll bite." Her brow furrowed. "Not as long as you're careful, that is."

Dawkins had returned to the hallway, the two breakfast room footmen at his heels. At least one maid lurked up on the balcony, eavesdropping, while he could hear Edward upstairs arguing with his tutor about Madagascar, of all things. Shrugging, he tossed the gloves onto the lid and then bent down and hefted the box.

Lucinda pulled open the front door before Dawkins could reach it. Rather than motioning for Robert to precede her, she marched down the front steps and turned right along the drive.

Well, this was odd, but at least it got him away from the curious eyes inside. Robert followed while she traipsed toward the stable, lifting her skirts above the damp grass as she left the carriage drive.

"This looks good," she said, stopping to turn a circle at the near side of the stable. "Plenty of sun, but with shelter from the worst of the weather." She faced him again, pulling on her own heavy pair of gloves. "Well, put it down."

Robert stood where he was, eyeing her. Once he saw her with the gardening gloves, everything began to make sense. For a brief moment he contemplated hunting down Georgiana and favoring her with a few choice words. Whatever she'd told Lucinda, though, Miss Barrett was the one who'd agreed to it.

Carefully he put the box down and took a

step back. "Good luck with your endeavors," he said, "but next time use a footman to cart your luggage. Good morning."

"Mister Carroway," she said to his back, "generally when someone gives someone else a gift of some rather rare and valuable rose cuttings, they are thanked for their efforts."

He stopped. "I didn't ask you for anything."

"Hence my use of the word 'gift.' There are also several books on rose cultivation in there. So you don't kill anything out of ignorance, I thought I might give you a brief introduction and some general instructions."

Robert strode back to her. "I don't want your roses, your instruction, or your damned charity," he snarled.

She blinked, and he realized he'd more than likely frightened her. *Well, good.* He didn't much like surprises, either.

"You came to see *me* yesterday," she said slowly, her gaze holding his. "When I saw Georgie this morning and she mentioned roses, I thought perhaps you'd meant to ask me for some clippings. So I don't consider this charity. I consider it my affirmative answer to a question you hadn't quite asked."

God, what was she thinking, to be willing to put up with such idiocy from him? And when he walked away, he would have no reason or cause ever to visit or talk with her again — about anything.

At the same time, her "gift," as she chose to call it, left him on very marshy ground. He needed a better tactical position if he ever wanted her to see him as anything other than a cripple. Just the fact that that concerned him was startling. "I actually thought I would suggest a trade," he lied, rushing his mind through several possible scenarios.

" 'A trade,' " she repeated, skepticism skimming across her face. "What sort of trade?"

Robert took a deep breath. This was what he'd meant to say yesterday. He'd blamed his leaving on hearing her father approach, but even as he'd escaped he'd known General Barrett was only an excuse. He hadn't spoken because he hadn't been certain he could carry through with what he wanted to propose.

Now or never, he told himself. If he meant to limp back into Society, he couldn't do it with his family as a crutch. No one would believe it, including himself. But Lucinda — she gave him something to focus on other than dread. And she still seemed to labor under the misconception that he was human.

"I thought if you would help me begin a rose garden," he said, encouraged that his voice sounded steady, "I would help you with Lord Geoffrey Newcombe."

"Lord Geoff . . . How would you help me with him?"

Damn. Now he needed an actual plan. "Whether you mean to teach him a lesson or . . . something more, in my company any of your meetings would seem more coincidental."

"I —"

"You know Georgie and Lady St. Aubyn can't be of as much help now that they're married. As a single gentleman, I also have insight into Geoffrey which you might find gives you a certain advantage."

Miss Barrett tilted her head, regarding him. "So you would avail me of your advice, and where necessary be my escort on drives or excursions, when my true purpose would be to encounter Lord Geoffrey."

"Yes." Until it killed him, anyway.

Slowly Lucinda walked to the crate and lifted the second pair of gloves off the lid. "Let's get started then," she said, handing them back to him, "shall we?"

★ ★ ★

Tristan couldn't find his wife. She'd gone out early on a brief errand, and he knew she'd returned, but she wasn't in their bedchamber, or her upstairs sitting room, or the aunties' frilly morning room, or the breakfast room.

Damnation. She was nearly eight months pregnant, and if she didn't begin to take things a little more slowly he was going to drag her off to Dare Park in Devon whether she wanted to go or not. "Georgiana!"

"Shh," came from the library. "In here. And be quiet, for goodness' sake."

More than a little curious, the viscount entered the library. His wife stood against the wall by a half-open window, peering through the glass.

"What the devil are y—"

She clapped a hand over his mouth. "Look," she whispered.

Following her gaze, Tristan looked down toward the stable — and froze.

Lucinda Barrett stood in the middle of an unruly clump of grass, an open book in her hands. Opposite her, gesturing with a scraggle of leaves and thorns in one hand as he spoke, stood Robert. As Tristan watched, Bit paced a limping square approximately fifteen feet per side and then returned to Lucinda.

"What is going on?" Tristan murmured, unable to take his eyes off his brother.

"Roses," Georgie answered in the same low voice. "I asked Lucinda to bring over some cuttings."

"But he's *talking* to her."

Georgiana slipped her hands around his arm, leaning against his shoulder. "Yes, he is."

Tristan continued to watch. Bit kept his distance from Lucinda, but he was definitely interacting with her. And he'd sought her out at the Wellcrist soiree. "Georgie, does he — I mean, how —" He stopped, taking a breath. "Does Lucinda like him?"

"Lucinda likes everyone," she murmured back, her hands tightening around his arm in obvious tension, "and everyone likes her."

"But —"

"I don't think so, Tristan. I can't say more, but I believe she has set her sights on someone. And no, it's not Bit."

Of course it wasn't. *Bloody hell.* "We have to go down there and stop this little meeting, then."

"No." Georgie shook him. "Leave them alone. If you interfere, Bit will resent it. They're just talking. And you don't know

anything about it. You are completely ignorant. Do you understand?"

Tristan sighed. With every fiber of his
being he wanted to protect his brother —
wanted to do . . . something to see that he
was all right, but obviously he was already
better than three years too late for that. At
the same time, he knew that Georgiana was
absolutely correct, as she usually was. "For
now, I don't know anything about it," he
agreed, turning to kiss her on one soft
cheek. "And neither do you. But I reserve
the right to be enlightened at a moment's
notice."

"Hopefully we'll both be able to remain
blissfully ignorant."

He tugged her away from the window,
pulling her into his arms. "I *was* blissfully ignorant, until five minutes ago. And I have a
very bad feeling about this, love."

"I know. But he wouldn't be down there if
he didn't want to be. And if he wants to be
there, then maybe that means he wants to
try to come back to us."

"I hope you're right."

As Robert listened to Miss Barrett instructing him about what kind of fish made
the best rose fertilizer, he glanced again at
the upstairs library window. Both Georgie

and Tristan would have made terrible spies. He knew Georgiana had arranged for Lucinda to visit this morning, but he hoped her eavesdropping didn't mean she intended to try managing him. That was *not* going to happen.

If he'd been himself, the Robert before the war, he would have thought Georgiana was matchmaking. Back then he would have pursued Lucinda, though in truth it would have been her looks that attracted him. Now she'd set her sights on someone else. And now it was her serenity, her peace, that drew him like a warm breeze on a cold day. And even though he enjoyed being around her, he resisted her, because he was supremely aware that he wasn't the old Robert any longer; he was Bit, a piece of what he'd once been.

Of course even now it would have been foolish to deny that he found her beautiful, almost medieval with her dark hair and eyes and her pale, smooth-as-cream skin. Her hair smelled pleasantly of roses, and he could imagine her bathing in a pool of red silken petals. But he hadn't been with a woman in four years, for God's sake, and this one happened to be Georgiana's closest friend, not to mention the only non-family female to whom he'd said more than a sen-

tence in what felt like decades. He scowled.
So he'd become a monk in his own private
monastery; at least his religion said he could
look.

"Mister Carroway," Lucinda said, jolting
him back from his worship, "I said, too
much fish will ruin the soil."

"I understand."

He turned the stumpy twig of a white
félicité parmentier in his hands. According to
Lucinda, he wasn't to be surprised if as
many as half of the cuttings she'd provided
didn't take. The thorny things, bare of soil
and roots, didn't look alive to begin with.
Were they? Were they awake, or asleep?
Would they feel something, or nothing, if
they died? If he killed them?

"I don't think this is a wise idea," he said,
hastily returning the cutting to the crate.

She eyed him. "Why is that?"

"I don't have time to go fishmongering or
plowing," he said, backing away, concentrating on breathing. He hated it when the
panic snuck up and hit him because of a
damned stray thought.

Miss Barrett drew a breath. "Very well.
The general doesn't like gardening, either."

His jaw tightened at the mention of her
father. "It's not that I dislike —"

"I suppose that means our entire agree-

81

ment is void." Setting the book on the ground, she pulled off her gloves. "Oh, well. No harm done, I suppose."

Robert watched as she walked back toward the front of the house. "What about your cuttings?"

She waved a hand in the direction of the crate. "I don't have room to plant a whole new rose garden. Just throw them away."

For a long moment he stood looking after her while she climbed into her waiting coach and vanished back into the street. That had been odd. The plants were obviously her pride and joy, and she'd said some of them were rare. Did she truly not care what he did with them? Or had she read his thoughts when *he* wasn't even certain what was bothering him?

With a sigh he tugged the crate into the shade of the stable and headed back to the house to change into some old clothes more fit for gardening than the ones he currently wore.

By the time he'd cleared off the grass and turned the soil, he was beginning to remember that he'd missed all but two bites of breakfast and that luncheon had already passed, as well. Reluctantly he returned the shovel to the stable.

This late in the day he'd never find the

quantity of fresh fish he required, so that meant a trip down to the docks along the Thames first thing in the morning. Lucinda had said the cuttings would survive out of the ground for a day or two in cool weather, so he secured the lid on the crate, collected the books she'd left, and returned to the house.

He'd been right about one thing: soil and plants didn't require conversation. In fact, silence actually seemed to suit them better. He couldn't, however, say the same about his family.

Normally whichever family members were home sought him out several times during the day, asking whether he was feeling well or whether he wanted to go riding or strolling or driving. After spending most of the day outside he'd seen no one but a few grooms, which of course meant that all of the Carroways knew what he'd been doing and didn't want to risk interfering.

As long as they didn't ask him to explain it, as long as they pretended nothing had changed and that he wasn't trying to pull himself out of the bottomless well where he'd been dwelling since his return to England, he was fine with the subterfuge.

The difficult part would be deciding whether he wanted to admit to Lucinda that he'd decided to try to grow the roses. Because once she knew, he would be obligated to carry out his part of their little agreement — and that would be the real test of whether he could be human again or not. He only wished he knew the answer to the question before he set out to prove it. And he wished he could convince himself that knowing what Lucinda thought of him didn't matter.

Chapter 5

Increase of knowledge only discovered
to me more clearly what a wretched
outcast I was.

— The Monster, *Frankenstein*

Lucinda charged into Barrett House and rushed upstairs to change into a gown more suitable for receiving visitors. The general had said that Lord Geoffrey would be calling after luncheon, but she'd lingered longer than she meant to at Carroway House and had no time for anything more than the peach her maid ran down to the kitchen to fetch for her.

She'd left things as well as she could with Robert Carroway, and she refused to feel guilty about abandoning him. It was up to him anyway, she told herself, to decide whether he wanted the garden or not. Nor

was she so thick-skulled that she didn't realize this was more than a simple planting
project for him.

Precisely what it was, she didn't know for
certain, but after spending more time in his
company, after seeing the haunted depths
behind those startling azure eyes, she hoped
her gift would help. Lucinda caught herself
staring sightlessly at her reflection in the
dressing-table mirror, and shook herself out
of her unaccustomed reverie.

Just as Helena finished fastening on her
necklace for her, she heard the front door
downstairs open, and the low, melodious
sound of Lord Geoffrey's voice as he re-
sponded to Ballow's greeting. Her heartbeat
quickened. He was here. It was time for the
lessons to begin.

She intentionally dallied upstairs for another few moments, fluffing curls and deciding on her strategy. She would have liked
more time for plotting, but the encounter
with Robert had taken all of her wits and attention. Interesting, that. She would have
thought that conversing with someone who
seldom spoke in return would have been
less . . . involving. Except that he *had*
spoken to her — and *with* her.

A scratch came at her door. "Miss
Barrett?" the butler said as Helena pulled

open the door, "your father requests that you join him in his office."

"Yes, of course." *Concentrate, Lucinda.* This wasn't just a social call, as her visit with Robert had more or less been. This was about setting the course for her future matrimonial status.

Trying to clear her head of the morning's events, she followed Ballow downstairs and slipped into the general's office. "Good afternoon, Papa, Lord Geoffrey," she said, dipping a curtsy.

"Miss Barrett," the Duke of Fenley's son returned, rising from his seat to grip her fingers. "General Barrett tells me that you've agreed to record our efforts."

"I have," she said, stepping around to plant a kiss on her father's cheek and motioning both men to sit. "I'll be by the window, so I won't intrude on your work."

"Nonsense." Lord Geoffrey pulled out the chair beside him. "I always tell a better story with an audience present. Especially an audience so attentive she's actually taking notes."

While Lucinda settled into the chair with a pencil and paper, the general opened the torn, half-burned and water-stained journal that contained his Salamanca notes. "Damned galley fire on the ship returning me to England after Boney sailed off to Elba," he grumbled, turning the pages gingerly despite the gruff nonchalance of his words. "My Pamplona journal was destroyed completely. All over a damned colonel wanting a slice of toasted bread for his bloody sea sickness."

"I hope you had him demoted," Lord Geoffrey agreed. "But it so happens that I saw some action at Pamplona, as well. Not as much as you did, I'm certain, but I'd be happy to offer my recollections if you think they could be of use."

"That's very kind of you, my lord."

" 'Geoffrey,' please. With three brothers ahead of me, the odds of my actually inheriting a title are something beyond abysmal."

The general smiled. " 'Geoffrey' it is, then. Salamanca was your first engagement, was it not?"

"Yes, it was — and quite the introduction to battle, if I may say so. A French musket ball took off my hat two minutes after I entered the field."

Lucinda listened to the two men talking, taking down notes on dates, weather conditions, troop movement, and personal observations. She could almost feel the heat of the battle, see the smoke and the ebb and flow of the troops as Wellington shadowed the forces of Marshal Auguste Marmont, the Commander of the Army of Portugal.

She actually gasped when Geoffrey described nearly being swept downriver as his squad crossed the Tormes River during a storm toward the end of the battle. "Apologies," she muttered, blushing, as both men looked over at her. "You tell a vivid story."

Geoffrey inclined his head. "I only hope it's not too horrific for a gently bred lady such as yourself."

Ah, opportunity. "I assure you, my lord, that while I never saw battle, I have read all of my father's notes and correspondence, and the drafts of his chapters. I also volunteered at hospitals for wounded soldiers directly after the war. One does not grow up as the daughter of General Augustus Barrett without knowing something about conflict and warfare."

"And the proper way to tell a tale," her father seconded, giving her a fond smile. "Not one to flinch, my Lucinda."

"I stand corrected, then," Lord Geoffrey conceded, "though in all honesty I think your father would agree that there are some aspects of battle that a gentleman does not speak of to a lady."

"I —"

"After all, what do soldiers fight for if not

to preserve a certain . . . quality of peace and amity at home?" he went on.

"Very good point, Geoffrey," the general said. "Do you mind if I have Lucinda take a note of it?"

"Not at all." He pulled out his pocket watch, consulting its time against that of the mantel clock. "I'm afraid I have a meeting with my finance man at four o'clock," he said.

"Of course." The general marked their place in the damaged journal and carefully closed it again. "We've made a good start." He glanced at his desk calendar. "Would you care to continue the skirmish on Tuesday for luncheon? My cook makes a fine roast chicken."

"It would be my pleasure." Geoffrey sent Lucinda a warm glance.

"Noon, then?" she asked, rising.

"Noon it is."

When Lord Geoffrey took her hand again she couldn't help noticing that his grip lingered a moment longer than custom dictated. My goodness, things were going well. And they'd have an even better opportunity for chatting at Evie and Saint's dinner, evening after next.

"Nice, upstanding lad," the general said, as Lord Geoffrey returned to his horse and cantered down the drive.

"He does seem to be, doesn't he?"

"And still a captain, not on active duty. If Boney had won at Waterloo, Captain Lord Geoffrey'd be a major by now. Perhaps even a lieutenant colonel. Has the right attitude for it. Just not enough war to go around."

For a fleeting moment, troubled azure eyes crossed Lucinda's thoughts. "Quite enough war, I think. I'm happy to see you employed at the Horse Guards and writing memoirs now rather than field journals, thank you very much."

"Yes, yes, my girl." The general turned back to the papers on his desk, where she knew he'd spend most of the evening outlining the next chapter of his book. "Even so, I'm glad you suggested that I consult with him."

"So am I," Lucinda murmured, heading for the library to look for a map of Spain and the town of Salamanca. She wondered whether Robert had fought there, and whether his recollections would be similar to those of Lord Geoffrey and her father. And she wondered whether she dared ask him.

As Robert pulled on his greatcoat and riding gloves he heard Edward pounding down the stairs behind him. *Damnation.* This was why he preferred midnight rides to those during daylight.

"Where are you going?" his youngest brother asked.

"An errand." He took his hat from Dawkins and rammed it onto his head, noting the butler's disapproving glance at his too-long hair.

"You always say that," Edward complained. "I want to go, too."

"It's boring," he said, waiting impatiently for Dawkins to pull open the front door.

"I still want to go. Shaw's going on a picnic with some chit, Tris has Parliament, and Georgie's going shopping."

Shopping with Lucinda Barrett, if he'd heard correctly. "What about Mr. Trost?" he asked, even as he remembered that it was the tutor's day off.

"He's visiting his mother. And I am *not* going to do lessons for no good reason."

Wishing their other brother, Andrew, didn't still have another week before he could come down from Cambridge, Robert sighed. "Then get your coat," he said.

"Hurray!" Edward thundered back up the stairs, but came to an abrupt halt on the landing. "You're not going to leave without me, are you, Bit?"

The thought had crossed his mind. "No. I'll be at the stables, having Tolley and Storm Cloud saddled."

"I'll be right down!"

Robert went outside, inspecting his patch of a garden while he waited for the horses. The family's apparent ignorance about his square of uprooted lawn had continued through dinner and his hasty breakfast, but he doubted anyone could stop Edward from saying something about it eventually.

He'd gone to bed tired and awakened at sunrise with aching shoulder muscles, surprised and grateful that he'd actually slept through the night and that he couldn't remember dreaming. That fact alone was enough to make him want to continue cultivating the rose garden.

He swung up on Tolley as Edward ran from the house. "Where are we going?" the Runt asked, stepping into John the groom's hands and hopping into Storm Cloud's saddle.

"The river."

They cantered down the drive and headed southeast. As they reached Pall Mall, Robert fought the urge to send Tolley into a gallop. It was still early, but Mayfair was bursting with people. Milk vendors, rag and bone men, vegetable and fruit carts, servants fetching this and that, coal and fire-wood salesmen, orange girls, and a few early-rising nobles all crowded onto the streets, pushing and yelling, shouting and singing.

"Why are we going to the river?" Edward asked.

"Fish."

"We're going fishing?"

He hid a scowl at the anticipation in the boy's voice. "No. I need some fresh fish for the garden."

"You can't grow fish in a garden, Bit. I'm not a baby, anymore, and you can't fool me with that nonsense."

"They're fertilizer, to help the roses root. That's the theory, anyway."

The boy opened and closed his mouth again. "Oh."

" 'Oh,' what?"

"I'm not supposed to ask about the rose garden. I'm not even supposed to say the word 'rose.' "

"Who told you that?"

"Everybody. First Georgie told me, then Tristan, and then Shaw nearly scared me to death when he jumped out of the drawing room to tell me not to talk about roses. I think I hate roses."

"If we're lucky, by the end of the morning

you'll hate fish even more."

"Are you going to let me help you with your garden, then? Because Georgie said I couldn't ask you that, either."

They passed out of Mayfair, but if anything the streets seemed even more crowded. Robert's chest began to tighten, and he fought to keep his breathing steady. If he went under here, there was no telling what might happen to Edward. He needed to distract himself while he still had some control. "Do you *want* to help with the garden?" he asked. "I thought you'd rather go riding with Shaw or Tristan."

"I like riding with you, too. You hardly even use the reins with Tolley. I want to learn to do that with Storm Cloud." Edward frowned. "But since nobody else will even talk about it, I'll help you with the garden. You shouldn't have to do it alone."

"Thank you, Runt."

Edward grinned happily, perfectly content at the rightness of the world. Robert envied him. He'd grasped that once, felt it, but somehow knowing what he'd had and lost only made things worse now. He could never tell anyone how far he'd fallen from that light, or that because of what he'd done, he could never return to daylight again.

"Is that a fishmonger?"

Robert blinked. "Yes." He dismounted and limped up to the withered old man and his weathered old cart. "I need to purchase some fish."

"Very good, milord. I have all kinds, very fresh. Cod, mackerel, smelt —"

"I need two dozen," Robert interrupted, hoping the catch smelled better than the vendor did.

"Two dozen? 'A course, milord. What k—"

"About this big." He held his hands up, about ten inches apart.

"Some of these is much better suited for the tables of good-bred folk such as yourself. Of course, them that tastes better do cost more."

"They're for fertilizer," Edward put in from his seat on Storm Cloud.

"Ferti—"

"This big," Robert repeated.

"You want to put my fine fish in the dirt?" the old man squawked. "If word gets around that my fish is good for nothing but burying, no one'll —"

"We're all good for nothing but burying," Robert growled. He needed to get home. And soon. "How much?"

The vendor swallowed. "Ten shillings."

"Eight shillings." He pulled the coins from his pocket.

"All right, milord. I won't vouch for the quality, though."

Once they'd dumped the fish into the cloth sack Robert had brought along for that purpose, he climbed back on Tolley. "Let's go, Runt," 'he grunted, tying the sack around the pommel.

It was a few minutes before he realized that Edward was being uncharacteristically quiet. He looked over at his youngest brother. The boy's eyes were fixed on his mount's ears, his lips tight and drawn. "What's wrong, Edward?" he asked.

"That was a bad thing you said," the Runt muttered, avoiding his gaze. "And you scared that man."

Robert swallowed his retort, surprised that he'd thought to make one. It would have been so much easier if Edward only saw him as the half-human wreck that everyone else did. Almost everyone else. A fleeting glimpse of Lucinda Barrett's smile crossed his thoughts.

"I'm sorry," he said. "I'm not feeling well. I need to get home."

"I remember when you came home," his brother said abruptly, "from fighting Napoleon. Shaw said you were going to die, but I knew you weren't."

"How did you know that?"

"Because of the letter you wrote me, where you said you were going to teach me how to jump fences when I was old enough. Andrew wanted to show me how last year when you were in Scotland, but I don't want anybody but you to teach me."

Robert swallowed. He'd forgotten about that letter. It was the last one he'd written, dropped in the mail satchel the night of . . . the night everything had changed. The night hell had begun.

Finally the house came into sight. "You should have let Andrew teach you," he muttered, kicking Tolley into a run.

As they reached the stables he slid out of the saddle, grabbed the sack of fish, and flung it beside the crate of rose cuttings. He strode for the house and shoved open the front door before Dawkins could reach it.

"Where the devil have you been?" Tristan snapped, as he emerged from his office.

"Out." Robert ignored his brother's angry look and headed for the stairs.

"With Edward."

"Yes."

Below him, Tristan cursed. "You are not to gallop off with Edward without telling someone where you're going first."

"Fine."

"Robert! I'm not finished talking to you!"

As far as Robert was concerned, he was. The panic grabbed hold of him again, clasping heavy, clawed fingers around his chest until he couldn't get enough air into his lungs.

"Damn it," he hissed, slamming into his bedchamber and shoving the door closed behind him. "Stop, stop, stop."

So Edward's faith in him was based on a stupid, naive letter, one he'd written before he knew anything. He remembered it now, remembered chatting about how cold it had been when they'd crossed the Spanish border into France, and how optimistic he'd been on hearing word that Bonaparte had abdicated. The fighting was over, they'd all thought. He'd intended to be home soon, hoping that his regiment wouldn't be one of those called on to remain in the area and enforce the peace. They had been, but he hadn't been with them.

"Robert!"

He ignored Tristan pounding on his door. In fact, he barely heard it as he paced the floor, trying to outrun the blackness coming up behind him.

He'd submitted papers asking for leave, and they'd been granted. What was left of his regiment had therefore thought he'd gone back to England, while his family had thought him still in Spain.

"Robert, open the damned door! I'm not joking!"

The anger and fear in Tristan's voice wrenched him back to the present. He stalked to the door and yanked it open. "I would never let anything happen to Edward," he rasped.

Whatever Tristan had been about to say, he closed his mouth over it. "God, Bit, are you hurt?" he asked instead. "You're white as a —"

Robert slammed the door again. "Go away," he snarled, leaning his forehead against the cool, heavy wood. "I just want some quiet."

"All right." After a few moments he heard Tristan's boots padding back down the hallway.

As Robert took another strangled breath and turned to resume his pacing, his gaze fell on his gardening clothes, which he'd left draped over a chair. He needed to get the fish in the ground before they attracted every stray cat in Mayfair, and if he didn't plant the cuttings today, he might as well do what Lucinda had suggested and throw them away.

His hands shook as he shed his greatcoat, slinging it over a bedpost. His coat and waistcoat followed, and he was able to concentrate enough to actually hang them back in the dressing closet.

Tristan kept offering to find him a valet, obviously not understanding how important it was that *no one* have free access to him, his private rooms, or his things. Dressing himself and tending to his own things was one of the few ways he had of demonstrating to himself that he could still function as a man.

By the time he'd pulled on his oldest pair of boots and grabbed up the heavy pair of gloves Lucinda had loaned him, he was surprised to realize that the desperate pounding of his heart had subsided, and that his breathing had slowed almost to normal.

Robert ventured a glance around him as he pulled open his bedchamber door and emerged into the hallway. He still felt the effects of it, the tiredness and the shaking, but he'd beaten it back this time. For the first time he hadn't let the blackness win. And he owed that to roses — and to Miss Lucinda Barrett.

Chapter 6

❧

**From this time a new spirit of life
animated the decaying frame
of the stranger.**

— Robert Walton, *Frankenstein*

Lucinda couldn't help slowing as she and the general reached the front steps of Halboro House. Before Evie and St. Aubyn had married, she'd crossed the threshold only once, and even then had ventured only as far as the foyer. And yet now, in the bowels of the house where until a few weeks ago virtuous females had feared to tread, she was popping in for an intimate dinner with family and friends — and a potential future spouse.

"Welcome, General Barrett, Miss Barrett," the butler said, ushering them in. "Lord and Lady St. Aubyn are in the drawing room."

"Thank you, Jansen."

The drawing room door was three-quarters closed, and at the last moment, remembering that Evie and Saint had only been married a month, Lucinda loudly cleared her throat. "You know, Papa," she said in a carrying voice, "I couldn't help noticing that you twice brought Madeira to Mrs. Hull at the Wellcrist soiree."

"Well, the heat in the ballroom was stifling, and Mrs. Hull had neglected to bring her fan," the general replied. "If —"

The door was pulled open. "Good evening," Evie said, smiling as she kissed Lucinda on the cheek and tugged the two of them into the room. "You're our first arrivals."

St. Aubyn appeared at his wife's shoulder to slide a hand possessively down her spine. "And you have fortuitous timing, too. I was just about to win an argument."

Evelyn blushed. "No, you weren't."

"We'll have to continue later, then," he drawled, green eyes assessing his bride. "General Barrett, allow me to challenge you to a game of billiards. I believe the ladies wish to chat."

The general lifted an eyebrow. "Considering the relationship of Lucinda and Evelyn, I believe you should call me Augustus."

The marquis nodded. "I do seem to have joined a larger family than I expected. This way then, Augustus. If I win, you may call me 'Saint.' In the unlikely circumstance that I lose, I will insist on being referred to as 'Your Most Beneficent Lordship, the Marquis of St. Aubyn.' "

Augustus chuckled. "Don't think that'll sway me, young man."

The two men vanished down the hall, and Lucinda watched after them for a moment. "I still can't quite grasp it."

"Grasp what?" Evie asked, taking a seat on the couch.

"His most beneficent lordship," Lucinda returned with a smile. "Michael Halboro. I mean, I know what lengths he went to in order to win you, but . . . my goodness, you married the Marquis of St. Aubyn."

"My mother refuses to believe it," Evelyn said with a small grimace, "and my brother still barely speaks to either of us."

"I know. I'm sorry."

"Oh, I'm not. Michael thinks it bothers me, too, but it really doesn't. I leave it to them to accept that I'm brave and independent and that I love Saint as much as he loves me. Because I'm not about to change now. Arriving here took far too much effort."

Effort. "Do you think I'm cheating?" Lucinda asked abruptly. "And please, *please* tell me the truth."

Evie grasped her hands to pull her down onto the couch. "Truthfully," her friend said, gazing at her closely, "I don't see how making a decision and then taking steps to realize your goal could be cheating."

"I meant about the lessons."

"Luce, you're not cheating. Whatever we thought we were talking about that day, I think we were actually expressing a certain . . . dissatisfaction with our own lives."

"I don't need a husband in order to be happy," Lucinda retorted.

"That's not what I mean." Evie sighed. "I *am* much happier now, with Saint. But I'm also happier because my family's not controlling my life."

"Maybe that's what's wrong with me," Lucinda said quietly. "I don't feel a driving ambition to do anything but see that the general is cared for, and to keep as much chaos from my life as possible."

Evie chuckled. "It's just as well you didn't fall in love with Dare, then."

A fleeting vision of Dare's troubled younger brother made her frown, but she shook it off before Evie could notice. For someone attempting to avoid trouble, though, she seemed to be spending an inordinate amount of time contemplating a certain pair of cobalt blue eyes. "Or with your Saint, for that matter, as much as I'm coming to like him."

Evelyn sat back. "Just because you require something different than Georgiana or I did, doesn't mean you're cheating."

For a long moment Lucinda sat and looked at her friend. "I have to apologize to you, Evie," she finally said.

"For what?"

"I always knew what a good, true, and generous friend you were," she continued, "but I didn't realize how very wise you have become."

"Oh, what did I miss now?" Georgiana said from the doorway. "It's Tristan's fault; he insisted on —"

"Darling, please," the viscount interrupted, leaning in behind her. "No need to go into that. Just ask them where the other gentlemen are."

"Tristan!" Georgiana flushed bright red.

Evelyn, though, laughed. "In the billiards room."

"Hurray!" Edward's voice came from deeper in the hallway. "Saint's going to teach me how to cheat!"

"Oh, good heavens," Georgiana muttered, vanishing again amid the clomping of boots. "Edward, you are not —"

"I definitely don't envy Georgie, sometimes," Evie stated, still chuckling.

"And with Andrew due back in London, she'll have five Carroway males to contend with." Lucinda smiled. She found herself wondering whether one particular Carroway had joined the group tonight or not, but she resolutely shook the thought away. She had other things to concentrate on — like allaying any suspicions Lord Geoffrey might have about why he'd been invited to the gathering.

If he planned on attending, that was. "Evie, are you expecting anyone else?" she murmured.

Gray eyes danced. "Yes. Any moment now."

With perfect timing a tall, dark form filled the drawing-room doorway. Lucinda looked up, expecting to see Lord Geoffrey, but the deep blue gazing at her could only belong to one man. "Mister Carroway," she said, surprised by her fast intake of breath. Well, she hadn't expected to see him there, for heaven's sake.

"Lady St. Aubyn," he said in his low voice, "Miss Barrett."

Evie looked at least as startled. "Mister

Carroway. I'm so pleased you decided to come. Won't you join us?"

He glanced at Evie, then settled his gaze again on Lucinda. "Might I have a word with you first, Miss Barrett?"

"Of course."

Avoiding Evie's curious look, she rose and followed Robert back into the relative quiet of the hallway. He'd dressed all in gray but for the white of his simply tied cravat. The color and the dim light darkened his eyes to twilight, and again she felt the unsettling sensation that he could read her thoughts.

"I planted the cuttings," he said abruptly. "And the fish."

"You did? Good."

"And I made you a bargain."

Oh, my. "Mister Carroway, you don't need —"

"Robert," he interrupted.

"Robert, then. I appreciate your offer, but it's really —"

Slowly he reached out a hand and touched her cheek, fingers drifting against her skin as though he expected her to evaporate. "I said I would help," he murmured, "and I will."

A tremor ran down her spine. Whether he had accepted the roses or not, she hadn't expected him ever to mention their agreement again. And she hadn't expected to feel . . . excited by his touch. Lucinda gazed up into his serious blue eyes. "Rob—"

"Good evening, Lucinda," the smooth voice of Lord Geoffrey drawled as he topped the stairs. "And Carroway. Surprised to see you here."

Robert lowered his hand. Lucinda realized both that Geoffrey had seen the gesture, and that Robert had intended for him to do so. With a glance from her to Geoffrey, Robert turned on his heel and vanished in the direction of the billiards room.

"Well, that was interesting," Geoffrey said, taking her hand and bowing over it.

"Yes." Lucinda resisted the urge to clear her throat. "He's a . . . friend of mine."

"So I saw. Will you assist me in locating our host and hostess?"

"Certainly. This way."

As she started off, Lord Geoffrey offered his arm. Wrapping her fingers around his sleeve, she guided him to the drawing room. How strange this evening had become. Five minutes ago she would have wagered both that Robert Carroway would never put in an appearance at Halboro House, and that despite his assurance whatever help he offered would be both useless and unwelcome. It seemed, though, that she would have been wrong — on both counts.

Surreptitiously she reached up to touch her cheek where he'd caressed her. Her skin felt warm. How very strange indeed.

With a slow breath Robert pushed open the billiards-room door and stepped inside. The rumble of male voices hit him first; it sounded as though everyone was talking at once. Then he made out Georgiana's higher, sweeter tones, aimed as usual at trying to dispel some of the chaos. He focused on her, mostly to give himself another moment before he faced the man in the back of the room. As he'd been telling himself all day, he'd entered into an agreement with Miss Barrett, and he couldn't fulfill his part of it from behind the walls of Carroway House — no matter who he might have to encounter along the way.

"I have your word then, Saint," Georgie was saying.

"You have my word. I will only pass on such skills of mine as may be deemed socially acceptable."

"Georgie, you're going to ruin me," Edward complained.

"No, I'm trying very hard to see that that

doesn't happen," she returned, and with a swift kiss to Tristan's cheek, she backed toward the door.

Robert sidestepped so she wouldn't crash into him. "Georgiana," he said, pulling the door open for her.

She touched him on the shoulder before she slipped from the room. Georgiana knew a little of what had happened to him, because he'd told her. She'd told Tristan, but he knew it hadn't gone any further than their immediate family. After all, what family would want it to be known that their brave soldier hadn't been wounded at Waterloo, but had missed the battle entirely? That he'd been kept in a prison for seven months, and had had no part in either of Bonaparte's two surrenders? What excuse would he then have for anything?

He pulled in a breath. And what would even his own family think if they knew everything about those seven months? Robert shuddered, deliberately lifting his gaze to the man who, for a time, anyway, he'd wanted to kill.

"Don't you worry, lad," General Augustus Barrett said to Edward, "I didn't promise anything. You stay close to me, and you'll learn a thing or two."

At that moment Lord Geoffrey entered

the room, and Robert edged farther away from the growing crowd. He wasn't surprised when the general stepped up to be the first to greet Newcombe.

"Geoffrey, you know everyone, don't you?" Barrett asked, shaking the hand of the Duke of Fenley's fourth son. "Our host, Lord St. Aubyn, and —"

"Saint," the marquis interrupted with a slight, dark smile.

"Yes, of course," Geoffrey replied. "Thank you for having me. The invitation was appreciated, if unexpected."

"I like surprises," Saint returned.

The general stepped in again. "All the rest are Carroways. Tristan, Lord Dare, and his brothers Lieutenant Bradshaw, unfortunately of His Majesty's Navy, Edward, and —"

"Call me Runt," Edward said proudly. "I'm the youngest."

"Runt," Geoffrey said, solemnly shaking Edward's proffered hand.

"And the other one there's Robert," General Barrett finished, barely sparing him a glance.

Geoffrey faced him. "Yes. We've met."

Robert inclined his head, his attention still on the general. So that's who he was to Barrett — "the other one." At least the contempt was mutual.

"Thank you," a low, deep voice came from close beside him. Saint leaned on his billiards cue, his gaze on the game.

"For what?" Bit muttered back.

"Being a new addition to the group, I'd begun to think it was me you were avoiding at our various gatherings," the marquis continued, keeping his voice quiet. "But it's not me, is it? It's Barrett."

"I don't know what you're talking about."

Saint nodded. "Fair enough. All the same, I wouldn't mind eventually hearing why. I generally trust my first impressions of people, and both of you seem to have ended up on my very small good side. I'd like to know if I've erred."

"You have," Robert returned. "With both of us."

"How interesting. You don't mind if I continue observing, then."

Robert wanted to tell him to bugger off, but he knew enough about the marquis not to want him as an enemy. "Suit yourself," he said instead.

"I always do." Saint signaled one of the footmen stationed around the room. "And in the meantime I think I'll make a change in the dinner seating arrangements. I believe Evie put you next to Augustus."

Bloody hell. He'd managed to make it there by concentrating on how he could assist Lucinda; dinner seating hadn't occurred to him. For Christ's sake, he almost never stayed anywhere long enough for dinner. "Thank you, then."

"You served on the *Dreadnought*?" Lord Geoffrey asked Bradshaw.

"I did," Shaw returned. "We saw more than a dozen engagements during the war."

"Ha." General Barrett looked up from instructing Edward. "A dozen engagements? How many of those were against French scows trying to run a blockade?"

Shaw only grinned. "A few."

"Enough for Shaw to be made captain," Edward said loyally.

"Congratulations, Carroway," Lord Geoffrey put in. "Perhaps I should have considered making my fortune in the Navy."

"Nonsense, lad. Much more opportunity for advancement in the Army."

"Bit met Wellington once," Edward offered, as he concentrated on lining up his next shot.

Gray eyes turned in Robert's direction. "I'm certain he did," the general conceded. "His Grace always made a point of calling on his wounded officers."

"It was before that. They shared a bottle of whiskey."

Geoffrey lifted an eyebrow. "Do tell. Why not regale us with the tale, Carroway?"

Robert returned his gaze levelly. "No."

Tristan and Bradshaw stepped forward at the same time. "It's your shot again, Runt," the viscount said, moving casually between Robert and Lord Geoffrey.

"I'd like to point out that I've been losing intentionally," Saint put in, shifting, whether by coincidence or not, to block Robert's view of General Barrett, "which makes me quite the generous host, does it not?"

The Halboro butler marched into the room. After giving a slight nod to St. Aubyn, he threw back the door. "Dinner is served."

As the relocation to the drawing room to join the ladies began, Edward found Robert. "Who am I supposed to escort?" he whispered.

Robert did a quick calculation. With three females present, Newcombe would be the last man to escort a guest of the opposite gender — and that would be Lucinda Barrett. "You may escort me," he said in a low voice.

"Good," the boy returned. "I'm glad you

came, or I'd have to escort myself."

Well, at least one of them was happy he was there. As they joined Shaw in back of the pairs strolling into the dining room, though, he had to modify that thought. Georgie made a point of smiling at him, while Tristan and Bradshaw both gave him a look while pretending not to do so.

All right, so all the Carroways were happy he'd managed to last till dinner. And maybe he owed it to them to last through the evening. He sent a glance at Lucinda, who was studying Lord Geoffrey's profile. If he'd been Geoffrey, he wouldn't have wasted time in the billiards room. Any thought of comparing himself with Fenley's son vanished, however, as he realized where St. Aubyn had decided to seat him.

"Miss Barrett," he said, taking the chair beside her.

She looked so elegant, and at the same time perfectly at ease. It was an emotion he could remember, if never hope to duplicate. He wondered if, despite her willingness to exchange words with him, she wished she hadn't run across him that afternoon in the spare bedchamber. At the same time, her breathing had stilled when he touched her cheek. He knew that, because it had felt as though his heart had stopped beating. Was it a sign, then, that he wasn't completely dead and decayed inside? Or did it mean he was simply becoming obsessed with Lucinda Barrett?

Who was he helping, then: her, or himself? Whoever it was, he needed to elevate himself from mute shadow to rival. He'd begun the process, but one touch, soft and breathless though it had been, was not enough.

"It occurred to me," he said quietly, waiting until boisterous conversation had begun around them, "that I might be of more assistance if I knew what appeared on your list."

"My . . . No!" she hissed nearly soundlessly.

You can do this, he shouted at himself, then forced a small smile. "If you don't want to tell me, I could guess."

Lucinda took a rather large gulp of Madeira. "Mister Carroway — Robert — I appreciate your offer, but I really do not need your help. The rose cuttings were a gift, nothing more."

He must sound as desperate as he felt. "What if I told you," he murmured, "that Geoffrey considers himself a hero, and that it is his opinion that has convinced everyone else?"

She looked sideways at him, then slid her gaze toward Geoffrey, who was deep in conversation with the general beside him. *Ah, ha.* No wonder Evelyn was sending infuriated looks at her husband. She'd meant for Geoffrey to sit beside Lucinda, and Saint had made new arrangements, putting the mute beside Miss Barrett. Robert apparently owed Saint a favor, then.

"Lord Geoffrey is assisting my father in re-creating missing portions of his field journals," she said. "So you see, I thank you again, but I have things quite well in hand."

"Very well. Tell me one item on your list, and I'll stop pestering you."

"I will not —" She closed her soft lips. At least he imagined they would be soft. "One item."

"Just one."

"Very well." Lucinda settled her napkin in her lap. "I will tell you one thing if you will tell me one thing."

Cold clenched into his chest. What if she asked something that he couldn't answer? What if he locked down into silence again, where he couldn't speak at all? It had taken him a year to crawl out of that hole — and he wasn't going back, not for anything, not for anyone.

"Do we have a deal, or not?" she prompted.

Stop it, he said to himself. His favorite mantra. She'd made a very simple challenge, one she expected him either to accept or to refuse. One she might make of any normal human. "Deal," he managed, his low voice hoarse.

"D . . . Really?"

For a moment, his expression softened into a fleeting smile. Lucinda could see it deepening into his eyes. In response, for the barest of beats, her breath caught. Good heavens. If he wasn't such a wreck, he would be irresistible.

"You didn't expect me to agree," he said.

She caught Lord Geoffrey looking at the two of them. This was silly. Playing with Robert was only going to delay her plans for Geoffrey, and might very well put them in jeopardy. Still, somewhere deep inside, Robert Carroway intrigued her. "No, I didn't." With a breath, Lucinda called to mind her list of lessons. "All right. This is the first lesson, more or less: 'When conversing with a lady, pay attention to her. Don't act as though you're just biding your time until someone more interesting comes along.' "

Robert gazed at her. "That's it?"

Heat rose in her cheeks. "It's only the first lesson, and *I* think it's important. Not just for me, but for any lady. And now you have to tell me something."

"What might that be?"

She could hear the tension beneath his words, and immediately altered what she'd been about to ask. Her curiosity about what troubled him could wait. She had no intention of hurting him. "Since you have roses now," she said, "where would I find the words 'Now 'tis the spring, and weeds are shallow-rooted/Suffer them now and they'll o'ergrow the garden'?"

Robert blinked. "Beg pardon?"

"You heard me."

For a long moment he gazed at her, while she wondered whether he would — or could — answer. It wasn't the best-known phrase in most circles. Then a slow smile touched his mouth. "It's from *Henry VI, Part Two*. By Shakespeare. But he wasn't talking about plants."

"I know that, but it seemed appropriate." Relieved, and oddly pleased both that she'd surprised him and that he'd known the origin of one of her favorite quotes, she returned his smile. "You do read more than *Frankenstein*."

"I read everyth—"

"Luce? Lucinda, listen." Evie motioned at her. "Lord Geoffrey is telling us about the night he crossed the Tormes River in Spain."

"Yes, listen to the fun," Robert murmured, closing off again and lowering his head to his dinner.

"That's mean," she returned in the same tone. "There's nothing wrong with being a hero."

"Heroes don't tell their own stories," he breathed back. "But I'll make certain he pays attention to you."

For a few moments she only half paid attention to Geoffrey's tale. She'd selected him in part because the choice had seemed amiable and painless. The goal remained precisely that, but with Robert Carroway's involvement, the hunt had become something else entirely. Lucinda took another swallow of Madeira, feeling the heat radiating off the tall, hard man beside her. One thing the lesson-giving *had* become was very, very interesting.

Chapter 7

Their feelings were serene and peaceful,
while mine became every day
more tumultuous.

— The Monster, *Frankenstein*

Outside the breakfast room, Robert stopped.
He'd risen later than usual, both because the
sound of the rain outside when he'd awakened had been soft and soothing, and because the nightmares, never far away, had
come calling again until almost dawn.

"— don't know why you always think I'm
up to something," Georgiana's voice came.

"Because you always are," Tristan replied. "I'm not completely blind, you know.
You and your scheming friends have picked
another victim for your lessons."

"I have no idea what —"

"Come now. It did take me a while to

122

figure out that Evie had targeted St. Aubyn, but since Lucinda's the only one left now, it's —"

"Stop it, Tristan," she interrupted, her tone more amused than angry. "You're not supposed to know anything about the lessons, anyway."

"You three happen to be rather consistent in your strategies," the viscount returned. "It's difficult to miss, once you know what to look for. Besides, suddenly inviting Lord Geoffrey Newcombe to one of our dinners? I only hope for Lucinda's sake that it wasn't as obvious to Geoffrey as it was to me."

Georgiana chuckled. "My goodness, you *have* become enlightened. You're actually sympathizing with Lucinda."

"I'm not sympathizing with anyone. Keep me out of it, if you please." He was silent for a moment. "But what does all this have to do with Bit?"

Robert leaned back against the wall. Whatever the common opinion about eavesdropping, he had a long time ago learned to appreciate its merits.

"Bit's not involved," Georgiana answered. "I wouldn't put him in the middle of something like this, and neither would Luce. You're the one who suggested he start a hobby. Lucinda is an expert in roses, and she's . . . not threatening."

Not threatening. If that meant the same thing as serene and insightful and compassionate, Georgie was correct. For three years he'd looked forward to seeing Lucinda, even from a distance. Close to her, interacting with her, she felt like daylight after a very long, very dark night. He couldn't help stretching his wings a little, yet he still lingered in the shadows, afraid the sun would burn him to ashes. But he'd made her a bargain, and she remained as alluring as candlelight to a moth.

He pushed away from the wall and strolled into the breakfast room. "Good morning."

Tristan and Georgiana looked up from their side-by-side seats at the table. "Good morning," Georgie returned. "How are you feeling?"

"Hungry." He headed for the food spread along the sideboard, wondering how things that he could remember coming easily to him seemed so far out of his grasp now. Robert drew a breath. "Tristan, are you still having luncheon at the Society today?"

He could almost hear the look that passed between Lord and Lady Dare. "I had planned to, yes."

"May I go with you?"

Silence. "Of course."

"Thank you."

His appetite fled as he considered what he'd decided to put himself through, but he dumped a few slices of bread and fresh fruit on his plate anyway. Being hungry only made him feel worse, and he would need every advantage he could conjure.

As Robert took a seat, Bradshaw strolled into the room, Edward slung over one shoulder. "I do weigh more than a bag of duffel," the Runt was protesting.

"You're more wiggly than most luggage," Bradshaw conceded, setting his brother on the floor. "I'll give you that."

"Pfftthh."

Bradshaw chuckled. "Good morning, family. Tris, may I still drag Perkins with us to luncheon? He's been trying to get a sponsorship to the Society for ages."

Dare cleared his throat, while Robert pretended not to notice his oldest brother's hesitation. Luncheon in public with family would be nerve-racking enough; if strangers were joining the spectacle, he wasn't certain he could do it.

"Just us today, Shaw," the viscount said. "You and Bit and I."

"B . . . Good idea, then. Don't want

125

someone else diluting our splendid Carroway-ness."

"Oh, good heavens," Georgiana muttered, chuckling.

"I want to go," Edward said, plunking himself down beside Robert and pilfering half an orange from his brother's plate. "I have Carroway-ness."

"You have to weigh more than a bag of duffel before you can go to the Society Club, Runt."

"I *do* weigh —"

"You may join me for luncheon with Lucinda and Evie," Georgie suggested.

"With a bunch of females?"

"At the museum," the viscountess continued.

"Can we — may we — go see the mummies?"

"Certainly. And I believe Evie has arranged for several of her charges to join us."

"The orphans?" Edward asked, piling jam onto his bread until it overflowed the crust and oozed onto his plate.

"A dozen of the youngest, yes."

"So I'll be the oldest."

Georgiana smiled. "You will be the oldest."

"All right, then. I'll go with you."

"Thank you, Edward."

With the aunties gone, Robert could have had Carroway House virtually to himself all afternoon. That was how most days went, though, and truth be told, he was growing tired of the endless repetition. Whether he would feel the same way after luncheon, he had no idea. Hell, he wasn't even certain he would survive luncheon.

He already knew, though, that as a recluse he couldn't possibly be of any assistance to Miss Barrett, or to himself. If Society thought he'd come back into its pretentious little fold, however, it would certainly notice to which lady he paid attention — and so would Lord Geoffrey Newcombe.

Robert shoved in another mouthful of toast. He tried not to think too much about it, but if he succeeded today he might actually be able to step a little out of the shadows. If mottled sunlight didn't burn too badly, who knew where his next step might lead him?

"I need to sit down for a moment." Georgiana found a bench just outside the Egyptian exhibit at the British Museum and sank onto the stone with a sigh.

Lucinda sat beside her, watching as Evie, with Edward's assistance, explained the theories of mummification. From the wrinkled noses and groans, the children thoroughly enjoyed it.

"I am going to make Tristan rub my feet for an hour," Georgie said, surreptitiously kicking out of one shoe.

"You shouldn't be doing this at all."

"Don't you start, too. I only have another three weeks before he whisks me off to Dare Park for my confinement. Whoever thought of that word, anyway? 'Confinement.' It sounds like I'm going to prison."

"Only three more weeks?" Lucinda repeated.

"I know. It's poor timing all around. Here you are in the middle of delivering your lesson, Bradshaw's about to get his own ship, and Robert's actually going to luncheon at the Society Club. If he's finally feeling well enough to . . . Well, if he needs Dare's or my support, I'll simply have to have my confinement here in London."

Lucinda blinked. Robert was deliberately going out in public? It had to have something to do with their agreement. *Oh, dear.* If he was somehow hurt, it would be her fault. She needed to call this off at once — except that in a small, wicked way, his attention made her life feel . . . larger than it was. Abruptly she scowled. Her life wasn't small; it was orderly. Robert upset the order. That

128

fact didn't explain, though, why she wasn't avoiding him, and why she seemed to think about him almost constantly.

"Luce?"

"Hm? I'm sorry. My mind must have been wandering."

"In any direction in particular?"

She looked at Georgiana. Her friend's expression had turned surprisingly serious. "Meaning?"

"Robert."

No doubt Robert would not appreciate anything she might say, but Georgie was her dearest friend, and honestly concerned about her brother-in-law's well-being. And so was she, she was beginning to realize. It was only because he was a friend, she decided. A new friend. An unexpected friend, when she seemed to have planned the rest of her life to the last detail. "This has to remain between us."

"Very well."

"I'm serious, Georgiana. Between *us*."

Georgiana looked down for a moment, obviously considering. "Between us," she finally repeated, nodding.

"I offered to help Robert with his rose garden," Lucinda said slowly, "and he refused. I think he felt I was there out of . . . pity, or something. He suggested that we make a trade, instead."

"A trade?"

"In return for my rose cuttings and advice, Robert proposed that he would assist me in getting Lord Geoffrey to comply with the items on my list."

Georgiana shot to her feet, no easy task for a woman as pregnant as she was. "You told him about our lessons?" she exclaimed, white-faced.

"No! Of course not. He broached the subject to me. He knew all about the lessons, Georgie — and about Dare and St. Aubyn."

Slowly Georgiana resumed her seat. "Damnation. I should have realized. He always knows everything that's going on."

"One of the benefits of being practically invisible."

"He's not — Oh, bother. I don't know why I'm arguing with you; you're not the spy. That big sneak."

"I don't think he meant any harm by it. He just seemed curious." She tucked her arm around Georgie's. "I tried to tell him that the roses were a gift, but he insisted that he was going to help me with Lord Geoffrey."

"So that's what all of this activity of his has been about. And he knows about your interest in Geoffrey?"

It was more a statement than a question, but Lucinda nodded anyway. "Oh, he knows. He was actually under the impression that we were each choosing a man in turn with the object of marrying him."

Georgiana scowled. "And he just came out and said all this to you."

"Y—"

The viscountess pushed to her feet again as the children filed out of the Egypt room. "Bit and I are going to have a little chat this evening."

"No, you're not. Not about anything I just told you. Whatever he thinks he can or can't do to help, I won't be responsible for . . ." She searched for the right words. "For making him feel ill again."

Young Edward emerged at the end of the parade of orphans. Lucinda wondered what it must be like for him, to have four formidable older brothers, and to have for the most part been raised by them. The boy obviously didn't lack self-confidence — how could he, with that family around him?

And then there was Robert. Whatever had happened to him, whatever he'd seen, it had profoundly changed him. And for some reason, he'd decided that they had something to offer to each other, he and she. Lucinda sighed. Whatever else she might tell herself, she wasn't simply doing a good deed. Altruism or charity didn't explain why she kept noticing that he had the deepest blue eyes she'd ever seen.

"Miss Lucinda?"

She started. "Yes, Edward?"

"I almost forgot. I'm supposed to give this to you." The ten-year-old dug a much-folded note out of his coat pocket and handed it to her.

"Thank you." She unfolded it to reveal Robert's hand, surprisingly neat, as though he'd thought out each word before he put pen to paper. It asked simply if she'd care to go riding in the morning. The missive was initialed only "R.C."

Lord Geoffrey would be calling for luncheon at noon, and she almost refused. At the same time, her appointment with Geoffrey gave her an excuse for a short outing with her purported co-conspirator — all for the cause, and she wouldn't have to decide yet whether allowing his continued involvement was simply a charitable act or not.

She pulled a pencil from her reticule and scribbled her answer across the bottom of the page before she folded the note again. "Please return this," she said, handing it back to Edward.

Georgiana looked at her expectantly, but she pretended not to notice. If Robert had wanted his family members involved, he would have included them.

So two gentlemen would be calling tomorrow; one to aid her in netting the second, and the other with no idea he was being hunted. And she claimed to like things uncomplicated. *Ha.*

When Robert came downstairs, Tristan and Bradshaw were already in the foyer pretending not to be edgy. They knew as well as he did that he hadn't set foot in one of London's gentlemen's clubs in better than five years, since he'd left England to join his regiment in Spain.

"I had the coach brought up," Tristan said as Robert reached them. "Unless you'd rather ride."

It wasn't an easy choice; sitting for fifteen minutes in a tiny, dark coach, or giving himself an easy opportunity to escape the entire venture aboard Tolley. "The coach is fine."

"Good. Ready?"

No! Robert nodded even though every muscle was taut, urging him to retreat. His breath was already coming too fast, and he forced himself to slow down. He could do this. It was just an hour or two, and then he could look forward to a ride in the early morning — with Lucinda. Or without her, if she had any sense and refused his offer.

Even the butler looked concerned as he pulled open the front door for them. Robert hung back as Bradshaw and Tristan climbed into the coach. He knew he could turn around now and that neither of them would ever say another word about it. And he remembered what Bradshaw had said, that he'd done nothing with his life.

Taking a deep breath, he stepped up into the coach. His brothers would see that he was reluctant and tense, but they wouldn't see that he was terrified — not of the coach or of the club, but that he wouldn't be able to hold the blackness at bay and that it would strike him when he was out in the open.

"I had a thought," Bradshaw said into the silence.

"Amazing," Tristan returned dryly.

"Very amusing. I was just going to say that with St. Aubyn now part of our alliance, we could recruit him and the Duke of Wycliffe, and apply for re-admission to White's."

Tristan lifted an eyebrow. "As I recall, *I* was the only one banned from White's, and it was *your* fault."

"Which is why I'm planning to get you back in."

"Don't bother, Shaw. I like being banned. It reminds Georgiana how much I love her."

Dark humor, and gratitude for the distraction, touched Robert. "It might also remind her how angry she was at you."

"And that is *also* my point," Shaw added. "I have many."

"No, that was Bit's point, but I'm still not interested. I'm going to be a father in a few short weeks, my lads, and oddly enough, that is more significant to me than just about anything else I can imagine."

Robert studied his brother's fond, amused expression. Tristan was obviously excited and pleased about his impending fatherhood. It seemed almost strange to be able to look forward to something with anticipation. Robert had spent so long dreading every night — and doubting that the following dawn would ever arrive.

The coach rolled to a halt, and a liveried Society footman pulled open the door and flipped down the step. Once again Robert hung back, then limped down to the ground. He could do this. He *wanted* to do this.

"Welcome, Lord Dare, Mr. Carroway," the host said, glancing at Robert and then leading them into the club's large dining room.

"By the window," Robert muttered, taking in the crowded room and close tables and heavy, dark wood paneling. *Breathe.*

"Watson, by the window if you please," Tristan drawled, nodding at some acquaintance or other.

A muscle in his round cheek twitching, their host changed direction. "I hadn't anticipated," he said, gesturing at a pair of footmen to clean and re-set a just vacated table. "Will this do?"

"Bit?" the viscount murmured.

Robert nodded stiffly, and the three Carroways took their seats. He'd done it; he'd made it inside. Now all he had to do was eat and leave.

"Carroway," a booming male voice came from behind him, "I hear congratulations are in order." A beefy hand reached past him in Bradshaw's direction. "Captain, is it?"

"Not yet officially," Bradshaw returned, shaking the hand, "but the paperwork's in process. You know my brothers, don't you, Hedgely? Dare and Robert? Tristan, Bit, Lord Hedgely."

"Oh, I know Dare. So this is the other one, eh?" Hedgely removed a chair from a neighboring table and dragged it closer to settle his large frame into it. "I heard you'd lost a leg or something at Waterloo. Or was it your mind you lost? You don't look like a Bedlamite."

Robert lifted his gaze from his hands to Hedgely. Brown eyes in a round, soft face met his and then flicked away. If Hedgely ended up being his most imposing foe, he'd been worrying over a great deal for no good reason.

"We met several years ago at the Devonshire ball," Robert said, his voice low but steady. "You were hanging on Lady Wedgerton, as I recall. Did her husband ever find out about your flirtation?"

For a moment Hedgely sat where he was, mouth hanging open and face growing red. A ripple of commentary flowed about the room, but Robert stayed there, unmoving, waiting for Hedgely's next move. In an odd way it was empowering to have nothing left to lose, to have toes clawed so hard into the rock at the edge of the precipice that nothing — *nothing* — could make him loose his grip in the stone.

"I don't know what you're talking about," Hedgely finally blustered.

"And I don't know what you're talking about," Robert returned. "Apparently we

137

have something in common."

"There's no cause to be rude. Here I am, trying to show a cripple a bit of charity, and —"

"And you have no idea how much charity I'm showing you, right now," Robert interrupted, aware that Shaw had started to his feet and that Tristan had motioned him to sit down. "How are your gambling debts these days?"

Hedgely shoved to his feet. "I will not sit for this," he snarled. "Dare, I suggest you either control your brother or put him back in his cage."

Tristan pulled a cigar from his pocket. "I'm enjoying the conversation, myself," he returned, "but if it upsets you, well, good day, Hedgely."

Bradshaw looked over as Hedgely stalked back to his own table and sat amid the sympathetic commiserations of his fellows. "That was interesting," he murmured, hiding a chuckle behind his glass of port.

"It was just a question," Robert said with forced lightness, unclenching one fist and feeling blood flow back into his fingers. His brothers had stood up for him. He hadn't really doubted that they would, but it warmed the tiny bit left of his soul. "Sorry about that."

"The day hasn't been a success unless somebody threatens to ban me from a club," Tristan said, "but that little byplay does make me wonder why you wanted to come to luncheon today. You had to know people would be curious to see you."

Of course he'd known. "They can gawk all they want," he grunted, suppressing a shudder, "but I'd prefer if they kept their distance. And I wanted to come to luncheon today because I wanted to. If that isn't enough, th—"

"It's enough. And after Hedgely, I don't think anyone else will be approaching to insult your health, if that's any consolation."

"It is."

Shaw cleared his throat. "Not that I'm asking for a punch in the eye or anything, but I didn't mean to upset you the other day."

Longingly fingering the glass of port Tristan had set in front of him, Robert shrugged. "I don't always know what might . . ." He trailed off, blanching. *Jesus.* He'd almost told them about the black panic. That would send him to Bedlam faster than anything else he could imagine. "Apology accepted." Slowly he nudged the glass away.

"I would think that might make today a little easier," Tristan noted, snapping a finger against the glass and making it ring.

Robert's hands trembled and he clenched them together once more. "It would, but then it's not real."

"Are you sure —"

"I'm not going to drink," he said, drawing a breath. "I don't think I'd be able to stop once I began."

Tristan signaled a footman. "Roast lamb all around, Stephen," he ordered, smiling at Bradshaw's grimace. "And lemonade."

"Very good, my lord."

As the footman vanished in the direction of the kitchens, Tristan lit his cigar and leaned back in his chair. "I had a letter from Andrew yesterday. He's taking the mail coach down from Cambridge, and should be in London by tomorrow after-noon."

"Good." Andrew probably had more fun at school, but Robert always felt better when he knew where everyone was. It made no sense, but he needed to know that his family was safe, needed to feel as though he could protect them. *Ah, that was amusing. As if he could protect anyone.*

"Are you coming back to Dare Park with us when Georgiana and I go?"

He shook himself. "You're taking Edward?"

Tristan nodded. "And the aunties. They insist Georgie will need their help."

Robert shrugged. "I don't know." Surprisingly, a face flitted across his mind — a kind, oval face with hazel eyes and dark hair that shone like bronze in the sunlight. Lucinda would still be in London, and still be in pursuit of Geoffrey Newcombe. None of it was any of his business, but she was the reason he was sitting in the Society Club right now.

"You don't have to decide yet."

"I'll be back at sea by then," Bradshaw put in, "so I'll comfort myself with the knowledge that you'll name the infant after me."

"I don't think 'Half-wit' will pass muster with Georgie, but I'll let her know that's your suggestion."

The food arrived, and Robert found himself calm enough that he actually had an appetite. That in itself seemed a victory — one tiny enough to require the use of a very strong magnifying lens, but a victory, nonetheless.

His first indication that he'd been far too confident didn't come until Tristan uttered a soft curse under his breath. Robert looked up to see his eldest brother scowling, his gaze turned toward the dining-room entrance.

As the crowd shifted, he spied the reason for Dare's frown; the Duke of Wellington, accompanied by a handful of officials from the Horse Guards headquarters, strolled in to take a table only a dozen feet from theirs. General Augustus Barrett sent a glance in their direction, nodding at Tristan, as he seated himself to the right of the duke.

Robert's first thought was to get up and leave — immediately, before any of the over-medaled officers could begin telling tales about the glory of war. He glanced at his brothers, both of whom had gone back to eating in silence, clearly waiting to see what he wanted to do.

If he left, they would accompany him. But walking out less than a minute after Wellington's arrival could have serious political repercussions. *Just ignore them,* he ordered himself, deliberately shoveling a forkful of roast lamb into his mouth. *You're invisible to them, anyway.*

"Bit," Bradshaw hissed.

"I'm f—"

"Captain Robert Carroway," Wellington's voice came from directly behind him. At the same time, the duke laid a

142

hand on his shoulder.

"Your Grace," he returned, the steadiness of his own voice surprising him. For the first time it occurred to him that compared to what had happened in Spain, this was nothing.

"I believe I still owe you a bottle of whiskey," the duke said.

"No nee—"

"And the thanks of a nation," Wellington continued, a smile in his voice. "Your contributions on the battlefield at Waterloo were invaluable."

He didn't know. Wellington didn't know a damned thing. "Thank you, Your Grace."

Applause circled the room, polite and aimed more at the duke than at the recipient of the compliment, thank God. If the duke asked him to stand and shake hands, he was going to vomit. Instead, after delivering another pat on the shoulder, Wellington returned to his seat.

"Robert?" Tristan whispered.

The black panic sucked at his heels. He could fall into it, drown in it, and no one would even know. Not even his brothers. If he was going to stay afloat, he would have to do it himself. Fighting for air, he shook his head. "Eat."

Fifteen minutes. If they stayed for fifteen

more minutes, they could leave without offending anyone — Tristan and Shaw could leave without offending anyone, that was.

He counted off every second of every minute. In one-second increments, he could survive. He made it through twelve seconds, through three minutes and twenty-eight seconds, through nine minutes. He'd lived seven months of his life by the second. This wasn't easy, but it was survivable, and while he counted, he couldn't drown. Besides, tomorrow he was going riding with Lucinda Barrett, and she had the gift of turning seconds into minutes.

Finally he reached fifteen. "I'm leaving," he said, pushing back from the table.

"We'll all go," Tristan said, signaling for the bill. He quickly signed for it to go to his account, and the three of them rose.

"That was actually a nice gesture on Wellington's part," Shaw said, climbing into the coach as it stopped beside them. "I very much doubt he thanks everyone for their contribution at Waterloo."

Robert pulled the door closed as he sat, for once grateful to trade the crowd for a small space. "He doesn't know anything," he growled, folding his arms so his brothers wouldn't see his hands shaking.

"Don't underestimate yourself, Bit. If he

thanked you, then you deserved —"

"Shaw," Tristan cautioned, "leave it be."

"I wasn't at Waterloo," Robert returned, then closed his eyes so he couldn't see the shock on Shaw's face. *Ha*. Now another brother could join in the general disappointment over his so-called life.

Chapter 8

You will rejoice to hear that no
disaster has accompanied the
commencement of an
enterprise which you have regarded
with such evil forebodings.

— Robert Walton, *Frankenstein*

"My father said that Wellington singled you
out yesterday."

Lucinda slipped on her riding gloves,
gazing at Robert from the corner of her eye
while he paced her front drive. His bay
walked a step behind him, gauging his
owner's turns to perfection despite the fact
that the reins were looped over the saddle,
and nothing connected one to the other.

"He thanked you for your service at
Waterloo," she continued, when he declined to answer. "That was nice of him."

"Why is that?" Robert grunted, then went back to his pacing as her groom brought Isis up from the stable.

And to think, she might have been weeding her garden this morning. "It's generally considered nice when someone thanks you for your efforts," she returned.

Robert threw a glance at her groom, then limped forward to offer her a hand into the saddle. "He was pointing out that *he* was in command at Waterloo, and that the nation actually owes *him* thanks," he said in his low voice. "I would imagine he's laying the groundwork for becoming prime minister. Where I was or what I did has absolutely nothing to do with it."

Lucinda stepped into his hands and let him boost her up into the sidesaddle. "Do you know all that, or are you just guessing?"

As he walked away from her, and then swung into his saddle in one fluid motion, she didn't think he would answer. It didn't matter what he said, she supposed; the most remarkable outcome of his outing yesterday seemed to be that her father had mentioned his name without scowling.

"Deductive reasoning," he finally said, nudging his animal up beside her. "Do you want to go riding, or do you want to go to Hyde Park?"

She understood what he meant; at this time of morning, managing even a steady walk through the park would take a near miracle. A ride, though, would mean heading north, out of London — spending more time with Robert and risking being late for Lord Geoffrey's visit this afternoon.

Dark blue eyes watched her. He probably knew about her father's scheduled meeting with Lord Geoffrey, because he knew everything, and he was daring her to make a choice. It would make sense if he were a suitor, but he was supposed to be helping her in regards *to* Geoffrey. Still . . .

"I would like to go riding," she said.

Something flashed deep in his eyes before he nodded. "I'll have you back for luncheon." With a shift of his knee he sent his mount down the drive.

"Um, Robert?"

He pulled up. "Changed your mind?"

"Did you bring along a chaperone?"

Robert looked at her blankly for a moment. Then he grinned. The change to his countenance was remarkable, with twinkling eyes that crinkled in the corners, and an openness to his smile that made her want to sigh — and to grin back at him. *My heavens.*

"I haven't —" he began, then stopped to clear his throat. "My apologies. I didn't think of it."

She twisted to face the house. "Benjamin? Please saddle a mount and join us."

"Yes, Miss Lucinda." The groom hurried back around the far corner of the house.

"Not very gentlemanly of me, was it?" he offered, the remains of his amusement still dancing in his eyes.

Lucinda smiled. "In a way, it's flattering."

"How so?"

"Well, a chaperone would protect good little me from big bad you. I choose to think that you see us on more equal footing than that."

"A nice way of saying that I have no teeth."

To her surprise, he didn't seem offended by the notion. Lord Geoffrey, if he ever offered to take her anywhere, would more than likely make some comment that she would need a chaperone to protect her maidenly virtue from his manly rakishness.

"It's not that," she returned. "I think you have teeth. It's just that you also have honor."

He looked at her for a moment, the expression in his eyes growing cool again. "You're wrong about that, but thank you."

Benjamin trotted around the corner of the house. With the groom following a few yards behind them, they headed down the drive and turned north.

"Georgiana always said you were a fine rider," she commented after they'd gone a mile in silence. "I see that she's right." In truth, he and his mount seemed so . . . connected that she doubted he even needed to use the reins.

"I like to ride. When I came back from Spain I wasn't certain Tolley would even recognize me, but he did." He patted the bay on the neck, affection in both the motion and his tone. "Better than I did," he continued in a quieter voice.

Lucinda swallowed. For the first time it felt as if this private, solitary man had let her inside, just a little. And abruptly she wasn't certain whether she was worthy of being there. It made everything seem . . . different. She wasn't performing an act of charity; a very private man was doing her the honor of letting her glimpse his life.

"Since we're working on getting Lord Geoffrey to comply with your first lesson," he said in a more conversational tone, "perhaps you might tell me your second."

She swallowed. Back to business. It was too unsettling to think this might be something other than a trade of favors. "Wait a moment. How are we getting Lord Geoffrey to pay his undivided attention to whichever female he is speaking?"

"Attention to *you,* you mean," he countered.

Well, she'd never admitted to him that she was plotting marriage with Lord Geoffrey, but denying it at this point didn't seem to serve much purpose. "All right, attention to me," she agreed. "How are you doing this?"

Robert hesitated. "It's complicated."

"I'm fairly intelligent," she said dryly, trying to set him back at ease. "Humor me."

He cleared his throat. "Apologies again. I . . . You'd think I would be better at choosing words, with the small quantity of them I use."

Laughter escaped her lips before she could stop herself. His sense of humor was so unexpected. She'd glimpsed it before, and Georgie had mentioned it, but she just assumed that he never showed that side of himself to outsiders. Again she felt honored. And surprised to realize that she enjoyed bantering with him. "Don't apologize," she said, grinning. "I'll let you know when I'm offended. And don't change the subject. How are we working on lesson number one?"

"Look to your right," he murmured, maneuvering Tolley closer.

She looked. They were passing by the front entrance of Gentleman Jackson's boxing establishment. As they crossed, Earl Clanfeld and William Pierce turned from their conversation on the steps to watch them.

"Lord Clanfeld and Mr. Pierce?"

"They're good friends of your Lord Geoffrey, and coincidentally they happen to be on their way to meet him at White's."

"How do you know that?"

He shrugged. "I pay attention."

Remarkable. She wondered whether he had everyone's schedule memorized, and how much he managed to overhear simply because he had the ability to make himself virtually invisible. No wonder more than a few people claimed he could read minds.

"All right, so they all meet at White's this morning. What good does that do us?"

"They know that Lord Geoffrey is meeting you and the General today for luncheon. You will come up in the conversation, and then so will the fact that you spent your morning with another man. We'll also manage to return you home slightly late, so he'll see you arrive at the front door with me."

"So we're making him jealous? It's a little premature for that tactic, don't you think?"

"We're not working toward jealousy. We're making certain that in his eyes you're not just your father's note-taker. You're a lady with admirers."

Admirers. Did Robert include himself in that category? Or was this truly just a repayment for rose cuttings? Lucinda focused her gaze on Isis's ears. It didn't matter what his motives might be. They were making a trade. The end.

"What if I'd decided we should go to Hyde Park?" she asked.

"I knew you wouldn't."

Lucinda lifted an eyebrow. "That's a bit presumptive. How could you know that for certain?"

"You're kind and considerate, and you knew I'd hate going to Hyde Park in the middle of the morning." His fleeting smile appeared again. "Just on the off chance you'd opted for the Park, however, Lord Geoffrey's sister-in-law, the Marchioness of Easton, leads an entourage through there every Tuesday and Thursday. She was only a contingency plan, though, because she won't see Geoffrey and the rest of the Newcombe family until evening after next."

"You are so devious," she exclaimed.

"But just for your information, I dislike Hyde Park myself."

"I'll keep that in mind."

No doubt he would. She shook her head at him, trying to pretend that his quiet tone didn't have an intimate edge that made her throat dry and her heartbeat quicken. "So is there anyone else we need to impress this morning?" she asked lightly.

"No, I don't think so. We can be as unpleasant as we like."

"That's reassuring, though I've found that it's easier to be pleasant when there's less need to be so."

As they left buildings behind and entered an area of glades and meadows, Robert slowed, his gaze again on her face. "Talking is that way for me," he said slowly. "I . . . got out of the habit of it, I think, and now I spend so much time thinking about it that the chance to speak sometimes passes me by."

"You talk to me."

"You're easy to talk to."

Her cheeks warmed. For goodness' sake, she hadn't been fishing for compliments. Before she could think of something to say in return, Robert kneed the gelding. He and Tolley set off across the meadow at a canter. Relieved herself that she didn't need to talk this time, she set off after him.

Lucinda was a fair rider. She'd obviously spent more time on sedate walks than gallops, but she had enough skill to know her limitations. After a few moments of watching, Robert felt reasonably sure that she wouldn't fall off her horse and break her neck.

For him and Tolley the day was a nice change as well. In daylight the sense of disconnection with the world wasn't as strong, but the fresh, warm air and sunshine were a fair compensation.

They spent two hours racing and riding, and as a bonus, not doing much talking. It was the most freeing experience of the last three years, and the smile on his face as he dug for his pocket watch felt easy and natural.

He flipped open the watch's cover, then shoved it back into his pocket. He sent Tolley in a tight circle around Lucinda and her mare, Isis. "We need to start back."

Her dark hair with its highlights of red and gold had come loose beneath her riding hat, and a long, tangled strand caressed her cheek as she grinned at him. "Time for the second part of our plan?"

He nodded, leading the way back to the

road. *Don't look at her like that,* he told himself. She was a friend, a rarity for him these days. And besides, she'd made it painfully clear both that she thought him toothless, and that she'd already chosen someone else.

She didn't even try to coax him into conversation on the way back to Barrett House. If his theory was correct, though, Geoffrey Newcombe would be watching for them when they turned up the drive. So, taking another breath and wishing they could have spent the entire day out of the city, he drew closer to her.

"You were going to tell me what lesson number two entails."

"No, I wasn't," she retorted, chuckling. "You haven't proven anything to me about your supposed success with lesson number one, yet."

"But I need to prepare a strategy for the next step. Surely you understand what a complex prospect all of this is. Plotting, planning, machinations, everything."

A blush crept up her cheeks. "It's actually rather silly, now that I think about it. And this one really isn't precisely for me — it's for all ladies."

"Tell me," he coaxed, noting that they were nearly at her house.

She blew out her breath. "Fine. It just

says that when a gentleman bothers to attend a dance, he should dance. Especially when there are always more ladies than men present. It's embarrassing to be the lone female not dancing while men stand about chatting."

"Geoffrey's already danced with you."

"Yes, but . . . he dances at his whim. Every young lady should be asked to dance at least once. I'm sure most handsome, popular men never even glance at who's sitting against the wall or trying to look busy at the refreshment table."

"But *you* notice," he countered. It made sense; she'd noticed him, as well. Dancing — that was one lesson where Lord Geoffrey definitely had the advantage. He'd said he was going to help, though, and he would find a way to do so. "I'll look into a plan," he said, gesturing her to precede him up the drive, and abruptly wishing that he didn't have to return her to anyone.

To his surprise, though, she stopped, luckily between two large shrubs and out of sight of the house. She put a hand on his arm. "Robert, the lesson is not a slight to you," she said, her face solemn.

Before he could convince himself of the idiocy of his impulse or think where their chaperone might be, he leaned over and touched his mouth to hers. For a second, for a heartbeat, time stopped. And then he made himself straighten, before she could pull away. "I know," he returned quietly, when he could breathe again. "You weren't thinking of me when you made the list."

She looked as stunned as he felt. Robert slapped Isis on the flank, and the mare jumped forward. He followed up the drive, noting that the curtains stirred in an overlooking upstairs room. *Ah, their audience.*

He swung down from Tolley and limped forward to take her hand. "Apologies again," he said, forcing a smile as he helped her to the ground. "Let me know how lesson number one proceeds."

Before she could answer, he returned to Tolley and climbed back into the saddle. For a moment, Lucinda watched him down the drive. "I'll let you know if you've offended me," she murmured, running her fingers along her lips.

Robert took the long way home. He hadn't meant to kiss Lucinda, hadn't intended to do any such thing. There he'd been, claiming to be her friend, claiming to have no ulterior motive, and then the need to touch her had simply overwhelmed him. Of course he could blame it on the fact that he hadn't touched anyone in a very long time, but that didn't excuse anything.

"Idiot," he muttered, and Tolley's ears flicked at him.

He'd probably ended whatever bargain they had; she'd be a fool to allow him to continue associating with her after that, and Lucinda Barrett was no fool. Had it been worth it, then, to trade his best chance to return to Society for a kiss? For a soft, sweet, hesitant, momentary escape from hell?

Yes.

John, the head groom, emerged from the stable to take charge of Tolley as he dismounted. Robert pulled a last carrot from his pocket and fed it to the gelding. All in all, it had been a very good morning.

By this time of day his family would have scattered to their various meetings, luncheons, and social outings. Even the Runt and his tutor, Mr. Trost, had opted to spend the afternoon at the London Zoo.

"Master Robert," Dawkins said as he pulled open the front door. "Shall I have Mrs. Haller prepare something for luncheon?"

"Just a sandwich," he said. "I'll be in the library."

"Very good, sir."

Between the foyer and the library, though, lay Tristan's office. Robert hesitated in the doorway and then slipped inside. All of the party invitations accepted by the family lay on one corner of the viscount's desk. Whether he'd ruined his friendship with Lucinda or not, he couldn't deny that he wanted to see her again. At the least he probably deserved a slap on the face. And besides, her second lesson had involved dancing. One had to attend an event in order to dance.

Dance. Aside from the constant ache of his left knee, he wasn't certain he even remembered the steps to the simplest jig. That would be a sight, Robert Carroway stumbling across the dance floor with the charitable Miss Barrett, then falling flat on his face. He grimaced. At least it might encourage all of the other males present to claim partners, if only to protect them from him.

He went through the short stack of invitations twice anyway. It couldn't hurt to know what was going on. Since Tristan and Georgiana would be attending them, Lucinda probably would be, as well. Thankfully, two or three looked to be fairly small and less formal, though he would have preferred knowing how disgusted Lucinda was with him before he talked himself into attending any of them.

The front door opened. Robert swiftly restacked the cards and strode for the hall door, but stopped at the sound of something heavy hitting the foyer floor.

"Master Andrew!" Dawkins exclaimed. "We didn't expect you until this evening."

"I managed a ride with a friend. Who's here?"

"Only Master Robert, at the moment. You will find him in the library."

"My thanks, Dawkins. And if Mrs. Haller could manage luncheon, I won't be forced to eat any furniture."

The butler chuckled. "Luncheon it is, Master Andrew."

Robert scowled as Andrew headed down the hallway. Not even he could manage to get from the office to the library without being seen, so naturally Andrew would think he'd been skulking. He seemed to skulk quite a bit, even when he didn't intend to. Smoothing his expression, he stepped into the hall.

"Bit!" Eighteen-year-old Andrew practically skidded to a halt. His arms lifted to deliver a hug, and then dropped again, as if he'd abruptly realized which brother he faced.

"You're taller," Robert said, offering a hand.

Surprise flashing in his light blue eyes, Andrew shook his proffered hand. "Nearly two inches. I think I've passed Shaw." His eyes angled past Robert to Tristan's office and then back again.

He had nothing to hide, Robert reminded himself. "I was looking at party invitations," he said. "Come to the library and tell me about your term."

"You want . . . ? All right." With a happy grin, Andrew headed down the hallway again. "What's that patch of weeds somebody's cleared out by the stables?"

"It's my rose garden." That reminded him; he needed to water the cuttings again. Lucinda had instructed him to do so daily for the first month.

"Your . . ." Andrew slowed, then faced him again. "You've been out riding," he said, gesturing at Robert's jacket.

Robert nodded. "I went with a friend." Though whether she was still a friend or not remained to be seen.

"With . . . Sweet Lucifer." Andrew lunged forward and threw his arms around Robert in a tight hug.

Robert's first instinct was to flinch backward, away from the restraint. *Be calm,* he shouted at himself, forcing a deep breath. *It's just Andrew.* He even managed a brief pat on his brother's back.

"Sorry," Andrew said, releasing him. "Are you all right?"

He nodded tightly. "You surprised me."

"And you surprised me." His brother looked at him closely, brief concern touching his blue-gray gaze again. "But I'll warn you next time."

They settled into the library, and for nearly an hour Andrew regaled him with a nonstop chronicle of the highlights of his second term at Cambridge. After a morning spent in the company of Lucinda and the subsequent idiocy of his actions, what Robert desperately wanted was just a few minutes of solitary silence. Andrew had been so obviously delighted at his "improvement," though, as he'd heard Tristan refer to it, that he couldn't stand the idea of disappointing him.

Even so, the strain of continuous sociability, of listening to tales of a happy, boisterous life so different from his own, began to make his hands shake. He grabbed a book and opened it, clenching his hands in his lap to hide the weakness from his brother. Shortly after that, though, the room began to close in, and his skin tighten across his muscles. *Damnation.* If he stayed any longer, he wouldn't be able to stop the blackness.

He lurched to his feet, surprising Andrew into silence. "I need to go," he grunted, already striding for the door.

"Do you need anything?" Andrew asked from behind him.

"No. I'll see you at dinner."

Robert made it into his bedchamber and slammed the door. "Breathe," he ordered himself. "Just breathe."

For several minutes he did just that, forcing himself to stroll back and forth to the window rather than stride, and keeping his breaths slow and even. To his surprise, the pace became easier, and finally he stopped to look out the window.

Late afternoon stretched across the stable yard, and his gaze fell on his small garden. He still needed to water, he remembered. Leaving the room, though, would mean facing servants and whichever family members had arrived home, and conversation, and politeness, and . . .

"Stop it."

This was ridiculous. All he needed to do was water a few small plants. Resolutely he went to the door. *It will be simple,* he told himself, and pulled it open. *Down the stairs,*

164

down the hall. Keeping his gaze on his next goal, he did it. *Out the front door, around the house.* Dawkins pulled the door open for him, apparently reading the moment well enough that he did it without inquiry.

Get a bucket, go to the well, and fill it. Once he made it out-of-doors, the motions became easier, and he let his mind move beyond each moment. He filled the bucket at the well behind the stable and carefully watered each cutting. After that it became necessary to pull out the weeds that had managed to sprout in three days, and then to rake the soil where he'd left boot prints and compacted the ground.

"Bit?"

He jumped, turning to see Tristan a few feet beyond the garden border. "What is it?"

"Are you going to join us for dinner?"

Blinking, Robert looked skyward. Not even a glimmer of sunset remained in the western sky. If not for a nearly full moon, he would have been gardening in complete darkness.

But that kind of darkness, he didn't mind. He'd done it. For the second time in a row, he'd beaten the blackness. "Andrew's home," he said, leaning the rake against the stable wall.

"I know. He's been announcing that the

only Carroway brother shorter than Shaw is Edward."

Robert grinned. "I'd wager that Shaw's not too happy about that."

"No, but I'm enjoying it, and that's what's important." The viscount hesitated. "You were in my office."

"Yes." He started for the door, Tristan falling in beside him.

"Don't be angry at Andrew; it only came out when he was telling us how he arrived home."

"I was looking at invitations."

"He said that, too. Which is why I thought I'd mention that the family will be attending the Montrose ball tomorrow night, if you'd care to join us."

"What about Edward?" He wasn't going to abandon the one person who seemed to rely on him.

"He'll be fine for a few hours. I'll have Mr. Trost stay late with him. He can stand to practice his mathematics a bit more, anyway."

"As long as Trost stays. The Runt doesn't like to be left alone."

"So you'll go?"

"Everyone's going?"

The viscount looked at him for a moment. "Everybody else in the house, Evie and

Saint, and Lucinda and the general, plus Wycliffe and Emma."

If even the Duke of Wycliffe and his wife were attending, then the event wouldn't be the small one he'd looked for. At the same time, the sooner he discovered how angry he'd made Lucinda, the better. "I'll go."

Chapter 9

A human being in perfection ought
always to preserve a calm and
peaceful mind and never to allow
passion or a transitory desire
to disturb his tranquility.

— Victor Frankenstein, *Frankenstein*

Her hand aching, Lucinda gratefully set
aside her pen and blew on the top page of
notes to dry the ink. Lord Geoffrey and the
general sipped brandy, their conversation de-
volving into a discussion of the merits or lack
thereof of various British officers with whom
they'd served.

"Major Scoggins?" Geoffrey said, chuckling. "Isn't he the one who had to be tied
into his saddle every morning?"

"Yes, that's him. I was never certain
whether those measures were necessary be-

cause of his poor horsemanship or because of his tendency toward drink." The general glanced at the small clock on his desk. "Damnation. Will you stay for dinner, Geoffrey?"

"I would love to, but unfortunately I have a prior engagement." He set aside his snifter. "In fact, I must take my leave."

Augustus Barrett rose to shake the younger man's hand. "Thank you again for your help."

"No need, Augustus. Any opportunity for me to boast about my heroics is welcome." He gaze slid once again to Lucinda. "And the audience is most definitely appreciated."

"And appreciative. I'll see you out, my lord."

"Geoffrey, please."

He motioned for her to precede him, and she led the way down the hall to the foyer. All afternoon he'd seemed to make a point of including her in the conversation. Twice he'd even risen to stand at her shoulder and watch her take notes.

"Thank you again for being so generous," she said, stopping beside the butler at the front door. "I've never seen the general so enthusiastic about his writing project."

"I'm happy to help." He took her hand,

brushing his lips across her knuckles. "Perhaps I might see you without a pen and paper in hand." Pretty green eyes lifted to hers. "I believe you enjoy going riding?"

So Robert had been correct; either he'd been watching for them, or Geoffrey's cronies had informed him of her activities. Or both. "I do enjoy it."

"I would be honored if you would join me for a jaunt in Hyde Park, then. Tomorrow morning, perhaps?"

Goodness. "I have a luncheon, but —"

"Ten o'clock?"

"Very well."

He smiled, squeezing her fingers gently and then releasing her. "I'll be by for you then. Until tomorrow."

"Good evening, Lord — good evening, Geoffrey."

"Lucinda."

She watched him claim his horse and trot down the drive, then returned to her father's office. He was already flipping through her notes, adding his own in some of the margins.

"I've been thinking," he said, not looking up. "Would it be imposing on Geoffrey to ask him to go over all of my journals with me? He does have a way of sparking my memory of certain events and conversations."

Lucinda sat down opposite him. "He's asked me to go riding with him tomorrow morning."

The general set the papers back on the desk. "Did you accept?"

"Yes. So if you're prolonging his involvement with your book for my sake, you may cease and desist."

Steel gray eyes, making an attempt to be stern and unyielding, met hers. "Are you accusing me of cultivating a friendship with Lord Geoffrey Newcombe in order to encourage him to pursue you?"

She returned his gaze, undaunted. "You are the master strategist, my dear."

He laughed. "You're the one who suggested I contact him."

"So I am," she said, refusing to be tricked into admitting anything.

"Ah. Well, I suppose he is genuinely useful. His recollections at least confirm my own."

"Then use him how you will, General."

"Thank you." His smile faded, and he sat forward, leaning both elbows on his stacks of notes and journals. "You also went riding with Robert Carroway."

Lucinda nodded, ruthlessly suppressing the thought of Robert's feather-light, soul-stunning kiss. "And you don't need to encourage him or his war memories for my sake, either."

"I won't." He patted her hand. "I know you've grown up around military officers and their stories. But for God's sake, Lucinda, there's no reason in the world for you to settle on someone like Robert Carroway. Not with all the better choices you have."

She pulled her hand free. "I went riding with him, Papa. He's the brother-in-law of my dearest friend, and it's sometimes . . . difficult for him to talk to people. He's not a beau, and he certainly doesn't regale me with war stories, fascinating or otherwise. And I would never settle, under any circumstances."

Sighing, the general pushed to his feet. "Perform your act of charity, then. I just hope for his sake that you've made your lack of interest clear."

"Of course I have."

For a long moment after her father left the office, Lucinda remained seated in the guest chair. The kiss Lord Geoffrey had placed on her knuckles had been flirtatious and frivolous, and was under no circumstance to be taken seriously. Robert Carroway, however, played by a different set of rules. Or rather, he didn't play at all.

She touched her lips again, then slapped her hands back into her lap. For heaven's sake, it had been a kiss by only the barest of margins. Lucinda scowled. Brief or not, it told her that she needed to end the agreement between them before things became even more complicated. She'd already realized that charity had nothing to do with her pleasure at seeing Robert. But she could never consider the wounded, broken soldier as a suitor, much less a potential spouse. Her father would never accept him, and even more than that, any further relationship with Robert would complicate her life a hundredfold. A thousandfold.

All she wanted was a nice, considerate, uncomplicated husband who would help her in the care of her father as he grew older, and who wouldn't resent the attention she gave the general. *Tranquility*. Was that too much to ask?

"Blast." If she was after tranquility, she probably shouldn't be thinking about either Robert or his kisses.

After some scavenging, Robert found three music boxes — two in the attic, and the third in the aunties' morning room. He hefted them in his arms and headed for the breakfast room.

"Good morning." Georgiana greeted him, looking up from her plate.

"Good morning."

As he looked around the breakfast room, Robert scowled. He'd been looking for Georgiana, so her presence was fine, but Tristan was also there eating. Hm. He could probably use a little extra assistance, but not from his damned brother.

"What've you got there?" his brother asked.

"Nothing." He shifted the cumbersome boxes. "Are you finished eating?"

Immediately Tristan pushed away his plate. "Yes. What do you need?"

"I need you to leave," Robert answered.

"Leave?"

"Yes."

Georgiana chuckled. "I have some correspondence, anyway."

"No, not you," Robert amended, feeling the unaccustomed urge to smile. "Just Tristan."

"Just me."

The viscountess patted her husband's arm. "So sorry, Dare. Give me a kiss, and go away."

"So that's how it is, is it?" Tristan said mildly, standing. "The patriarch of the family banished without ceremony."

"Good-bye," Georgiana said, chortling.

"Well, I can tell when I'm not wanted." He looked at the two footmen standing by the window. "You can't stay if I'm being forced to leave. Out." Kissing Georgie on the cheek, Tristan nabbed an orange from the sideboard and slipped out the door behind the servants.

"So what can *I* do for you, Bit?" Georgie asked.

Now came the hard part. Blowing out his breath, Robert set the music boxes on the table. "I need to know if I can . . . dance, without looking like a complete looby." When the viscountess didn't scream or double over with laughter, he flipped open the music boxes, one after the other. "I found a waltz and two country dances. Do you —"

"I think we should move this to the morning room," she interrupted. "None of your other brothers have eaten yet, and we don't want them barging in on us." She lifted a music box, leaving two for him, and marched out the door.

Tristan lurked in the hallway and pretended to inspect a vase of purple irises as they passed him. Robert had already begun to think this was a bad idea, but he tried to ignore the ice creeping along his skull. Apparently waking in the morning after a good night's sleep spent dreaming of nothing more troubling than a horseback ride was enough to make him insane.

He just needed to know whether he could still do it, he told himself. Determining whether he had the skills and ability to dance didn't mean he'd decided to perform in public or not.

"What are you doing?" Edward asked, emerging from the west-wing hallway.

"Cleaning," Georgiana said. "Go have some breakfast."

They made it to the pink crinoline-draped refuge of the aunties without running into any other Carroways. Robert set his music boxes in the windowsill and faced his sister-in-law.

"I should tell you," he said, clenching his jaw, "I don't know if I can —"

"No excuses," Georgiana cut in briskly. "Shall we begin with a waltz?" Before he could answer, she flipped up a music-box lid. She lifted her arms into position and waited.

Georgiana was safe, he reminded himself, moving forward. The closest thing he had to a sister. She understood at least part of what troubled him, and he'd trusted her enough to tell her a little. Surely he could dance with her.

Swallowing, he took Georgiana's hand in his, and placed his other palm on her waist. Smiling her encouragement, she laid her free hand on his shoulder.

She felt warm and alive and feminine, and revulsion — not at her, but at himself — flooded through him. With a strangled growl he pulled away from her, clenching his fists so tightly his knuckles went white.

"Bit?"

"Apologies," he managed, backing for the door. "This was a mistake."

"It wasn't a mistake," Georgiana said firmly. "I'll be here, any time you want to practice."

This time it hit him hard, the panic nearly doubling him over before he even reached his bedchamber. He stumbled into his sanctuary and slammed the door closed.

Sweet Lucifer. What had he been thinking? That he could go back to who he used to be, that he could dance and laugh and find a woman attractive as if nothing had ever happened? He had no right to any of it. For God's sake, he was supposed to be dead. And the dead knew nothing but darkness.

He hunched down in the corner, rocking back and forth. *Stop it, stop it, stop it.*

"What in the devil did you do to him?"

Tristan snapped, striding back and forth in front of Bit's door.

"I didn't do anything," Georgiana returned, keeping her own voice quieter than her husband's. "He tried something, and it was more than he was ready for. That's all."

"But —"

"Keep your voice down, Tristan. He doesn't need to know we're debating him, for heaven's sake."

"But he was getting better," Tristan hissed.

"He *is* getting better — I think." She sighed. "It's been nearly two weeks since he had an attack this . . . violent."

"That doesn't help him." Dare paced in silence for a moment. "I know what they do when women are in hysterics."

"Tristan? Tristan! He's not a woman, and he's not hysterical."

Robert shoved himself upright, stumbling to the door to listen, and trying to control his shaking enough that he could grip the door handle. It didn't make him feel any less like vomiting, but he didn't want to be discovered curled up on the floor.

Think of something else, he bellowed at himself. It had worked before. A distraction. Some other thought besides the reality that it wasn't just the seven months of deprivation and pain and terror that haunted him. Nor was it the fact that he'd been shot five times. It was what had come when he'd given up — when he'd broken.

And it was that he couldn't tell anyone about any of it. The way they looked at him now was bad enough. If they found out what had truly happened . . .

He yanked open the door. "Go aw—"

A bucketful of freezing cold water dumped full into his face.

The shock of it stunned him for a bare second. Acting on instinct, he knocked the bucket out of his attacker's hands and shoved him hard against the opposite wall.

"Bit! Robert! It's me!" Tristan was bellowing at him, pushing at the hands Robert had locked around his throat.

Robert blinked water from his eyes. "I know it's you," he grunted, letting go with what he hoped looked like disgust. "Don't do that again." He shook cold wet from his hair, backing away. His clothes down to his trousers were soaked, and he swore water had even managed to seep into his boots. "Damn it, Tristan."

"I told him not to do it," Georgiana said, wringing water from the edge of her shawl. "Let's at least get you out of those wet clothes."

He evaded her reach. "I'll take care of it."

It had begun to dawn on him, though, that while his heart still raced and his breath came in short gasps, it felt . . . normal. For Lucifer's sake, he'd just nearly drowned. And it seemed to have worked. The black panic still lurked at the edge of his mind, as it always did, but something had sent it into a hasty retreat.

Robert lifted his eyes to Tristan, who stood looking out of breath himself, his cravat soaked and wilted from where he'd been choked half to death. The viscount didn't look the least bit angry, however; rather, he looked concerned, and a little amused.

"I take it back," Robert said slowly.

"Take what back?"

"When I told you not to do that again. I changed my mind."

"Oh. Well, I thought it might help you t—"

"I'm going to change." Backing into his room, Robert slammed his door again.

Slowly he shrugged out of his coat and unbuttoned his waistcoat, dropping them to the floor. This morning had made two things clear, anyway, he decided, as he dug into his wardrobe for a clean shirt. One, he had a great deal of work to do if he meant to dance with Lucinda tonight. And two, he'd learned a second way to distract his mind and keep hell at bay. Thinking of Lucinda and rose gardens was certainly less damaging to his wardrobe, but he supposed a bucket of water would work in an emergency.

"Wonderful," he muttered, stripping off his ruined cravat and tossing it on the growing stack of wet clothes. "Now I just need to figure a way to carry buckets with me at all times."

". . . and so I decided it might be prudent to withdraw."

Lucinda chuckled. " 'Might be prudent,' " she repeated.

Lord Geoffrey lifted an eyebrow. "I could have been in error."

"A hundred French cavalry make camp twenty feet from where you've set out your luncheon. I would say, with confidence, that withdrawal was without a doubt *extremely* prudent."

The sedate walk they'd been forced to observe in the midst of the crowds had finally brought them back to the east end of Hyde Park. And Lucinda had to give Robert Carroway credit for keen insight once more — Geoffrey had barely looked away from her long enough to choose their riding path.

She'd done her own part to encourage his interest, of course, having decided to wear her crimson military-style riding jacket and skirt. Being charming and attentive in his presence was simple, and unless she was greatly mistaken, his own attention was based on more than mere manners.

Entertaining as the morning had been, one small part of it troubled her. She hated to admit it, even to herself, but a sedate walk in Hyde Park couldn't quite compare to a hair-tangling gallop in the countryside. And being charming, while she liked to think it was a natural part of her character, made her feel a little self-conscious. With Robert she didn't even need to speak if she didn't feel like it.

Lucinda blinked. That was silly. Galloping and a comfortable silence did not an acceptable beau make. She needed to concentrate. She had a respectable family name and a respectable fortune, but Geoffrey came from the most auspicious of families. A union would bring honor to everyone concerned. In addition he was as charming as he was handsome, and it seemed as though a hundred other young ladies were also in close pursuit of his hand.

"Do you attend the Montrose ball tonight?" he asked.

"I intend to, yes."

"Say you'll save a waltz for me, Lucinda."

She smiled. "I will save a waltz for you."

"And a quadrille."

Two dances in a single evening with the same gentleman wasn't uncommon, though it would send a message to the *ton* at large that he held her in high regard. "And a quadrille," she repeated.

"And a country dance."

"You're in danger of depriving everyone else of your company," she returned, hiding a frown. Three dances could damage her reputation.

"I've stepped too far," he said. "I apologize."

"Oh, for heaven's sake, Geoffrey. You knew I'd say no, and you're only trying to flatter me."

Geoffrey laughed. "At least tell me I succeeded."

"You've succeeded — if you haven't made me late for my luncheon engagement."

He pulled out his pocket watch, scowled, then gestured at his groom, whom he'd brought along as their chaperone. "I don't suppose you'll allow me to send Isaac ahead to inform your party that you'll be a little late?"

"I don't think so."

"Ah. Perhaps I'd best get you home, then."

She laughed again. "Yes, perhaps you should."

At her front door he insisted on helping her down from Isis himself. If she'd been an eighteen-year-old debutante she probably would have swooned from the attention by now, except that she'd never been the type of woman who fainted. Six years past that, she *did* feel flattered, but more than that, she was aware of an almost smug satisfaction.

This was progressing exactly as she planned: The general approved of Geoffrey, she liked him; he definitely seemed interested in her; and no betrayal, heartache, or undue excitement looked to be in the offing. If not for one cool-eyed distraction, everything would be perfect.

"I had a wonderful time, Geoffrey," she said. "Thank you."

He drew her gloved hand to his lips. "Thank *you*, Lucinda. I hope this may be the first of many mornings we spend in each other's company."

She only smiled. For heaven's sake, she

wasn't going to succumb to a glib tongue, though his efforts were certainly appreciated. It was nice to hear, but it wasn't why she'd selected him. "I'll see you tonight."

"Until then."

It wasn't until she entered the house that she realized her luncheon companions were already there, waiting for her. "Am I late?" she asked, following the butler into the morning room.

Evelyn came forward, her eyes dancing. "We're early."

"And we hope this will be the first of many times we are," Georgiana added, her own expression far too bland.

"Very amusing," Lucinda grumbled, blushing. "Next time I'll have Ballow close the windows in here."

"Things do seem to be going well," Evie said, kissing her on the cheek. "Shall we go? I brought the barouche."

"Do you mind if I change first?" Lucinda asked. "I won't be a minute."

"Of course not. We'll be down here gossiping about you."

Lucinda hurried upstairs, summoning Helena as she went. Inside her bedchamber she threw off her hat and riding jacket. The gown she'd chosen to wear at luncheon lay on the bed already, waiting for her.

When someone tapped at her door and pushed it open, though, it wasn't her maid. Georgiana stood just inside the room, looking uncomfortable. "Let me help you with that," she said after a moment.

"Helena's on her way —"

"No, she isn't. I'm substituting."

"Ah. Why?"

"Because I want to talk to you, and I don't want anyone else to overhear. Not even Evie."

Lucinda immediately knew it was about Robert. Slowly she set her hairbrush aside. "I like Robert," she said quietly. "As a friend. But with the general my life is . . . complicated enough. It sounds selfish, but I want a husband who will make things easier. Not more difficult."

Georgiana took a deep breath. "That's not selfish, Luce. It's practical. *You're* practical. And I'm not trying to do any matchmaking. But Bit's been hurting for a long time, and he seems to see you as someone he can talk to."

"I argue with him," Lucinda said. "Or I should say, I don't back away from arguing with him."

Georgiana nodded. "Maybe that's the secret. We're all so worried we'll push him farther away if we say the wrong thing."

"Georgie, I'll be happy to fight with him whenever he wants."

"Thank you." She smiled a little. "All right. This is extremely complicated, and I won't involve you if you don't want it that way."

Ah, guilt. If it had just been that, she would have simply changed the subject. If he hadn't kissed her, and if that kiss and his presence hadn't been more interesting than she felt comfortable admitting, she wouldn't have said anything more. Lucinda sighed. "I *have* been wondering why I've seen more of him in the past ten days than I have over the past three years."

"I think he's trying to come back," Georgiana said, helping Lucinda into her blue muslin gown. "I only know a little of what happened to him, but . . ." She stopped, swallowing. "It was terrible, Luce. So anything you can do to help him, I would appreciate."

Deep down, Lucinda badly wanted to know what terrible things he'd been through. If she asked, though, if she found out, everything would change. Things had begun to change already, but she could certainly manage to keep her interest in check around Robert. "I'll do what I can," she agreed.

★ ★ ★

Andrew was walking past the library when Robert grabbed him by the arm and hauled him through the door. "What the dev—"

"I need your help," Robert said, speaking quickly, before he could change his mind. "But if you tell anyone, I'll —"

"I won't say a word," Andrew stated, stumbling to catch his balance.

"Hold out your arms."

Looking baffled, Andrew complied. Not giving himself time to wonder whether he would succeed or fail, either prospect of which he found troubling, Robert grabbed one of his brother's hands, and attached the other to his shoulder. Snagging Andrew's waist with his free hand, he clomped into a waltz.

"Get off my foot," Andrew blurped, stumbling again.

Robert closed his eyes, trying to conjure the music and remember the steps. "Stop trying to lead."

"Oh. Right."

Though he couldn't possibly mistake Andrew for a female — one of the main reasons he'd made the selection — his brother made a fair partner. Within a few moments Robert could feel himself relaxing, the steps coming easier and more smoothly. His knee ached, but no worse than it generally did, and it felt sturdy enough. The unsteady, boneless feeling from his earlier attack remained, but he knew how to hide that.

He opened his eyes again as Andrew began humming something in the correct meter but horribly off-key. "Did it seem . . . stupid?" he asked, coming to a halt and releasing his brother.

"Other than the sensation that I was going in the wrong direction, I didn't notice anything untoward." His brother offered the easy, charismatic Carroway grin. "You're not a bad dancer, actually."

"Thank you."

Abruptly the smile collapsed. "You're not going to make me dress up like a chit tonight to dance with you, are you? Because really you were quite good, and I don't think any girl would have an objection to —"

"No, I'm not making you wear a gown," Robert returned, relief at his success making him smile. "I just wanted to be certain I remembered the steps."

"Oh. You do. And —" Andrew looked over his shoulder, toward the closed door. "I'm actually supposed to meet a few of my friends for lun—"

"I'm finished with you," Robert said. "Go away now."

"Right. Thanks."

Closing the door again behind his brother, Robert practiced a few quadrille turns and bows on his way to the window. He could do it, though despite Andrew's approval he could feel a certain rustiness in his steps. But considering how he'd begun the morning, he couldn't help feeling somewhat satisfied.

That pleasant feeling lasted for nearly thirty seconds, until he realized that he couldn't expect simply to walk up to Lucinda, waltz with her, and escape. No, to help her with lesson number two, to maintain a reason to remain in her company, he was going to have to lead by example — and in this instance that would mean dancing with other ladies, *for every dance of the evening.*

He sank into the deep windowsill. There was simply no way he could do that. Robert let out a curse, pounding a fist against the wooden frame. He sat there for several minutes, hating himself and whatever was wrong with him, when he remembered precisely what Lucinda had said. Her lesson was meant to help the girls who remained by the refreshment table or in the corner — the ones with no dowry, the ones without looks or charm or wit or grace to recommend them. The ones without hope.

A lady with a choice between sitting out yet another dance or partnering with him would surely at least hesitate before she refused. And if anyone could understand someone without hope or prospects, it was him. And hopefully in dancing with someone like that, they wouldn't expect much from him, and he would retain a slight chance of remaining unnoticed by everyone but Lucinda — and Geoffrey Newcombe, of course, who'd be a fool not to keep an eye on an unexpected, if unlikely, rival.

A rival. Him. It was unimaginable, except that he *could* imagine it. Lucinda Barrett. He liked her, enjoyed her company, but it was more than that. He craved her, craved her serenity, and her independence, her sense of self — she felt like hope to a man who hadn't known any for a very long time.

For that reason, he knew he should stay away from her, if only for her sake. He couldn't help that he wanted to glimpse heaven, but to try to bring an angel into his world . . . One or both of them would catch fire and burn to cinders.

No, she thought of them as friends, and so friends they would be — even if it killed him. That part should be easy. He'd been dead for years.

Chapter 10

I was encouraged to hope my
present attempts would at least lay the
foundations of future success.

— Victor Frankenstein, *Frankenstein*

"Is it me," General Barrett said, "or is every
resident of Mayfair in attendance tonight?"

"I don't think it's you," Lucinda answered, holding onto his arm. "Heavens. Is
that a juggler?"

The sight didn't surprise her all that
much; Lady Montrose had been trying for
the past four years to have someone declare
one of her parties the event of the Season.
Thus far, she hadn't succeeded.

"I see Geoffrey's made a point of arriving
on time," her father pointed out.

"In all fairness, he's not the only one,
Papa," she returned. "You did just note

that all of Mayf—"

"You know what I meant, girl. I won't be monopolizing him this evening, so that task will be up to you."

"I'm not going to monopolize anyone." Her wandering gaze found an acquaintance across the room, and she smiled. "Ah, look. It seems Mrs. Miller has returned from her painting tour of Venice."

"Lillian? Where?"

Lucinda nudged him in the widow's direction and released her grip on his arm. "Remember, you promised me a waltz," she said.

"I'll hold it safe for you, but I will give up my spot if necessary."

The fact that her father was willing to leave her side said a great deal about what he thought of her prospects with Lord Geoffrey. She smiled as the Season's Adonis reached her.

"Good evening, Geoffrey."

He kissed her knuckles. "Lucinda." His gaze swept the length of her. "You look lovely."

"Thank you." The deep blue silk gown with silver trim was a particular favorite of hers, and it was nice to know that he appreciated it.

"And you've saved two spaces on your

dance card for me?"

"Other than my father, you're the first gentleman to ask for a spot."

Geoffrey took her card and pencil, marking his name by the waltz and quadrille of his choice. "It's a shame there aren't enough men here to keep Francis Henning off the dance floor tonight," he commented. "Are you certain you'll only allow me two dances?"

For a moment she was annoyed that he and his friends were still blackballing poor Francis, until she decided that perhaps he was just baiting her. Additionally, he was correct about one thing: The ladies far outnumbered the gentlemen tonight, and quite a few girls would be left by the wall.

"Two dances," she repeated, smiling to soften her refusal. "But don't despair; I doubt you'll lack for partners."

"None of them will compare with you."

He excused himself to go greet her father, and in what seemed like less than a minute the remainder of her dances had been claimed. Finally, through the crush of people, she glimpsed the tall forms of Lord St. Aubyn and Lord Dare, and she made her way in that direction.

"Luce, isn't this mad?" Evie exclaimed, hugging her. "And I told you that blue would look divine on you."

"Yes, you were right. I admit it," she replied, turning to greet Georgie.

Evie, though, snagged her arm. "Not yet," she whispered. "Dare's trying to talk her into leaving. He's afraid the room will be too stifling with all these people."

"He's probably right."

As she watched, Georgiana placed a finger over her husband's mouth and then replaced it with a kiss. "I promise, as soon as I feel the least bit uncomfortable I'll tell you, and we'll leave."

"You promise?"

Saint, meanwhile, leaned down and whispered something in Evie's ear, which made her blush wildly. Before she could answer, he'd strolled off to find a footman with some punch.

"What did he say?" Lucinda murmured.

"He was just . . . never mind," her friend answered, clearing her throat. "But come say hello to Georgie. You'll never guess who else is in attendance tonight."

But Lucinda had already looked across the room, and she knew. "Robert Carroway."

He stood gazing at her, his unruly dark hair down to his collar and hanging across one blue eye. His black jacket and trousers called attention to the lean hardness of his frame, while his crimson waistcoat stood out as bright and surprising as blood. He looked like a wolf again, hungry and definitely on the prowl.

She expected him to approach, but instead he inclined his head and then vanished back into the crowd. *Well.* According to Georgiana, he viewed her as his savior of sorts. The least he could do was say hello and come close enough so she could see the expression in his eyes and wonder if he thought of kissing her again.

"Who's your partner for the first dance?" Georgiana asked, joining them.

"Lord Geoffrey."

"I see."

"It seems like good strategy to me," Lucinda said, ignoring Georgie's smug tone. "The first dance and the last waltz."

"Absolutely," Georgiana agreed. "But I've seen your lesson list, my dear. I think we can safely say that Lord Geoffrey has acquitted himself admirably on lesson number one."

"Ooh, I have a question," Evie put in, stepping closer and lowering her voice as Geoffrey approached. "If he offers for you before we're satisfied on all four lesson points, do we allow you to accept him anyway?"

"You tease now," Lucinda said, grinning, "but I don't remember you being nearly so sure of yourself when you began instructing St. Aubyn."

"Enough about me, Luce. It's your turn, my dear."

The orchestra signaled that they were about to begin the first dance of the evening. At the same moment, Geoffrey arrived beside her. "Lady St. Aubyn, Lady Dare, I'm afraid I must claim Lucinda."

"Of course," Georgie said, nodding.

Evie was less reserved. "Have fun," she called, blowing Lucinda a kiss.

"Your friendship with them is quite remarkable," Geoffrey said, guiding her to their place in line. "I almost feel as if I'm courting them and both their families in addition to you and your father."

Lucinda started to answer, then as the music began to play, she realized precisely what he'd said. He wasn't after her heart any more than she was after his. Interesting. They were both being mercenary. That certainly made things easier, even if deep down where she could pretend it didn't affect her, the realization hurt just a little.

She yanked her mind back to current events as the dance's meanderings brought them back together again. "I admit, the general does seem taken with you — or your memory, at least."

Geoffrey chuckled. "I'm pleased to be of ser . . . Well, I'll be damned."

Turning to look in the direction he gazed, Lucinda felt speechless herself. Miss Margaret Heywater had joined the dance. Cursed with the abominable combination of a nonexistent dowry and a tendency toward squinting and simpering, at this moment with the high color in her cheeks and flounce of her secondhand gown, she actually looked attractive. And Lucinda knew without a doubt that that miracle was due to the man on Miss Margaret's right, who held her fingers and smiled at her and stepped and turned with a rusty elegance that made Lucinda abruptly want to weep.

More people had begun to notice, and the resulting lift of her chin gave Miss Margaret an even more elegant line. Robert, on the other hand, gave no sign at all if he realized that half the guests in attendance were watching him.

When Lucinda nearly crashed into Lord Charles Daymore, she blinked, catching his hand just in time to avoid throwing the entire dance into chaos. The lines of men and women twisted around one another, touching and releasing hands and moving on to the next.

As she reached Robert she realized she was holding her breath. "Hello," she said, as their fingers met.

He nodded, blue eyes meeting hers. "Lesson two," he murmured, and then was gone again.

All the partners rejoined, and she caught Geoffrey looking over his shoulder at Robert and Miss Margaret. "That cripple never dances with anyone," he muttered. "What does he know about Margaret Heywater that I don't?"

"Please don't call him that. And perhaps he's just being nice."

"Half her dance card's bound to be empty, anyway, so it shouldn't be too difficult to find out."

Lucinda hid a sudden smile. Robert had managed a miracle again. Once Geoffrey danced with Margaret, every single gentleman in attendance would want to know what the fuss was about.

Abruptly Geoffrey gripped her hand again, more tightly than before. "I don't mean to say that another female could take my attention from you," he amended.

"Of course not," she returned, wondering at his declaration. Had he expected her to be jealous? Was she supposed to feel jealous?

"You truly don't have any idea why he's dancing with her?"

"No," she lied. "None at all."

"But you claim to be his friend."

"I didn't ask him, any more than he asked why I'm dancing with you," she said, beginning to feel annoyed. "I think the key would be for you to ask her to dance, and find out for yourself."

He looked over at her from beyond their joined hands, then smiled. "My apologies again, Lucinda. I am dancing with you, and you shall remain the focus of my thoughts."

She smiled back to show that she wasn't offended. "You have two dances with me. The remainder of the evening is your own."

As soon as the dance ended, and as she'd suspected, half a dozen men, Geoffrey among them, approached Margaret. Robert, though, had disappeared again. He'd certainly done his good deed. One young lady who would have spent the evening as a non-participant would now have a partner for every dance. And a few of the young men who typically would have been standing around talking about horses or wagering would find themselves doing something useful.

"Madeira?" Saint asked, appearing at her shoulder.

"Yes, thank you." She accepted the glass he offered and took a grateful swallow. "Where's Evie?"

"Testing my patience with Bradshaw," the marquis answered, gesturing to the couple taking their places for a quadrille.

She looked for her own partner, but Charles Weldon was still part of the cluster surrounding Miss Margaret. "Are you dancing this evening?" she asked Saint.

"Only with Evelyn, unless you require a partner, of course."

"I believe I have a full quota, but thank you."

She — and the rest of London — had been aware of St. Aubyn for years. That devilish reputation of his had been well warranted, but the change in him since he'd met Evelyn had been remarkable. Still, though Lucinda had come to appreciate his dry wit and intelligence, she was never entirely certain what he might say — or do.

"I'm curious about something," he said, his gaze still steady on Bradshaw and Evie.

"About what?"

"Your family and the Carroways are close, but what was it that happened between your father and Robert?"

She faced him, an uncomfortable something thumping in her gut. Surely her father had never mentioned his misgivings about Robert to anyone — especially not to anyone within their circle of friends. "I don't know what you mean."

Saint shrugged. "Maybe I'm misreading Robert." He favored her with a dark grin. "I do tend to look for trouble."

Saint had never misread anything that she'd ever noticed. Of course her father didn't think much of Robert, but she'd had no idea it might be mutual. Lucinda frowned. "What do you think you know, Saint?"

His smile deepened. "I think your partner is waiting for you," he said, then took her arm, leaning closer. "I don't mind having my own curiosity satisfied," he murmured, "but I don't share."

"Humph. That's convenient." Charles lurked behind her, and she spun around to take his arm. "Lead the way to the quadrille, if you please."

The dance had barely begun when she spotted Robert again, this time in the company of Hyacinth Styles. A pleasant girl, but excruciatingly shy, her presence on the dance floor was nearly as surprising as Robert's. The couple ended up in a group halfway across the room, which served somewhat to annoy Lucinda — mostly because it meant she had to admit to herself that she badly wanted to talk to Mr. Carroway.

Evie and especially Bradshaw kept looking in his direction as well, though privately Lucinda thought Shaw would be better served keeping a close eye on Evie's husband. She glanced at Saint, standing with Tristan and Georgiana. He wouldn't have mentioned a problem between Robert and the general unless he knew for certain one existed.

What was it? And why hadn't she realized it before? Of course, for years Georgiana's feud with Tristan had limited her own exposure to the Carroways, but they'd all been united now for over a year. And still, until recently her father had never even mentioned Robert's name — not in her presence, anyway.

"Lucinda, do you plan to go to Vauxhall on Saturday?" Charles asked as they circled each other. His desperately cheery tone reminded her that she'd scarcely said a word to him. He smiled as she looked up at him. "I've heard that the Regent himself intends to make an appearance."

"I'll be attending with a group of friends," she answered.

He gave her a hopeful smile. "Yes?"

"Yes," she returned, searching for a diplomatic way to tell him that he wasn't invited. "It's a shame that we were only able to rent one small box," she commented. "If we'd known about Prinny, we would have tried to find something larger, so we could accommodate everyone."

"Of course."

Now that Charles had mentioned Vauxhall, she couldn't help wondering whether Robert would attend or not. Lucinda sighed. She needed to be more concerned about whether Lord Geoffrey would be joining them or not. Tristan was supposed to invite him; she would have to check with Georgiana.

As the dance ended, Charles escorted her back to Lord and Lady Dare. Once they were alone, Georgie put an arm around her. "How much did you tell Bit about the items on your list?" she whispered.

"I might have mentioned to him that it's embarrassing to be a female left on the sidelines during a dance when gentlemen are on hand," she hedged.

"I see."

Lucinda frowned. Now Georgie would be angry with her, or worse yet, accuse her of somehow leading Robert on. But she hadn't done anything wrong, for goodness' sake. And if anyone knew that her interest lay with Lord Geoffrey, it was Robert. "He asked me to tell him," she whispered back. "He knows that I've selected Geoff—"

Georgiana kissed her on the cheek. "He's here, and he's dancing," she said, her voice catching. "Whatever's inspired him, I'm not about to complain."

A hand touched Lucinda's shoulder, and to her surprise Tristan leaned down to kiss her other cheek. "I don't know what the devil's going on, but Georgie seems to think you're partly responsible."

She cleared her throat. "I think Robert wanted this, and that maybe I provided an excuse for him to act. But good heavens, thank Robert. Or yourselves. Not me."

The rest of the evening passed in a swirl of silk gowns and evening jackets. Robert Carroway danced every dance — and none of them with her. As the night progressed, she thought the lines of his shoulders grew tighter and his face grimmer, but he stayed. And because of his efforts, a host of young ladies who might not have been asked on the floor at all instead found names on their dance cards and even an invitation or two for picnics later in the week.

She saw nearly as little of Geoffrey as she

did of Robert. Even during the numerous refreshment breaks, he'd been busy writing his name on the dance cards of ladies with whom he'd probably never even spoken before. For a moment she wondered whether his absence was part of the plan as well, but that was just a little too much to expect, even from someone with Robert's powers of insight.

The last dance of the evening was the waltz, and Geoffrey finally approached her again. "Shall we?" he asked, holding out his hand.

She took it, walking with him to the dance floor. "You've been busy this evening," she said, trying not to laugh as he sent her an exasperated look.

"At least someone's noticed. And look. There he goes again." He gestured toward one side of the room as Robert escorted Miss Jane Melroy onto the floor. "The cripple seems determined to ask every ugly chit in London to dance." He snorted. "Maybe that's all he can manage, these days."

Lucinda pulled her hand free. Perhaps a simple "act like a gentleman" hadn't appeared on her list, but he knew quite well that she and Robert were friends. She'd told him often enough. "Excuse me, Geoffrey," she said, backing away, "but my father is quite tired. I need to see him home."

His smile dropped. "I've offended you. I apologize, Lucinda."

"I asked you not to call him that. I'm not the one you've insulted, Geoffrey."

He reached out, gripping her arm. "I'll see you at Vauxhall, yes?"

"I'll be in attendance." Lucinda blew out her breath. This was *not* how she'd wanted the evening to end, but neither was she going to tolerate one friend verbally abusing another. "Good evening."

"Lucinda," he protested, still holding her sleeve.

She pulled her arm free. "I'm certain you were trying to be amusing, but I don't appreciate humor at the expense of other people. So good evening."

The general seemed to sense that something was amiss, because he left his group of cronies to join her. "What is it, my dear?"

"I'm making a point. Are you ready to leave?"

"Anything to provide an exclamation to your point," he replied.

Lucinda took his arm. "Thank you."

"We aren't giving up on Geoffrey, are we?" he muttered, guiding her through the crowd toward the ballroom doors.

"No. But we are encouraging him to be more considerate of those less perfect than himself."

"He doesn't look pleased."

"Good."

As they passed through the double doors she couldn't resist taking one last look over her shoulder. Geoffrey stalked toward the opposite door, anger in the straight, stiff line of his back. Closer by, though, Robert gazed at her over the head of his partner. After a moment, he gave her a slight smile.

Lucinda frowned as she and her father climbed into their coach. Perhaps Robert really could read minds. If so, she was in a great deal of trouble.

Chapter 11

The different accidents of life are not so changeable as the feelings of human nature.

— Victor Frankenstein, *Frankenstein*

When Robert awoke in the morning, it was well past daylight. He'd expected to be tense and wakeful after an evening spent in the crush of so many people, but instead he felt tired and relaxed and even a little satisfied. He'd done it. He'd lasted the evening and had danced every dance. Admittedly his conversation had been somewhat sparse, but hell, he could work on that.

He sat up, swung his legs over the side of the bed, and stood. And then collapsed to the floor.

"Damn it!"

His knee throbbed, refusing to take his

weight as he pulled himself up the bedpost. Well, that figured. He'd been so worried that the black panic would find him in the middle of the ballroom that he hadn't taken the time to consider what four hours of dancing would do to his game leg.

Still cursing, he hopped to his wardrobe and grabbed a pair of trousers, dropping into the chair at his dressing table to pull them on. This would have been one of the times when having a valet would have come in handy.

That, however, simply wasn't possible. Robert looked up, facing himself in the mirror. The mop of disheveled hair and a night's growth of beard didn't concern him; he was used to seeing that. Generally, when he faced his reflection, though, he'd already pulled on a shirt.

Now, bare-chested, his gaze automatically went to the damage they — he — had done. The small round scar just beneath his left shoulder, matched by another high on his back where the ball had passed through. Another, larger scar puckered above his left hip, with a white blotch almost directly opposite, where the Spanish surgeon had dug for an endless twenty minutes looking for the lead ball. He still carried it inside him, somewhere.

Another white streak of a scar marked his right arm where the first shot had grazed him. The last had been the one to his left knee, the shot that had brought him down.

Robert leaned toward his chest of drawers and managed to grab a clean shirt with his fingertips. Shifting away from the mirror, he yanked the fine white fabric over his head. There. Gone now, but not forgotten. Never forgotten.

After he'd shaved and washed and finished dressing, he made a dive for his boots and ended on the floor beside the bed again. He'd discarded his walking cane two years ago, a gesture that this morning he was beginning to regret.

Just as he was beginning to wonder how he was going to make it downstairs for breakfast, someone knocked on his door.

"Come in."

Edward pushed open the door, looking toward the window where Robert usually sat, reading. A brief frown touched his young face, until he spotted his brother sprawled on the floor with one boot on.

"What are you doing?"

"Getting dressed. What are you doing?"

"I came to find you. You're sitting on the floor."

Robert finished pulling on his boots. "Am

211

I? I must have missed the bed. Who's here this morning?"

"Everyone. And —"

"Good. Fetch Shaw or Andrew for me, will you?" They'd ask fewer questions than Tristan.

The Runt blew out his breath. "First, may I tell you something?"

Leaning back against the bed, Robert folded his arms. "Yes."

"You have a caller downstairs. That's what I came to tell you."

His heart missed a beat. "Who is it?"

"Lucinda. She's talking with Georgie right now, and she said there's no hurry, but —"

Robert scrambled for the bedpost and hauled himself upright again. The dread over who he might be forced to converse with was gone, but the anticipation coursing just beneath his skin didn't feel much better. "Thank you for telling me," he said, noting that Edward was staring at him now, open-mouthed. "Please find Shaw or Andrew for me."

"Is your leg broken again?"

"No, it's just tired. And I'm trying not to be rude and make Lucinda wait. So will you please find me a taller brother, Runt?"

Instead of leaving, Edward marched up to

him. "I'll help you."

Wonderful. "I'll squash you, and then we'll both need help."

Squinting one eye, Edward assessed him again. "Yes, I suppose you probably would squash me," he finally conceded. "All right. Don't go anywhere. I'll be right back." He charged out the door.

"And please be —"

"Shaw! Andrew! Bit hurt his leg! He needs help!"

"— discreet," Robert finished, sighing, and amused despite himself.

Before he'd counted to five, footsteps charged up the stairs for the third floor. Robert grimaced. The last thing he wanted to do was alarm his family again. He'd put them through enough hell when he'd come back from Europe.

"Bit, what —" Shaw stopped in the doorway. Out of breath and his expression going from concerned to baffled, he took in the sight of his brother leaning, one leg slightly bent, against the oak bedpost.

"I'm f—"

"What happened?" Tristan and Andrew asked at the same moment, plowing into Bradshaw from behind. The butler and three footmen crowded into the hallway on their tails.

An alarming thought occurred to Robert. "Please tell me Georgie's not running up here."

"No, I made her stay downstairs with Lucinda. What the devil happened?"

"Nothing." Robert paused at their skeptical looks. "Truly. I — my knee stiffened up overnight, and I asked the Runt to send me some assistance to get me downstairs. Edward just . . . overreacted a little."

Shaw made a face. "The Runt and I are going to have a little chat about the proper circumstances under which it's allowable to give people apoplexies," he grumbled, turning to Dare. "Do you have this?"

"Yes."

"Good. Let's go, boys." He made his way back through the crowd.

"You heard him," Tristan said. "Dawkins, Henry, everyone, downstairs."

"Yes, my lord." The butler herded the footmen and gathering maids out of the hallway.

"Are you in pain?" the viscount continued, entering the room with Andrew behind him.

"No," Robert lied. Hell, he was always in pain these days. He'd gotten used to it, for the most part.

Tristan looked at him for a moment.

"We'll get you downstairs, and then I'm sending for a physician to take a look at your knee. You shouldn't have pushed yourself so har—"

"No," Robert interrupted, shuddering. "No physicians."

"Bit —"

"No." He'd had enough of that drivel to last a lifetime; the sympathetic clucking and the ham-fisted poking and prodding. He preferred his torture straight — not accompanied by patronizing protestations that it was for his own good.

Tristan blew out his breath. "No physicians," he agreed, "unless it gets worse."

Robert didn't reply to that. They would only argue, and he would win, because Tristan wouldn't risk upsetting him. And at the moment, he would much rather go downstairs. "Just give me a hand, will you?"

With Andrew bracing him under his right shoulder and Tristan under his left, he managed a moderately dignified limp down the stairs and into the breakfast room. Shaw had evidently informed everyone that he wasn't in mortal peril, and from the subdued look on Edward's face, the Runt had been lectured about the dangers of sounding false alarms.

He shrugged free of his brothers as soon

as he reached an empty chair to lean against. Once he'd satisfied himself that no one remained unduly alarmed on his behalf, he turned his attention to Lucinda. He'd wanted to look at her from the moment he'd entered the room, but he knew he wouldn't be able to disguise how pleased he was to see her. They were just friends, after all.

Hazel eyes, though, swept down to his bent leg and up to his face again. *Yes, we can't have anyone forgetting that Robert Carroway's a cripple, now, can we?* he thought. *The madman decided to go dancing, and now he can't walk.* Well, now that she'd been reminded, no doubt she would make some excuse and leave.

Lucinda smiled. "I was going to ask if you would care to go walking with me," she said, "to show me how your roses are progressing. Now, perhaps, we should forget the walking and you can just describe them to me."

Robert swallowed. God, she'd worn yellow muslin. She looked like sunshine. "Aunt Milly's walking cane should be in her bedchamber," he said. "Would you fetch it for me, Runt?"

Edward seemed happy to escape. "I'll be right back."

"Robert," Tristan hissed in his ear, "you need to res—"

"I had a question for you, anyway, Miss Barrett," he interrupted, "about one of the cuttings."

"Oh, good," Lucinda replied, her warm smile deepening. "I do like to pretend to be an authority about things."

Edward reappeared in a few moments with the cane. Robert took it, cautiously testing his weight on it. It was too short, and his knee hurt like the devil, but he could stand it. He could stand nearly anything.

"Shall we?" he asked, gesturing for Lucinda to lead the way.

By some miracle he made it out the front door and down the shallow steps. Despite his efforts the strain must have shown on his face, because abruptly Lucinda took his free arm.

"I can manage," he grunted, shuddering at the contact. "I don't need help."

Hazel eyes lifted to meet his, and his mouth went dry. "I'm not helping you," she stated. "I'm forcing you to behave like a gentleman and escort me."

That said, she wrapped her left hand around his arm as well. Beneath short, puffy sleeves, her arms were bare to her wrists, with thin lace gloves as fashionable as they were impractical covering her fingers. The warmth of her seeped through his sleeve, heating his own skin. "Is that another of your lessons?" he forced out, thankful that his voice sounded normal.

"No, it's just a general rule."

Thanks to her feigned lack of assistance, he navigated the carriage drive fairly easily, and they reached his small garden beside the stables without his falling on his face.

"They look very healthy," she said approvingly.

"I used flounder."

"Ah. Only the best for the roses. I even see the beginnings of new leaf growth. You see? There and there."

Robert kept his gaze on her face, aware that either the library curtains were suffering an apoplexy or his entire family was spying on them. "You didn't come here to evaluate my leaf growth."

"No, I didn't," she returned without hesitation. "I came to thank you for last night. However I might have tried to implement that particular lesson, I could never have been that successful. It was wonderful. You were wonderful."

He shrugged. "It worked because of you. If Geoffrey hadn't thought you might have had some interest in me, he wouldn't have noticed anything I did. No one would have."

Some interest in Robert. More like a schoolgirl's infatuation — which wasn't helpful at all. Lucinda kept her gaze on the roses, and wondered whether he was truly that unaware of what a mesmerizing sight he'd been. She and Geoffrey hadn't been the only ones watching him last evening. With that dark, disheveled hair and those intense blue eyes, he was a poet's vision. And the quiet mystery that seemed to surround him only made him more attractive. And not just to her. She'd heard enough females muttering to be certain on that front.

"However you managed it," she said, "thank you. Those girls looked so happy. I know it couldn't have been easy for y—"

"I'm fine," he interrupted.

It sounded like something he said a great deal, an automatic response to anyone expressing their concern over him. Lucinda frowned. "No, you're not," she stated. "You hurt your leg for my lesson."

He didn't move, but all the same she could feel him pulling away. "It's just my knee. It gets a little stiff when I'm on it for a while. You and Geoffrey argued."

Lucinda blinked. Of course he would have noticed. He noticed everything. "He made a . . . disparaging comment about some of the young ladies dancing last evening. I didn't appreciate it." She paused. If Robert could jump into any subject he chose, she could do the same. "You were shot in that knee, weren't you?"

A muscle in his cheek jumped. "Yes. And Geoffrey's comments weren't just about the ladies, were they? He said something about me."

"He . . . might have." She drew a breath. "I didn't appreciate that, either."

"But I set myself up as a potential rival," he returned, as they slowly made their way along the front of his garden in the direction of the stables. "It's a good sign if he insults me."

"It's never a good sign to insult anyone," she retorted. "You and he went through the same experiences. If he can't sympathize with a fellow soldier, I —"

"We didn't go through the same experiences," he interrupted. "He just thinks we did. Everyone does. That's why . . ." Robert cleared his throat. "What do aphids look like?"

"You don't have to worry about aphids until you get blooms," she said, pulling him to a halt. If his leg hadn't been injured, she didn't think she would have been able to

220

stop him. "That's why what?"

"Nothing."

"No. It's not 'nothing.' Finish your sentence."

Robert shook his head. His gaze had gone past her, to the stables, as though he wanted to escape. Well, he could go, but she was going with him. Georgie had hinted at things, and Robert avoided discussing them. And she wanted to know why he hurt so much.

"I was just going to say that's why they despise me," he muttered.

"You're wrong, Robert. And they have no right to despise you," she snapped, as angry at the thought as she was at herself for goading him into saying it. "You were wounded, several times over. Wellington even called you a hero for your efforts at Waterloo. You can't —"

He yanked his arm free and limped for the stables. "I didn't make any efforts at Waterloo," he hissed, vanishing inside.

She followed him through the door. At her quick gesture, the three grooms inside exited, leaving the two of them alone with the horses. "Of course you did. Whatever Wellington's political agenda, you —"

"I wasn't even there, goddammit." He limped up to his bay's stall. Tolley stuck his head over, nuzzling Robert's arm. "Now go away."

Lucinda stared at his back. Everyone knew he'd been wounded at Waterloo. She remembered when he'd returned to London, one of the first soldiers to do so. In fact, he'd arrived only three days after the battle. She frowned again. It had taken Wellington's messenger two days to get the news to Prince George, and he'd been on horseback with a dispatch ship waiting specifically for him on the coast.

"You're figuring out the timing, aren't you?" he said in a quiet voice. "You're General Barrett's daughter. You know the different routes along which information and troops travel. I was so glad the news arrived in town before I did. No one would think to ask any questions."

My God, she kept thinking. *My God.* "What happened to you, Robert?" she asked, slowly approaching him and laying a hand on his shoulder. She felt his muscles flinch beneath her touch. "How were you hurt?"

He lurched around to face her, haunted eyes burning into hers. "You don't want to know."

"Yes, I do."

"No. You would tell your father."

He started around her, but taking advantage of his game leg she pushed him back against the stall door again. Snatching the cane from his fingers, she swept it behind her. "I wouldn't tell my father."

"Why not?"

"Because you don't want me to."

Robert closed his eyes for a moment, his breathing harsh. When he looked at her again, she couldn't begin to read his expression. "Why do you want to know?" he asked.

"Because . . . because we're friends, Robert. Friends care about each other." She reached up, putting a hand over his heart. Touching him was probably the wrong thing to do, but it seemed to be the only thing guaranteed to get a reaction from him. It was funny — touching Geoffrey didn't give her goose bumps. "And friends *can* keep secrets. So if you want to tell me, tell me. If not, I'll still be your friend."

He stared into her eyes for a long moment. "Have you ever heard of Chateau Pagnon?"

She frowned. "It sounds familiar. In southern France, isn't it?"

"Yes. I spent seven months there."

He made it sound like he'd been there on holiday, but she knew it would have been nothing like that. "Why?"

Robert opened his mouth, but all that came out was a low growl. "I . . . don't want to talk about this anymore," he whispered, and leaned down to capture her mouth with his.

Almost on instinct, Lucinda leaned up, twining her fingers into his lapels to draw herself closer against his hard chest. Hunger and need. The sensation crashed through her as he molded his mouth hard against hers. It was as if he was breathing through her, breathing *her,* even. Heat and longing spiraled down her spine as his hands swept around her.

His previous kiss had been tentative, as if he didn't quite remember how to do it. Not so, this one. She knew exactly what he wanted: her.

Her mind began to catch up with her body, and she became aware that she was moaning, drinking him in. "Stop!" she commanded, pushing against his chest. "Please stop."

Robert abruptly released her. "I'm sorry," he said, wiping a hand across his sensuous mouth. "I didn't mean —"

"You didn't mean to kiss me," she interrupted, backing away and nearly tripping over his borrowed cane. "That's all right."

"No, I didn't mean to upset you," he countered, limping forward to retrieve the cane from the tangle of her skirts. "I meant to kiss you."

"Oh. Why?" she asked, still stammering and uncomfortably hot beneath her thin muslin gown.

"If I told you that, I don't think we would be able to remain friends," he said, his gaze still on her mouth. "And we are still friends, aren't we?"

She wanted to point out that she'd never had a friend kiss her like that, so that her heart felt as if it was going to pound right through her chest. But if she complained that he'd overstepped the bounds, he would close off from her again, never touch her again — and certainly never kiss her again. And she wasn't quite ready to give any of those things up yet.

"Yes, we are friends," she agreed, straightening the front of her dress. Did he mean that he desired her? It was certainly mutual. But if he hadn't meant to upset her, hadn't been in earnest, then whomever he did kiss with those intentions was going to die in his arms of ecstasy. "Of course we're friends."

He shook himself, looking around them as if he'd forgotten they were in the stables.

"I'd best get you back to Georgiana," he said, hitching forward with the cane and offering his arm again.

"Oh. Yes. Your family will be wondering what we've done to your roses by now."

As they reached the stable entrance, Robert stopped again. "Do you go to Vauxhall for the fireworks?"

"Yes. Are you going to attend?"

He nodded. "I'll try. And you'll have to tell me there what your third lesson for Lord Geoffrey might be."

Robert left her with Georgiana in the morning room while he vanished somewhere back into the depths of the house. Much as she enjoyed Georgiana's company, this morning Lucinda wanted nothing more than to cut the visit short and return home.

Aside from the fact that she wanted to spend a bit more time thinking about why Geoffrey hadn't kissed her yet when Robert had done so twice, her father had several journals she hadn't even begun transcribing. And unless she was mistaken, one of them mentioned something about a Chateau Pagnon. Lucinda suddenly felt like doing some research.

Chapter 12

Some time elapsed before I learned
the history of my friends.

— The Monster, *Frankenstein*

"Good morning, Miss Lucinda," Ballow
said, pulling open the front door. "We didn't
expect you back until luncheon."

"Is the general home?" she asked brightly,
wishing she had Robert's skill at evading inquiry, subtle or otherwise.

"He was called to a meeting at the Horse
Guards, miss. May I have Albert bring you
some tea?"

"Oh, no thank you. I'm going to go
through some . . . I'll be in the general's
office," she said, handing over her bonnet
and shawl.

"Very good, miss."

With a grimace Lucinda stepped past the

butler and walked as casually as she could to her father's office. Just because she felt as jittery inside as if she'd drunk a dozen cups of coffee all full of sugar didn't mean she needed to make a spectacle of herself. It had just been a kiss — a kiss that should never have happened and one that had practically set her toes on fire, but only a kiss, nonetheless.

The journals her father hadn't yet edited for his book lay in date order on a side table. Depending on how fast-moving a particular campaign had been, his notes could be very sketchy — hence his use of Geoffrey's recollections — or extremely thorough. Several times his entries had hinted at some fairly gruesome incidents, but he never went into detail. A gentleman wouldn't, he always said.

She flipped through the top journal, looking for place names. Mostly she found towns where battles or sieges had been fought, like Càdiz or Burgos or Tarragona, or British officers like General Rowland Hill or Major General Galbraith Cole.

In the spring 1814 journal, she found what she was looking for. In the middle of a brief account of the battle of Bayonne in the Pyrenees, the general mentioned a chateau half dug into a mountainside just inside the

French border. Pagnon Castle, he wrote, thankfully didn't overlook a main road or pass, because in his opinion it would take half the Peninsular army to get inside.

She turned another few pages and then went back again. Nothing more. From the brevity of her father's account of the Bayonne battle, he'd been extremely busy.

Lucinda sat back. So now she knew that Chateau Pagnon was just north of the town of Bayonne, and that it was highly defensible. And she knew that Robert Carroway had spent several months inside. Was that where he'd been sent to recuperate after he'd been wounded? The way her father wrote about it, the chateau didn't sound as though it was under British or Spanish control. And his wounds had been fresh when he'd returned home, not nearly healed at some monastery or other.

"Well, you've made a mess."

She jumped. Her father stood in the doorway, arms folded across his barrel chest.

"I was just . . . looking for something." Half the journals lay open across the credenza and his desk, and she busied herself closing them and putting them back in order.

"Military secrets?" he asked, strolling into

the room and closing the door behind him.

Lucinda forced a smile. "As if you would put any of those in writing." Clearing her throat, she vacated his chair. "You mention a place called Chateau Pagnon. Was it a military hospital or something?"

His expression cooled as he crossed the floor. "Why?"

She slipped toward the door. "It's just a question. Your notes are fairly sketchy during the Bayonne battle."

"Yes. It was a confusing campaign." With a scowl he sank into his chair. "Not the British army's finest moment. Or mine."

She paused, one hand on the door handle. "I've never heard you talk like that before," she said quietly.

He blew out his breath, opening the Bayonne journal again. "Chateau Pagnon. I remember some of the foot soldiers mumbling about it." The general snorted. "From the way they talked about it, you'd think it was where Mary Shelley got the idea for that monster book of hers."

"*Frankenstein*?" she asked, her hands beginning to shake.

"Yes, that's the one. Just rumors flying about." He looked at his notes again. "Yes. All I wrote is that from a military stand-point, it would have been a nightmare to storm. So who mentioned it to you, my girl?"

He knew more than he was saying. She wanted to ask, but she had given her word to Robert, and was pushing it as it was. If she pursued her inquiries further, her father would start asking questions of his own. "Just a friend," she returned. "In passing. And thank you."

He stirred. "You're welcome."

Distracted as she was by what she was hearing, something in her father's tone caught her attention. She released the door handle, coming toward him again. "Is something wrong, Papa?"

"Eh? No, no. Just some things went m . . . Just a few entanglements at the Horse Guards."

"Anything you can tell me?"

The general smiled. "Nothing that important. Anything you'd care to tell me? About your sudden interest in Chateau Pagnon, for example? Which friend were you talking with?"

"Oh, I don't remember," she returned, uncomfortable. She had always been able to speak freely with her father. But Robert had made it clear that the general was not to be included in any of this. "It just caught my attention, and the name seemed familiar."

"I see." From his expression he already had a good idea which friend she'd been speaking to, but to his credit he didn't say anything. "You have interesting conversations, my dear," he continued instead. "Now go on, and let me get some work done."

Lucinda left the office with more questions than she'd found answers. She always did her best thinking when she was out working in her rose garden, so she went upstairs to change. As she sat to fix her hair, though, she found herself examining her own reflection in the mirror.

What was she doing, digging through her father's things? Her lessons weren't about Robert. His whole involvement had been an accident, anyway. And yet seeing him to thank him for his efforts at the ball had been her first thought this morning. Discovering the importance of Chateau Pagnon had consumed her afternoon, and in between had been that kiss. Lucinda sighed. She desperately needed to re-assess her plan of action. For goodness' sake, she'd argued with her chosen potential future spouse last evening, and had scarcely given it a second thought.

But what Robert had told her — what he'd begun to tell her — how could she ignore that? How could she forget it? And how could she keep from wanting to know more about what had happened to him?

"No," she said, looking sternly at the figure in the mirror. "Do what you set out to do."

However arousing his kisses, Robert was trouble. Nothing about him could possibly make her life any easier. He wouldn't — couldn't — banter or trade stories with her father. If St. Aubyn and her own growing suspicions were correct, Robert didn't even like her father. Nor did she think he could be the kind of man to offer her comfortable companionship.

Someone scratched at her door, and she quickly finished putting up her hair. "Come in."

Ballow cracked open the door. "Miss Lucinda, you have a caller." He held out his silver tray, an elegant embossed calling card set in its middle.

She picked it up. Lord Geoffrey Newcombe. And there she was dressed in her old gardening gown. "Drat."

"Shall I inform him that you're out, then?"

"No, no. Please let him know I'll be down in a few minutes. And send Helena up to me, will you?"

"Yes, miss." The butler nodded, pulling the door closed again.

Quickly she chose another gown. When her maid arrived, Helena helped her throw on the blue muslin and fix her hair for the second time. In less than five minutes she was ready, and hurried down the stairs.

Ballow caught her attention as she headed for the morning room. "Lord Geoffrey has joined your father in his office."

Of course he had. If anything, Geoffrey seemed more interested in bonding with the general than with her. Well, that served her right; she'd spent her morning with Robert rather than trying to find a way to make amends with her supposed student.

"Hello," she said, stepping into the office.

Immediately the two men stopped their discussion and Geoffrey came to his feet. "Lucinda. I'm so pleased to find you at home."

"I returned early from a visit."

Geoffrey glanced toward her father and back again. "I was hoping I might convince you to join me for luncheon."

That was bold of him, if he expected to simply drop by and find her schedule free. And it was lucky of him, because she did have nothing planned for the remainder of the afternoon. "Consider me convinced, then," she said, smiling.

They left in his curricle, Helena seated behind them, as soon as Lucinda put on her walking bonnet. For a few minutes she could almost believe she was riding with Robert Carroway, since Lord Geoffrey sat in silence beside her, his jaw working though he made no sound.

She supposed she was expected to start the conversation, chat about the weather or Edmund Keane's latest performance at Drury Lane Theatre, but the image of a fog-shrouded stone castle with Robert inside pulled at her. Damn it, she wanted to know why he'd been there, and obviously no amount of pondering on her part would answer the question. Only Robert could do that.

"You're still angry with me, aren't you?" Geoffrey asked abruptly, glancing at her and then back at his team.

"I —"

"I apologize again, sincerely," he interrupted. "Name what it is I need to do for you to forgive me, and I'll do it."

She started to tell him that none of this groveling was necessary. Being General Augustus Barrett's daughter, however, gave her good instincts. Perhaps it was time to have Geoffrey at least answer some questions, since no one else seemed willing or able to do so. "Clarify something for me," she said.

"Anything."

"Why are you and I here?"

His familiar grin flashed. "Do you mean why are we in my curricle? Because I made you angry at —"

"You know what I mean."

"A lady really isn't supposed to ask such questions, Lucinda."

Probably not. "Indulge me, Geoffrey. It's important. And please be honest."

A slight grimace twisting his handsome features, he nodded. "Very well. We are here for two reasons. The first is that you're lovely and pleasant and practical, and familiar with a military lifestyle, and I desire you."

"And the second reason?" she prompted, though she had a fairly good idea.

"The second reason." He glanced around the curricle as if to make certain no one else approached closely enough to overhear. "The second reason could be somewhat . . . embarrassing, and I would appreciate your discretion."

"Of course."

He smiled at her again. "You are your father's daughter. And I am my father's son.

The fourth son, to be more specific." Geoffrey cleared his throat. "I'm still with the Army, you know."

"My father mentioned it."

"I'm on extended voluntary leave, at half wages. My commanding officer suggested it. As you're no doubt aware, during the Peninsular War His Majesty had a great need for large numbers of soldiers, and officers. The war, however, is over, and I find myself . . . in a predicament."

Lucinda nodded. "Pay and advancement, I presume?"

"You presume correctly. My funds through my family are limited. I was expected to make my fortune through my career, and though my prospects were good, the war ended before my promotion could be processed. Not even taking a ball at Waterloo could do the trick. And as you know, military advancement during times of peace is nearly impossible. Your father, though, is a senior member of the Horse Guards. If you and I were . . . allied, my chances of becoming a major with a command posting in India would be increased a hundredfold."

So there it was. Lord Geoffrey had found himself in the unenviable position of needing either a war or an influential mentor. She'd been right; he *was* courting her father as much as he was pursuing her. For the moment she put aside the news that he wanted to serve in India. Husbands frequently left their wives behind to maintain their social status in London — but that was for later consideration, anyway.

"And now you're even angrier," he said, sighing. "You asked me for honesty."

"I know I did. And —"

"Please know that I intend to win your heart, Lucinda."

"Geoffrey, I suspected your motives from the beginning," she said. All of his protestations of . . . whatever it was he was protesting were actually just what she expected to hear. "I can't fault you for being practical, when it's a trait you say you admire in me."

He looked over at her. "Then you're not angry."

"I'm not angry."

"And I may continue to call on you."

"Of course you may."

The curricle turned up Pall Mall, and he drew the team to a halt alongside her favorite outdoor café. Jumping to the ground, any reserve he'd demonstrated earlier seemingly gone, Geoffrey trotted around to offer her his hand. Lucinda stood, but before she could take him up on his assistance he put both hands around her waist and lifted her to the ground.

"That wasn't —"

He bent his head and touched his lips to hers.

"Geoffrey!" she gasped, pulling away.

"That, I won't apologize for," he returned, taking her hand and tucking it over his arm. "I intend to enjoy and take advantage of your loveliness. It is another aspect of you for which I am exceedingly thankful."

A footman showed them to a table. Lucinda sat, nodding at several acquaintances at nearby tables as she did so. *Hm.* She had asked for Geoffrey's honesty, and she seemed to have received it in spades. He confessed himself thankful for her pretty face, because if she'd been ugly he wouldn't have enjoyed courting her nearly as much — but he would have pursued her, nonetheless.

Was she the same? Or worse? Had she chosen Geoffrey for his mild demeanor and appeal to her father, or for his handsome countenance and heroic reputation? Neither choice sank very deeply into his character. Or hers. At least she wasn't so practical that she couldn't appreciate his kiss. He'd done that quite well, with obvious skill and at just the right moment so that no one would see, and so that it would provide the appropriate punctuation to their conversation.

She took a grateful swallow of Madeira as soon as a footman poured her a glass. It was a toast to her success so far, she decided — not a delaying tactic while she tried to think of something innocuous and charming to say in order to change the subject.

Yes, everything was proceeding swimmingly. And she wasn't thinking about seeing Robert Carroway on Saturday evening, or about how she would have to tell him now that the list and lessons were moot, because she and Geoffrey had a mutual understanding. And she certainly wasn't thinking about *his* kiss, and how it hadn't melted into her as much as it had seared and burned. She didn't want to be seared. She wanted peace and calm. So, no, she wasn't thinking of Robert at all. Not a bit.

Robert sat on the library couch, reading. He'd stretched both legs out along the seat cushions, trying to rest his bad knee, after his family had finally given up on asking him how he felt. The last of them, Andrew, had vanished nearly an hour ago to some afternoon entertainment or other.

The question of how he felt was becoming increasingly complicated, anyway. His knee was easy — it ached dully, a great improvement from the raw throbbing of earlier. For the first time in a long while, though, warmth seemed to have swept into him, soaking bones and muscles and veins with . . . life.

That was it. He actually felt alive. And when he'd kissed Lucinda, he'd remembered some things he'd thought long forgotten: the way a woman tasted, how it felt to have warm, soft skin touching his, the arousing smells of sweat and sex.

"Robert, you are insane," he murmured to himself, turning the page.

When Lucinda had stumbled across him hiding that day, he'd been genuinely curious to know her lesson plans. Her choice of Lord Geoffrey Newcombe had been both a surprise and something of a disappointment, but if she'd already set her heart on someone else, it also made her safe. Safe for him, and safe from him.

They could be friends, and he could tell himself he was helping her — while that made it easier for him to venture out into Society. Success or failure didn't matter so much when it was on someone else's behalf.

Or so he could tell himself, which was the only reason he'd been able to accomplish any of it at all.

Lucinda didn't feel safe any longer. In fact, he wasn't certain she ever really had, or whether that was another lie he'd told himself when the truth would have meant facing the black panic again.

So now the cripple wanted Lucinda. It would have been funny, if he hadn't felt her kissing him back, stretching her body along his. That made it real, and it made coming up with an easy, comfortable lie impossible.

He heard the front door open, and then voices. Dawkins, of course, then the lower tones of Tristan and surprisingly, Greydon Brakenridge, the Duke of Wycliffe. Parliament must have ended session early.

The two of them approached along the hallway, likely heading for Tristan's office. They were best friends, probably the reason the duke hadn't shot Tristan when the viscount had ruined Georgiana. He smiled a little at the memory. First cousins could be very protective of their female relations, and Grey and Georgiana were closer even than most siblings.

"Bit?"

He looked up at the doorway. "I'm fine."

"I wasn't going to ask that," Tristan returned. "Have you been here all day?"

Robert nodded. "Why?"

"I just don't want you attempting the stairs without help. By the way, Grey wanted to borrow the Runt's old saddle. Do you remem—"

"It's still in the tack room, wrapped in burlap," he interrupted, nodding at Grey. "For little Elizabeth?"

"I'm going to try to convince Emma that fourteen months isn't too young to begin riding," the duke rumbled.

"He's going to lose," Tristan put in, grinning, "but the argument should be fun to watch. That's why I'm supplying the props."

"Edward's old hobby horse is in the attic, if you want to try that first." Robert went back to his book. "Less arguing that way."

"I always said Tristan wasn't the smart one in his family," Wycliffe drawled.

"And I never argued with you about it, either." Tristan started out, then stopped again. "What are you reading?"

"*The Care and Cultivation of Roses*," Robert answered. "Miss Barrett loaned it to me."

"My thanks, Robert," Grey said. "We'll see you at Vauxhall, yes?"

Apparently everyone meant to attend the fireworks. "I'll make an attempt."

"Good."

The two of them vanished into Tristan's office. He had a feeling the visit wasn't about saddles or hobby horses; both men had seemed too on edge for a casual visit. And Tristan had wanted to know where he was, and where he'd been. Interesting, that. He was used to being checked on, but it usually wasn't done with friends in tow. He shrugged. Maybe Tristan really did think he was getting better. He felt like he was.

It would have been easy to listen in on the conversation; the room upstairs from Tristan's office was unoccupied except for stacks of spare dining-room chairs and an old wardrobe or two. The problem would be getting upstairs with his bad knee.

Robert settled back again. If they were talking about something important, someone would tell him eventually.

Eventually turned out to be dinner, and the someone, Andrew. "Did you hear?" he asked, around a mouthful of roast ham.

"Should I just have Dawkins collect your silverware, then, and you can use your hands?" Georgiana queried.

"Apologies." He swallowed. "You've heard, haven't you, Tris?"

The viscount sighed. "Probably. *Where* did you hear it?"

"It was all over Tattersall's this afternoon. You can't tell me they know more at the horse auctions than they do at Parliament."

Georgiana scowled. "What in the world are you two talking about?"

"Nothing much," Andrew said with a grin. "Just rumors, unless they're not. Not just rumors, I mean."

"Andrew! Tell us!" Edward demanded.

Amid the general round of chuckling, Robert kept eating. His appetite had certainly improved over the past few weeks. As he glanced up, though, he abruptly didn't feel quite as hungry anymore. Tristan sat gazing at him, a surprisingly serious expression on his face.

"No one's confirmed anything," Tristan said slowly, "but there's a rumor that some papers were taken from the Horse Guards yesterday."

"Which papers?" Edward asked.

"Maps of St. Helena Island," Andrew chimed in, "and lists of Bonaparte's supporters still on the loose, things like that."

Bradshaw set down his fork with a clatter that made Robert flinch. "Someone's trying to free Bonaparte!"

"Shaw, you're jumping to conclusions,"

Tristan said sharply. "This could all just be a nasty rumor. It probably is. No one from the Horse Guards has confirmed anything."

Robert closed his eyes, the excited chattering of his family blurring into a buzzing roar and flooding into his ears. The last time Bonaparte escaped an island prison, it had taken the combined armies of England and Prussia — and the battle of Waterloo — to stop him. No one would make him go this time, but he would know — know what other soldiers faced, and wonder whether the French would again inhabit Chateau Pagnon.

"Bit? Sit down."

He blinked. Tristan had him by one arm, and he stood at the table, his chair pushed over backward. Shrugging free of Tristan's grip, he grabbed his borrowed cane and backed for the door. *Breathe.* "I'm fine. I just need some air."

His knee slowed him down, but he lurched for the front door. Yanking it open, he half stumbled down the steps. He stopped at the rose garden — his rose garden — and sat on the ground at one side of the cuttings.

"Robert, I'm sorry," Tristan said from the edge of the carriage drive. "I should have s—"

"You should have said something before," Robert grunted, picking up a dirt clod. He wanted to throw it. Throw it and break something. Instead he tightened his fist around it so hard the dust sifted out through his fingers. "You knew. You and Grey. What were you doing, checking to see whether I'd heard or not?"

"Bit, you —"

"Too late, Dare," he interrupted. "Just go away."

"Bit —"

"Leave me alone!" He drew a breath. "I'll be in later."

Robert didn't move until he heard Tristan leave the drive. It was dark; the moon wouldn't be up for another hour, and clouds drifted in over London, anyway. They'd have rain before midnight.

He liked the rain. When it had rained in the Pyrenees, he'd been one of those fighting for a place by the window, stretching out his hand with a bit of torn cloth to hold the moisture. It had meant he might stay alive for another day or two.

The news about the thefts shouldn't have struck him that hard. After all, he hadn't known until much later about Bonaparte's exile to Elba, or of his subsequent escape, or of the hundred days of war which had ended at Waterloo. But he did know what the war had done to him — and to others who hadn't been as lucky.

Robert shredded a leaf in his fingers. Perhaps the former emperor would have been less anxious for battle if he'd spent time at Chateau Pagnon rather than a pair of nice, cozy islands. Perhaps then all he would want was the scent of fresh air and never to smell the sweet copper odor of blood again.

He should never have mentioned Pagnon to Lucinda. Hopefully she would forget the name — few knew much about the fortress, anyway. Few who were alive, that was.

When the rain began, he was still sitting at the edge of his garden. He tilted back his head, letting the cold droplets run down his face. It was just rain now, he told himself. And Andrew's story was just a rumor, or at worst just a few missing pieces of paper. He didn't have to go back. Tristan had sold away his commission before he'd even been able to sit up in bed.

The rumors, true or not, couldn't hurt him, regardless. He was safe. He was still safe.

Chapter 13

It was a strong effort of the spirit of
good, but it was ineffectual.
Destiny was too potent, and her
immutable laws had decreed my utter
and terrible destruction.

— Victor Frankenstein, *Frankenstein*

Even after a night of showers, Lucinda
almost wished it would rain again. True, the
fireworks display at Vauxhall looked to be the
best of the Season, and the Regent along with
most of the population of Mayfair planned to
attend. She'd even found the prettiest of outdoor evening gowns to wear, a soft lavender
with deep purple lace and beading.

She loved such events, the crowds and the
spectacle, but over the past days it had occurred to her that Robert hated them. And
yet, he meant to attend. And as a reward,

she planned to tell him that Geoffrey had told her the items on his own list — a wife and a promotion — and that their marriage was practically arranged. She was finished with delivering her lessons, and his assistance was therefore no longer required. *Thank you very much, and goodbye. And no more kissing.*

"Good morning, my dear," her father said, emerging from his office to join her in the breakfast room.

"Good morning, Papa. How long have you been working?" She looked at him more closely. "Have you even slept?"

The general handed her a plate and motioned for her to precede him along the sideboard. "I rose early. Just trying to straighten out a few tangles."

"But I thought the chapter was going well," she said, selecting a peach and a few slices of toasted bread.

"The chapter *is* going well. This isn't about that. Oh, and by the way, Geoffrey was here already this morning. He left a letter and a box of chocolates."

"For me, or for you?" she couldn't help asking.

"We chatted about a few things, but I'm fairly certain the things are for you. He apologized for leaving, but he had an appointment with his tailor."

She glanced back at him again. He'd put a few pieces of fruit on his plate, and nothing else. When the general didn't have an appetite, something was seriously wrong. "Is there anything I can do to help?"

Her father took his usual place at the head of the table, while Lucinda sat to his left. When he refused the footman's offer of tea in favor of coffee, she knew for certain that something was troubling him.

"Papa?"

He blinked, looking up at her. "Ah, no. It's nothing, really."

"Are you still attending the fireworks tonight?"

"I don't know yet. I'll certainly try." His steel gray gaze focused on his plate. "You know, perhaps you *can* help me."

"Anything, Papa."

"Who mentioned Chateau Pagnon to you?"

The blood drained from her face. She had nothing to hide, but Robert had asked specifically that she not say anything about their conversation to her father. As for why, she meant to ask him tonight. "I told you that I don't remember," she said lightly. "Pass the jam, will you please?"

The general slid the jam in front of her.

"Lucinda," he said slowly, "it's important. None of your friends will be in any trouble, but this could be a clue to something else."

"Your tangle?" she suggested.

"Yes, my tangle. I can make a very good guess, of course, but I need you to confirm it for me."

She drew a breath. "I made a promise to be discreet," she told him. "I'll tell you because you're my father, but . . . please. I don't want to hurt anyone."

"I understand," he said simply. "At this point, I would just like to know for my own peace of mind. Was it Robert Carroway?"

"Yes." Even as she spoke she felt dirty and evil — it had only been yesterday morning that she'd given her word, and already she was betraying it. "We were talking about the war, and he said he hadn't been at Waterloo, and that instead he'd spent several months at Chateau Pagnon. I thought it might have been a hospital, since he was so badly hurt."

Her father sat in silence for a long moment. "Did he say how he ended up there or how he left?" he asked finally, his expression unreadable.

"No." Lucinda frowned at her breakfast plate. "You do know more about that place than you told me, don't you?"

"What I know about Pagnon isn't fit for a lady's ears, Lucinda."

"Papa, I want to know —"

The general pushed away from the table. "I have a meeting this morning." He stopped, then leaned down and kissed her forehead. "If you go out today, don't say anything about our conversation to anyone." Her father grimaced, then smoothed the expression away again. "Especially not to a Carroway."

"Papa! What is going on?"

He left the room, and a moment later she heard the front door open and close. His breakfast sat untouched beside hers.

This was wrong, and so strange. She couldn't shake the feeling that she'd just done something terrible to Robert. That her father had known something terrible about Robert, and she'd confirmed it.

Slowly she set her napkin on the table. She knew where she could find some answers, if he would talk to her. And if she had the courage to ask the questions.

If she went to see Robert again this morning, after a visit yesterday, people would begin to talk. Even Georgie, who knew of the agreement she had with Robert, would doubt she had only her lessons with Lord Geoffrey in mind. And she would be right.

Lucinda went upstairs to change into a visiting dress. One good thing about Robert's reticence was that he tended to stay at home. So she would go call on Georgiana — who would be at breakfast with her aunt, the Dowager Duchess of Wycliffe. Lucinda took a quick breath as a thrill of excitement went through her — anticipation which had nothing to do with asking questions and everything to do with seeing Robert again.

Dawkins pulled open the door of her coach as she arrived at Carroway House. "Good morning, Miss Barrett," he said, handing her to the ground.

As she stepped down she spied Robert around the side of the house. His jacket off and his shirt sleeves rolled up, he was crouched down, pulling weeds from his flowerbed. With dirt smudged across his arm and lanky black hair fallen over one eye, he looked so delectable that her mouth went dry.

"Miss Barrett?" the butler said, looking at her curiously.

Concentrate. "Is Lady Dare at home?" she asked, forcing her gaze and her attention away from the garden. As soon as the butler told her Georgie was out, she could pay a visit to the roses — and whomever happened to be tending them.

"She is indeed, Miss Barrett."

"Oh, well, in that c— Oh." *Drat.* "Is she receiving callers? I don't want to disturb her."

Dawkins guided her into the front sitting room. "I shall inquire."

What was Georgiana doing at home? She and the duchess had scheduled this breakfast over a week ago. Lucinda scowled out the front window. Now she would have to think of a reason for making the visit.

"Miss Barrett, Lady Dare is upstairs in the music room."

"I know the way." With a nod of thanks to the butler, she climbed the stairs to the second floor.

Georgiana sat at the piano, arms outstretched to reach the keys beyond her rounded belly. She looked up, smiling, as Lucinda strolled into the room. "I'm so glad you're here, Luce," she said, bringing the Haydn tune to a halt. "I am desperate to go for a walk without being surrounded by large, overprotective men."

Despite her frustration, Lucinda chuckled. "Well, I'm not large, or a man, but I can't promise not to be overprotective." She helped Georgie to her feet. "I was halfway here when I remembered you were going to breakfast with the duchess," she lied. "I'm surprised to see you here, actually."

"Aunt Frederica sent over a note cancelling." Georgie grinned. "I think she was out late playing cards with her friends, and wanted to sleep late."

"She must have won."

"She always does."

They headed downstairs, Georgie holding the rail with one hand and Lucinda's arm with the other. It was the first time Lucinda realized just how far along in her pregnancy Georgiana was. Seeing her nearly every day, the change hadn't been all that noticeable. "Are you certain you want to go walking?" she asked.

"I'm certain I don't want to stay shut up in the house all day while my men are at the boat races." She sighed. "I don't know how Bit can stand being alone all the time, but he seems to find it peaceful."

"He's actually outside right now, working in his rose garden. I saw him when I drove up."

"Did you? His knee didn't seem to be bothering him as much this morning. A short walk might do him some good."

Lucinda hadn't meant to suggest he be dragged along. Yes, she wanted to talk with him, but not with Georgiana present. He probably wouldn't talk in front of Georgie, anyway — except that he had. Georgie knew things about Robert that she didn't, and Lucinda abruptly realized that she didn't like that much.

Oh, that was stupid. Stupid and wrong. Georgiana was Robert's sister-in-law, for heaven's sake. And *she* was just a friend. A friend who was going to marry Lord Geoffrey Newcombe as soon as he asked her. A friend who really had no business gawking at another man — and especially not at Robert Carroway.

Robert looked up from his weeding a moment before Georgiana and Lucinda rounded the corner of the house. He straightened automatically, which amused him. Apparently he still remembered some manners. Or rather, he remembered them when Lucinda was present.

She looked like spring in her white and green sprig muslin, her brown hair topped with a matching green bonnet. He couldn't take his eyes off her. *Stop it,* he told himself. She didn't belong to him. He didn't deserve her, and she would be much better off without him.

"Bit, care to escort us on a short stroll?" Georgie asked.

Since he was already on his feet, he didn't

have grounds for much of an excuse. Shrugging, he rolled down his sleeves and pulled on the jacket he'd tossed over a phaeton wheel. His limp was more noticeable than it had been for over a year, but he'd discarded Aunt Milly's cane as soon as he could stand it.

They started down the street, passing by pretty front gardens and mansions with dozens of staring glass windows. Lucinda and Georgie walked arm in arm, while he stayed close by Georgie's other side in case she stumbled.

"We make a fine group, don't we?" Georgiana said after a few moments. "Luce, you may end up having to carry Bit and me both back home."

Lucinda laughed. "One at a time, if you please."

"Did General Barrett go to view those silly boat races, too?"

"No, he had a meeting."

A meeting. Robert could guess what it was about. A shudder of uneasiness went through him. If the old generals of the Horse Guards chose to meet on a Saturday morning rather than attend boat races on the Thames, something serious was amiss.

They made a circle of four blocks, and by the time they returned to Carroway House,

Robert wasn't certain who was more grateful to be back — himself or Georgiana. Ignoring the sharpening ache in his knee, he put a hand under his sister-in-law's elbow to help her up the front steps.

"Dawkins, I would be extremely grateful for a glass of lemonade," Georgie said, collapsing on the sitting-room couch.

Because he was always aware of where Lucinda was, Robert knew she was going to touch him a heartbeat before she did so. He tensed his arm, but flinched anyway. She burned straight through the material of his jacket.

"Georgie, are you all right here for a few minutes?" Lucinda asked. "When we were outside I noticed a mildew on some of the roses. They're still quite delicate, and I —"

"Go, go. I'm not moving. Ever."

Robert followed her back outside. He could play aloof; he was an expert at that. On the inside, though, he was imagining kissing her again. Kissing her, and peeling her out of her springtime gown and running his hands along her warm, smooth skin.

"I lied," Lucinda said abruptly, stopping to face him.

"I know," he answered.

"You do?"

He couldn't help a brief smile. "I've seen

mildew. My roses don't have any."

Her cheeks darkened. "But you came out here, anyway."

"I thought you probably wanted to talk to me about something."

Lucinda's shoulders heaved with the breath she took, and abruptly she began pacing toward the street and back again. Cursing under his breath at the pain to his knee, he shifted backward so he could keep her in sight.

"Yes, I do. After we spoke yesterday, I went through some of my father's journals. I knew he'd mentioned Chateau Pagnon, but I couldn't remember what he'd —"

"Forget what I said. It wasn't important," he interrupted, trying to ignore the jolt to his insides. After three years, he still couldn't even stand hearing its name.

"Robert. Why were you there? The general wrote that it was well fortified, but not a place of strategic interest. But it was significant, or you wouldn't have mentioned it."

He'd known this would happen. With anyone else, he would simply have walked away. He could talk to Lucinda, though. And her presence eased the distance between himself and the world.

"I was a prisoner," he forced out.

"A pr—"

"This has nothing to do with our agreement," he broke in, shoving his hands into his pockets so she wouldn't see them shaking. "Tell me about your third lesson, why don't you? I may need some preparation time."

Lucinda began pacing again. This time he followed her, catching her arm as they reached the end of the drive. She shrugged free even before he could release her. "Don't change the subject," she said stiffly. "I want to know about Chateau Pagnon."

He studied her face for a long moment. "No. Lesson number three."

Her lips twitched. "Has anyone told you that you're stubborn?"

"Yes."

"Robert, I . . ." Frowning, she turned her back on him. "I came here to find out more about you."

Her bonnet blocked his view of her face. "Why?" he asked, touching her shoulder and drawing her around to face him again.

"Because."

He lifted an eyebrow. "I thought I was the one with the limited vocab—"

"Blast it, tell me," she interrupted.

Robert studied her expression, a growing suspicion pulling at him. He knew why he resisted talking, but he wasn't certain why she was doing so. "Something's happened. Did Geoffrey disagree with your . . . tolerance for me?"

"It's not tolerance, for goodness' sake, and we can discuss Geoffrey later."

Something was definitely troubling her. "Lucinda, you can tell me anything."

Lucinda stopped at the foot of the steps. It was the first time he'd called her by her given name, and she liked the sound on his lips. "We are friends," she returned, facing him again. A very odd pair of friends who kissed and who, for her part anyway, thought of kissing each other quite a bit. "But if you won't talk to me, why should I talk to you?"

Sky blue eyes met hers and slid away. It seemed to be the one advantage she had, that he had a keen sense of fair play. If she could remind him of that, perhaps he would stop pressing her for information — information she hadn't yet decided how to tell him, about how she didn't need him any longer, but wanted him there, anyway.

"What do you want to know?" he asked quietly.

The pain and reluctance in his voice almost stopped her. She might have given in, if her father's "it's important" hadn't been so fresh in her thoughts, along with

Robert's specific request that the general not be told. At any rate, she wasn't going to make him shout it halfway across the drive. "Shall we go inside?" she suggested.

Robert shook his head. "I don't know how much I can tell you," he said, "but I . . . need to be outside."

She returned to him. "Give me your arm, then, and we'll take another walk. A short walk."

For a moment she didn't think he would comply. "What about a chaperone?" he muttered.

"Hang the chaperone," she retorted. "We're walking around the block, in the open, for heaven's sake."

He held out his arm, and she wrapped her hand around his sleeve. His leg did seem better, but it gave her a pretext for touching him, for leaning into him. He smelled of fresh earth and leather, and more faintly, of shaving soap. She caught herself gazing at his sensuous mouth, and resolutely looked away again. *Friends.* They were friends.

As they continued on in silence, she realized she was going to have to begin the conversation. It wouldn't be an easy path to tread. The last thing she wanted to do was cause him more pain, but she wanted, she needed, to know more about him. And not

263

just to satisfy her curiosity about her father's comments.

"In the general's journals," she said, sending up a quick prayer, "I've noticed that he has three reasons for leaving out details. The first is that the campaign was so involved or was moving so quickly that he simply didn't have time to record everything. The second is that the incident or battle was too . . . disturbing, and he didn't want to record the details. The third reason is that he intentionally didn't note certain things for reasons of security or to ensure the safety of his men — in case his journals were lost or captured."

"Lack of detail could also be because of simple lack of significance," Robert put in.

"Yes, I suppose, but he tended not to mention insignificant things in the first place."

He looked at her sideways, surprising her with the appreciation in his gaze. "Does General Barrett have any idea you've figured him out to such a degree?"

"Oh, I think he has a fairly good idea." She smiled. "I ask a great many questions."

"I've noticed that." They walked past another house and turned the corner. "You're very fond of General Barrett, aren't you?"

"Yes, I am. He's never treated me like an

inferior because of my sex, and he saw to it that I received a first-rate education."

" 'I had begun life with benevolent intentions and thirsted for the moment when I should put them in practice and make myself useful to my fellow beings,' " he recited, his fleeting smile appearing again.

"That's from *Frankenstein*, isn't it?" she asked, remembering the tattered pages of the book he'd been reading the day all of this had begun.

"Are you guessing, or do you know?"

"I used deductive reasoning," Lucinda returned. "I'm good at that, too. For instance, I have deduced that my father's brevity concerning Bayonne and Chateau Pagnon was for all three reasons: time, content, and security."

She felt his arm muscles draw tight beneath her hand, but his expression didn't change. "I couldn't begin to deduce what General Barrett might have been thinking," he said in a low, hard voice, "but I would guess that *you* are correct."

Lucinda swallowed. She could ask him why he disliked her father, or she could ask him about the thing her father had deemed important. From what she'd begun to learn, she had the feeling they were connected. With another swift glance at his tense, handsome face, she decided. "So Chateau Pagnon was a prison."

"Of sorts."

"Of what sort?"

With a ragged intake of breath, he began speaking, his voice low and rough and distant. "I didn't see much of it, but as far as I could tell, it was a prison for British officers. A place where they — the French — tried to get . . . information."

He meant a place where British officers were tortured. Where *he* had been tortured. "I'm so sorry," she whispered.

"It wasn't your fault."

"You've never told anyone about this before, have you?" she asked, tightening her grip on his arm.

"No. I mean, I told Georgiana a little, about not being permitted to talk. That's all. She didn't need to know anything more than that. She may not have realized it, but she didn't *want* to know anything more than that."

"You weren't permitted to talk?"

"Not to each other. If a guard heard anyone even whisper, even one word, they would drag us out and beat us."

"But you said they wanted information. If you weren't allowed to speak, how —"

"We were only allowed to talk to him." A

266

violent shudder went through his lean frame.

"Robert?"

He closed his eyes for a moment. "I've spent three years trying to forget this," he murmured. "I don't like remembering it again."

"You don't have to, then." She meant it. Her father's quest for information, and her own curiosity, could wait.

They walked a few steps in silence. "No, I think maybe I do. It's . . . strange, but if I can remember and not die, I think it might help."

My God. Abruptly the question wasn't whether he would talk about it, but whether she could stand to listen. She'd heard so many tales and anecdotes from her father and his cronies, but none of them had been so immediately and plainly . . . horrific. "Tell me what you can, then," she said hoarsely.

He looked over at her, a hundred things passing behind his eyes. "I'm sorry."

"For what?"

"You don't need my nightmares, Lucinda. You talk to me like I'm human, and that's enough."

They passed between a tall stand of pink rhododendron and an empty coach stopped

267

at the edge of the street, and abruptly she couldn't stand it any longer. If she couldn't touch him, comfort him, do something, it would cause her physical pain. Tightening her grip on his arm, she pulled him around and leaned up to tangle her fingers through his hair, drew his face down, and kissed him. Heat flooded her. Making a small sound deep in his chest, Robert pressed her back against the side of the coach.

Her mind couldn't seem to grasp anything beyond the need to be closer to him. His pain, his frustration, his damaged pride and anger all melted into her with such ferocity that it was almost tangible. If she could have taken it all into herself, she would have.

His hands slipped down her shoulders, brushed the outsides of her breasts, and slid warm and solid around her waist. At the same time his mouth broke from hers, dipping to taste the line of her jaw and the base of her throat. Her knees went weak, and she fleetingly thought if not for the coach at her back, she would have fallen to the ground.

Robert pulled away from her. "Lucinda," he whispered, "st—"

"Shh. Kiss me."

She tried to pull him closer again, but she could as easily have moved a stone statue.

That was interesting. Before, when she'd tugged at him and he'd acquiesced, she hadn't realized how much he'd simply been letting her get away with.

"Carriage coming," he breathed, setting her back from him a second time.

A heartbeat later she heard the curricle rattling down the lane toward them. Thank goodness Robert had very good hearing. Swiftly she took his arm again, and resisting the urge to straighten her bonnet, started back up the street beside him.

"You still haven't told me about your next lesson for Geoffrey," he said, his voice stronger, as if he hadn't just a moment before been discussing torture and death — or half a moment before, kissing her.

Kissing her. That was why he'd brought up Geoffrey again; to remind her that she hadn't chosen Robert Carroway for lessons, or for anything else. At least one of them remembered what they were supposed to be doing.

"I'm still planning on telling you tonight," she returned.

"It must be bad."

It *was*, for him — and maybe for her. "Nonsen—"

"Bloody traitor!"

Robert whipped his head toward the

269

street, stepping in front of Lucinda and blocking her view. She leaned around him.

The curricle hugged the far side of the street as it passed them at high speed. "Who was that?" she asked.

"Sir Walter Fengrove and Lady Daltrey," he said absently, watching the carriage as it bumped down the lane past them.

"Was he talking to us? Why would he say such a thing?"

He shrugged once more, finally facing forward again. "I don't know," he said, but his face had gone gray.

"Robert?"

"I'm fine," he said. "We should get back to Georgie."

Lucinda had the distinct feeling that he wasn't fine, but she had no wish to distress him more than she already had this morning. "Yes, you're right," she said. "Back to Georgie."

Chapter 14

Now all was blasted.

— Victor Frankenstein, *Frankenstein*

Robert had talked a little about Chateau Pagnon, and he hadn't died. As he'd told Lucinda, that in itself was something of a success. Or it would have been if Sir Walter Fengrove hadn't driven by.

Something had happened, something was wrong; he could feel it in his bones, and he wasn't surprised. He'd been feeling too well, even begun thinking about a future. He'd felt himself coming alive again — some parts of him more than others, at least when he was near Lucinda.

Almost as soon as the two of them returned to the house, she took her leave from Georgie and drove off in her coach again. Hesitating, Robert went back to the sitting room. Georgiana still sat on the couch, looking uncomfortable. "You shouldn't have gone walking," he said, after a moment spent leaning against the doorjamb, watching her fidget.

"Yes, I should have," she argued. "I feel like a hippopotamus, wallowing about."

"And you feel better now?"

She made a face at him. "At least I don't have mildew."

Ignoring that, Robert pushed upright. "I'll fetch you some pillows."

Before he could leave, Georgie sat up a little straighter. "Lucinda seemed out of sorts when she left. Did she say whether anything was troubling her?"

The last thing he intended to do was upset Georgiana. "When we were on the drive, somebody rode by yelling. An escapee from Bedlam, no doubt."

"I thought I heard something." She smiled, the expression warming her soft green eyes. "Would it embarrass you if I said that you seem . . . happier these days?"

Robert forced a return smile, hoping Sir Walter had simply been out all night drinking, and that he'd been calling everyone he passed on the street a traitor. It was possible, he supposed. Fengrove did drink. "I'll get the pillows. And would you like a book?"

"I think I left one on the breakfast table. Thank you, Bit."

He nodded. "Happy to help."

Georgie waved him away with a chuckle. "You see, I *told* you that you were happier."

Maybe he was. And hopefully he'd learned enough to enjoy it while it lasted. He went to fetch her things for her, hoping this tense uneasiness was all just a reaction to nothing, a lingering sense of hopelessness that prevented him from believing anything could go well. Because judging by the way Lucinda had kissed him, some things were going better than he ever could have imagined.

He delivered the book and pillows to Georgiana, then headed down the hallway to the library to read. His sister-in-law claimed to be feeling fine except for tired feet, but he wanted to be within earshot in case she should need someone. She hated hovering nearly as much as he did, so the library seemed the best compromise.

An hour later he rose to look in on her, to find her dozing on the couch. As he turned back down the hall, the front door rattled and opened.

"That is not true," Edward said loudly,

marching into the house in front of his brothers. "I would have won ten quid if you'd let me wager on —"

"Hush," Robert said, limping up to throw a hand over the Runt's mouth. "Georgie's aslee—"

"Tristan, did you bring me a lemon ice?" Georgiana's voice came.

Dare pushed to the front of the group. "Yes, my dear." As he passed, he put a hand on Robert's arm. "Wait for me in my office," he muttered.

Robert's first instinct was to go find somewhere dark and quiet so he wouldn't have to hear whatever it was that Tristan wanted to tell him. As he'd discovered in France, however, dark and quiet had nothing to do with safe.

Edward stood telling Dawkins about the boat races, but he seemed to be the only Carroway brother who didn't realize that something was amiss. Both Bradshaw and Andrew remained in the foyer, their faces solemn and even angry. And neither of them would look at him.

With dread sinking deep into his gut, Robert went to Tristan's office. Despite his tired knee he couldn't make himself sit still, and instead paced slowly in front of the window.

He heard Tristan come in a few minutes later, but didn't turn around. The sound of the door closing was like the crack of doom.

"Bit, have a seat."

"No."

The viscount sighed. "All right. I wanted you to know that I think you should stay in tonight."

"Why?"

"Will you at least look at me while I'm talking to you?"

Taking a deep breath, Robert turned around, sinking back against the window sill. "For three years you've been trying to get me to go places, Tris. Why don't you want me at Vauxhall tonight?"

"It's complicated." Tristan dropped into one of the guest chairs that faced Robert and the window. "And I truly don't want to hurt you. So I'm asking you to stay home tonight. For my sake."

Sometimes the blanket his brothers threw over him for his own protection could smother the life out of him. "You couldn't possibly hurt me, Tristan. Tell me what's going on. I presume it has something to do with why Sir Walter Fengrove called me a traitor an hour ago."

Tristan blanched. "He . . . God dammit."

This was getting them nowhere. "Fine.

I'll guess. Something did go missing from the Horse Guards, and people think I'm the one who did it."

"A few people think that. They're wrong."

Robert frowned. "I know they're wrong. But why do they think it was me?"

Shooting to his feet again, Tristan began his own pacing by the door. "Because some idiot started a rumor that you'd been imprisoned at Chateau Pagnon, and everyone knows that the only soldiers — officers — who left there alive were the ones who'd turned traitor."

Robert stared at his brother. He couldn't think. Silence roared up and around and into him, and he dug his fingers into the windowsill to keep from being blasted away. God, he'd been wrong. Stupid and wrong. He'd finally spoken about Chateau Pagnon, and it *had* killed him.

"It's ridiculous," Tristan snapped, real anger in his voice, "and I intend to find out who the bloody liar is and beat the truth out of him. They have no idea what they're —"

"I *was* at Pagnon," Robert interrupted, his voice a rasping whisper.

It stopped Tristan cold. "No. No, you weren't."

"If I can accept it," Robert returned,

every word as painful as a knife stabbing into his chest, "you should be able to."

"But —"

"I didn't take anything from the Horse Guards."

"Of course you didn't." His brother gazed at him, hurt and horror in his light blue eyes. "But *I* didn't even know where . . . How did anyone else know about your being a prisoner?"

In the black, dying depths of his heart, Robert knew. She'd betrayed him, just when he'd begun to trust her. Just when he'd begun to see daylight again. And she'd played so innocent and concerned — and bewildered when men began shouting epithets at him. "I have a good idea," he growled, pushing upright. "Excuse me. I have an errand."

"Bit, no." Tristan moved to block the door. "You're not going anywhere until I get an explanation. How did someone else know this, when you didn't even tell your own family?"

Growing fury screaming just beneath his skin, Robert shoved his brother aside. "Later."

"Rob—"

Throwing open the door, he strode for the foyer. Bradshaw and Andrew were still there, but Shaw at least seemed to read his mood, because he dragged Andrew away from the door just as Robert flung it open.

His leg shrieked at the abuse, but as he stalked up the carriage drive, Robert didn't care. He was used to pain. The clawing anger and disappointment inside him, though — that was new. And worse.

General Barrett opened the front door himself when Lucinda returned home. "Papa," she exclaimed, taking in his flashing eyes and stern countenance with some alarm. "What's happened?"

"My office," he said, turning on his heel and marching down the hall.

Uh-oh. Even as a child she'd rarely been the victim of one of her father's tirades. Acknowledging a fleeting wish that she could go somewhere quiet and think about Robert, she followed him, removing her bonnet as she walked. Robert. It was interesting that, for someone who so seldom talked, he could have such a sensuous, capable mouth.

"Door," the general ordered briskly, making for his chair. He sat, straight-backed and rigid as a statue.

She closed the door, leaning back against it. "What's wrong?"

"I asked you to stay in this morning," he said without preamble.

"No, you didn't. You asked me not to spread about anything we discussed this morning, and I haven't."

"Then why, on my way back here from luncheon, did three separate people stop me, all to ask whether it was true that Robert Carroway stole papers from the Horse Guards?"

Lucinda couldn't have felt more stunned if he'd slapped her. "*What?* Why — why would anyone say that Robert stole anything? Much less from the Horse Guards. Is something actually missing?"

He looked at her for a moment, drawing a deep breath into his barrel chest. "Where did you go this morning?"

"To see Georgiana," she answered, weighing her promise to Robert against her trust in her father. Judging by what he'd told her, anything and everything could be important — except for the kiss and the way it had made her feel. "And to ask Robert what he knew about Chateau Pagnon."

"So you *did* go out gossiping," he snapped. "Lucinda, I —"

"I did no such thing," she said firmly. "Robert has told no one but me, and I've told no one but you — and even that was

279

against his wishes. So no rumors about anything came from me, Papa."

"You're saying this is my fault, then? I think I know —"

She put out her hand. "Stop shouting and tell me what's going on. Then maybe we can make some sense of it."

The general rose, striding to his window to gaze out at the street. "At times your level-headedness is very aggravating," he rumbled.

Lucinda fought the surprising urge to smile, despite her growing dread. "Yes, I know."

He glanced over his shoulder at her. "Very well. I suppose since I've bellowed accusations at you, you have a right to know the facts."

"Thank you."

"Firstly, yes, some items were taken from the Horse Guards. Items that would have no use to anyone except as instruments to free Napoleon and begin another uprising in Europe."

"G . . . good heavens," she faltered, moving away from the door to take a seat in one of his comfortable office chairs. Then, as she realized what he was saying, her heart dropped into the pit of her stomach. "Robert couldn't — *wouldn't* — have done any such thing. Why is he being blamed?"

"I admire your loyalty to your friend, Lucinda, but I suggest that for the time being you keep it to yourself."

"*You* don't think . . . How could you?"

"What did he tell you about Chateau Pagnon?"

She hesitated, but under the circumstances clearing Robert's name seemed more important than keeping his confidences. She would explain it to him tonight; she had so much to explain to him anyway — though her lessons seemed trifling compared with this.

"Papa, Robert Carroway didn't do anything wrong. All he said was that only captured British officers were imprisoned there. They were beaten if they spoke a single word to anyone but . . . He didn't tell me who."

"That would have been General Jean-Paul Barrere. Bonaparte's information officer, and a very . . . persuasive madman."

For a long moment Lucinda sat quietly. "It must have been horrific," she whispered, half to herself, then straightened. "But I still don't understand why Robert is being singled out as some sort of traitor, simply because of where he was imprisoned."

Traitor. That was exactly what Sir Walter

Fenley had called him.

"Nothing is for certain yet, or he would be under arrest. However, the —"

"Arrest!" She shot to her feet again. "Papa, you can't be serious." And if this was because of something — anything — she'd said to her father, it was her fault. Robert had told her to keep quiet. *But why?*

"The truth of the matter is, we've only found three officers who left Pagnon alive. One of them tried to murder his commanding officer, and the second was assigned to Elba just before Bonaparte's escape. Which leaves us with Robert Carroway. Unfortunately the Horse Guards didn't know he'd been a prisoner of Barrere's until yesterday."

"Until I told you," she whispered. Feeling light-headed, she sank back into the chair again.

"Don't feel guilty, Lucinda. I figured it out yesterday. You claim one new 'friend,' a former soldier, and then ten days later you begin asking me about Chateau Pagnon. You might very well have saved a great many English lives by your actions."

She closed her eyes, wishing everything would just go away. "But you don't know it was him."

"Not yet." The general moved to stand in

front of her, putting a hand on either arm of her chair. "Until this is resolved, I want you to stay away from him, from the rest of his family, and from that house. Is that clear?"

"But Georgiana is my —"

"She's your dearest friend. I know. And I'm sorry. But whoever is guilty of this is an infamous . . . blackguard, and you won't want to be *anywhere* near him." He straightened. "I'm afraid we won't be joining the Carroways at Vauxhall tonight, or anywhere else, for the foreseeable future."

Lucinda couldn't think. Mostly she wanted to scream, to shout that none of her friends were traitors. Two of the Carroway brothers had risked their lives against Bonaparte's army, for heaven's sake. *Oh, God.* Bradshaw would lose his command over this. And Robert . . .

Before she could complete that thought, the butler scratched at the door. "I'm sorry to interrupt, sir," he said, "but Miss Lucinda has a caller."

"Who is it, Ballow?"

"A Mr. Robert Carroway, sir."

He knew. He knew she'd said something after she'd promised him that she wouldn't. He knew that people were shouting at him and accusing him of things because of her.

Her father strode for the door. "I'll take care of this."

She stood, grabbing his arm. "Papa, you said nothing's certain yet."

"If he is the one who took those papers, harming you would be a very small matter. Stay here."

Shaking, Lucinda did as he asked, but cracked open the office door just enough so she could peer down the hallway. *Please let this be a misunderstanding. Please let it be a mistake.*

Robert's face was pale, his expression absolutely still as the general reached the foyer. "My daughter isn't receiving callers," her father said, his voice clipped. "I suggest you leave."

For a moment she thought Robert meant to strike her father, but his clenched fists remained at his sides. "This is your fault as much as it is hers," he finally said in a black, cold voice that made her shiver. "And to think, I'd almost thought I could forgive you."

"Forgive me?" the general snapped. "For what?"

"Bayonne." Robert pulled open the front door. "Keep her away from me. You both keep away from me."

As the door slammed, Lucinda flinched.

She'd seen Robert amused, frustrated, and upset. But she'd never seen him truly angry until now. And it frightened her — because it was her fault, and because he was angry with her.

Worst of all, she deserved it.

More people knew about Chateau Pagnon than Robert had realized. It had been stupid and naive to assume that just because he never spoke of it and he never associated with anyone who would have reason to discuss it, it would cease to exist. As if he, by force of will alone, could make the place and his memories of it crumble into dust.

As he left Barrett House he caught the accusing gazes and heard the muttering all along Bond Street. Apparently he'd managed to go from solitude and obscurity to infamy, all in one day. One hellish day.

Back at home he would face more questions and scrutiny, and the devil knew what else. Home was the only place he'd ever thought himself safe from that. The only questions his family had ever asked were how he was feeling and whether he needed anything. And now he had lost that — and them — as well.

He leaned forward to stroke Tolley's

neck. "Let's go for a ride," he said.

They headed north, out of London, past the meadow where he and Lucinda had spent that one morning of peace, and kept going. He did have one safe place left — Glauden Abbey in Scotland, an old, half-forgotten Carroway estate that Tristan had given him outright last year. A place with two footmen and one cook, where he'd spent the past two winters cleaning and renovating and repairing, doing all the work himself and in perfect silence.

It would take him a good five days to get there, four if he pushed Tolley. He could stay there in the wilds until the mess in London was forgotten, until they'd found whoever had stolen the damned papers, until everyone forgot that he'd tried to become human again.

It was early evening when he stopped at the Devil's Bow Inn to eat and to rest Tolley. No one there looked askance at him any more than they did any well-dressed traveler, and he tried to force his mind to slow its spinning a little.

When he didn't return home they would know where he'd gone, or at least Tristan would know. Edward would be angry, but the rest of the family would understand — probably, unless his confession to Tristan that he'd been held at Chateau Pagnon was enough to convince them, as well, that he was guilty. In that case, nowhere would be safe.

The edges of the black panic pulled at him, and he downed an ale with his roasted chicken, then asked for another pint. It couldn't happen now. He wouldn't let it happen.

Usually it helped a little if he could concentrate on something else, but today was different. This, he realized, was the first time he'd actually been threatened by anything more potent than nightmares since the Spanish freedom fighters had found him. And what was he doing? Running. Giving up. Abandoning hope. Just as he'd done once before.

Lucinda had talked, obviously. He considered it a betrayal — or he had, when he'd stalked out of Barrett House so furious he couldn't think. But it didn't quite fit. If she'd felt righteous about it, then her father wouldn't have been the one confronting him in the hallway. If she'd done it reluctantly, then she had a reason.

This was the woman, after all, who'd reminded him that places other than darkness existed. She'd begun to melt the ice and stone that encased him. She was lovely, yes, but it hadn't been her looks that had convinced him to take his first limping steps into daylight. It had been her heart.

He hadn't been wrong about that; he couldn't have been. Because if she wasn't what he thought, then there was no such thing as hope. And hope was all he had. If she'd spoken his secrets to her father, then she'd had a reason to do so. He needed to find out what that reason was.

Pushing to his feet, Robert tossed a few coins on the table and went outside to the inn's courtyard. General Barrett hadn't been certain of anything, or a squad of soldiers would have awakened him this morning at Carroway House.

He collected Tolley, giving the gelding the carrot he'd pocketed during dinner. "What do you think?" he asked, and the bay's ears twitched at him.

For three years he hadn't cared what anyone else thought of him, but the truth was, that had been easy — because he'd been less than a shadow, and no one had spared him a thought at all. Well, he had their attention now. This wasn't the test he'd wanted, but obviously it was the one he'd been given.

Robert frowned as he swung back into the saddle. "Change of plans, Tolley," he muttered. "We're going back to London."

Chapter 15

⚜

I closed not my eyes that night.

— Victor Frankenstein, *Frankenstein*

By the time the sound of fireworks faded in the distance, it was well past midnight, but Lucinda still couldn't sleep. The look on Robert's face haunted her, and if she fell asleep, she knew it would be a hundred times worse.

She wondered whether the Carroways had gone to Vauxhall, and whether Saint and Evie had joined them. She hoped so, because the thought of Georgiana and Tristan sitting there alone tormented her. Robert had said he would attend as well, but surely he would have reconsidered. Belatedly she remembered that she'd also had Dare invite Geoffrey. The evening was a disaster all the way around, then.

The tea she'd brought with her to her bedchamber had grown cold, but she sipped at it anyway as she slowly paced. Her father had obviously known all about Chateau Pagnon, but yesterday he'd only said enough to whet her curiosity. Had he known she would go to Robert for more answers? Had he used her to do his spying?

Her window rattled. Lucinda whipped around, grabbing for a vase as it slid open. A dark figure slipped over the casement and into the room. With a gasp, she lifted her weapon and charged forward.

A hand gripped her wrist, spinning her around and yanking her backward against a hard, solid form. She took a breath to scream, but another hand covered her mouth before she could make a sound. The vase fell to the carpet and rolled with a hollow clank beneath the bed.

"Finished?" a low, familiar voice whispered in her ear.

Robert. *Robert.* Her heart pounding so hard and loud she thought he must be able to hear it, she nodded.

"No screaming, Lucinda."

With that he released her, his hands leaving her body so suddenly that she stumbled forward. "May —" Her voice squeaked, and she took a breath, trying to calm down. She didn't believe he'd stolen anything, but he *was* here in her bedchamber — and in the murky dark she couldn't help but remember that he'd wanted Pagnon kept a secret, and her father's words about what a small thing it would be for him to harm her. "May I turn up the light?"

She heard her curtains being pulled closed. "A little."

Hands shaking so hard she could barely grip the lamp, she turned up the wick. She'd wanted a chance to talk with him, to explain herself, but as yellow light flickered across his drawn, tense face and glittering eyes, she wasn't certain he would listen.

"Robert, I didn't mean for this to happen," she said anyway. "I'm so sorry."

"You told your father, after I asked you not to say anything. Why?" He prowled her room as he spoke, not touching anything but examining everything, as though he was trying to figure something out. Trying to figure *her* out.

"I only asked my father what Chateau Pagnon was," she returned, voice breaking. "When he asked where I'd heard the name, I told him I didn't recall. But he said it was important." A tear ran down her face. "He wouldn't have said that if he hadn't meant it."

"Did he say why it was so important?"

She shook her head. "He said he was trying to straighten out a tangle — he was so worried about something, Robert. But I didn't know about the theft or that Pagnon was a prison. Not until afterward."

"Who else did you tell?"

"No one."

He sank into the chair at her dressing table. "Then the rumors came from the general."

At least he believed her, though she didn't like the dark cold that came into his voice when he mentioned her father. "He knows I told him in confidence."

"You knew that, too."

"Yes, but why? Why didn't you want my father to know?"

Robert ground his fist into his thigh. "I have my reasons. But they don't have anything to do with stealing from the Horse Guards."

"Robert, I —"

"Someone passed it along," he continued. "If it wasn't you, then — I would like to know who, exactly, the general might have spoken to."

They could continue arguing over her father's integrity all night without agreeing, but his last comment concerned her even more. "You want me to spy on my father for you?"

"No, I want to know where the rumors came from. I would wager that it's someone without your sense of right and wrong."

His tone wasn't as tight or as furious as she expected, after the way he'd left her house that morning. Obviously he was still angry, but it didn't seem to be aimed at her any longer. *Thank goodness.*

Letting out a breath, she couldn't help the slow swirl of lightning curling up her spine as she watched him pick up her hairbrush and turn it idly in his elegant hands. She could imagine him brushing out her hair, the gentle pull and tug, the soft . . . She shook herself. "The rumors are out there, and so is the thief. Knowing who gossiped about it won't help anything."

For a long moment he sat in silence. "It might help my peace of mind." He stirred. "You were going to tell me your third lesson tonight."

"You want to talk about that, when people are accusing you of . . ."

"Of high treason?" he finished.

"Yes. You can't possibly be that calm about it, Robert."

He faced her, blue eyes nearly black in the dim light. "Believe me, I'm not about to forget it. But you're my friend, aren't you? Are we still friends?"

Another tear ran down her cheek. "I'm the one who should be asking that question, Robert. If you'll have me for one, then yes, we're still friends."

"Then as my friend, I'm asking you to distract me. Tell me your lesson."

God, they seemed so infantile now. "The lessons are finished."

"Are they? Or are you just saying that to be rid of me?" Something dark crossed his face. "I am dangerous to be with, after all."

"No!" she hissed. "That's not it. It was just that I had a talk with Geoffrey. He wants a promotion, so he can take a command position in India."

The expression in Robert's eyes changed, though she had no idea what he might be thinking. "So Newcombe marries you, and the general gives him a major's commission."

"Yes."

"And it doesn't bother you that he doesn't care for you? That you're going through all this for him, and —"

"It's not like that." Lucinda sat on the edge of the bed, then had to get up and walk again. He thought she loved Geoffrey, when in truth, no one made her feel . . . electric, like Robert did. He said he'd come for answers, to be distracted, but she was the one who couldn't think straight. Heavens, she was four-and-twenty — not some simpering schoolroom miss. Simply because a handsome, haunted, dangerous man chose to climb through her bedchamber window, it didn't mean she had to lose all use of her brain. "My father likes Geoffrey, and it'll please him that I'm marrying someone he approves of, and someone whom he knows will take care of me. It's very simple and straightforward, really."

"You're settling," he said, managing to make it sound like a statement and an insult all at the same time.

She'd never thought of it like that before, but he was correct. Absolutely correct — and it truly wasn't any of his business. "And what's wrong with that?" she protested, abruptly embarrassed. "Everyone's happy, and everyone gets what they want."

Robert shoved to his feet. "You can't do it."

"Why not? I'm fortunate to have found such a simple, amiable solution to everyone's problems."

He strode up to her, taking her shoulders and pushing her back against the wall. "Simple? Amiable? With all of the passion and life you have in you, you want to feel 'amiable'?"

She could barely breathe with him standing so close and her heart beating so fast. "Everything else is too complicated," she whispered.

"And thank God it is," he growled. "I have nothing left. Do you know what I would give to . . . ?" He closed his eyes for a moment. When he opened them again, they were filled with heat, and anger, and something she couldn't put a name to, but that seemed to start a fever just beneath her skin.

"Robert?"

"Let me teach *you* a lesson," he said, his voice soft and deadly. "It has a moral and everything. It's about an officer, a captain in the army. He and his squad were ambushed when they were supposed to be on a simple reconnaissance, and then his men were killed, all around him, until only he was left alive.

"Figuring there was a reason the French hadn't killed him, he decided to make a fight of it. There were too many of them, though, and they clubbed him into unconsciousness. He came to in a small cell with one small barred window and six other British officers for company. Next door were six or seven more men, though he wasn't certain, because they could only communicate with very slow, very quiet taps on the stone wall in between."

"I'm so sorry," she whispered.

"I'm not finished yet," he hissed. "For seven months he watched and listened to friends, fellow officers, being tortured until they told everything they knew. When they did, they were killed." He gave a snort of laughter, full of anger and empty of any amusement at all. "That was the choice. Talk and die, or be silent until you were tortured to death. And the really amusing thing was, this officer didn't know anything to begin with."

"Robert —"

"Believe me, if he — I — had known anything, I would have told him. Barrere. But he didn't believe me; he thought I must know something. So there I was, trying to die, and with no one willing to oblige me."

Lucinda tried to cover her ears with her hands, but he grabbed her wrists and pinned them to the wall above her head. "Please stop," she whispered. "I can't stand that you were so hurt you wanted to . . ."

"Kill myself? I did kill myself. I finally couldn't stand it any longer. I grabbed one of the guards while they were shoving me back into the cell, and I pulled his knife, then ran at the commandant so they would have to shoot me. They did. I woke up at the foot of the chateau. They must have thought I really was dead, and thrown me over the wall. I crawled into the woods so they wouldn't be able to bring me back inside, and then I waited to die."

Another tear ran down her cheek, warm against her skin, and then another. His face, inches from hers, was drawn and gray, as if even remembering hurt him. Lucinda flexed her wrists beneath his steel-strong fingers, then leaned up and kissed him.

"I never thought you stole anything," she muttered, kissing him again and again, pulling against his grip to try to bring him closer.

He jerked away, backing up. "It's not about that. I've been dead for the past three years, Lucinda. And then I thought I could help you, and by doing that I could help myself. I know it hurts my family that I'm . . . like this. It's just that I'm supposed to be dead."

That simple statement horrified her more than anything else he'd said. "But you're not dead."

"No, I'm not. And every day that I wake up is a . . . a miracle. And you can't settle for Geoffrey Newcombe just because it's

298

simple and amiable. Don't you understand?"

"There is nothing wrong with peace and simplicity."

"It's not peace. It's hollow. For you, simple and amiable means that nothing will upset you, or excite you, or touch you."

She scowled at him. "No. It means that . . ." Lucinda trailed off. He was right, but going through life without a sea of troubles around her — what was wrong with that? "Simplicity is what makes me happy."

He tilted his head at her, his gaze dropping down the length of her thin cotton shift and back up to her face again. "Liar."

"I am not —"

He took her mouth again. This time there was no mistaking the message. She didn't think she could have stopped him if she'd wanted to, but stopping him was the farthest thing from her mind. Death had so very nearly taken him — it stalked him still, and she wanted to hold onto him, make him know that he was alive, that he made *her* feel alive.

Her heart pounded in her chest as their mouths molded together. His tongue danced along her teeth, and with a groan she opened to him. Agile fingers pulled the ribbon from her hair and combed with surprising gentleness through the dark waves that tumbled past her shoulders.

Heat coursed through her, out to her fingertips as she slipped her hands beneath his coat and shoved it from his shoulders. It coursed down her spine, too, as he slid his hands around her waist and drew her close against him.

"Robert," she murmured, her voice breathless and throaty and sounding like a stranger's to her own ears. She sounded like a wanton — but as he slipped her shift from her shoulder, placing kisses down her throat and along her bare skin, she felt wanton. Wanton and wild and on fire. Peace and simplicity could wait until tomorrow.

Lucinda pulled his shirt from his trousers and ran her hands up under it, along his flat abdomen and hard chest. Muscles jumped at her touch. His hands covered hers, drawing her seeking fingers away from him and up over her head again.

As he kissed her mouth and throat he gathered her shift in his fists, slowly raising the hem to her calves, to her knees, past her hips, and on upward. The thin cotton whispered against her skin, and the cool breeze ruffling through the closed curtains felt like more hands on her body. Robert lifted the material further, gathering it in his fingers as he went, slowly and steadily uncovering her waist, her breasts, her shoulders, and drawing it over her head and arms to cast it aside.

For a long moment he didn't touch her. Hands so close to her skin that she could feel their heat, his palms coursed along her curves, down her back, as though he were memorizing her and sculpting her in his mind. She felt so hot inside that it made her tremble.

"Say something," she whispered, as breathless as if she'd been running.

Azure eyes met hers. "You're beautiful," he murmured. "Warm, and soft, and . . . a great deal more than amiable. You're so . . . real, and I —"

She stopped him with a finger across his sensuous lips. "You're alive, Robert. You're allowed to feel alive. Touch me. I *am* real."

His gaze lowered again, and feather-light fingers traveled down her shoulders to the curve of her breasts. Slowly, carefully, almost as if he was afraid she might vanish, he ran his thumbs across her nipples.

Lucinda gasped, arching against him. He kissed her again, pressing her back against the wall with the pressure of his mouth and his hands on her breasts.

"I haven't done this in a very long time,"

he said huskily, his nails across her nipples making her moan again.

Oh, goodness. He used to have the reputation of a rake; she knew that. Since he'd come back from that awful place, he'd barely been able to touch anyone. Until tonight. Until her. She kissed him again, breathing him in. "And I've never done it at all," she returned.

Fleeting concern flashed across his face. "I want you to enjoy it. If you —"

"You talk too much."

His disarming grin made her knees weak. He bent, lifting her in his arms. When he laid her on her bed, made down for the night but not slept in, she kept her fingers locked around his neck. Kissing him, though, wasn't enough. She wanted more, wanted inside him.

Robert sank onto the bed beside her, shifting his attention from her mouth to her throat, and then slowly trailing his lips down her sternum. When he took her left breast into his mouth, stroking her nipple with his tongue, she bucked. Lucinda reached for his shirt again, wanting to feel his warm skin against hers, but again he took her hands, this time lowering them to his belt.

He leaned over her, sucking her breasts,

while she unfastened his belt and opened the buttons on his trousers. Her fingers shook and her mind had closed down completely, but she knew she wanted to see him, and to feel him. This was what it felt like to be alive. Her heart pounding and her breath coming in harsh, shallow gasps, she couldn't possibly feel otherwise. And as much as she felt it, she hoped he did, too. She would do whatever she could to make certain he felt as . . . electric and vibrant and excited as she did.

She pushed down his trousers and he came free. Large, erect, and impressive, he was definitely as aroused as she was. "May I . . . may I touch you?"

"Boots first," he breathed, sitting to yank them off and set them on the floor. He kicked out of his trousers altogether, then sank onto his knees over her. As he leaned down they kissed again, hot and open-mouthed. "You touch me by letting me be around you," he murmured, taking her hand to guide her to him.

She wrapped her fingers gently around the warm, hard length of him, noting that he flinched, his jaw clenching. "Does it hurt?"

Robert shook his head. "No. But as I said, it's been a long time. I want to be inside you, Lucinda. Do you want me?"

So much she could barely breathe. "Yes," she managed, reaching for his shirt once more.

Again he caught her hands. "Don't."

"Robert, I know you were shot. You're here now, and I want to see you. I want to feel you."

Swallowing, he sat back a little. For a moment she was afraid that he was going to change his mind and leave. Then he took the bottom of his shirt in his hands and in one swift, violent motion, pulled it off over his head.

White, puckered scars, two on his abdomen and one on his shoulder, immediately caught her eye. Did he think they made him flawed, less than he'd been before? Lucinda ran her hands over his warm chest, deliberately crossing the old wounds and just as deliberately not pausing over them. He sat very still, his eyes closed as if he didn't want to see the look on her face.

She sat up and kissed him again, hard and deep. "I have a scar, too," she said, pulling him down over her. "On the back of my right knee, from when my dress got caught in the coach steps." Her breath quickening, she ran her hands down his back, and along his hard, muscled buttocks. Oh, dear God, she wanted this — she wanted him.

His eyes opened again. "Do you, now?" he breathed, lying full length along her and then sinking down along her body, marking his course with his lips and his tongue and his teeth. "A scar?"

"Yes," she gasped, as he slowly descended along her body, caressing every inch of her with his mouth as he lowered himself past her waist. "It was quite frightening. The coach dragged me halfway down the drive before the driver heard my governess bellowing at him to stop."

Kissing her thighs, he slid down farther, all the way to her ankle and her foot, and then meandering back up the other leg. At her knee he stopped, lifting her leg a little and bending it. "This leg?"

"Yes, right there. You can feel it with your — oh, my."

The tip of his tongue flickered along the short length of her scar, then trailed back up the inside of her thigh. Oh, she was going to melt, or to burst into flames. Or both, she decided, as his tongue dipped between her thighs.

"Robert!" she rasped, twining her fingers into his hair. "Please."

He lifted his head, gazing at her along the length of her body. The small, secret smile was on his lips again. "You do want me," he whispered.

"Yes, I want you," she said, beginning to feel tight in her skin and hot and exasperated and expectant all at the same time. "Now, blast it."

Robert didn't answer, though, but only lowered his head to torment her some more with his lips and tongue and — *oh* — teeth. She was panting, moaning helplessly, when his fingers joined in, gently parting her folds as he leaned in again.

Lucinda gasped. "Robert, please stop. I can't . . . I'm going to catch fire."

"You are fire."

She couldn't stand it any longer, poised on the edge of this . . . ecstasy. She grabbed his hair, pulling until he relented, slowly, deliberately making his way back up to suck her breasts again and then kiss her deeply.

He settled over her, nudging her knees farther apart, then sinking down on her. She felt him pressing at her entrance, already exquisitely aroused thanks to his attentions, and she arched her hips. Slowly, very slowly, he pushed inside. The feeling was indescribable. More than she could possibly have imagined. Just as she began to feel a tight pressure, he stopped.

"Lucinda," he breathed, his arms shaking

a little as they held his weight, "this is your last chance to esc—"

He was not going to change his mind and leave her feeling . . . unfinished like this. She lifted her hips, gasping a sharp breath and wrenching her eyes closed as he filled her completely. She'd heard Georgie and Evie talk about it a little, though they hadn't told her much. It hurt, but no more than she'd expected. Robert held still, his gaze on her face when she opened her eyes again.

"I didn't want to hurt you."

"Make me forget it, then," she said breathlessly, kissing him again.

He began to move, lifting and lowering his hips as he thrust into her. Moaning in time with his movements, Lucinda wrapped her ankles around his thighs, and her arms around his back. She dug her fingers in, unable to do more than keep breathing as his relentless, rhythmic plunging continued.

"Robert, Robert," she repeated, lifting her hips to meet his downward thrusts. Her skin grew tighter and tighter, the humming in her mind louder and louder, until with a gasp she shattered.

He lowered his head, kissing her with his tongue matching the rhythm of his hips, faster and harder until with a deep groan he pushed against her and then came.

Breathing hard, she loosened the grip of her limbs around his body and drew him down on her. His weight felt so . . . comforting on her, his pounding heart beating into her chest, matching the fast rhythm of her own.

"Was it like you remembered?" she finally murmured.

"Better."

They lay that way for a few minutes, while Lucinda fought to keep her eyes from closing and her relaxed mind from slipping into sleep. She didn't want to miss a moment of his presence. Abruptly he pushed up on his hands again, pulling out of and away from her to sit up. "I need to leave," he said.

She would have protested, but as he turned away from her, bending down to grab his trousers, she caught sight of his back in the lamplight. Thin white streaks crossed and crisscrossed his skin from high on his back down to his buttocks.

"You were whipped," she said, lifting her hand to run her fingers along one of the scars.

As Robert slipped out of the moment, the close contact and the intimacy became too much. He wanted to stay with her, but at the same time he needed a space to breathe. Upside down. Everything had turned upside down tonight.

He lurched upright again, trying to cover his flinch at her gentle touch by shrugging into his trousers and reaching for his boots. "Among other things," he grumbled.

She hadn't fainted or screamed or turned away from him, but he knew he was less than a pretty sight. The first valet Tristan had brought in to assist him in dressing, while he was still healing and his wounds raw and painful, had actually vomited. That had been the end of that. No one had seen him since. Until tonight.

"We'll figure this out, Robert. The talk about you — it's just rumors," she said, sitting up behind him and running her fingers along his shoulder again. "They'll stop when the Horse Guards finds the real thief."

Except that no one would be looking in any direction but his. "In an ideal world, you would be right. But I happen to think that a little more action on my part will be required."

"On *our* part," she corrected.

What remained of his heart clenched and released again. "I didn't come here tonight to gain your assistance," he returned, pulling on his shirt. "And I won't have my family ruined by rumors that I tried to kill myself. You *can't* say anything about that to your father, Lucinda. Promise me." With the information he'd given her, he was even more vulnerable than he'd been before he'd climbed through her window. And so was his family.

"I won't say anything."

"Keep your word this time."

"I will. I promise." She stood, slender and beautiful in the lamplight, her long, wavy dark hair partially obscuring her breasts, like Botticelli's *Venus* rising from the clam shell.

He wanted her again, immediately. And if he stayed any longer, he would begin babbling that she'd become his beacon, his hope, his obsession, his reason now to stay alive. He needed to leave. But she'd made him human again, so he couldn't resist her entirely. "Lucinda," he murmured, stroking her cheek with the backs of his fingers. "The last part of my lesson is very simple. The next time you see Geoffrey, think how amiable he is. And then think of this." Leaning in, he kissed her slow and deep, floating as her mouth molded to his. God, she made him ache inside.

"Good night, Lucinda."

"Good . . . good night, Robert."

Chapter 16

⚜

**Thus ended a day memorable to me;
it decided my future destiny.**

— Victor Frankenstein, *Frankenstein*

When Robert slipped into the foyer of
Carroway House, he immediately sensed
that someone else was already there. He
raised his arm defensively as a shadowed
figure grabbed for his shoulder. "Get away,"
he growled, smelling Tristan's brand of soap.

"Andrew and Shaw were about to pack
for Scotland," the viscount said, turning
away to light a candle on the side table.

Despite his brother's mild words, his face
was hard and set. Robert took a breath. He'd
left Lucinda's actually feeling more hopeful,
but he also knew that reality hadn't changed
a whit in his favor. "I'm going to bed."

"First you need to come with me to see

Georgiana and let her know you're safe," Tristan countered, not moving. "She was worried. We were all worried."

"I'll tell her in the morning."

"No, you'll tell her now. She's not asleep. None of us is. Her maid's upstairs with her, trying to keep her calm."

Robert's fleeting sense of satisfaction fled. His trouble hadn't ended just because he'd gone to see Lucinda. And as usual, he seemed to be hurting his family in his quest to escape his own pain. "Is she well?"

"So far. But don't you ever . . ." Tristan swallowed, equal parts anger and concern shredding his voice. "Don't you ever disappear without a word like that again."

Robert started up the stairs. "I told you I went to run an errand."

"That was fifteen hours ago, Bit. If you'd vanished, no one would need anything more than those damned rumors. You would have been ruined."

"And you would have been ruined. Unless you started spreading talk that I've been unbalanced since I returned from the Peninsula. You might try that."

Tristan grabbed his shoulder, yanking him around and nearly sending him back down the stairs on his head. "You are my brother," the viscount growled, his expression dead serious. "None of us will distance ourselves from you. So yes, if you run, we're all ruined. I suggest you think about that next time."

For a long moment Robert stared at his eldest brother. "I didn't do anything wrong," he finally said in a low voice, resuming his ascent.

"I know that. We all do."

"The rest of London doesn't. Don't be noble on my account, Dare. For your sake, and especially for Shaw's, if this gets worse I want you to stay clear of me. I mean it."

"We'll discuss that later if we need to. At the moment it's just nasty talk." Tristan gestured at the half-open master bed-chamber door. "Go on."

Robert pushed open the door. "Georgiana?"

She was propped up in bed, surrounded by pillows and reading a book while her maid sat darning socks by the window. The viscountess looked up at the sound of his voice, a smile wiping the concerned, wan look from her face. "Bit. Thank God. Are you well?"

"I'm fine," he answered automatically. "I apologize if I upset you."

"Come here," she demanded, holding out her arms.

Suppressing a shudder, he did as she asked, letting her wrap her arms around his

313

shoulders and place a sound kiss on his cheek. To his surprise, the close contact didn't bother him, and after a moment he returned the kiss with a light one of his own.

"Where have you been?" she asked.

Behind him the rest of his brothers began trooping into the room. Shaw and Andrew were both dressed for riding; they *had* been about to track him to Scotland. He wasn't certain whether that information made him feel better or worse.

"I went riding," he said, straightening again. He couldn't very well tell Georgiana that he'd been in her dearest friend's bed, or that he'd taken what he wanted — what he needed — and then left her to contemplate Lord Geoffrey and their simple, amiable match.

"Riding where?" Edward asked, stumbling sleepily into the room.

Shaw put an arm around his shoulders. "Go back to bed, Runt. Everything's well."

"No, it's not," the boy insisted, pushing free. "You left." He jabbed a finger at Robert. "And you didn't tell us where. We were worried."

Wonderful. Being chastised by a ten-year-old. "I know, and I'm sorry."

"Where did you go?"

Obviously no one was going to shut Edward up, because he was asking the ques-

314

tions they wanted answered. Tristan only lifted an eyebrow, looking at Robert expectantly.

"I started north," he said. "I thought things would be quieter at Glauden."

"But you came back."

He shrugged. "I'm tired of running. I've done nothing wrong, and I think I can stand a few rumors." His ability to withstand innuendo, though, wasn't the entire issue. "If *you* can tolerate them, that is."

His gaze went to Bradshaw, the one besides himself who had the most to lose from this. His older brother smiled, though his eyes remained somber. "As long as you stand, so will I."

Robert understood the sentiment, and the warning. If he ran again, it was every Carroway for himself. He nodded. "Fair enough."

Tristan stirred in the doorway. "Now that we're all back where we belong, everyone will please get out of my bedchamber. Except for you of course, Georgiana."

"But —"

"Tomorrow, Andrew," the viscount interrupted, though his attention remained on Robert. "Get some sleep. If we need a strategy, we'll figure it out in the morning."

That made sense, Robert decided, as the lot of them shuffled off to bed. By tomorrow the real culprit in the robbery might very well have been apprehended, and everyone could go back to forgetting the Carroway cripple. That suited him fine, except for one problem: Lucinda. Lucinda Barrett and her damned simple, amiable plans for Lord Geoffrey Newcombe.

He might want her for himself, but he knew better than to dream she'd ever accept more from him than a dark night of sin. After tonight, however, the least he could do was make certain that Newcombe had learned the lessons from her list. *All* of the lessons, whatever they might be. That was what the three ladies' agreement had been anyway, hadn't it? To each teach a student a lesson in behavior?

Robert gave a small smile. Something was definitely wrong with him if he was more concerned about Lucinda's agreement with her friends than about people accusing him of treason.

As he shed his clothes and sank into bed, he could still smell her scent on his skin. If he lived through the next few days, he was going to have to figure out a few things — like how he would be able to keep everyone — and her prospective husband in particular — from realizing how much she'd come to mean to him.

For once, Lucinda made her way downstairs before her father, and she managed to snatch a quick breakfast and slip out to tend her roses before he appeared. Her advantage at rising early was simply because she hadn't slept all night, but she had no intention of telling him — or anyone else — about that, or the reason behind it.

She snipped away at yellowing leaves and wilting blooms. She'd received offers of marriage before, and offers to engage in sin, and she'd declined both without a second thought, simply because neither the offer nor the man had interested her. Robert interested her, and intrigued her, and engaged her senses in a way no one else ever had.

Low heat rose in her again as she remembered his battered, scarred, and still beautiful body in her bed. Inside her. And because of that, she'd stepped into the least simple thing she could ever have imagined — and right in between Robert and her father.

The general had said that whoever had stolen those documents from the Horse Guards was a rogue. An infamous blackguard. Well, that described Society's current view of Robert Carroway to perfection, though her own view was radically different.

And whether he'd forgiven her or not, she had broken his trust and allowed the rumors to start. The coincidence of the theft happening at the same time everyone learned about his imprisonment was the blackest kind of luck, but it didn't prove anything.

Robert could probably dispel the worst of the rumors by confessing how his stay at Chateau Pagnon had ended. But he was right to be worried that the truth could be just as harmful. The circumstances in his case were extreme, but Society wouldn't understand that, or even care. The only part of the tale they would carry was that a soldier from a prominent family had tried to commit suicide rather than fight Napoleon.

And she'd been the one to tell her father about where Robert had been in the first place. The general wouldn't have betrayed her trust — not for anything less than the safety of the kingdom. This was obviously that important. Logically, then, he'd told someone else in authority at the Horse Guards. It would have been his duty to do so. So while she did trust him, his fellows were a different tale. "Damnation," she muttered.

"Did you prick yourself?"

Lucinda started, blushing as her father joined her in the rose garden. "No, no. This

318

breeze is drying out the petals. That's all."

"Ah." He stood there for a moment, watching her prune. "Did you sleep at all last night?"

"Wh . . . what?" *Oh, good heavens, he hadn't heard Robert and her, had he?* "Why do you ask?"

"You look tired." In a gesture that seemed awkward coming from him, he bent down to pick up some stray cuttings and dump them into her waste bucket. "I heard the Vauxhall fireworks last night. I know you wanted to go, and I'm sor—"

"Papa, I don't care about the fireworks," she said, snapping off a perfectly good bud. "Drat."

"It's the Carroways, isn't it? And Georgiana. We're holding another meeting today, and hopefully we'll be able to put together a little more complete list of what was taken, and gather information on any suspected Bonaparte sympathizers in London. That might —"

She turned to look at him. "You don't even know for certain what was taken? And yet based on that, and on secondhand information that Robert Carroway was taken prisoner, you —"

"*I* haven't done anything, Luce."

"Well, *I* didn't tell anyone else what I told

you. No one. How much do you trust the men you told?"

Slowly he sank onto the stone bench at one end of the row. "So that's what this is about. You want to blame me for betraying the confidence that you betrayed."

"No! Ye— I don't know. Maybe. If there was anyone I thought I could trust to keep the secrets of my friends, it was you. He was so angry." So angry, and so alone. She sniffed as a tear ran down her cheek. Impatiently she wiped it away with the back of her gardening glove.

"You heard him in the hallway, did you? I thought you might have been listening."

What? Oh, that. "Yes," she improvised, swallowing at the thought of what she'd almost given away.

"It's for the best, my dear. Truly. This investigation needs to be carried through. If Robert Carroway's innocent, you can apologize to him, or tell him and Georgiana later that you simply weren't feeling well or something, and that's why you stayed away from Vauxhall. If he's guilty, then you won't need to explain anything."

"He's *not* guilty. For heaven's sake, Papa, you know him."

"Not well. You're better acquainted with him than I am." He scowled. "In fact, per-

320

haps you can explain why he threw that reference to Bayonne in my face yesterday."

"I don't know." And she was *never* going to tell the general another confidence that came from Robert, anyway. She'd learned that lesson, at least. The other lesson, the one that heated every thought, was going to be much more difficult to resolve.

"Who was his regimental commander?"

"I don't know, Papa. And I don't think he's likely to talk to me about any of this now — not that I would be permitted to see him. So please stop asking me. I've hurt everyone enough as it is. I won't do it again."

The general sat quietly for a few moments while she pretended to keep pruning. Without even realizing it, she'd apparently become some sort of awful army informant, and even worse, she'd slept with the object of their investigation — and practically promised to get him information, as well.

Finally he stood again. "I almost forgot. Geoffrey sent over a note. I don't suppose you sent him a thank-you for the chocolates yesterday?"

"Not yet." Actually, she'd forgotten all about it. Shame on her.

"Well, despite that, he'd like my permission to escort you to the Hesterfield soiree tonight."

"I'm not going. I don't want to hear all of that nasty muttering."

"Of course you're going. You can't become a hermit just because one of your friends did something wrong." He raised a hand before she could protest. "Is suspected of doing something wrong," he amended.

"Papa, you don't understand. Georgiana and Tristan will probably be there. You told me to stay away from them, and they won't have any idea why."

"If they've heard the rumors, which I suspect they have, they'll have a very good idea why you're keeping your distance. And they'll understand. Neither of them is a fool."

"You've always told me to stand by my convictions."

"I know. This time, this once, I'm asking you to stand by mine. Whoever did this is trying to begin a war."

"They are my friends," she said, as calmly as she could. He knew it as well as she did. This mess was desperately serious — but she was just as serious in her belief that Robert was innocent.

"Lucinda, I won't let you speculate over what might happen, but I won't let you lie to yourself, either. Yes, you may lose a friend-

ship or two over this. I can't help that. But you haven't done anything wrong."

Yes, she had. Being the strategist and leader that he was, though, of course the information would matter to him more than where he — or she — had acquired it. Well, if she had to, she could play that game, as well. "I suppose even Wellington knows about this?"

"He's aware of the problem, but only the five senior officers are involved in the investigation."

Five men, then, including her father, would have known about Robert and Chateau Pagnon before the rest of London. Which left four men who might have told anyone. "This is awful," she muttered.

"It's more awful that someone is trying to free Bonaparte and start up more of this damned bloodshed. Now, you've had a bad few days. Go enjoy yourself tonight. Geoffrey's becoming quite fond of you, and if I'm not mistaken, you rather like him. Think a little of yourself, my sweet. In the long run, no one will blame you for any of this. You may even turn out to be quite the heroine."

"I don't want to be a heroine," she muttered. "You may take all the credit you like." Lucinda took a deep breath. "I need

323

to finish tending my roses."

"I'll send Geoffrey your acceptance."

She nodded the back of her head at him. Arguing obviously wouldn't do any good; he expected her to be a good soldier and continue with her duties. At the worst, at least in Geoffrey's company she wouldn't feel completely alone at the soiree when she couldn't speak with her friends. At best, she would see Robert in the shadows and he would know that he had an ally in the room.

Lucinda and Geoffrey arrived just past fashionably late at the Hesterfield ball. Lord Geoffrey had actually driven up to Barrett House exactly on time; she was the one who had dawdled and fidgeted upstairs for nearly an hour before descending with Helena, who was serving as their chaperone. The delay had been completely intentional. If they were late, they wouldn't be announced, and she could slip in unnoticed and scout out the territory.

"We've missed the first two dances," Geoffrey said, standing at her side and taking in the guests, as well.

"My apologies," she said, flitting her fan in front of her face so she could search the crowd around its edges. "My maid couldn't find my green slippers."

He ignored the sound of Helena behind them clearing her throat, and instead swept his gaze down her figure and back again. "Don't apologize. It was well worth the wait. And your father and I had time for another nice chat."

"Did you?"

"Yes. He, ah, informed me that all of this gossip has upset you."

Lucinda hid a frown. Obviously her father wanted this match, but he had used to be much more cautious about passing along private confidences. She wished she could make him see that; if he would at least admit that the Chateau Pagnon rumors had come from someone he'd told, she would feel a little better about the whole disaster. A very little better, but she would take anything she could get.

"Did he inform you about anything else?" she asked.

"Only that he's requested you to stay away from the Carroway family."

Dash it all. "That was his request," she stated, "not mine. Please do not repeat it."

"I had been about to make the same suggestion to you, anyway, though with Robert's odd behavior over the years, the rest of his family would probably not be hurt overmuch by news of his activities. Still, it's better to be cautious."

"Nothing has been proven," she snapped. "May we please discuss something else?"

"Of course, Lucinda. As the daughter of a respected army officer, though, I'm certain you know it's better to face facts than to ignore them."

"I will be happy to face facts," she retorted, wishing he didn't sound so much like a parrot of her father. "I haven't see any yet."

"I admire your loyalty to your friends. But I would still urge you to stay away from them."

Her jaw clenched. "Listen, a cotillion," she said stiffly, practically towing him toward the dance floor. "Shall we?"

The floor was crowded, which was both a blessing and a curse. She could hide easily among the swirl of gowns, but neither could she see anyone else who might be there. Of course Georgiana wasn't doing much dancing these days, but there were three Carroway males who *could* be dancing at the soiree, and that wasn't counting Robert. But after yesterday, no one in London was likely to ever see him at a social gathering ever again.

"They probably won't be here at all," Geoffrey said after a minute of silence.

"They weren't at the fireworks last night."

"They weren't?"

"No. If St. Aubyn and his wife hadn't been in the box, I would have thought someone was playing a jest by inviting me."

Oh, dear. She'd forgotten about that again. "Something came up last evening." Several somethings, as she recalled, at least one of them supremely memorable.

"You don't need to explain, Lucinda."

She hadn't even thought to look for Evie and Saint, and as the dance came to a close she spotted them, seated against one wall and deep in conversation. Evelyn looked collected to anyone who didn't know her well, but Lucinda saw the tight clasp of her hands and her pale skin. As dear friends of the Carroways, tonight had to be miserable for them, as well. Taking a deep breath, she excused herself from Geoffrey.

"Lucinda," Evie exclaimed, rising to take her hands. "You've heard, haven't you?"

"Yes, I have." She sat on the far side of Evie, though her attention was on the tall marquis. Saint undoubtedly knew far more about what was going on than anyone else in the room, except, perhaps, for her; he always seemed to. "I'm sorry Papa and I abandoned you at Vauxhall last night; he wasn't feeling well."

"I imagine he's been having a busy few days," Saint drawled. "Do they have a suspect, yet?"

"She couldn't tell you that, Saint, even if she knew," Evie countered, still twisting her fingers. "Could you?"

"No, I couldn't. I do know he's doing everything possible to sort this out."

"When the rumors of the theft came out, Georgie might at least have warned us that Robert could be considered a suspect," Evie went on in a low voice. "I nearly had to punch Melissa Milton yesterday for even mentioning his name in connection with this. We might have been downplaying his imprisonment, if we'd known about it."

Lucinda tried to keep her breathing steady and wished she could just sink through the floor. "The Carroways may have been surprised, as well. He doesn't say much, after all."

"He told someone, obviously," Saint put in mildly, meeting Lucinda's surprised gaze. "And if it's true that he was held at Chateau Pagnon, I'm not sure I would blame him for this, even if he *did* do it."

"He didn't!" Lucinda said, more sharply than she meant to.

"And I'm sure they'll appreciate your support," he returned, nodding past her shoulder. "I was wondering if they'd make an appearance."

As hard as she tried, Lucinda couldn't help flinching as she turned her head. They'd all come: Tristan and Georgiana, hand in hand; Andrew and Bradshaw bringing up the rear; and in the middle, surprisingly, Robert himself.

None of them looked particularly happy, and concerned as she was over Georgie's health, she couldn't turn her eyes from Robert. The haunted look deep in his eyes made her heart physically hurt, and she hoped no one else knew him well enough to see it. Other than that, he looked as strong and stoic as he always did, aloof and completely unconcerned with the buzz of voices rising around him.

She wanted to run up to him and throw her arms around him and just hold onto him. She wanted to feel his mouth on hers, and his hands on her skin. Her face warmed, and she knew she was blushing. And she knew she couldn't stay away. Not from him, and not from her friends.

At that moment, he turned his head and looked at her, as if he'd known exactly where she was all along. His family would have asked him how the news of his imprisonment had reached the ears of Society, and she wondered whether he'd told them. He had the power to destroy — or at least to badly hurt — her friendship with Georgiana, and probably with Evie as well. He hadn't seemed angry when he'd left her bed last night, but if she couldn't forget that she'd betrayed his trust and told her father one of his deepest secrets, she didn't see how he could.

"Come on, we can't leave them standing there alone," Evie said, and she and Saint rose.

Lucinda followed suit, then stopped, surprised, when Saint stepped in front of her. "Perhaps you should stay here," he said, just loud enough for Evelyn to overhear. "Your father's directly involved in the investigation, and your being seen with Robert could compromise that."

"But —" Evie stopped. "You're right, Saint. Stay here, Luce. I'll explain it to Georgie."

"No," she returned, not certain whether to be grateful or not for another voice of reason — especially after she'd made up her mind to be foolish. "I'm not losing friends over a rumor." *Especially not one she'd caused.*

She started across the corner of the ballroom behind Lord and Lady St. Aubyn.

Before she'd gotten more than a few steps, a hand grabbed her elbow. "Don't do it," Geoffrey murmured, guiding her toward the refreshment table.

"Did my father tell you to supervise me?" she asked, pulling free as nonchalantly as she could.

"He asked me to keep an eye on you, yes," he returned. "But as I have an interest in you, and in your father's influence as well, I don't want either of you compromised."

At least he was honest. Lucinda sighed. "Everyone knows that we're friends. My staying away will only make things worse. My standing with them will hopefully help, if just a little."

"Until the cripple gets arrested, and the rumors start that you and your father were the reason he was able to get into the Horse Guards in the first place. There's more at stake here than your peace of mind, Lucinda."

"I realize that," she retorted, barely remembering to keep her voice lowered. "It's not only my peace of mind that concerns me, Geoffrey. It's about loyalty and friendship, as well."

He took her arm again. "I need you, Lucinda. Don't step into this mess."

"I'm already in it, I'm afr—"

"Miss Barrett," a low, soft voice came from beside her. "Have you already been claimed for this waltz?"

Robert stood two feet away, as if he'd simply materialized. His expression was cool and collected, but she knew that he was testing her, waiting to see whether she would cut him in public or not. "I —"

"Yes, she's spoken for, Carroway," Geoffrey interrupted. "Go home, and spare everyone the indignity of your presence."

Bottomless azure eyes met frustrated green ones. "I don't believe you own her yet, Newcombe," Robert said quietly. "She may accept or decline my invitation all on her own. I'm certain she's taken your reservations into account."

For someone who didn't do a great deal of talking, Robert certainly knew how to put a sentence together. Lucinda looked from one gentleman to the other: fair and beautiful opposing dark and soulful, the angel and the devil. "I will waltz with you, Robert," she said.

He held out his hand, and she took it. Not until then did she realize how quiet the ballroom had become, or that despite his quiet demeanor, his fingers weren't quite as steady as his voice. He'd been tortured, and now his own fellows were doing it to him again. Thank heavens she'd decided to help put things right; she wouldn't have been able to stand watching this from the safety of the shadows.

"I'm surprised you came here tonight," she said, as they slipped into the dance. Belatedly, other couples joined them on the floor, though Lucinda and Robert seemed to have an unusually wide space around them. Her father was going to be furious, but she would deal with that later. At the moment, all of her attention was on Robert.

"I wanted to dance with you," he murmured. "I didn't get a chance to, the last time."

His warm hand about her waist and his fingers clasping hers sent heat spearing down her spine. "Have you told . . . Did you . . ."

"Did I say anything to Georgiana about where the rumors began?" he finished for her, his gaze touching hers and then sliding away again.

"Did you?"

"No, I didn't. It wouldn't serve much of a purpose. And I wouldn't hurt you, Lucinda. Not as long as you keep your word not to hurt my family."

Relief made her feel weak kneed. "Thank you."

He inclined his head. "How is your amiable friend?"

"Stop that. We all have responsibilities and duties, and I really don't want to talk about it right now, anyway. I'm more worried about you."

"And I'm worried about you." A brief frown touched his face. "I've been thinking. I'm not going to ask you to betray your father's confidences. It . . . I can't do that."

Lucinda took a breath. He had given her an easy way out, but she'd learned enough about him last night to know why. "Robert, I'm not being tortured, and believe me, I have been considering the consequences. And despite your dislike of 'simple' things, that's what this is. I did something that hurt you, and I intend to put it right."

Robert studied her face for a moment as they danced. He waltzed well, she realized, easy and graceful and his limp barely noticeable. His knee would hurt tomorrow, probably, but she had to think that that was the least of his worries at the moment.

"I'm beginning to wish I was amiable," he murmured.

She swallowed, because she'd been thinking the same thing. Part of what attracted her to him, though, was the depth behind his eyes. Depth that she'd begun to

334

realize Geoffrey didn't have, and probably didn't even see. "My father's meeting was with the four other senior officers at the Horse Guards. You know who they are, yes?"

He nodded. "I know who they are."

"They're some of the most trusted members of the military."

"I know that, as well."

"For some reason they don't seem certain of everything that went missing, but they're putting together a list of Bonaparte supporters in London."

" 'Putting together' a list?" he repeated, something sparking in his eyes.

"Yes." She'd said something important. Hiding a scowl, she considered what she'd said and how he'd reacted to it, trying to become a participant instead of just a witness. "They should have had a list already."

Nodding, he favored her with his fleeting, breathtaking smile. "I'm certain they do."

"That was one of the items that went missing." She grimaced. "I probably shouldn't have told you that, then."

"Too late," he drawled. "Anything else?"

"Oh, so *now* you have a sense of humor."

"Sometimes. Did the general say anything else?"

"He warned me to stay away from you —

and from your family — until this is all settled."

The humor in his eyes faded. "He really *does* suspect me. And you're going to be in trouble. You should have told me before. I thought I was just lesson-helping."

"I'll only be in trouble if someone tells him we danced."

"Ah. And will your amiable friend keep his mouth shut, then?"

Lucinda glanced at Geoffrey, dancing now with Lady Desmond and still managing to glare at the two of them. "No. But there are plenty of other gossips here, anyway."

She hated this. All of her instincts told her that Robert was innocent, but so was her father. Neither of them had done anything wrong, and at least one of them was going to suffer, whatever her decision.

The waltz ended before she was ready, and Robert slid his hand from around her waist. "He'll want to know what we talked about," he said, glancing past her shoulder.

Lucinda sighed. "I know. I'll tell him you were anxious to discover whether my father had mentioned anything further about the thefts."

"Which would be the truth." He started to lift his hand toward her cheek, then abruptly lowered it again. "I won't ask you for anything else. Thank you, Lucinda."

He meant to exclude her from the rest of this mess — and from him. Her breath faltered, and she had to stop herself from grabbing his arm. "How shall we meet again?"

"I don't think we should."

"I do." In fact, she almost suggested that he climb back through her window. Given how drawn she felt to him and how precarious his position in Society remained, that, however, would be extremely unwise. "I'll go see Georgie tomorrow."

"Not if your father has asked you to stay away."

"But —"

"She'll understand, Lucinda. I'll make certain of it."

His simple reassurance convinced her more than the vehement protestations everyone else had been making all evening. "Then I'll be calling on Evelyn tomorrow, at noon. Perhaps you could visit Saint."

A slow smile curved his mouth. "Very well. I'll manage it. And so you know, Georgiana's refusing to leave London now. Tristan says he's angry, but I think he's actually relieved. Because of this damned mess, she's going to have the baby here."

"Don't blame yourself."

"I don't. I blame whoever stole those bloody papers."

She risked putting a hand on his arm. "We'll find him."

"We'd better."

Chapter 17

❧

**You have determined to live,
and I am satisfied.**

— The Monster, *Frankenstein*

"What the devil were you thinking," Tristan hissed at Robert as he returned to the Carroway group, "going out on the dance floor?"

"I was thinking I might dance," Robert answered.

"Bit, you could be placing Lucinda and her father in a difficult position," Georgiana said, laying a hand over his arm much as Lucinda had.

Robert looked from one to the other. "You're right about that. Lucinda wanted to stand here with us tonight, and to call on you tomorrow, Georgie, but I asked her not to." He hesitated, looking down at his sister-in-law. "The general suggested she stay away from us."

"Then she should stay away," the viscountess returned promptly. "Were you able to convince her?"

"I think so."

His brothers had ranged themselves in a loose circle around Georgie, looking aggressive and angry, and practically daring anyone to approach with less than polite things to say. Tristan in particular bore a sullen look as he eyed the crowd, Saint at his side. "You know," the viscount murmured, "this is beginning to make me rather annoyed."

"So much for a united front." Bradshaw signaled a footman for a tray of drinks. "How long do you think we'll last before Hesterfield asks us to leave?"

"I've never been booted out of a soiree before," Andrew put in. "I'm almost looking forward to it."

"Well, I have been," Saint said, "and interesting as it is, I don't think we'll be helping the situation by brawling."

Across the room, Geoffrey had claimed Lucinda again, and appeared to be plying her with chocolates in an attempt to distract her. Robert wished him success. As difficult as this was on his family, it had to be equally so for her. And as much as she valued trust and fair play, her involvement in this — and with him — must be excruciating. Yet when he'd given her the opportunity to be free of him, she'd declined. His heart jumped. She'd wanted to be around him. Tonight, though, was less than ideal for anything.

"Perhaps we should go," he suggested.

"What? And let the wags win?" Bradshaw folded his arms across his chest, looking even more belligerent. "I'm not leaving until I get to punch someone."

As grateful and surprised as Robert was by their show of support, his family members weren't helping anything, nor were they becoming any more popular with their fellows. This was *his* problem, and he'd done it to himself, in the long run — by his silence, mostly. He would take care of it without involving them any further. If he could, he would have done it without Lucinda, but as much as he needed her assistance, he wanted an excuse to be near her even more.

Angry as everyone was, they were still fighting only rumors. But knowing how important it would be to find someone to blame for this, to make the citizens of England feel safe again, he wasn't certain how much effort the Horse Guards would be making to discover the real culprit, when they had a ready-made scapegoat to hand.

The thought of ending up in jail, even by

mistake — even for a short time if by some miracle the true thief should come forward — sent Robert falling toward the black panic. He couldn't be locked behind bars again. Not even for a minute.

"Robert," Georgiana said quietly, "we won't let them blame you for this."

He forced a smile. "It's a little late for that, Georgie. But letting everyone see us standing here like a herd of angry rhinoceros isn't helping. I want to leave, but if you —"

"We'll go, then," Tristan interrupted. "Hesterfield looks as though he's about to have an apoplexy, anyway."

Good. Robert had already accomplished what he needed to. He'd seen Lucinda, and she'd told him who had heard the Pagnon story first, and a little of what had been taken. He needed, though, to know more. The only way to save himself would be to figure out who the real burglar might be, a difficult task under normal circumstances, but even worse now with himself as the main — the only — suspect, and with very little time before the rumors were enough to get him locked up.

Unable to resist a last look at Lucinda, he risked a glance as they waited by the coatroom for Georgiana and the aunties' wraps. He'd already memorized what she wore, the pale green of her silk gown, the sea-foam lace at her cuffs and along the low neckline, the ivory elbow-length gloves, and the emerald hairpin that perfectly matched her delicate dancing slippers.

Some men complained that she was too tall, too regal, but he knew the truth. She was smarter than most of them, more independent, more honest, and she frightened the hell out of them. She frightened him too, but for a very different reason: he couldn't imagine trying to return to life, to humanity, without her. He wasn't certain he would want to.

"Bit," Andrew muttered, nudging him, "we're leaving."

He shook himself. "Good. Let's go."

Lord and Lady St. Aubyn stayed behind, ostensibly to keep Lucinda and Lord Geoffrey company, but more likely because their presence would at least force the rumor-spreading to remain at a discreet noise level. The Carroways climbed back into their carriages and returned home, where Shaw and Andrew disappeared upstairs to play billiards. The rest of them headed for the drawing room, where after five minutes of silence, Georgiana suggested they play a game of whist.

That was the cue Robert had been waiting for. "Why don't you play?" he suggested.

"My knee's a bit tired, anyway. I thought I'd wrap it in a hot towel and go to bed, if that's all right with you."

Tristan nodded. "This idiocy won't last, Bit. You'll be fine."

"I know."

It would be even finer if he helped it along. Upstairs in his bedchamber he pulled off his fine evening clothes and exchanged them for his old, threadbare gardening ones. He didn't do much sleeping anyway, and tonight, with an actual plan forming in his mind, he'd never close his eyes.

He pushed his window open a little farther and leaned out. Over the past three years he'd managed to train the vine which crawled up the terrace beneath him so that it looked dense enough but left plenty of handholds. He swung one leg over the windowsill, then stopped.

Georgiana was eight months' pregnant, and the rest of his family practically became hysterical every time he was out of their sight. And Tristan had asked him not to vanish again without a word. Sighing, he slipped back inside and dug into his writing desk for a piece of paper.

A year or two ago it would never have occurred to him that his troubles affected his family, or his friends. He supposed he had

Lucinda to thank for the change. She *had* done something to make him human again. And because of that, he wouldn't — he couldn't — hurt them anymore. That seemed as important a vow as finding out who in England had turned traitor. It wasn't just about him, as everything had seemed to be since he returned. Not *his* pain, not *his* name, not *his* loneliness. Swiftly he scrawled out a note detailing his whereabouts and left it on his bed, just in case anyone came in to check on him.

He was halfway out the window again when someone rapped on his door and pushed it open. "Damn," he muttered. His room was dark; maybe no one would notice him if he didn't —

"What the devil are you doing?" Bradshaw hissed, striding into the room. "Is this supposed to help you look innocent? Damnation, Bit, I warned you — we all warned you — about running off ag—"

"I left a note," Robert interrupted, jabbing a finger at the bed. "Now keep your voice down, or you'll wake Edward."

Eyes narrowed, Bradshaw closed the door and stalked to the bed. He lifted the note, tilting it toward the window to read it in the dim moonlight, then with what might have been a snarl, tossed it down again. "You are not going to the Horse Guards, Bit. That's insane."

"I need to know who else they suspect of being a Bonaparte supporter — and how simple it would be to get inside."

"And you think you'll be able to tell that from sneaking around in the dark, in a place where they would like nothing better than to catch you with evidence in your hand?"

Robert scowled. "I can't do anything from here! Who do you think they're looking for, Shaw? No one. And do you know why? Because they're going to accuse me. So go back to bed. This is my problem, and I'll take care of it."

"This is *not* your problem. You said yourself, right now it's just rumors. Let the Army do its job, and stay out of trouble."

"I can't, Shaw."

"And why not, for God's sake?"

For a moment Robert sat in the window sill, gazing at his hands. How could he explain, when he didn't even understand it all himself? "If I'd . . . come back differently," he began slowly, trying to piece together what he wanted to say from the thousand scattered splinters of thought in his mind, "if I hadn't spent my time hiding, then all of this would have been in the open already."

Bradshaw sat on the edge of the bed.

"You barely spoke a word for over a year, Bit," he said quietly. "I remember. It didn't look like a choice, or something you were doing to torment the rest of us. It looked as though something unspeakable had happened to you, and that was your way of coping with it. We don't blame you for it."

He'd known he'd put his family through hell, but hearing Shaw say those things touched him in a way he couldn't even express. Robert swallowed. "Thank you."

"The point being, I'm not going to let you put yourself at further risk for something that's only connected to you by a damned rumor. If you go tonight, then the connection becomes real."

Bradshaw had a point — a very good one. Even so, the thought of doing nothing while someone else controlled his fate, unsettled him deep in his bones. He'd let that happen once before, and he would never do it again. Not now, when he'd begun to have hope again. "All I have left is my name, Shaw."

"You have your life."

Taking a breath, he leaned back against the casement. "I learned, at Chateau Pagnon, that there is a difference between being alive and living. And over the past few weeks, I realized that while I've been walking and breathing, I hadn't been living for a long time."

"What changed, then?"

"If you repeat a word of this, Shaw, I —"

"Oh, please. You never told Tris that I was the one who put glue on his saddle."

The recollection made Robert smile. "That's right; you owe me a secret."

"So why the change, Bit? We've all noticed it."

"Lucinda Barrett."

Bradshaw looked at him for a long moment. "She's got her cap set at Lord Geoffrey Newcombe."

"I know."

"You're . . . not in love with her, are you?"

This had obviously been a mistake. "It's not that," he countered, though he wasn't quite certain whether it was true or not. He certainly had become obsessed with her, and taking her to bed hadn't lessened that feeling one whit. Just the opposite. "It's more of an . . . appreciation. A hope. I can't explain it."

"All right, but what does that have to do with you risking your life by breaking into the Horse Guards?"

"I want her to know the truth. And I want her . . . I want General Barrett to know the truth. If I don't supply it, there'll always be that suspicion, those glances while everyone whispers that if it wasn't the Horse Guards, he must have done something else, because, well, look at him. Look what happened to him."

"Bit —"

"No, Shaw. Don't you understand? I'm an object of pity, of disgust. I'm half a man." He took a deep breath. They were wasting time, and he needed to get going. "I want to be whole again."

"And you think this will do that."

"I think it might help."

Slowly Bradshaw stood again. He uttered a curse, then walked to the window. "Let's go, then. I don't have all night."

Robert blinked. "You're not going with me. I told you, this is my problem. I'll take care of it. Alone."

"I'm not staying here to face Dare's wrath when he figures out where you've gone. Get moving."

Whatever Bradshaw's excuse, Robert had to admit that he could use the assistance. And the support. Nodding, he slipped out of the window and climbed down the trellis.

Bradshaw reached the ground a moment after he did. "That's handy," he said, looking back up at the window. "But why do I have the feeling that you've left the house that way before?"

"Because I have. And shut up. Dare's still in the drawing room."

"Right. Not much stealth required in the Navy, you know. Just a strong stomach."

Hiding his grin in the darkness, Robert made his way through the shadows and around the back of the house toward the stables. With Shaw present, at least he had a distraction from his own black thoughts. That, however, was more than likely Bradshaw's intention.

"What about the grooms?" Shaw breathed as they stopped in the dark gloom of the stable's shadow.

"They'll all be to bed by now, except for Wiest, and he's three-quarters deaf. We'll saddle the horses in the yard."

"And how do you know all this? Wait, don't tell me. I don't want to know."

Moving quickly, they led out Tolley and Shaw's mount, Zeus. Tolley was used to midnight rides and barely batted an ear when Robert saddled him, but the big black Arabian snorted and refused to take the bit when Shaw shoved it at him.

"Damn it, Zeus, hold still," Shaw growled.

"Here." Robert pulled a lump of sugar from his pocket and handed it over. "Try bribery."

It worked. "Hm," Bradshaw muttered as he fastened the bridle over the black's head, "the next time I have a midnight rendezvous with Lady Daltrey, I'm taking you along."

"Her husband knows about you, anyway. He doesn't mind, because then she doesn't complain about his affair with Lady Walton."

Shaw lifted an eyebrow. "Beg pardon?"

"I go out at night a lot," Robert said, swinging up into the saddle.

They went down the drive at a walk, only moving into a canter when they were well away from the house. The Hesterfield soiree and any number of other parties would still be going strong, but most of the vendors and cart drivers had abandoned the streets in preparation for tomorrow morning. With several miles to go, they settled into a trot heading south and east along Grosvenor Place and then past St. James's Park and north along Whitehall. Outside the Treasury Building, they stopped.

"So do we ride straight through the parade grounds?" Bradshaw asked, his gaze on the street.

"There'll be sentries posted at either end of the building," Robert said, wishing he'd spent more time at the headquarters. "And

351

the offices are on the second and third floors."

"How many offices?"

Robert shrugged. "I don't know. Thirty? Forty?"

"That'll take all night."

Slowly Robert dismounted, walking Tolley toward the massive white building. It was surrounded by open space to accommodate the parade and old jousting grounds, and even at night anyone trying to approach would be easy to spot. Four sentries stood in clear view at the gate and along the parapets, and he would wager that at least that many more waited in less visible areas.

"I didn't bring a rope," Shaw murmured, walking beside him. "Any ideas?"

"I want to circle the building. It's been a while since I've seen it up close."

They walked for a few minutes in silence. Robert knew they'd been seen, but hopefully, in the dark they — he — hadn't been recognized. With stables on the bottom floor and a literal maze of offices above, navigating wouldn't be easy under the most ideal circumstances. Sneaking about in the dark would make finding anything significant almost impossible.

"Do you remember, Bit, when we used to

play chess, and you'd sit down and after four moves you would announce that I'd lost and then proceed to annihilate me?"

"Mm-hm."

"You have that look on your face again. What are you thinking?"

"I'm thinking that breaking into the Horse Guards would be a waste of time, and would probably get both of us arrested." Trying not to envision that scenario, he finished the circle and stopped at the corner where they'd begun.

"And?"

"And so whoever took those papers has spent time inside that building, Shaw. I mean, even if I knew what I was looking for, it would have taken me hours to locate the file room and then the correct maps and papers."

His brother nodded. "That makes sense. May we go, then? I'm beginning to feel a little conspicuous."

"Yes. We can't do anything else here."

Luckily no one else had gone into his bedchamber while he and Bradshaw were absent, and after Shaw left, Robert sank into his reading chair beneath the window. Since the imprisonment of Bonaparte the need for recruiting and promoting had lessened considerably, and the staff at the Horse Guards had been substantially reduced or reassigned to the larger War Office. Consequently, a large portion of the offices were now used for storage or simply stood empty.

All he needed to do was discover who had had access to the Horse Guards last week, and who knew the building well enough to find what they wanted and get out without being stopped. Simple. Or it would have been, if *he* had any access to personnel information or even anyone at all who worked at the Horse Guards.

Well, in a sense he did have that access — through Lucinda. He would have to explain it to her, though. For some reason she wanted to see him again, and she seemed to want to help. Whatever the grounds for her generosity, he wasn't going to ask her to do anything she felt uncomfortable with.

As he turned up the lamplight and opened the book he'd left waiting, he wondered whether she was still at the ball with Lord Geoffrey, and whether she was enjoying herself. By his best guess she still had two lessons she hadn't gone through, but as she'd said, that probably didn't matter any longer. She and Geoffrey had their amiable understanding, and when the *ton* had seen them together enough and had tacitly approved the match, he would ask for her hand, and they would have their amiable marriage. Robert stared at the open page, not seeing the words. Would things have happened differently if she'd chosen *him* for her lessons?

He'd beaten Geoffrey to her bed, but given who he was and who her father was, anything more was highly unlikely. If he'd returned from the war cocky and carefree and full of heroic tales, perhaps General Barrett would have thought better of him, though as it was, *he* didn't think much of Augustus Barrett.

Lucinda made him feel . . . hopeful, and after four years of pain, hope was as hard to ignore as sunshine. And he wondered what he would have been doing right now in the face of all the rumors if she hadn't pulled him a little out of the shadows. Robert sighed. He would probably be in Scotland, barring the manor doors and waiting for the British army to come after him.

The idea of being killed wouldn't have bothered him much, except that he'd found a reason to live. What he would do when his reason married someone else, he had no idea.

Chapter 18

I hope to see peace in your
countenance and to find that your
heart is not totally void of
comfort and tranquility.

— Elizabeth Lavenza, *Frankenstein*

". . . Luckily, they left before anyone was
forced to throw them out."

Lucinda stopped just outside the doorway
of her father's office. Geoffrey must have arrived before breakfast to tell her father the
news about the Carroways. She leaned
against the wall, waiting to see what he had
to say about her.

"It has to be an uncomfortable position
for them. After all, no one's been accused of
anything yet," her father was saying.

"*Yet,*" Geoffrey repeated. "And I don't
want to carry tales, but I think perhaps a

sterner talk with Lucinda might be in order. She insisted on greeting them, and even danced with Robert. I understand her sentiments, but she's not helping anyone. I tried to warn her, but I got the distinct impression that she was displeased with me."

From the other side of the door Lucinda could almost see her father's frown, hear him tapping his fingers on the stack of his latest chapter. "She's as stubborn as her mother. But she's very logical. I'm sure she understands your concerns. I've found that apologizing usually works."

Humph. What worked was the liberal use of common sense.

"So perhaps you should tell me a little about your own sentiments, my boy," the general continued.

Geoffrey chuckled. "I think you know what they are. Lucinda's wonderful, and I would like to think that she's becoming fond of me."

"I think we can safely assume that your suit is being well received."

"Then I would like your permission to ask for her hand in marriage."

Lucinda's stomach lurched. He made it sound so matter-of-fact. That's what it was, of course, practically a business arrangement, but to hear it like that was so . . . cold.

So simple and amiable.

"Under the circumstances, I think making an announcement now would be in poor taste. She can't be allowed to stand by the Carroways, but she is their friend."

"Of course. Once this little mess is concluded, though, may I assume that I have your permission?"

"You may."

"And the position in India?"

"Don't worry, lad. I have enough influence to see you with a command in Delhi. So long as you comply with Lucinda's wishes regarding whether she stays here or goes with you."

"Of course," Geoffrey repeated.

Signed, sealed, and delivered. It was just too bad that the "mess" they were discussing was the possible imprisonment of Robert Carroway. True, Geoffrey didn't seem to have much love for Robert, but referring to this catastrophe as a "little mess" was a bit callous.

"Very good, then, sir. Do you think she'll be down soon?"

"Any minute now, I would think. Have you had an opportunity to read chapter two?"

"I'm nearly finished with it. It's quite good. You capture the excitement and chaos of the march to Ciudad Rodrigo with amazing clarity."

The general snorted. "I already agreed to give you my daughter. No need for flattery."

"I'm completely serious. In fact, might I drop off the chapter to you this afternoon and see the next one?"

"You'll have to bring it by the Horse Guards. Chapter three is there with General Bronlin, but he should be finished with it today — unless something new has happened with the investigation."

"Have you heard anything?"

"Nothing." He sighed. "In addition to the searches of all ships leaving for the Continent, we have a detail beginning a watch on Robert Carroway this morning in case he tries to hand off the papers or leave the country himself."

Lucinda blanched. She hadn't even considered that someone might be watching Robert. Heavens, what if they'd been following him two nights ago? She needed to let him know, but that had just become trickier.

However straightforward she preferred things, though, she'd certainly learned the art of subterfuge — and under the circumstances, she was perfectly willing to use it. She didn't abandon her friends, and neither

— she was beginning to discover — did she care to be managed. Squaring her shoulders, she backed up and then strolled into the office.

"Good morning, Pa— Lord Geoffrey. I didn't expect to see you this morning."

Geoffrey rose, a bouquet of daisies in his hand. "These are for you, my dear. I thought you had enough roses."

She accepted them with a small curtsy. "Thank you."

"I also wondered if you'd care to go riding."

"I hope you understand, Geoffrey, but I'm a bit distracted this morning. If I'm permitted, I would like to write a letter to Georgiana."

"Lucinda." Her father stood. "There's no need to be rude."

"Am I being rude? Heavens, forgive me. I only meant to say that I miss seeing my friends, and I wish to let them know they have my support."

"How could you miss them," her father countered, "when you spoke with them just last night?"

And the men stepped right into her trap. She looked at Geoffrey. "My goodness, do you carry everyone's tales, or just mine?"

"Lucinda!"

Geoffrey, though, looked contrite. "I have your best interests in mind, Lucinda. I hope you understand that."

"I think it's *your* best interests you have in mind." She drew a breath, trying to remember that this was the man she'd decided to marry. If not for the theft, or for Robert, Geoffrey might already have asked for her hand. "If you'll excuse me, I feel very out of sorts this morning."

"No, it's I who should go. I only wanted to apologize. Obviously I have poor timing." He reached out and took her hand. "Please tell me that we're still friends."

All the men wanted to be friends with her, apparently. Lucinda shook herself. *What was wrong with her?* "Of course we are. I just . . . I need a morning to myself."

The general stood to walk Geoffrey out, but reading the look on his face, Lucinda stayed where she was. Yes, she'd behaved abominably, when all Geoffrey had done was echo the sentiments of half of London Society. He might have considered her feelings, though, rather than how he might look to his fellows.

"You danced with Robert last night," her father said, resuming his seat at the office desk.

"He asked me to."

"And I asked you not to."

"Papa, I'm sorry, but I do not choose my friends lightly, and I will not abandon them because of a rumor."

He glared at her, but she met his gaze and refused to look away. How long they might have sat staring at each other she didn't know, because Ballow scratched at the half-open door. "You have received a note, sir," he said.

"Let's see it."

The butler handed it over and vanished again. Lucinda watched her father's face as he opened and read the short missive, and something in his expression froze her heart. "What's happened?" she asked.

The general slammed the note onto his desk with such force it made her jump. "Your 'friend' was seen last night, outside the Horse Guards."

She blanched. "No! It's a mistake."

"The sentries were given his description and told to keep watch for him. He and another man rode up at half past eleven, walked their horses around the perimeter of the grounds, and then rode off again."

Her mind flying madly, Lucinda searched for an excuse that wouldn't sound completely ridiculous. "He's been accused of breaking in," she managed. "Perhaps he wanted to see the building firsthand."

"And perhaps he wanted to see whether our security remains as lax as it was last week. It isn't, I assure you." He stood, leaning over the desk. "I don't want to have to tell you again, Lucinda. Stay away from him."

Tempted for a bare moment to announce that Robert had already spent a night in her bed, Lucinda gave a stiff nod and pushed to her feet. "As you wish, Papa."

"Where are you going?"

"I'm going upstairs to read, and then I'll be going out to Lady St. Aubyn's for luncheon." She caught his frown as she turned away. "Don't worry. Georgiana won't be there."

"When this is finished, you'll see that it's all been for the best, daughter. All ships leaving Dover or Brighton for the Continent are being searched. If those papers are on their way to France, we'll find them."

"I'm sure you will."

"And you owe Lord Geoffrey an apology. He's done everything he can to please you. You have no reason to snap at him."

"Yes, Papa." She pulled open the office door the rest of the way.

"Lucinda?"

With a tight breath she stopped, her fingers clenched around the door handle. "Yes?"

"In all fairness, Geoffrey Newcombe is a better man than Robert Carroway, even without this disaster. Geoffrey is kind, handsome, popular, and has a brilliant career ahead of him. Robert . . . can barely put two words together and has no future that I can see."

Abruptly she wanted to cry. "Thank you for your opinion, Papa," she muttered. "I'm the one who suggested you bring in Lord Geoffrey in the first place, if you'll recall."

"So you were."

Lucinda hurried upstairs and closed herself in her bedchamber. She hated the tension between her and her father, when until now they'd always dealt so well together. And she hated that she couldn't stop thinking about Robert, when everything told her that Geoffrey was the better choice for a husband. And she hated that no one knew what Robert really was like — not even Robert, himself.

For the next hour she did more pacing than reading, finally summoning Helena to help her dress for luncheon when she could excuse the time as being only marginally early. Evie wouldn't mind, and there were things that Robert badly needed to know.

The Horse Guards probably had men watching him already.

She scowled. That would be a problem, if they reported that the two of them were at Halboro House at the same time. Well, if that happened she would deal with it. Someone owed them a little luck, and today would be the day to pay up.

When she arrived at Halboro House, Evie was just coming down the stairs. "Luce! Lucky you caught me. I was just about to go down to Bond Street for a new hat. Care to join me?"

In retrospect, Lucinda decided it might have been a good idea to inform Lord and Lady St. Aubyn that she and Robert were going to call on them today. "Actually, I think we should stay in for luncheon," she suggested with a sheepish grin.

Evie stopped tying on her bonnet. "You do?"

"Yes. Definitely."

"Any particular reason?"

Lucinda glanced at Jansen, the Halboro butler, standing unobtrusively beside the coat rack. "The weather is frightful outside."

Evie looked out the front windows on either side of the door, squinting a little against the bright, reflected sunlight. "So it is," she agreed, pulling off her bonnet again. "Jansen, please have Mrs. Dooley prepare some cucumber sandwiches and lemonade."

"Yes, my lady," he said, and vanished into the bowels of the house.

Evie took Lucinda's arm and pulled her into the morning room. "All right, what's going on, Miss Barrett? You seemed terribly distracted at the ball last night, and now this?"

"Is Saint here?" Lucinda asked, wishing she could stop fidgeting. She'd make a terrible spy, she decided.

"He's in the stable, looking at a hunter he purchased from Lord Mayhew. Why?"

"I, um, he may have a caller, as well."

"Oh, he may." Evie sat on the couch, making a show of smoothing the skirt of her pink and yellow muslin while a footman brought in a pot of tea and vanished again. "Lucinda, it may surprise you to know that I can keep a secret better than just about anyone you — or I — know."

"Yes? What does that have to do with —"

"For instance," she continued, pouring tea and handing Lucinda a cup, "earlier this year, when I had just begun delivering my lessons to Saint, and he vanished for a week. Do you remember that?"

Slowly Lucinda sat opposite her friend, taking a long swallow of tea and wishing it were brandy or whiskey or something. "I remember."

"Yes, well, the reason he vanished was because I kidnaped him."

Lucinda choked, spitting tea across Evie's fine Persian carpet. "You *what?*"

Evelyn nodded matter-of-factly, sipping her own tea. "Yes. He and I had an argument, and he announced that he was going to tear down the orphanage I'd been working to save, and so I locked him in its cellar for a week to convince him to change his mind."

For a long moment all Lucinda could do was stare at her friend. And to think, she and Georgie had considered Evie the most timid of the three of them. "It . . . worked."

Evie smiled, completely composed but for the twinkle in her gray eyes. "Yes, it did. Anyway, the reason I'm telling you now is because I want to assure you that whatever it is you're up to, you can trust me."

"I —"

The morning-room door opened. Saint strolled in, Robert on his heels. "Good afternoon, Lucinda," the marquis said.

Lucinda shot to her feet, missing the rest of the marquis's greeting as she looked at

Robert. Last night in the ballroom had been bad enough. But today, it took all of her self-control not to run across the room, throw her arms around him, and kiss him until the pain left his eyes, and until the heated yearning in her was satisfied.

Saint leaned back against the doorjamb. "Is someone making sandwiches or something, Evelyn?"

"Yes."

"Good. I wish you'd tell me when we're having friends over for luncheon."

"I would, if they would tell *me*."

"Hello," Robert said, ignoring the byplay around him and taking Lucinda in from head to toe.

Warmth crept up her cheeks at his scrutiny, and lust tugged at her again like a warm breeze. It would be nice if Geoffrey made her feel that way, she reflected, but no, it had to be the one man her father truly seemed to dislike. "We forgot to tell Evie and Saint that we were calling on them today," she offered.

"Yes, well, you're here," Saint interrupted, "so have a seat. Unless you'd like Evie and me to leave."

"We are *not* leaving," Evelyn stated. "I insist on some propriety in this house."

Robert blinked, as though he'd forgotten

anyone else was in the room. "It might be better if you *did* go," he said, facing Saint again. "I'm something of a pariah at the moment."

"You've already come through my front door. Obviously you needed a safe place to meet," Saint countered. "And this is it. Have a seat." He walked to the table set beneath the window. "Brandy?"

Shaking his head, Robert sat in the chair beside Lucinda. He didn't look as if he'd done much sleeping over the past few days; neither, though, had she. Something other than weariness lurked in his blue eyes, however; worry, unless she was greatly mistaken. And she was only going to make it worse.

"Did anyone follow you here?" she asked, lowering her voice.

"They tried," he returned. "Two men. Soldiers, I presume?"

She blanched. "Yes. They can't know I'm here talking with you, Robert. My fath—"

He took her hand, and despite the reassuring touch and the blaze of heat that ran through her at the contact, she could feel the tension along his fingers. "They think I'm in Piccadilly, Lucinda. It's all right. I've been expecting it."

"Because of last night?"

Robert frowned. " 'Last night?' " he repeated, surprise touching his eyes for the first time.

"Someone from the Horse Guards sent my father a note saying that you were seen there last night. You and another man."

"Bradshaw," he supplied, scowling. "I wanted to take a look at the building, to see how easy it would be for someone to get inside."

"You shouldn't have gone yourself," Saint put in, sinking onto the couch beside Evie.

"I couldn't very well ask anyone else to take the risk," Robert returned stiffly. She could read his reluctance at letting anyone else into this, but at the same time she was relieved that he'd done so. "I wouldn't have taken Bradshaw," he continued, "but he caught me escaping out the window."

"The window?" she murmured, and caught the brief amusement touching his gaze. At least there were some secrets they wouldn't have to share.

"Being that you're here," Saint said, "and being that that could potentially harm my standing in Society if I gave a damn about it, I do have a few questions, Robert."

"Too many people know more than they should, as it is," Robert retorted.

"You can't expect —"

"That's my fault, Robert," Lucinda said stiffly, standing again. "Not Saint's. If I hadn't relayed to my father what you told me in confidence, no one would suspect you any more than they would suspect . . . Wellington."

Robert looked as though he wanted to speak, but instead he stood to look out the front window. "This was a bad idea."

Lucinda looked at Evie, and jerked her head in the direction of the door. They couldn't force Robert to trust them; under the same circumstances, with the same past he'd faced, she wasn't certain she'd be keen to trust anyone, either. The fact that he trusted *her*, even after what she'd done, both astounded her and left her feeling un-worthy.

Evie cleared her throat. "I need to go check on luncheon," she said, rising. "Michael, please fetch me a shawl."

Saint crossed his legs at the ankle. "I'm staying."

"No, you're not."

"I thought we were being chaperones."

Lucinda looked from Saint to Robert, standing unmoving by the window. "Five minutes. Please."

She wasn't certain he would change his

mind, but after a moment Saint blew out his breath and stood. "Five minutes."

When they were gone and the door closed behind them, Lucinda forced a chuckle. "I definitely see drawbacks to including Saint in any of this."

Robert turned around. Stalking up to her, he took her face in his hands and kissed her with a desperate ferocity that stole her breath. Heat speared from her toes through the top of her scalp. With a moan she sank into him, slipping her hands beneath his jacket and twining them into the back of his shirt.

Whatever this was, it intoxicated her. *He* intoxicated her — and she knew that wasn't supposed to happen. His mouth molded to hers, pressing her against the back of the couch as he deepened their embrace.

Finally he lifted his head. "It's not your fault," he breathed. "The way I am . . . Something was bound to happen sooner or later."

"No, Robert. There is nothing wrong with the way you are. You lived through what would kill most men."

"It did kill me, Lucinda."

She shook her head. "It hasn't killed you yet. And I don't think it will."

A soft smile touched the corners of his

mouth. "I'm beginning to see more mornings where I agree with you." Slowly the somber look came into his eyes again. "I thought I might have been seen last night, but I needed to know something."

"I hope it was important." Finding that she wanted to run her fingers through his dark, lanky hair, she backed away and sat again. They had five minutes, and they had best use them.

"It was. I'm fairly proficient at getting in and out of places, and —"

"So I've noticed."

Appreciation flickered in his eyes. "The Horse Guards is a rabbit warren. Did your father say whether anything other than the sympathizers list and the maps were taken?"

"No."

"Then someone had to know where they were in advance, and had to have fairly easy access to the building." He grimaced, pacing to the window and back again. "I think that whoever did this —"

"Works at the Horse Guards?" she finished. She pondered that for a moment. "I'm not so certain, Robert. I've been there a great many times myself. Men, soldiers, come and go all the time. Wellington and his entourage, old friends of my father and the other senior officers, anyone Papa's

talking to about his book, messengers to
and from Parliament and the War Office,
the —"

He muttered a curse. "Do visitors or
workers have to report to anyone? Is there
any record of who goes in and when?"

"Visitors only. There's a book everyone's
supposed to sign by the front entry." For a
moment hope flared, until she remembered
how quickly they'd spotted him last night.
"Inside the front entry and under guard,"
she amended.

"It's a start," he said, shrugging.

"Oh, it's useless." Blowing out her
breath, she went to the liquor table and deliberately poured herself a whiskey. "I've
tried and tried to tell my father that you had
nothing to do with this, and all he cares
about is that I not offend Lord Geoffrey,
and that I keep my nose out of trouble."

"You offended Lord Geoffrey?"

"I disagreed with his suggestion that I stay
away from my friends in order to preserve
his chances at promotion."

"And what did he do?"

"He brought me flowers this morning —
though I think he spends more time
courting my father than me."

"What kind of flowers?"

She looked over at him. "All of this, and

you want to know what kind of flowers I received?"

He stood there watching her pace, eyeing the drink in her hand, an absorbed expression on his face. "I would guess daisies," he said.

"How in the world could you know that?"

"You grow roses, so he would conclude that you have enough of those. Daisies are in abundance this year."

"You mean they're less expensive."

"I mean they're simple," he corrected. "Easy to find, easy to please."

"I see. And what kind of flower would you have brought me then, pray tell?"

"Lavender roses," he answered promptly.

Lucinda's heart flip-flopped. "Why?"

"Because lavender is your favorite color, and roses are your favorite flower." He approached her again, slowly running the back of his finger along her cheek.

She couldn't breathe, didn't want to move. Abruptly she wished they could stand like that forever, just looking at one another, just barely touching. "How did you know that? I mean about lavender being my favorite color."

"I pay attention," he said quietly, leaning down to kiss her again.

This time he was slow, gentle, and

feather-light, like a breath of warm air across her lips. Lucinda closed her eyes, leaning up toward the embrace of his mouth.

"Lucinda?"

She opened her eyes again, looking up into bottomless blue. "Yes?"

"Has Geoffrey kissed you?"

Whiskey. Lifting the glass, she tilted it down her throat. It scalded, making her cough and hack, and her eyes tear up. "Good . . . good heavens!"

The morning-room door opened again. "Five min—" Saint strode forward, taking Lucinda's shoulder and rapping her on the back. "Are you all right?"

"F . . . fine." She coughed again.

"She drank whiskey," Robert supplied.

"Well, I wish I'd seen that. Come along. Luncheon is served."

The marquis led the way down the hall to the dining room, but seeing Robert hanging back a little, Lucinda slowed as well. "Why did you have to ask me that?" she whispered.

"Because if you're going to marry him, you should at least try kissing him," Robert murmured back.

"And then I suppose we should stop kissing?"

He flashed his breathtaking grin, then sobered again. "I don't think I can do that."

That was the problem. Neither could she.

Chapter 19

⁘

My future hopes and prospects are
entirely bound up in the expectation
of our union.

— Victor Frankenstein, *Frankenstein*

Robert leaned against a stall door, watching
one of the grooms brush and put away
Tolley. The two of them had certainly gotten
their exercise over the past few days. Riding
three miles out of his way before luncheon
hadn't been part of his plan, but evidently he
now needed to factor in time to lose anyone
who might be following him. The subterfuge
had been worth it, to see, to touch Lucinda
again.

She had given him a better clue than she
realized. A guest book. Being that he didn't
visit the Horse Guards, the fact that people
who didn't work there might do so hadn't

even occurred to him. Neither had the idea that they might visit on a regular-enough basis to be familiar with the place.

Of course it could be one of the staff — that was far too likely a possibility for him to dismiss. But a guest, in his mind anyway, made more sense. The officers and staff and guards at the Horse Guards tended to be lifetime military. They didn't need a war to secure their incomes or their futures.

Money didn't have to be the motive either, he supposed. Some Englishman or other could be a rabid supporter of Bonaparte. The war, however, had ended three years ago. Wouldn't anyone that fond of Napoleon have been discussed by the wags, or arrested by the Crown, before now? Unless it was a spy of some sort. That could —

"What're you doing?" Edward asked, strolling into the stable with Tristan on his heels.

"Making my head hurt," he answered. "What're you doing?"

"Tristan's taking me fishing. I was supposed to go riding with William Grayson and his uncle, but they sent over a note that William is sick."

Tristan met his gaze over the Runt's head. That answered that. William's family had been sick at the notion of their youngster being seen with a Carroway. "I'm certain he'll feel better soon," he offered, trying not to choke on his own words.

"I hope so, because Shaw promised to take us to Portsmouth next week to see his ship."

"Runt, why don't you go help John saddle Storm Cloud?" Tristan suggested, nudging his youngest brother in the back.

Edward dug his heels in. Facing his brothers, he folded his arms across his chest. "I'm not stupid, you know. If you want to talk about something and you don't want me to hear, just say, 'Runt, go away for a minute so I can talk to Bit.' "

Tristan gave a lazy grin. "Runt, go away for a minute so I can talk to Bit."

"Fine. Eventually, though, you're going to have to tell me what's going on."

"Out, Edward." They both watched him exit the stable, and then Tristan faced him again. "How was your luncheon with Saint? That's where you went, isn't it?"

"I notified you, as ordered. He and Evie say hello, and want to know if there's anything they can do to be of help." Robert shredded a piece of hay in his fingers.

"They're good friends."

Robert nodded. "Yes. Have fun fishing."

"Robert, wait." Scowling, Tristan edged closer. "I know you blame yourself for this. And —"

"How do you know that?"

"Because I know you. And I have eyes. But don't. Blame yourself, I mean. The good thing about having a family is that you don't have to stand alone."

"Tristan," he began, then had to stop and take a breath. They needed to know. They needed to know why he had to do this alone. "Tristan, I do blame myself, because I tried to do something three years ago that would have taken care of all this, and I failed."

The viscount's pale blue gaze studied him for a long moment. "What did you try to do?"

"Kill myself. Or make the French kill me, which is the same thing."

Tristan went white. "Robert," he whispered.

"I couldn't see any other way out of Chateau Pagnon, and I couldn't stand to be there any longer. I couldn't stand it, so I . . . convinced them to shoot me to death. Except that the Spanish resistance found me before I could crawl off to die."

"You wouldn't . . ."

"Try it again? No. Not voluntarily. But that's why I can't explain to anyone else

381

about Pagnon, and that's why I have to take care of this, because it *is* my fault, and because if any of you get caught doing something to help me, I . . . couldn't stand it. For God's sake, Tris, you're going to be a father in a month."

Tristan grabbed his arm. "I know that," he hissed. "And I want my child to have an uncle."

"He'll have at least three uncles." Robert tried to wrench free, but Tristan wouldn't let him go.

"Yes, but I want him to have one who has some common sense and intelligence. And that's you." With a growl, the viscount let him go. "All I'm trying to say is, don't exclude me — or any of us — because you think it's for our own good. Let us decide that."

"I'll consider it." He closed his eyes for a minute, because he knew he could never include them. It wasn't that he thought it was for their own good; he *knew* it. "Just so you know, Dare, the Horse Guards are having me followed."

"What? How —"

"I lost them in Piccadilly. They'll be back here any time now."

"Sweet Lucifer," Tristan swore. "Is there anything else you'd like to tell me today?

Because I'd really like to have a drink first, if there's more."

"That's all I can think of at the moment." Except for Lucinda, of course, but Robert didn't think he could put that into words any more than he thought Tristan would be able to understand his obsession.

After the horses were saddled, he boosted Edward up onto his mount and watched them trot down the drive. A groom followed behind, his horse laden with fishing poles.

"Anything else, sir?" Gimble asked as he led Tolley into his stall.

Robert patted the gelding's neck, receiving a nuzzle on the shoulder in return. "No, we're fine."

"Very good, sir."

He needed to think, but he knew he made the grooms nervous when he hung about the stable, so he wandered out to his rose garden. The plants amazed him; two weeks ago they'd been sticks with a few leaves and thorns, dead-looking but for the faint green in the leaves. This afternoon new shoots and leaves sprouted everywhere, and on one of the larger plants he swore he could detect the beginnings of a bud.

A few more weeds had managed to spring practically full grown out of the soil as well, and he squatted down to yank them out of the ground. It would have been nice if villains were as easy to find among his fellows as were weeds among roses, but since he'd spent three years looking and feeling rather like a weed himself, he supposed — and hoped — that the analogy wouldn't work.

And of course there was the extended metaphor of the impossibility of a tranquil existence for him, once again as the scrawny, half-dead weed, and Lucinda as the blooming, blushing rose — but that didn't help much, either. Not that it mattered; he'd held her in his arms, told her his deepest secret, and she still planned to marry Geoffrey Newcombe.

Geoffrey Newcombe. Robert had never thought much of him, and since Lucinda had named him as her matrimonial mate of preference, the indifference had become dislike. Now with this disaster before him and Geoffrey looking like the portrait of a young patriot while Robert's own appearance seemed to become more foul each day, it wasn't even dislike any longer. No, Robert realized, as he dug out the last of the weeds with his fingers, it wasn't dislike. It was hatred. He hated Lord Geoffrey Newcombe with a passion that surprised him.

Robert slammed his fist into the earth.

And what was he supposed to do? Sit there in the dirt and let Lucinda settle for someone else simply because the other fellow was amiable? Who, though, if not Geoffrey? Himself? He snorted. Him, marrying. And not just anyone — Lucinda Guinevere Barrett. As if he could, even if he wanted to, with a hangman's noose practically around his neck for treason. If nothing else, he needed — wanted — to prove everyone wrong about that.

"Bit, are you punching earthworms?" Georgiana's soft voice came from behind him.

He jumped. "No. Just thinking." Unclenching his fist, he dusted the dirt off his knuckles.

"About what?"

"About how I might obtain a piece of paper I'm not supposed to have access to from a place I'm not permitted to go. While I'm being watched by men I'm not supposed to know are lurking out there in the shrubbery."

"Oh. Have someone else get it for you, then."

He swung around to look at her. "That would mean involving someone else in this mess."

She pursed her lips. "Well, I could state

the obvious, that other people already are involved. Or I could say, why don't you ask and see whether any of your family or friends might be willing to help?"

"And how could I possibly ask —"

"Why, yes, I'd love to help. Which piece of paper did you say you needed?" she interrupted.

"Georgiana, you can't —"

"Too late. I've already volunteered." She smiled, humor and a surprising determination in her eyes. "I dislike seeing people I love accused of things they didn't do. It irritates me. Which piece of paper?"

Robert stood. All of the Carroways' lives had changed when Georgiana had moved into the house, his perhaps more than anyone's but Tristan. If nothing else, her coming had brought Lucinda into his small, dark world, and blasted it into the sunlight. "It's a page from the sign-in book for visitors at the Horse Guards. I need to know who was there last week."

"And where is this book located?"

"Just inside the front entry. It's manned by a sentry."

"Do you think it'll still be there? With an investigation going on?"

He nodded. "From everything I've heard, they suspect a robbery by a stranger, not by

386

someone who was an accepted, regular visitor."

"Good." She glanced down the front drive. "Are men actually lurking in the shrubbery?"

"They came back about five minutes ago. I . . . have it on good authority that they're here to watch me."

"When this is over, General Barrett and I are going to have a little chat," she said, her eyes glinting. "Very well. You stay here in the garden until I leave."

"Leave? You're not —"

"I never thought I'd say this to you, Robert, but be quiet. This is women's work. Now I have a quick note to write. Remember, don't return to the house until I've gone."

Apparently she was more annoyed by this than he'd realized. He lifted an eyebrow as she stomped back inside. A footman charged out a moment later and hailed a hack. Robert fetched a watering can, deliberately turning his back on the house and the carriage drive. Whatever she had planned, he wasn't going to complicate it any further.

Ten minutes after the footman vanished, a coach rumbled onto the drive. He managed a glance in that direction as he pretended to pluck an insect from a leaf. The red-and-yellow St. Aubyn crest glinted on the carriage door. Whatever Georgie had written, it had been effective.

She strolled out to the coach and climbed inside with ample assistance from her maid and Evelyn, and the two ladies, along with the servant, departed in the conveyance. Robert finished watering and returned to the house. Whatever she had planned, he was going to have to wait.

"Lucinda!"

Lucinda started, nearly tripping as she descended from her father's coach to the ground. "Geoffrey?"

He pulled his bay to a stop and jumped down, striding up the drive. "I need to speak with you."

Lucinda glanced toward the house, where Ballow had already pulled open the door in anticipation of her return. "I've just returned from luncheon," she stammered. She should have felt guilty; twenty minutes earlier she'd been kissing Robert Carroway. Her first emotion as this man took her hand, however, was annoyance. She needed to figure out how to obtain a list of Horse Guards personnel without alerting her father, and she didn't have time for a row with Geoffrey. "If you'd care to wait in the sitting room for a few mo—"

"No, please, walk with me. I need to see you now."

Geoffrey wrapped her fingers around his arm. She'd never seen him so passionate about anything. Beginning to feel a little alarmed, she nodded, gesturing toward her rose garden, where at least they wouldn't require a chaperone. "A brief walk."

Their pace as they rounded the side of the house was closer to a trot, and she pulled back against his arm to slow him down. He merely changed his grip to her hand, towing her to the stone bench at one side of the garden.

"There," he said, gesturing for her to take a seat.

"Geoffrey, what is going on?"

"Sit, please."

She complied, but he continued pacing back and forth in front of her. Until this point nothing, including her snapping at him, had elicited anything stronger than an apology from him. What could have upset him?

"Geoffrey, whatever it is, please tell me."

He came to a stop in front of her. "I followed you," he said.

Ice ran through her heart. "What?"

"I'm not blind, Lucinda. I've seen the way you look at that . . . at Robert Carroway. And since we argued this morning, I thought you might . . . go to see him. So I followed you to St. Aubyn's residence."

For a moment she thought her heart would pound right through her chest. *Oh, no.* If her father found out that she'd gone behind his back yet again, he would never forgive her. "I didn't know he would be th—"

"It doesn't matter. You're a female. I understand your kind's penchant for taking in stray dogs and wounded birds." He sat beside her, grasping her hand again. "I told your father I would wait until this mess is settled, but I find that I'm not that patient."

Lucinda fought the abrupt urge to run shrieking into the house. This was what she wanted, she reminded herself. This was why she'd selected Geoffrey for her lessons. *Be calm, be calm.*

He reached out with his free hand and slowly tilted up her chin. Leaning in, he touched his lips to hers. Back in the stable she could hear the low chatter of the grooms, while closer by, a phaeton rolled down the street and a pair of crows cawed at each other up on the roof.

After a moment he sat back, smiling and

much more in control. "You see, we are suited for each other."

Lucinda studied his face, the confidence in his straight shoulders. How odd, that she'd felt more moved when her father had accepted her word correction on one of his manuscript pages than by handsome Geoffrey's kiss. If this was what Robert meant by an amiable existence, she wasn't certain she liked it all that much.

Geoffrey slid off the bench and sank to one knee. "Call me forward, or accuse me of impropriety, but I need to know, Lucinda — will you be my wife?"

"My friends are in trouble, Geoffrey. You can't expect me to forget about that in favor of something else."

"We don't need to marry tomorrow. I only want to know if you will do me the honor. When this is over, if you prefer."

All she had to do was say yes, and her father would be happy, she would have a secure, comfortable future, and Geoffrey would have his major's command in India. Heavens, if she wanted to, she could even join him there. The general would probably travel with them as well. Still, she couldn't rid herself of a vision of someone else's eyes, someone else's voice, someone else's touch. "I'm not certain yet," she said slowly. "My mind is . . . my concern is elsewhere right now."

He gazed at her for a moment. "I've just asked you to marry me, and you're telling me you're too busy to consider it?"

"No! For goodness' sake, no. It's just that you and I can have this discussion to-morrow, or next week, or next month. Robert Carroway needs help now, or it will be too late."

Geoffrey straightened. "I have to admit, I do admire your loyalty," he murmured, sitting beside her again. "For your own sake, though, I hope you've considered one very small possibility: that Robert Carroway might be lying to you."

"He's n—"

"If he took those papers, do you think he would admit to it? To you? You're General Barrett's daughter. Who better to have on his side than you? I would imagine that over the past week or so he's gone to great pains to ingratiate himself with you, Lucinda. *You* are his best, last, and only real hope."

"You shouldn't say such things," she said, dismayed that her voice was as shaky as her nerves. The problem was, she realized, that Geoffrey was right. Guilty or innocent, she *was* Robert's best chance of escape from this.

"I know I shouldn't, and I don't want to upset you." Taking a deep breath, he stood again, pulling her up after him. "I have asked you a question. Let it remain that way, while you consider. And I want you to know that whatever might happen with your friend, *I* will not abandon you."

"Thank you, Geoffrey." She forced a smile. "I do need to do some thinking." *What was wrong with her?* She'd been offered everything she wanted, and she needed to think about it? And people said Robert was mad.

"Take all the time you need, my dear."

With that, he took his leave, this time placing a more chaste kiss on her cheek. Lucinda sank back down onto the bench and lowered her head to her hands. What a mess. What a disaster. This was precisely what she'd wanted to avoid: entanglements, questioned loyalties, complications. All she needed to do was say yes to Geoffrey, and with the wave of a magic faerie wand, her life could be simple and amiable again.

She blew out her breath. At least she still had a little time.

When Geoffrey rounded the house, out of Lucinda's sight, he cracked his riding crop so hard across his thigh that the flimsy thing broke into two pieces. He cast it into the shrubbery and collected his horse. He hated complications. Nor was he very fond of Robert Carroway.

The front door of Carroway House opened. Before it could close again, Robert dashed out the library door. Bradshaw and Andrew stood in the foyer, handing over their hats and coats to Dawkins.

"Damnation," he muttered.

Shaw looked over at him. "Hello to you, too."

"Hello. Apologies. I'm waiting for Georgie."

"Ah. And would you know anything about the pair of men hiding in the bushes across the way?"

"They're spying on me," he answered.

"Not very well, I have to say. Shall I go roust them?"

Robert shook his head. "I'd rather they know where I am."

Bradshaw frowned as he dumped his gloves into his hat. "Well, I feel the need to thrash someone." He looked sideways at Andrew. "Up for a game of billiards?"

"Very amusing." Andrew snatched the stack of letters Dawkins handed him. "For-tunately, I still happen to have friends who don't know anything about what's going on in London." He glanced at Robert, a half-apologetic, half-angry look on his face. "I need to write them back, and see if I can keep it that way." He stalked toward Tristan's office.

"Andrew," Shaw snapped at him. "That was uncalled for."

"Leave him be," Robert said. "This affects him as much as it does you."

"Which would be about a quarter of how much it affects you," Shaw returned, climbing the stairs. "Play billiards with me."

Robert decided that he might as well, and followed his brother. He'd read the same page of *Frankenstein* nine times in a row, and still couldn't remember what it said. "It's funny," he said, pulling down a pair of cues and tossing one of them to Shaw, "now that I'm not supposed to go anywhere, I find myself wishing that I'd spent more time outside."

"You're not going to prison, Bit. I won't allow it."

"That's a little self-important of you, wouldn't you say?"

Shaw shook his head as he lined up the balls. "I don't know if you've realized it, but you've taken on a rather frightening resemblance to the Robert I used to know, say five years ago. I like having him around again." Leaning down, he aimed and took his shot. "And just to keep you informed of current events, my ship is about three days away from being finished with its refitting in Portsmouth."

Robert's heart lurched. "At least you'll be clear of this, then."

"You misunderstand me. I'm taking another few weeks' leave, until this idiocy is resolved. What I meant to say is that if it should prove necessary, I'll have clear sailing to the Americas, on a ship their President would no doubt be happy to add to his navy."

For a long moment Robert stared at his brother. "Bradshaw, you can't be serious."

"I'm deadly serious. No one's taking you to prison, Bit. Not after what you went through at Chateau Pagnon." He paused. "I ran into Tristan in Hyde Park. He told me about . . . what you told him this morning. But don't worry, Andrew and Edward don't know."

"No." Robert shook his head. "Promise me you won't throw your career away for me. No matter what happens."

"The Runt always said I should turn pirate, anyway." He grinned. "It's your shot."

Before he could decide whether Shaw had merely said that to throw off his billiards game or because he actually meant it, he heard female giggling coming from the stairs. Thank God. At least Georgie and Evelyn hadn't been arrested on his behalf. Everyone was going insane. And it was a sad state of affairs when, out of everyone in the group, *he* made the most sense.

"Bit?"

"We're in here," Shaw called.

The two ladies marched through the gaming room doorway and then collapsed on the chairs along the near wall. Both of them were laughing, and Lady St. Aubyn in particular seemed close to collapse.

"What have you two been up to?" Shaw asked, leaning on his billiards cue.

Sobering a little, Georgie glanced at Robert. "It's something of a secret," she chortled.

"You may as well include him," Robert said, indicating Shaw. He'd offered to turn criminal, after all, so he probably had a right to know what was going on. "Did you get it?"

"Get what?"

Georgiana cleared her throat. "Well, we went to the Horse Guards, and I asked —"

The cue hit the floor. "You did what?"

Bradshaw asked, ashen-faced.

"Oh, it's all right. We had a plan."

"I need to sit down." Shaw sank into the chair beside Evelyn, but his glare was at Robert. "You knew about this?"

"Of course he did," Georgiana cut in. "And don't mistake; we know it's Robert's safety at risk here, not ours."

"I trust them," Robert said, leaning back against the billiards table and fighting the surprising urge to grin. If there was one thing he wasn't afraid of, he was beginning to realize, it was being killed. He'd been there once already. And it meant he didn't have to go to prison, no matter what happened.

"May we tell our story now?"

"Oh, please do," Bradshaw said weakly, gesturing with his hand for them to continue.

"We walked into the Horse Guards, and I demanded to see General Barrett. Evie tried to hold me back, but I was quite indignant, since the general had forbidden Lucinda to see me." She leaned against Evie's shoulder. "And I'm quite irrational, being that my child is due any day now."

"Give or take five weeks," Evie added, chuckling.

"Of course the sentry became very flustered, and tried to tell me that the general wasn't at the office today, but I wouldn't listen."

"And then she shrieked and fainted right into the sentry's arms," Evelyn took up. "It was an amazing performance. You almost had *me* convinced that the poor man was going to have to deliver the baby."

"Oh, good God," Bradshaw muttered, lowering his face into his hands. "Dare is going to kill all of us. You realize that, don't you?"

"This is the best part," Georgiana said. "Evie became hysterical, and everyone started pouring out of their offices, trying to help. She grabbed the sign-in book and started fanning my face, and then after a minute or two I sat up and started crying that I needed to get home to Tristan. They tried to make us stay while they summoned an army surgeon, but when I insisted, they helped us to the coach and we drove off. And here we are."

"And?" Robert prompted. "This wasn't all just for fun, was it?"

"And," Evie repeated, reaching down the front of her dress to produce a crumpled paper, "here it is."

Robert took the pages from her and uncreased them. The two women had done this for him. And whatever they said about who truly faced the risk, there might have been consequences for either or both of them. Serious consequences. "Thank you."

Shaw stood to look over Robert's shoulder. "What is it?"

"The signatures of all of last week's guests to the Horse Guards," Robert answered, running his finger down the list.

Lucinda had been right. Dozens of visitors had been to call, at all hours and for varying lengths of time. Most of the names were at least familiar, though a few were little more than an illegible scrawl.

"So these are your suspects," Shaw muttered. "Fifty or so different names? That's quite a collection, Bit. And I have a feeling that sooner or later someone's going to piece together our ladies' rather spectacular visit and the missing log pages."

"I know," Robert said absently, barely paying attention to the conversation. One name on the list recurred several times over the three days Evelyn had ripped free: a man who'd consistently included his rank with his signature, even though he was on voluntary extended leave at half pay. Captain Lord Geoffrey Newcombe. "Now that's interesting," he murmured.

Chapter 20

Should I by my base desertion leave
them exposed and unprotected to the
malice of the fiend whom I had let
loose among them?

— Victor Frankenstein, *Frankenstein*

Lucinda sat in her bedchamber, spending as
much time studying her own reflection in the
window as she did looking down at the stable
yard — and trying to convince herself that
she wasn't a fool. She had a completely legitimate excuse for not accepting Geoffrey's
offer of marriage, after all: She'd only delivered two of the four lessons from her list.

But the problem was much more than a
simple matter of mathematics. Sighing, she
unfolded the worn paper on her lap. A little
over a year ago, when she'd written them
out, they'd seemed important. The willing-

ness to pay attention to one's companion, to dance in mixed company, to have interests other than oneself, and the honesty to be straightforward in one's opinion of people.

"Rubbish," she said, wadding up the paper and throwing it into a wastebasket.

She hadn't delayed answering Geoffrey because of her lessons. She'd delayed answering him because of Robert. Because when she thought of quiet evenings by the fire it was Robert's voice she heard, and when warm fingers touched her skin they belonged to Robert.

It didn't make any sense; her father would never approve, for one thing; and for another, Robert would never ask. And unless someone came forward and confessed to committing treason in the next few days, he would never have the opportunity to ask, anyway.

The thought of Robert dragged off in chains and thrown into some tiny, windowless cell made her throat constrict until she couldn't breathe. They couldn't do that to him. If someone would just take a moment to think, they would realize that Robert was the least likely man in London — in England — to want a war to recommence with Bonaparte. He was one of the few men who understood the true cost of war.

Who, then? Who had taken those papers? Frowning, Lucinda rose to pace the length of her room. It could have been anyone. A supporter of Bonaparte, a mercenary who made money whenever two sides fought in battle, someone else who thought they had something to gain by starting a war.

Something tapped at her window, and she whirled around, hand to her breast. Nothing. "For heaven's sake, Lucinda, did you think it was going to be Robert, coming to call again?" she muttered at herself.

The idea, though, didn't displease her at all. For something she hadn't even partaken in until a few days ago, thinking about having sex again seemed to occupy an inordinate amount of her time, and her imagination. After Geoffrey had handed her his kiss and his marriage proposal she'd tried to imagine being in his embrace. He was handsome enough, and his kiss had been technically proficient, but other than a slight murmur of nervousness at the idea of being intimate with someone so perfect, it hadn't moved her at all.

The tap came at her window again. Deciding it must be the starling that had nested in the eve just above, she went to the window and opened it. "Shoo."

Looking up, she could just see the bird's

beady little eyes gazing at her from the safety of its nest. Her pulse stirred, and she turned her gaze downward. At first she didn't make out anything but the stable and the line of trees and bushes bordering it from the street, until something stirred beside the nearest oak. Robert.

"What are you —"

He put his fingers to his lips, then motioned for her to join him. A faint smile touched his mouth, and her heart lurched.

Before she could change her mind, Lucinda nodded and pulled the window closed again. Her father would be in his office, but since they weren't speaking, she didn't expect to be stopped. Just in case, though, she went out the back way, through the servants' hall and the kitchen.

"Robert, you shouldn't be here," she whispered. "If my father —"

"He won't." He took her hands and pulled her around the side of the stable.

"What about the men following you?"

"They're still at Carroway House. I needed to talk to you."

"You should have sent a note through Evie or something," she returned. "Don't you realize how terrible things could become for you?"

"They already are terrible." He ran a

finger along her cheek. "You make them better. I could wish for your sake that you didn't, but you do."

She wanted him to kiss her, but obviously he was making an attempt to be a gentleman. Considering that another man had proposed to her an hour ago, his restraint seemed appropriate, if unwelcome. "Why did you need to talk to me, then?" she asked, her own fingers twitching with the desire, the need, to touch him.

"I got hold of the list," he returned, sending another glance around them. "The guest list at the Horse Guards."

"You what?" She froze.

The soft smile touched his mouth. "Actually, some friends of mine nicked it."

Her eyes narrowed. Allies were welcome, but completely unexpected. "Which friends?"

"Georgiana and Lady St. Aubyn."

"Georgiana and Evie? What —"

"It's a long story. Hopefully they'll be able to tell you themselves in a few days."

"What did the guest book tell you, then?"

He hesitated. "It told me I have a very good reason to stay away from you. Better than the reason that you're practically betrothed and it's simply not right for me to be here."

She couldn't have helped her scowl for anything. "Stay away from *me?* Do you think I stole those papers?"

"No. But . . ." He drew a breath. "For the next few days, just be cautious. About everything."

It sounded as if he wasn't planning to be around. Lucinda's voice caught. "What are you talking about?"

"I'm not certain, yet." Blue eyes studied her face for a long moment. "Nothing, I hope." He glanced past her again, obviously uneasy there. "I shouldn't have come. I just wanted to see you again. Be careful, Lucinda." With a slight nod, he turned around.

Lucinda grabbed his shoulder. "No. You don't get to vanish away from me. Tell me."

"I —"

She knew one way that might convince him to talk to her. Lucinda twined her fingers into his lanky hair, pulling his face down to hers and covered his mouth with hers. At his response, warm dampness immediately started between her legs.

She wrapped her arms around his neck, stretching herself along his lean body. She could tell herself this was to put him at ease, but it had much more to do with wanting him so much she couldn't stand it. It seemed like forever, rather than a few hours, since she'd seen him last, and even when he wasn't in her sight, every thought seemed to be of him; hoping he was well, praying that no one had gone to arrest him, wanting to talk with him about everything and nothing at all. He wasn't going anywhere. Not without touching her again.

With a groan he sank with her to the grass, leaning back against the stable wall and pulling her across his thighs. His hands caressed and kneaded her breasts through the thin muslin of her gown, leaving her breathless and aching. In the late afternoon most of the servants would be in the kitchen, eating, but it wouldn't take much noise on their part to arouse someone's suspicions. And only a water barrel and a curricle would shield them from curious eyes if someone came looking around the side of the stable.

She didn't care. Nothing could make her let this moment pass without acting. His arousal beneath her bottom strained at his trousers, and with shaking fingers she shifted to unbutton them. "Oh, God," she whimpered, kissing him hot and open-mouthed.

Robert lifted her in his arms, pulling her dress to her thighs, and then let her sink down on her knees, onto his engorged member. He made her feel so full and so tight, and she clung to him as he moaned and dug his fingers into her hips, shifting her up and back again, up and down on him.

"Lucinda," he rasped, tilting his head back and pushing his hips up against her.

It wasn't enough. "More, more," she chanted, rocking back and forth on him. His deep blue gaze caught hers, bottomless, timeless, as tension speared down her spine, tightened, and then released.

She cried out, but he muffled the sound against his mouth, heaving a groan into her as he came. Breathing hard, she leaned her forehead against his chest while she soared into the air and then back down to the ground again.

Slowly he slid his palms up her thighs, beneath her gown. "Sometime I would like to do this when we can have all day," he murmured.

Lucinda shut her eyes, drinking in the thought. "Or all night." Kissing the line of his jaw, she settled her arms around his shoulders. "This is my stable yard," she said quietly. "In the middle of the day, fifty feet from my back door. I'm only saying this to illustrate how much I trust you, Robert. When you decide you can trust me, tell me your news."

She would have pulled away, but he pressed his hands down, holding her against him, keeping him inside her. "Stay."

The word reverberated through her heart. She kissed him again, slowly this time, and he leaned back against the wall, letting her explore and caress him as she wanted. The feeling was glorious, with him still filling her and she having the satisfaction of knowing that she aroused him, that she'd been the only woman he wanted after four years of his self-styled hell.

Taking a slow breath and shifting her hands to caress his hard, muscled chest through his fine shirt, she looked him in the eye. "Then tell me your news."

"I looked through the names on the list," Robert returned, wishing he'd listened to his instincts and left while he could — despite the pure delight of being with her.

"And?"

He heard the kitchen door open, and drew in his legs. "Shh," he breathed, though with her moving about on him, he was having some difficulty with silence, himself.

A potful of water dumped into the bushes behind the house, and then the door opened and closed again. They'd probably pressed their luck far enough, and with great reluctance he shifted her off. Her hazel eyes sparkled in the late afternoon sunlight as she stood, settling her skirts around her. He climbed to his feet as well, fastening his trousers and feeling far more self-satisfied than he probably should under the circumstances.

"I recognized most of the names, but nothing odd struck me about their being there. Except . . ."

" 'Except'?" she prompted after a moment.

She wasn't going to like this, and he couldn't blame her. Still, he'd learned to listen to his instincts, and she needed to know. "What was Geoffrey Newcombe doing at the Horse Guards?"

"What?"

"He was there four times last week. Do you know why?"

"He's . . . he's reading my father's manuscript. I know he's dropped off or picked up pages there."

" 'Picked up pages'?" Robert repeated. If everyone knew he was carrying papers in and out, one or two more wouldn't rouse anyone's suspicions.

"He was there to see my father." Lucinda folded her arms across her pert bosom. "Who else is on the list?"

Robert pulled it from his pocket and

handed it to her. "It won't be long before someone realizes who took this, and why. If you can think of anything, Lucinda, you need to tell me."

She looked at the list, but before she could possibly have read all the names she handed it back again. "It's not Geoffrey. He's already got his life planned out — marrying me, being promoted to major, going to India, and making his fortune. Why in the world would he risk stealing papers that could either get him thrown in prison or start another war with France?"

"I don't know. How confident is he that he's going to marry you?"

Color crept up her cheeks. "What does that have to do with anything?"

Something had happened between her and Geoffrey. Robert was certain of it. "Marrying you is the base of his pyramid, Lucinda. Without that, he has no plan. So it has everything to do with this."

Her brow furrowed. "I don't like this, Robert. Don't you think it's convenient for you, that you can go directly from being suspected to suspecting Geoffrey?"

"Maybe it is." He paused for a moment, listening to the sounds of Barrett House. "You said you trusted me. I'm only asking for your opinion."

For a long moment she searched his gaze. "No," she finally said. "I believe *you,* and likewise I have no reason to suspect *him.*"

"Lucinda!"

At her father's bellow, both of them jumped. "Robert, hide," she hissed.

"He's probably heard about the uproar at the Horse Guards."

"Oh, no."

She would have hurried around the corner to meet her father, but Robert caught her arm. "Did Geoffrey ask you to marry him?" he asked, trying to pretend that he didn't care one way or the other.

"Rob . . . yes. He did ask me. This morning, as a matter of fact."

Ice trailed through his chest. "And what was your answer?" He couldn't breathe, but he needed to know. They'd just made love again, but she seemed determined to separate her feelings from her thoughts where her future was concerned. That was how she meant to keep things simple and amiable, he supposed. For his part, though, if she'd agreed to marry Geoffrey it changed how he meant to approach this.

"I said . . . I said I needed a little more time to consider," she said slowly, then shoved at his chest before she strolled around the corner away from him. *"Go."*

She hadn't agreed to marry Geoffrey. For a moment nothing else mattered. An out-and-out refusal would have suited him better, but a plea for time meant something as well. He could use a little time himself to figure out what he was going to do and what she would think of him as a consequence. One thing he'd lost all patience for, however, was dishonesty. Whoever had stolen those papers should have simply taken them and left — not stayed lurking in the shadows and allowed, even encouraged, someone else to take the blame.

Heavy footsteps clomped in his direction. "I asked what you were doing behind the stable," General Barrett's voice came.

Robert faded back into the shrubbery, crouching in the deep shade of an over-hanging elm. The general stalked around the corner, his fists clenched and his color high. Clearly he expected to see one of her friends or other, and he spun a circle to glare into the bushes.

"I told you, I was thinking," Lucinda said, joining him. "What in heaven's name is wrong? You frightened me half to death, yelling like that."

Good girl. She had to hate lying to the general, but it meant that she did trust in Robert if she'd decided to keep silent about his visit. Still, he tried not to let it mean too much.

Whatever had upset Barrett, Lucinda managed to get him into the house before the neighbors could hear any of the arguing. Robert disliked leaving her there, but if he stepped into the middle of it, things would only get worse for all of them. And besides, he had some things he needed to look into, which he couldn't do if General Barrett had him arrested.

He slipped down the street and hailed a hack to drop him off behind Carroway House. From there it was simple, even with his game leg, to hop a fence and climb the trellis back into his bedchamber. To cover for Lucinda in case her father wanted to know if he'd been lurking about earlier, he then headed downstairs and out around the side of the house to water his roses again. Both of his watchers remained in the bushes across the street, and obviously had no idea he'd gone anywhere. If he wasn't careful, he was going to kill his plants with overwatering.

"I wish the Runt attended to his studies as well as you attend to those roses," Tristan drawled, coming outside to watch him.

"I'm just making an appearance," Robert returned, jerking his head in the direction of their skulking audience.

"Did Lucinda have any insights?"

Robert straightened. "I wasn't going to ask her for any, but it doesn't matter anyway. She won't help. She said it's not fair that she trusted me and isn't supposed to trust Geoffrey." The fact that she refused to differentiate between the two of them angered him, but he would dwell on that later.

"She has a point."

"Yes, she does. Which means I'll have to go about this the hard way."

Tristan blew out his breath. "I wish you'd stop saying that."

"Saying what?"

" 'I.' And yes, I know, you're going to tell me again that this is your problem, and that you'll deal with it, and that the rest of us need to stay out of trouble."

"Exactly," Robert agreed, tossing the watering can back beside the stable.

"Bullocks."

Lifting an eyebrow, Robert folded his arms. "Beg pardon?"

The viscount took a step closer, putting a hand on Robert's shoulder. "Think about it, Robert. Where do you want to be tomorrow? Next week? If you don't care, then definitely keep us out of this. If you do, we're here for you."

With that, he strolled back around the front of the house. Robert dusted off his trousers and followed. A few weeks ago, he wasn't certain he would have had an answer to Tristan's question. How could he possibly know where he wanted to be in the future, when he didn't deserve one?

Recently, though, the question — and its answer — had become much more complicated. Where did he want to be tomorrow? With Lucinda. Next week, forever? With Lucinda. Robert stopped on the front step, ignoring Dawkins holding the door open for him.

Good God. He was eight and twenty years of age. Of those, he'd served in the British Army for three years, and had been all but dead for nearly four. He'd known he'd been getting better, slowly, in the last two years or so, though it felt more like clawing his way out of a pit than making improvement. But in the past weeks, things had changed. He felt . . . alive. And even the accusations and the mutterings served to bring his emotions — his anger and his long-buried instinct for survival — back into play.

And along with that, he'd been rediscovering his sense of humor, and his passion — and for that he needed to thank Lucinda. It wasn't gratitude that he felt most strongly, though. He wanted her, and he wanted to hold her, and talk with her, and protect her, and just look at her. And he definitely did not want anyone else to have her.

"Bit, are you coming in?" Tristan called.

"I'll be right there."

So he did have a reason to want Lord Geoffrey Newcombe to be the culprit in this whole mess. And he wanted to tell Lucinda Guinevere Barrett something that wouldn't have been easy for him even before he'd been captured and taken to Chateau Pagnon. He wanted to tell her that he loved her. And even if it didn't change her plans for a simple life, he wanted to know whether she could ever, possibly, perhaps, love him a little, as well.

If he ever wanted the opportunity to find out, he needed to solve this — and quickly. And so he would have to do something else he wouldn't have been able to do a few weeks ago: He needed to ask for help.

Lucinda wanted to tear her hair out. Instead, she sat in her father's office, hands folded on her lap, while he paced the floor and ranted about her dearest friends.

"And Lieutenant Staeley's report says that pages are now missing from the visitors

417

logbook! Am I supposed to believe that's a coincidence?"

Since she knew it wasn't, and she'd even seen the pages, Lucinda kept her mouth shut. She needed to think anyway — as difficult as it was to do with her father yelling like that. But out of all the names on those pages, Robert had chosen to be suspicious of Geoffrey. Was he jealous? A shiver of goose bumps ran down her arms.

"Apparently the damned Carroways have managed to dupe Lady St. Aubyn into playing their little games, too! Hopefully, St. Aubyn has more sense."

When she looked at all of this logically, with no stake in either Geoffrey or Robert's innocence, it didn't point at one or the other of them. Robert had been a survivor of Chateau Pagnon for three years, so she had no reasonable explanation as to why he would select last week to begin life as a traitor. As for Geoffrey, the general had enlisted his help with the Salamanca chapter . . . what, four weeks ago? And . . .

And he'd taken to visiting her father at the Horse Guards since then. Lucinda shook herself. No. It was a coincidence, just as the news about Robert and the theft had coincidentally come to public notice at the same time.

"I don't think I have a choice, any longer," her father was saying. "I've tried to give him the benefit of the doubt for your sake, but this debacle aside, we now have a theft, obviously on his behalf, made in broad daylight — and again at the Horse Guards! How much more evidence do you need, Lucinda?"

She blinked. "From what you said, at least thirty people were in the entryway during the time those log pages went missing, Papa."

"Ah, so this *is* another coincidence? Do you really expect me to believe that?"

"I expect that you know Georgiana and Evelyn almost as well as you know me," she returned. "They aren't criminals."

"I didn't say they did it for themselves. It's Dare's damned brother. Again." Growling, he dropped into his desk chair, threw open a drawer, and yanked out a piece of paper. "And it's time he answered some questions. Officially."

"You're going to have him arrested?" she squeaked, abruptly glad she was sitting down.

"I'm going to request that he report to the Horse Guards for questioning. If he refuses to cooperate, I will have him arrested, yes."

"No!" She shot to her feet, yanking the pen out of her father's hand.

"Lucinda! Are you mad? Give that back at once!"

Oh, she should never have refused to help Robert. All he needed was a little time — either to solve this mess, or to flee to Scotland or abroad. A tear ran down her cheek. She didn't want him to go anywhere. She wanted him here, in London, with her.

"Lucinda!"

"You will give him one more day, Papa," she said, her voice shaking. "If you don't —"

"If I don't, then what?" he snapped, his color high.

"If you don't, then I will never speak to you again," she said slowly, another tear following the first.

"You . . ." He trailed off, the blustering anger in his face fading as he studied her expression. "You're serious."

"Yes, I am."

The general lowered his head. When he straightened again, he looked more tired and old than she'd ever seen. "A few years ago, I would have had him in jail and confessing by now," he said in a quieter voice, "damn the consequences. Now, however, I find that my daughter's affection comes before my career, and my duty to my country."

"Papa."

"This is Wednesday. I will give him until noon on Friday," the general said. "I suggest you send him a note to inform him of that deadline. But he will be watched during that time. And if he leaves, he'd best not take those papers with him. If we don't find them here in London, I *will* see him hunted down."

"Thank you, Papa," she whispered, standing.

"And Lucinda, I suggest you make it clear that running would be a good idea. I don't want him in England, regardless of his involvement with this theft."

She looked at her father for a moment. From the vehemence of her protest, he no doubt realized that she considered Robert more than a mere friend. So the general had his own reasons for wanting to be rid of a rival to Geoffrey — the man he obviously favored. For heaven's sake, he'd already granted permission for them to marry. That should have made her happy. But it didn't. "Robert is innocent," she said firmly.

"I hope you're right, for both our sakes."

She hoped so as well. Because if he *did* run, she wasn't certain she could let him go alone.

Chapter 21

My heart beat quick;
this was the hour and moment of trial,
which would decide my hopes
or realize my fears.

— The Monster, *Frankenstein*

Robert was halfway inside the front door when the messenger from Barrett House arrived. He took the missive himself, which didn't please Dawkins overly much, but as he saw the addressee and the handwriting, he didn't care whether he'd offended the butler or not.

If Lucinda had written to him and sent one of her father's footmen, then the general knew about the correspondence. His heart pounded. What else did her father know? If the general had found out about him and Lucinda . . .

Her handwriting, though, was clear and neat, with small flourishes here and there — just like her. Robert smiled a little as he opened the note. *Robert, my father knows about the log sheets,* he read silently, his grin fading. *He has convinced himself that you are to blame for both thefts, and insists that you meet him at the Horse Guards for questioning.*

"Uh-oh," Bradshaw said, coming down the stairs. "You don't look happy."

"Quiet, I'm reading," Robert returned, otherwise ignoring him. *I have asked, and he has granted, that you be given until noon on Friday to do what it is you need to accomplish. At that time, if you are still in London he will send soldiers to escort you, and I'm to inform you that you will be watched until then.*

"Who's that from?"

"Lucinda."

Bradshaw turned on his heel and vanished into the drawing room. When he emerged a moment later, Tristan was right behind him. "Bit, what —"

"Just a damned minute," Robert retorted. "At least let me finish reading it." He lowered his head again. *Please be careful, Robert. And know that until four weeks ago, I don't think Geoffrey had ever been to the Horse Guards. Yours, Lucinda.*

He handed it over to his brothers, who

immediately began a loud argument over whether General Barrett had lost his mind or not. Robert, though, found that something else occupied his thoughts at the moment — the way Lucinda had signed the letter. *Yours* meant his — "Mine." Did it signify something, or was she being polite?

"Why does she mention Lord Geoffrey and the Horse Guards?" Andrew wanted to know, snatching the letter for himself when Tristan began waving it in the air.

"She's giving us a clue," Robert returned.

"A clue about what?" Edward asked, as he too, joined the fracas, his tutor in tow.

"I thought she wasn't going to help you," Tristan said, eyeing Robert.

"Who?" the Runt demanded.

Robert shrugged. "Something changed her mind." And obviously, he needed to find out a few more things about Lord Geoffrey Newcombe. Things other than the fact that Newcombe wanted to marry Lucinda and become a major with his own command in India.

"He's only giving you a damned day and a half," Shaw growled. "Does he really expect you to clear yourself by then?"

"I think he expects me to leave England by then," Robert returned slowly. That made more sense than anything. Whatever

Lucinda had used to convince the general to give him more time, it had also convinced Barrett that Robert needed to get away from his daughter.

"You can't leave England!" Edward protested, then stomped both feet. "Someone tell me what the devil is going on here!"

"Edward!" half the adults yelled at him at the same time.

"I don't care! Devil, devil, devil! You tell me what's going on!"

Robert snagged his arm, crouching down in front of him while Bradshaw got rid of Mr. Trost. "I'm in a little trouble," he said quietly, damning himself for not keeping this away from Edward. "We're just trying to straighten some things out before it gets any worse."

"Is this the same thing you were worried about before?" the Runt asked.

"Yes. But it's almost over with."

"I want to help."

Smiling, Robert tousled the boy's dark hair. "You are helping, by being my brother."

Abruptly Edward threw his arms around Robert's shoulders. "Promise you're not leaving," he said.

Every moment he seemed to realize more of what he had to lose if he let this go — or if he ran. "I promise," he said, hugging the Runt back.

"So what are we going to do, then?" Andrew queried, stepping sideways as Georgiana joined them, reading the missive in turn.

"First, I think we need to get out of the hallway." Robert motioned the group toward the drawing room.

"Lucinda must be very upset by this," Georgiana said, leading the way into the large room and taking a seat on the couch. She perused the letter again, glancing up at Robert as she finished.

"I'm very upset by it, too," he returned, sitting close to the door. As soon as everyone was inside and the door closed he sat forward. "All right," he said slowly, praying none of them would pay for his poor reputation, "I'm asking for your help."

"Tell us what you need." Tristan entwined his fingers with Georgiana's.

Robert took a breath. "First of all, I need someone who can converse with Geoffrey without making him suspicious."

"That lets all of us out," Shaw said. "What about St. Aubyn?"

"He might do." Robert furrowed his brow, then turned his gaze to Tristan. "Tattersall's auction is tomorrow, isn't it?"

"Yes. It's fairly wide open, there, though."

"That's what I want. Somewhere I can watch him without being seen."

"Why don't Dare or I watch him, and you stay here, out of trouble?" Bradshaw countered, scowling.

"Because I've done enough sitting about to last me a lifetime," he returned. "Saint by himself might rouse Newcombe's suspicions."

"Evie will go," Georgiana said, with a small smile. "She's already volunteered any assistance necessary."

"That should help. It would be even better if . . ." Robert trailed off. Lucinda had given him a hint, but she'd also made her feelings about getting involved in this quite clear. "Nothing. This should do."

"I'll ask Evie to send Lucinda a note," Georgie offered, demonstrating her usual keen intuition. "In fact, we should have Evie and Saint here now, while we're planning."

She rose with help from Tristan, and hurried into the office. A moment later a footman left, and Robert could hear Georgie informing Dawkins that they would have two more for dinner.

"I don't understand," Edward said, sitting on the floor in front of Bradshaw and looking far too serious for his age. "Why are we spying on Lord Geoffrey?"

Tristan stirred. "Runt, why don't you go dress for dinner?"

"Because this is my family, too, and I want to know what's going on. I won't get in the way."

"Runt, there are things you should know, but not until you're a little older," Robert said slowly.

Large gray eyes filled with tears. "But I can help," he whispered, as if he couldn't trust his normal speaking voice.

Well, that was that. There was no way in hell that Robert was going to let his youngest brother and greatest champion cry. He nodded. "All right. We want to spy on Lord Geoffrey because we think he stole something and managed to blame me for it."

"How did he blame you?"

Andrew blew out his breath. "This isn't helping."

"Hush," Georgiana warned. "It's a valid question. How did he manage to time things so well?"

Robert cleared his throat. Some of this definitely would have been easier without Edward being present. "I told one person about my . . . stay at Chateau Pagnon."

"Lucinda?"

Edward bounced onto his knees. "She could've told Lord Geoffrey! They're getting married, aren't they?"

"No," Robert snapped, before anyone else could answer. He swallowed. "I mean, she only told one person — the general."

"Then General Barrett told him," Edward insisted.

The room went quiet. Part of Robert had wanted to suspect the general of leaking the rumor from the beginning, but little liking as he had for the man, he was, after all, Lucinda's father. "Barrett told the senior command at the Horse Guards. It could have been any one of them."

Andrew was shaking his head. "But if we're thinking Lord Geoffrey stole those papers, he would be the one to see your . . . news as something he could use to his advantage."

"Would the senior officers spread that kind of news around without investigating it first?" Tristan put in.

"Probably not." Bradshaw sat forward, sipping from the snifter of brandy he'd poured for himself. "If they're anything like the Admiralty, they hate sharing a juicy tidbit until they've squeezed all the fun and possibilities for self-promotion out of it."

Damn. It did make sense. "Considering

that General Barrett's chomping at the bit to get Lucinda married to Geoffrey, he might have felt comfortable confiding in him. It's unfortunate that we can't confirm that with Barrett, though."

"Maybe we can't," Georgiana said, "but Lucinda can."

"No. I won't ask her to spy on her own father."

"Bit, be reason—"

"If she'll help us get Geoffrey to Tattersall's, that'll be more than enough." He didn't like it. She'd made it clear that she didn't feel comfortable suspecting Geoffrey; asking her to question her father had to be even worse. At the same time — and he felt like an idiot even admitting it to himself — he missed her already. Anything that brought her into close proximity held a definite appeal for him.

"I'm not convinced she should be included at all. She's the daughter of the man trying to put Bit in prison," Andrew pointed out.

The argument over whether to include Lucinda in their plot went on for several minutes. Robert let them talk; he needed a few moments to think things through, anyway. Lucinda was right about one thing: he *wanted* to suspect Geoffrey. He wanted to hate the pretty, charming, popular bastard for thinking that being grazed in the arm and telling stories of other soldiers' foibles and misfortunes made him a hero. And he wanted to hate him because everyone — even Lucinda — considered him a better candidate for a husband than himself. He wanted to prove them wrong.

"This isn't getting us anywhere," Tristan said, annoyance edging his voice. "General Barrett's given Bit a day and a half." His frown deepened. "I don't like ultimatums, but much as I hate to admit it, with the bloody rumors going about, Barrett can do whatever he damn well pleases."

"Then we find Lord Geoffrey and beat a confession out of him," Shaw suggested, his tone dark and deadly serious.

"That won't help." Georgiana looked as serious as Robert had ever seen her. "We need evidence, and we need a motive. At the moment we don't have either." As the Viscountess Dare and the cousin of the Duke of Wycliffe, she obviously wasn't used to being in a powerless position.

Robert, on the other hand, had spent seven months relying on nothing but luck and the whim of English-hating soldiers. "We'll get what we need," he said, "because I don't want to leave England. It took me four years to get back."

The front door opened. "Is everyone well?" Lady St. Aubyn asked, hurrying into the drawing room before Dawkins could announce her. Saint was on her heels, and they were both dressed for an evening out.

Wordlessly Georgiana handed over Lucinda's note. The marquis read it over his wife's shoulder, his gaze sliding to Robert as he finished. "I would assume we're here because you require our assistance?" he commented, running a hand along Evie's arm. "Or further assistance, rather, since apparently my wife has become a burglar now."

"It was for a good cause," Georgiana protested.

"I didn't say I minded," Saint returned, a slight smile touching his mouth. "She told me all about it. I particularly enjoyed hearing where she hid the evidence."

Evelyn blushed. "Saint, that's quite enough. This is serious."

He nodded, guiding her to an empty chair and then sitting on the arm beside her. "Are we arranging for you to leave the country, Robert, or are we going after . . ." He eyed the letter again. ". . . Lord Geoffrey Newcombe?"

"Lord Geoffrey," Edward answered.

Everyone began chiming in with their ideas and theories. For a moment Robert listened. Seeing so much activity and passion erupting on his behalf was supremely interesting. From the flow of the argument, Tristan was trying to take command of their small band of troops, and Saint was challenging him. What they needed to realize, however, was that this game — and its outcome — was his responsibility.

"This hinges on Lucinda," he said loudly, noting that his interruption startled everyone into silence. "She needs to convince Geoffrey to join her at Tattersall's, where she will be joining Saint and Evie."

"And what will we be doing there?" Saint asked.

"Looking at teams — and trying to convince Geoffrey to buy a new mount."

"Why do we want him to buy a horse?" Edward wanted to know.

"We don't. We want to hear what he says about his finances." Robert gazed at Saint. "And if possible, we want to know what he plans to do for a career if Lucinda doesn't agree to marry him."

"Is he even going to think that's a possibility?" Georgiana broke in. "Lucinda's fairly straightforward, and she has been —"

"I have reason to believe that Geoffrey

will be nervous about her answer," Robert said calmly.

"That's simple enough." Saint brushed at an imaginary fleck of dust on his midnight-colored jacket. "But what will you be doing, Robert?"

"I'll eavesdrop until I'm convinced that we're on the correct trail, and then I'll make a visit to Geoffrey's home." He glanced at Edward. "Which is a very bad thing, and should only be condoned under the most dire of circumstances."

"What about us?" Andrew asked.

"I rather thought you might join me," Robert answered. "We won't have much time to search the house for the missing items, and I'd like to have at least one of you there to attest to the fact that I didn't plant them in the first place."

"It would be better if we had someone who wasn't a family member to witness that," Bradshaw countered.

Tristan cleared his throat. "I believe I can take care of that. I mean, what's the use of having the Duke of Wycliffe as your closest friend if you don't embroil him in some of your schemes?"

"As long as he knows the risks." No one else was going to become involved by accident. Too much of that had happened already, as far as Robert was concerned. He faced Saint again. "The three of you will have to keep Newcombe occupied long enough to let us make a search."

"How polite do we have to be about it?"

"With his access to Lucinda and General Barrett, I don't want him suspecting anything, if we can help it."

Saint nodded, though he looked a little disappointed. "And what if you don't find anything?"

"I'd better," Robert answered. "Because I'm not going to prison, and I promised not to leave England."

Dawkins scratched at the door to announce dinner, and everyone trooped into the dining room. Georgiana hung back a little, and curious, Robert followed suit.

"I have two questions for you," the viscountess said, taking his arm.

He could guess what they were, but gestured for her to continue anyway. "I'm listening."

"First, what will you do if you *do* happen to find the missing papers at Lord Geoffrey's residence?"

"I'll turn him in."

"To General Barrett?"

A slight shudder went through his frame. Hoping she hadn't noticed, he nodded. "He would seem to be the official heading the investigation."

"And he also has a reputation to think of. Everyone knows of his friendship with Geoffrey." She walked in silence for a moment. "And his dislike for you."

"It's a shared emotion," he said stiffly. "I can deal with Barrett." And to his surprise, in part he was looking forward to it. "What's your second question?"

"How do you know Lucinda didn't accept a marriage offer from Geoffrey?"

"She told me."

"She seems to confide in you a great deal."

Robert smiled. "I'm a good listener."

Georgiana gazed up at him with warm green eyes. "I have a feeling you're a great deal more than that, Robert Sylvester Carroway."

He ushered her into the dining room. "Time will tell, I suppose." A very short time, one way or the other.

Before he could make his way to his chair, a small hand tugged on his coat. As he turned, Edward gestured for him to turn back into the hallway.

"What is it?" he asked.

"Did I help?"

Robert squatted, trying not to favor his

bad knee. "You provided what may turn out to be the key to this entire investigation, Runt. That's more than helping."

The boy blinked. "What did I provide?" he whispered.

"The main piece of the puzzle is whether or not General Barrett talked to Lord Geoffrey about my stay at Chateau Pagnon. You suggested that."

Edward's chest puffed out. "I'm very intuitive," he said. "But I didn't know you stayed at Chateau Pagnon. What is it?"

Slowly Robert pulled his brother into a tight hug. "I'll make you an agreement," he whispered into his youngest brother's ear. "If you keep all of this conversation tonight a secret from your friends and Mr. Trost until Friday at noon, I will tell you about Chateau Pagnon."

"I agr—"

"Wait. I'm not finished. I will tell you about Pagnon — in seven years."

Edward pulled away, eyeing Robert doubtfully. "Seven years?"

"That's the best I can do, Runt." He stuck out his hand. "Do we have an agreement?"

After a short moment Edward sighed and shook Robert's hand. "Yes, we have an agreement."

★ ★ ★

"You're going to bed already?" General Barrett asked, one hand on his office door handle.

Lucinda looked down from the landing. "I thought I would. I'm a bit tired."

Her father nodded. "Shall I have Helena bring you up some dinner?"

"No, thank you. I'm not hungry." She started up again.

"Lucinda?"

"Yes, Papa?"

"Please face the fact that Robert Carroway is the most likely candidate to have committed this crime. You need to be prepared for the worst."

She slowed, wishing she could explain the pure panic that ran through her when anyone suggested that Robert would be sent to prison — or worse. It hurt that her own father could say such things, even more because until a few weeks ago she'd been able to confide in him about anything. *Why was this so different?* Because she had a stake in the outcome? Because it was something — someone — she actually cared about? Perhaps she'd found the key. Life could be simple and amiable only as long as nothing about it felt particularly important.

Some of the general's peers had thought

the job of editing his memoirs would prove to be too dreadful for someone of the female persuasion, and now she thought perhaps it *should* have bothered her. But it hadn't. None of it had, none of it affected her, until she'd learned the truth and the horror of war from Robert.

Lucinda leaned over the balcony, looking down at her father. "Why is he the most likely candidate?" she asked, making an effort to keep her voice quiet and her tone even. "Because he was tortured and survived? What if I hadn't told you about that? Who would be the most likely candidate then?"

He grimaced. "The fact is, I *do* know about it, and I thank you for informing me. It's made the investigation much easier."

"Did you ever discover who informed the rest of London?"

"Lucinda, I told you already, it doesn't matt—"

"It matters, Papa. Can you think of anyone you told who might have anything to gain from another war? Or from the money that selling those papers would earn him? Because frankly, neither of those things would benefit Robert Carroway, and I think you know that. And I think that's why you were willing to give him a little more time."

"I did that for you."

She took a deep breath, not quite willing to believe she was about to ask the question. "Did you, by any chance, mention Chateau Pagnon and Robert to Geoffrey? In one of your tales about the war, maybe?"

He opened his mouth and closed it again. "You suspect *Geoffrey?*"

Quickly she shook her head, and at the same time reversed course and practically flew back down the stairs. If she couldn't change his train of thought now, she'd never get any information out of him. And she needed some answers, because she was the only one who could get them.

"No, no, no. I do think that Geoffrey, at the beginning of our friendship, might have been jealous of Robert. Of my friendship with him. What better way to make him unpopular than to spread a little gossip, especially if he had it from a reliable source and knew it to be the truth?" She frowned. "If Robert did steal those papers, *he* certainly wouldn't have been the one to spread the rumors."

"Lucinda, this is ridiculous. If Robert Carroway is innocent, the sooner we take him in and have him answer some questions, the better off all of us will be."

"Not Robert," she said quietly. If

Geoffrey hadn't spread the rumors, it could have been any of her father's cronies, getting as old as he was, and unable to discern between a piece of juicy gossip and something that could ruin a man's life. And then they would again have little to point to anyone but Robert. "Good night, Papa."

"Good night, Luce. And I'm certain that no matter how 'jealous' you think Geoffrey might have been, he wouldn't have told anyone. The lad knows how to keep a confidence, if anyone does."

Lucinda nearly tripped on the stairs, and made a show of adjusting her slipper to cover it. Geoffrey had known. Her father had told him, and Geoffrey had known.

Oh, she needed to tell Robert. She'd been half hoping he would be lurking in her bedchamber, waiting for her, but now her heart beat so fast she feared she might faint. It didn't mean Geoffrey had done the other things Robert accused him of, but it did mean he was less innocent than she'd believed.

Nothing would happen tonight, she told herself. First thing in the morning, she would get word to Robert. Apparently her neutral stance had ended. She'd just taken sides.

Chapter 22

I devote myself,
either in my life or death,
to his destruction.

— Victor Frankenstein, *Frankenstein*

Lucinda didn't sleep much at all. Her mind refused to relinquish the riddle of whether Geoffrey had acted out of jealousy, or something far more nefarious. As soon as the sun rose, so did she, going straight to her writing desk. She had her note to Robert half written, and was just beginning to wonder how in the world she was going to get it to him, when a missive arrived from Evelyn.

" 'Lucinda,' " she read, " 'Saint and I would very much appreciate if you and Lord Geoffrey would accompany us to the horse auctions at Tattersall's this morning, though it would be better if you could contact Geoffrey yourself and mention your desire to attend in his company.' "

Something was afoot. And apparently Robert had taken her mention of Geoffrey in the note she'd sent as a concession that she would be willing to help, after all. Thank goodness for that. She went on, reading the time and designated meeting place, but Evie didn't mention a reason for the rendezvous. Perhaps, though, that was better, in case her father had happened to intercept the note.

Lucinda frowned. Now not only was her father excluded, he wasn't to be trusted. It couldn't go on like this. Her heart wouldn't be able to stand it. She dashed off a note to Evie, accepting the invitation, and then went about composing one to Geoffrey that would convince him to join her.

"Lucinda?" her father's voice came, while he knocked at her bedchamber door.

Drat. "Come in, Papa," she called, sliding the notes to and from Evie under her appointment book. "What is it?"

"I have a meeting this morning," he said, glancing at her writing desk. "Before I leave, I want to make certain that . . . nothing untoward will happen while I'm gone."

" 'Untoward?' " she repeated, indignant. "Do you mean will I elope with a fishmonger or something? I assure you that I won't." She drew a slow breath. "In fact, I was just writing Geoffrey a note, asking if he'd allow me to accompany him to Tattersall's today. He was going to look at a new hunter, and, well, I may have been a little sharp with him yesterday."

"In what way?"

"He . . . he asked me to marry him."

Both the general's eyebrows lifted. "He did? Why didn't you tell me? How — what did you say to him?"

"I told him I wished to wait until this mess with Robert is resolved," she answered, relieved to be able to tell the truth, however poorly it sufficed. Things were so complicated. "I think he may have taken that as a refusal, and I want to assure him that is not so."

"I can't fault you for your loyalty or your compassion," her father said, "though I could wish you had better taste in friends." Nodding, he backed out of the doorway. "Please tell Geoffrey I said hello, and ask him if he's finished the chapter."

"I will, Papa."

Robert and Bradshaw arrived at Tattersall's a few minutes before Saint and Evelyn. Thankfully, a large crowd was already gathering at the corrals and beneath the open tents of the market, so remaining unseen wouldn't be too much of a challenge. Overhearing conversation would be a much stickier proposition, but Robert was nothing if not determined.

"Where do you want me?" Shaw asked, as they left Tolley and Zeus in the care of a pair of likely-looking urchins.

"Up high, if you can," he answered. "You'll have to make certain that if Geoffrey leaves here, you'll be able to get to his lodgings before he does. Otherwise I may not be the only one in trouble."

Shaw nodded. "*If* he says something incriminating, and *if* you decide it's enough to break into his home and look for those papers. Because you won't do it otherwise, right?"

Robert looked at his older brother. "I may dislike Geoffrey, but I dislike the thought of being arrested even more."

"Good enough." Shaw cuffed him on the shoulder. "I'll be about, then. And you?"

"I'll be here. Hopefully, out of sight and within earshot." He turned away, but Bradshaw caught his arm before he could vanish into the crowd.

"And please tell me," his brother said, a slight grin on his face, "where you found those clothes."

"In the back corner of the stable. I didn't want to be recognized."

"I don't think you'll have to worry about that."

His goal had been to look like one of the men working the stables at Tattersall's. To that end, aside from the battered hat pulled low over his eyes and the dirty clothes, he'd borrowed a pair of John the groom's mud and manure-covered work boots. Thankfully, they fit well enough that he wouldn't cripple himself any further wearing them. Now, as long as no one recognized him, he'd be able to wander fairly freely about the grounds, virtually unnoticed. And not smelling particularly inviting, either, but if anything, that helped his disguise.

Once he emerged onto the crowded grounds he hung along the fringes, waiting for Saint and Evie to arrive. Belatedly it occurred to him that with the combination of the hordes of milling people and the tension running through him, he should be on the verge of a blind panic. It stayed at bay, though, back in the dark recesses of his mind that he simply didn't have time to contemplate at the moment.

He spotted Shaw almost immediately, up on a nearby balcony and chatting happily with a pretty young lady there. Robert grinned. That figured. Somehow Bradshaw always knew how to make the best of a situation.

As he finished a circuit of the grounds, he saw Lord and Lady St. Aubyn arrive. He still couldn't believe they were willing to do this for him. Apparently he had better friends than he knew — or deserved.

Saint looked perfectly at ease, but he was more used to subterfuge than his wife. Evie kept peeking over her shoulder, gazing into the crowd, obviously looking for him or Bradshaw. He started to approach, to let them know that everything was in place, but the crowd didn't move aside for a horse handler. It took a few moments, and some apologies, before he reached them.

"Good morning, milord, milady," he drawled, tipping his hat at them.

Evelyn covered her mouth. "Wh— For heaven's sake! You startled me."

Saint, though, grinned. "You smell," he noted.

"It's part of the plan. Shaw's up over my shoulder." He focused on Evie. "Try not to notice either of us. We're not here, remember?"

She drew a breath. "I remember. Lucinda sent a note that she would try to persuade Lord Geoffrey to accompany her here, but I haven't heard anything since. I'm certain she'll manage it."

"So am I."

Lucinda meant to help them, meant to help him. He tried not to grin like an idiot as he faded back into the crowd, but he wanted to smile, and sing, and dance. She'd made her decision. Of course in truth it only meant she didn't trust everything about Lord Geoffrey, not that she'd chosen *him* above Society's golden boy. She'd be a fool to do so.

If she did suspect Geoffrey, though, she was also being foolish to put herself in his company. For that, Robert blamed himself. If it looked as though Geoffrey suspected anything, he would end the charade himself — even if it meant having to flee England. He wouldn't let Lucinda be hurt. Not for him, not for anyone.

He sensed her arrival before he saw her. Warmth ran soft along his skin, like an unseen breeze, and when he turned around, she was there. With *him.*

She'd worn a low-cut, close-fitting muslin that clung to her figure and drew his attention to the soft, creamy curve of her breasts. His mouth went dry. No wonder Geoffrey seemed so attentive, and no wonder Robert wanted to smash the man's face into a pulp

— whether he'd turned traitor or not.

As Evie beckoned to the two of them, he worked his own way closer. Everyone shook hands and exchanged hugs, as friendly as if they were just out for a day at the horse auctions. Robert found himself studying Geoffrey, looking for some external sign that he could possibly have done what they now suspected. Amiable and handsome, he looked the embodiment of the perfect English gentleman.

Perhaps if Robert had looked — had behaved — more like one himself, the *ton* wouldn't have been so quick to believe the rumors. He glanced at his rough, smelly clothing. No one would have any trouble believing the worst of him at the moment. All he could do was hope no one recognized him.

". . . make a purchase for the general's birthday, but you know how particular he is," Lucinda was saying, her hand around Geoffrey's arm.

"It's always good to know who's producing the quality animals," Geoffrey returned, "whether you buy one today or not."

"I don't know about that." Saint took Evie's arm and led the way through the crowd toward the front of the bidders. "One

449

good horse from a breeder doesn't neces- sarily mean the rest will be of the same quality. If you see one you like, you should purchase it. You can always sell it again later, if your father doesn't approve. Don't you think so, Lord Geoffrey?"

"Just Geoffrey, please. And while I admire the sentiment, I tend to be a little more cautious in my purchases."

"That's right, you're the fourth son, aren't you?" Saint said, striking just the right tone between commiseration and insult. "I don't know Fenley well at all, but the rumor is that his grip can be rather — how shall I put it — tight."

Geoffrey chuckled. "Yes, it can be. It's always been his philosophy that the 'extra' sons make their own way."

"That's rather severe." Lucinda gave him a sympathetic look. "I hope he's proud that you've done so well."

Robert wanted to kiss her. She was playing the game. From what he knew and what he was learning, Geoffrey wanted a promotion, and the choice of assignment the rank would gain him. If he couldn't get it through marriage, a war would be his next most likely opportunity. Of course if he married he would have to have someone else take the blame for the thefts — which was probably where Robert and the rumors had come in extremely handy.

Flashing his famous smile, Geoffrey lifted Lucinda's hand to kiss her knuckles. "He'll be even more proud to see me settled and with a tenable career."

"Which career would that be?" Saint asked. "You're still in the Army, aren't you?"

"I am. And there are still opportunities there. I intend to take one, and make it my own." He smiled again at Lucinda. "As I intend to make Lucinda my own."

Bastard. If he wasn't guilty, Robert was going to have to seriously consider several methods of getting rid of him anyway. He edged closer, leaning against a wagon wheel and lowering his hat brim past his eyes.

"I'll wager the Carroways wish that Robert hadn't chosen a career with the Army," Saint drawled.

Evie flushed. "Saint! Georgiana's my friend. That's a terrible thing to say."

"It's also true," he returned.

"I . . . have to admit, this whole thing's made more than enough problems for the general," Lucinda said slowly.

Robert looked up. She gazed straight at him, and for a moment his heart stopped. Then she deliberately faced Geoffrey again. "Robert is my friend, and I won't forget that, but it would be nonsense to say that we're all happy this happened."

"They're almost finished with the teams," Saint announced.

Lucinda looked startled. "So soon?" Facing Geoffrey, she extricated her hand. "Will you excuse me for just a moment?"

"Of course. You shouldn't go anywhere alone, though. Shall I fetch your maid from the carriage?"

"I'll go with you, Luce," Evie said. "I could use a bit of refreshment myself."

Thinking fast, Robert pushed away from the wagon, leading the way toward the nearest building. The alley behind was empty, and he turned into it. Lucinda and Evie followed a moment later. He couldn't help smiling as Luce appeared. "How in the world did you know I was —"

She grabbed his lapels, leaned up, and kissed him. Robert wanted to wrap his arms around her and hold her close, but even as he remembered how filthy he was, he heard Evelyn gasp.

"Lucinda," he managed as he backed away, kissing her once more because he simply couldn't help himself. "Careful. Someone will see."

"I saw," Evie noted, her eyes still wide. "How long has this been going on?"

"I don't think we have time for that right now," Lucinda returned, her gaze still on him.

What he saw in her clear hazel eyes filled him with more hope and more terror than anything he'd faced in the past five years. He stroked his fingers along her cheek. "I'm sorry to put you through this. I know you didn't want to be involv—"

"I changed my mind," she interrupted, then took a moment to run her gaze down the length of him and back. "You look . . . interesting."

"Um, excuse me, but if you don't have time to tell me what's going on, you certainly don't have time for this," Evie put in. "We need to get back. Did you hear enough to convince you?"

"Almost," he returned. "Evie, I need a moment."

Lady St. Aubyn grimaced. "Yes, of course you do. I'll be over there." She stalked back to the entrance of the alley, folded her arms across her chest, and turned her back on the two of them.

"What do you want to know?" Lucinda asked, tugging at his sleeve.

"You're the reason I have another day, aren't you?" he murmured, searching her eyes.

"We'd best be right about this, Robert," she whispered back, "or I will have a great deal of apologizing to do to my father."

"Speaking of General Barrett, I . . . need to know if you would be willing to ask him about the source of the rumors again. No one else needs to hear about it, but it would answer the last question for me about this."

"About Geoffrey, you mean," she said quietly.

"Lucinda, I don't know how else to do this. I'm sorr—"

"My father told Geoffrey about you and Chateau Pagnon. It had to have been the day before he went to his meeting," she interrupted. "It was before I confirmed that you were the one who told me, but he already knew it was you."

White-hot relief pierced through him. They'd been right. It had to be Geoffrey. His lips curved in a smile, even though he knew it wasn't appropriate, even though he knew how much she had to have hated asking her father the question. "Thank you."

"I like that," she whispered.

"Like what?"

She lifted her hand, running her fingers along his mouth. "When you smile." Leaning up, she kissed him again, slowly, as if she savored the touch as much as he did. "We have to get back."

"And I have an errand to run. Can you keep him occupied?"

"Yes. Be careful, Robert. And if you have to leave the country to save yourself, then leave. But you had best get word to me about where you are."

He touched her cheek. "You're the reason I smile," he murmured, and strode away. He had a house to break into.

Chapter 23

When I found so astonishing a power placed within my hands, I hesitated a long time concerning the manner in which I should employ it.

— Victor Frankenstein, *Frankenstein*

"Stop stalling," Robert snapped, stalking back and forth. "I don't like leaving Lucinda there to keep that bastard at bay."

"I believe St. Aubyn and Evie are with her," Tristan said dryly, his gaze on the small house beyond the row of shrubs. "And I prefer not to be seen breaking in somewhere."

"He's not home, Dare. That's the point. Jesus Christ." Robert pointed at the leopard-shaped face piece Tristan held in one hand. "And we have masks. Let's go." Their third companion leaned against an elm tree, but he wasn't watching the house. Rather, he'd been staring at Robert for the past three minutes. And it was becoming rather annoying. "What?" he finally snapped, turning.

The Duke of Wycliffe tilted his head. "I'm merely trying to get used to a few things," he drawled. "Your clothes, for one."

"I told you, it's a disguise. Bloody hell."

"And your increased vocabulary, for another."

"Get used to it later." Robert threw up his hands. "I'm going. You two can talk each other to death if you want, but don't expect me to listen to it."

Grumbling, he drew the tiger mask over his face and started across the street. A moment later he heard Wycliffe and Tristan fall in behind him, and he increased his pace, trying not to limp. If anything could give him away, it would be that.

"Ready?" he murmured, lifting his hand to the door knocker. "Office first, then library, and then bedchamber. If it's not any of those places, we tear the damned house apart."

The other two nodded, and he knocked at the door. A moment later it opened. The butler, a dignified older man, gave them one look and shrieked. "Robbers!"

Scrambling backward as Robert pushed his way into the house, the butler grabbed a walking cane and swung it. Robert intercepted, blocking the blow with his arm and then wrenching the cane from the butler's hands. "Get in there," he growled, gesturing at the closet off the morning room.

"But —"

"Inside," Wycliffe echoed in his lower rumble, half lifting the servant off his feet and tossing him into the storage room.

A pair of footmen emerged from the servants' hall. Pointing the cane like a pistol, Robert advanced on them. "Both of you, in there with the butler."

"Six servants total," Wycliffe called, releasing the butler's neckcloth.

"And only three of you," the larger of the two footmen said, fisting both hands.

"We're not after anything that rightfully belongs here," Robert snapped, losing patience, "and we don't want to hurt anyone. But don't get in our way."

"Bugger that."

The footman swung at him. Ducking, Robert brought the cane around and thwacked it into the side of the man's head. He dropped like a stone. Robert looked at the second man. "In the closet or on the floor. Your choice."

With a grimace the man lifted his hands and sidestepped toward the storage room. Tristan crouched to grab the downed servant under the arms and drag him inside, as well.

"Next time," he said, panting, "only knock out the scrawny ones."

"Three more," Robert said, heading down the servants' hall toward the kitchens. "Check upstairs."

He heard Tristan pound up the stairs while Wycliffe kept watch on the three in the closet. It was doubtful the servants knew anything about Lord Geoffrey's activities, but neither did he want them fleeing the house and bringing half of Bow Street back with them. The search needed to be done quickly, and they needed to be gone before Geoffrey returned.

A cook and her helper washed pots in the kitchen, and it only took a moment's persuasion to convince them to join their fellows. Dare came downstairs at the same time, a large, panicked-looking-housekeeper preceding him. As soon as the servants were closed in, Wycliffe locked and barricaded the closet door.

"All right," Dare muttered. "Let's find those damned papers."

"That's a fine-looking bay," Geoffrey said, leaning so close to Lucinda that she could feel his breath on her cheek.

"Yes, he's lovely," she agreed, using every ounce of willpower to keep from edging away from him. "I've seen him at auction before though, haven't I?"

"You have," Saint agreed. "He threw Lord Rayburne last week, and that was after he bit Totley's son last autumn."

"Hm. Probably a bit headstrong for Papa, then." She'd spied Bradshaw a few moments earlier, seated on a balcony with half a dozen young ladies of questionable reputation. With Saint beside her and Shaw keeping a watch, she should have felt perfectly safe. She couldn't help thinking, though, that the man standing next to her had been inside her house, had chatted and lied about God knew what with her father, had even kissed her and asked her to marry him.

And if they were right, he'd stolen papers that could have no purpose but to start a war. He'd spread a rumor knowing the damage it would do to another man — counting on the damage it would do. Why? Had Robert just been convenient? Or had Geoffrey considered his victim, and figured that Robert would be an easy target? Either way, they were in the process of proving him wrong.

"Half the fun with a headstrong animal is breaking it," Geoffrey observed.

Lucinda kept her gaze on the pen before them, hoping he'd been speaking in generalities and hadn't meant to send anyone in particular — her — a message. And she knew that wasn't so.

"Lord Geoffrey, you're hoping for a posting in India, are you not?" Evie said brightly.

"Yes, I am. Wellington served there, and it didn't do *him* any harm."

"And would you wish your spouse to join you there?"

Geoffrey turned his pretty green eyes on Lucinda. "I expect that she would wish to be by my side."

But her father had made it clear to Geoffrey that the decision of whether or not to travel to India would be hers. She couldn't mention that, though, without him realizing that she'd been eavesdropping. How odd, though, that even before she'd known about his involvement in this mess, the idea of Geoffrey going off to India without her for several years hadn't caused her a moment of hesitation — while just the thought of Robert fleeing London sent her into a panic of yearning and need.

Thank goodness this friendly conversation was only a pretense now. She forced a smile. "I've heard so many enchanting things about India. The spices, the music — it all seems so exotic." She paused as another thought occurred to her. As long as they were looking for evidence . . . "I'm certain the general would enjoy it there, as well."

Something passed behind those emerald eyes, so quickly she couldn't be certain what it was. "General Barrett? He'd be welcome, of course, but I hardly think he'd find it interesting. None of his old cronies would be there, after all, for him to regale with his stories."

"But you and I would be there."

"Yes, of course. Having a superior officer of General Barrett's reputation in the house would be very prestigious, to be sure, but he is becoming elderly, Lucinda. Don't you think he'd be more comfortable here? The ocean voyage itself can be quite harrowing."

Well, this was interesting. General Barrett's "reputation" for honesty and fairness would also have the effect of making it more difficult for his son-in-law if said relation intended to engage in smuggling, or coercion, or profiteering, the swiftest, surest ways for an enterprising young major to make his fortune. "My goodness. 'Harrowing?' I'm not certain *I'd* be comfortable there," she returned. "If I even survived the journey."

His smile tightened. "Surely this is a conversation best left for another time and another setting," he murmured.

"I'm merely familiarizing myself with your plans," she said. "It occurs to me that you haven't told me much more than the basics. If you wish us to marry, I think I have some right to know where I'm expected to live, for instance."

"You're a general's daughter. Surely you're accustomed to a military lifestyle."

"I was practically a child when my father fought on the Continent. I stayed with my aunt, and at various finishing schools. He didn't want me traveling about in soldiers' camps."

He gazed at her. "So your delay in answering my proposal wasn't in deference to Carroway's troubles," he said slowly. "You don't wish to marry me at all."

Drat. Suspecting him as she did, he'd made her more angry with practically every sentence he spoke, and she'd stepped too far. "That's not what I said. I merely wish to have all possible information first."

"Look, Lucinda," Evelyn broke in, "that bay is gorgeous."

"And you chose here to have this conversation?" Geoffrey pursued, ignoring Evie.

Oh, hang being amiable. "You're the one who said you enjoyed breaking headstrong animals," she retorted. "How am I supposed to interpret that?"

He wrapped hard fingers around her upper arm. "Answer me this, Lucinda. After this mess with your good friend is concluded, do you intend to accept my proposal? Or are you merely baiting me to amuse your friends and waste my . . ."

This time she didn't want to interpret what flashed across his eyes. Closing his mouth, he turned on his heel.

"Geoffrey!" she called after him. "Where are you —"

"Damnation," Saint hissed. "A little hard on him, weren't you?"

"If I'd fluttered and giggled he would have known something was wrong," she returned, turning her frantic gaze toward Bradshaw. He'd vanished as well, hopefully to warn Robert that Geoffrey was most likely on his way home. "Blast it. I'm so stupid."

"No, you're not," Evie countered.

"You're right. Once this began, one way or another he was bound to realize we were delaying him here for no particular reason. That's why Bradshaw was keeping an eye on things, as well."

"What vehicle did you arrive in?" Saint asked, taking one of the ladies' hands in each of his and heading away from the pens.

"A curricle. My maid was waiting for us there. Oh, goodness. He wouldn't hurt Helena, would he?"

"I don't think so. It would take him a moment to remove her, though. Shaw's on horseback, so he should end with a five- or six-minute lead on Newcombe. I hope."

"What do we do?" she asked, still cursing herself. If she'd held her tongue for just a few more moments — oh, what if they hadn't had time to find the documents? She might have just condemned Robert.

"You said your father had a meeting this morning," Saint prompted.

"Yes, at the Horse Guards."

"Then we go to the Horse Guards and find him. If Robert has the evidence, he'll need someone to show it to."

"It's not here, either," Robert growled, shoving the mask up on the top of his head. Damnation. The office had been immacu-

465

late, as if no one had ever done a minute's work inside, though they'd left it in less than pristine condition. Likewise the books in the library didn't look as though they'd ever been opened. The fact that most of them now rested in haphazard stacks on the floor didn't bother him in the least. Lord Geoffrey had made far more of a shambles of his life than they were making of the bastard's house.

"Not in the cabinet either," Tristan seconded. He straightened from his crouch, glancing at Wycliffe as the duke went through the scattering of books and papers on the oak credenza. After a moment, Wycliffe shook his head.

Robert cursed. "It's here somewhere. It has to be. If you had papers which could either make you a great deal of money or get you thrown in prison, you would want them somewhere close by, so you wouldn't have to worry about someone stumbling across them. At the same time, you wouldn't want your servants to be able to find them, and you wouldn't want to hide them somewhere you'd look conspicuous retrieving them or checking on them."

"That still leaves a great many hiding places," Tristan noted, brushing his hands across his thighs.

Pacing around the room, Robert ran the floor plan through his mind. It was a small house, a rented lodging. That in itself pointed to the fact that Geoffrey was not plump in the pockets. He was, however, a self-professed war hero with a great deal of pride in his looks and his reputation. A war hero. One who would either marry to become a major, or start a war to receive a battle promotion.

"His uniform," he said, heading out the door and toward the stairs. "Where do you think he keeps his uniform?"

"His uniform?" Tristan repeated. "Why —"

"He's still in the army," Robert said over his shoulder. "He would have had it pressed and put away — ready for whichever special occasion could give him the most use out of it — with no one else allowed to touch it. It's his pride and joy; his future, one way or the other."

"But the papers would make him a traitor," his brother protested, topping the stairs behind him and striding down the hallway toward Geoffrey's private rooms. "Isn't keeping them with his uniform a bit odd?"

"Not if you're him. They're his way to a promotion. How does that make him a traitor?"

Wycliffe gave a low whistle. "You're turning me into a believer, and we haven't even found anything yet."

"I've been thinking about it quite a bit." Robert shoved open the bedchamber door.

Considering what he'd deduced to be a modest income, the number of wardrobes in the large double suite bedchamber was startling. Obviously this was where the majority of Lord Geoffrey's money went.

"And I thought Georgiana had too many clothes," Tristan muttered, heading for the wardrobe farthest to the right.

Robert flung open the one next to it, rifling through jackets and waistcoats, trousers, and breeches. Apparently shirts were located in a different section of the room altogether. Kneeling, he yanked open the bottom drawers to find stockings and neckcloths, but no uniform.

Quiet as the house was, the sound of the front door opening sounded as loud as a pistol shot. He jerked to his feet, striding for the hallway. Bradshaw's suggestion of beating the truth out of Lord Geoffrey was beginning to seem like a good idea.

"Any housebreakers here?" Bradshaw's voice came, a loud, whispered yell.

Robert leaned over the balcony railing. "Upstairs."

"He's left Tattersall's," Bradshaw panted. "And he didn't look happy."

"What about Lucinda?"

"He left her there," Shaw returned, climbing the stairs as he explained. "It looked as though they were arguing, and then he rode off. He was heading straight for his carriage. He can't be more than five minutes behind me."

"I found something!" Wycliffe called.

Robert sprinted back for the bedchamber. The duke dragged a small oak trunk from beneath the raised bed.

"It's locked," Wycliffe said, pulling it further into the open. "And I don't suppose we'll find the key anywhere in the house."

"No, if that's his uniform, he'll have the key with him," Robert said, squatting down to examine the mechanism. By the time he'd made his accidental escape from Chateau Pagnon, all he had left of his uniform were torn mud- and bloodstained shreds of his trousers and a ripped undershirt. If he had somehow returned with a wearable jacket or boots, he would have burned them.

Geoffrey, though, was proud of his uniform, proud of the prestige it gave him, and the money it would eventually earn him. The lock was good quality, better than the chest demanded. "This is it." It had to be.

"Can you pick it?" Bradshaw asked, joining them.

"I'm a recluse, not a burglar," Robert returned with a half smile. In truth, he probably *could* have picked it, but with Geoffrey on the way, he didn't want to take the time. Instead he pulled a pistol from his pocket.

"Robert," Tristan said, his expression startled. "What did you bring that for?"

"Unforeseen circumstances," he answered, pulling back the hammer. At least his hand wasn't shaking; it had been when he'd retrieved the thing from Bradshaw's room and loaded it.

"Fire in the hole," he muttered, and pulled the trigger.

In the closed room the roar and spit was louder than he remembered, and he couldn't help flinching from the explosion. He hadn't fired a weapon in just under four years, but at least his aim hadn't faltered. The front of the trunk had splintered, and the lock had been obliterated.

"I don't think anyone outside heard that, do you?" Bradshaw said sarcastically, scowling. "For the devil's sake, Bit."

"We're in a hurry." Robert shoved open the lid. Inside, marred only by a bullet hole through the left side of the jacket, lay a neatly folded, perfectly pressed, captain's uniform.

"Good shot," Wycliffe noted, grabbing the jacket and shaking it. "Right through the heart."

A flutter of folded papers thunked to the floor. For a brief moment, Robert closed his eyes. Thank Lucifer. He'd been right. "Check them," he barked, digging deeper into the trunk. Maps were supposed to be missing as well, and they needed to find everything — not just to convict Geoffrey, but to ensure that England didn't end up having to go to war against Bonaparte again.

"I'll be damned," Tristan said slowly, anger dripping from his voice. "These are the lists. Englishmen with sympathies for Napoleon. It's a shame we can't hang onto these for a few days and make a few visits."

Robert barely glanced up as he dug through the trunk. "They can sympathize with whomever they want, as long as they don't do anything about it."

His fingers touched a rolled parchment, lodged in the deepest corner and covered by Geoffrey's dress sword. He pulled it free, opening it across the top of the trunk. St. Helena Island spread out before him, with notations of elevation and distance, and detailed blueprints of the fortress there.

"The maps," Tristan said, gripping Robert's shoulder. "You did it."

"And now let's get out of here, if you don't mind," Bradshaw suggested. "I would enjoy being a hero, but I could do without being arrested for burglary and doing something nefarious with the household staff."

"They're locked in the storage closet," Tristan supplied, stacking the papers and tucking them under his arm.

They headed down the stairs and out the front door. No sign of Geoffrey yet, but he wasn't going to be happy when he arrived. They'd left Tolley and the other horses around the corner, but Robert stopped Tristan before he could mount.

"I need those papers," he said, holding out his hand.

"I'll get them to the Horse Guards," the viscount said, frowning. "Don't worry about that. I want you somewhere safe."

"They aren't going to the Horse Guards."

Wycliffe went very still. "Beg pardon?"

"Lord Geoffrey got these by going through General Barrett. The general's career could be destroyed if we go straight to his headquarters and announce that his prospective son-in-law is the traitor everyone's been looking for."

"Um, Bit, I was under the impression that

472

you weren't overly fond of General Barrett."

"I'm not," he answered, taking the papers from Tristan and folding them into his worn livestock handler's jacket. "I *am* fond of his daughter." Hurting Barrett would hurt her, and he wouldn't allow that to happen. In addition, the animosity he felt toward the general was entirely personal; he'd begun to realize that he had no real wish to ruin a man who in everyone else's estimation was honorable and honest.

"So we're going to Barrett House?"

He swung up on Tolley. "No, *I'm* going to Barrett House. You're going to Carroway House and be prepared to either tell the authorities I left for America or attest to the fact that we found these things in Geoffrey's uniform trunk."

"This is your play, Bit," Tristan said reluctantly. "But for God's sake, be careful."

"I will be," Robert answered, clucking to Tolley. Of course his health would depend on how General Barrett received the news, but he was willing to take the risk. The stakes were much higher than Geoffrey's future, or his own, anyway. The stakes were Lucinda's future, and her happiness.

Chapter 24

The tale which I have recorded would be incomplete without this final and wonderful catastrophe.

— Robert Walton, *Frankenstein*

Lucinda could tell from the looks on the sentries' faces that they were none too happy to see Evie calling at the Horse Guards, even in the company of General Barrett's daughter. Having St. Aubyn there had to make them even more nervous, and truth be told, she was somewhat relieved that her father had been there and gone already. He certainly wouldn't have been pleased to see her in the company she was keeping, either.

"He must be home, then," she said, as Saint handed her back into his curricle. "That's probably better, anyway. I can talk to him and try to make him see reason. If we all jump in at once, he'll just become defensive."

"You shouldn't confront him alone," Evie said, the worried lines of her face deepening.

"It's not so much confronting him as making certain he keeps an open mind," she returned, hoping that in this grand scheme of Robert's, someone had been assigned to let her know that he'd found the papers and gotten away from Geoffrey's house safely.

"You're taking quite a risk, Lucinda," Saint said, his gaze on the street ahead. "Once you level an accusation at Geoffrey, you can't go back. And Robert . . . isn't the most likely man in the world to stand by anyone. Are you sure you —"

"Michael, she knows," Evie interrupted, putting a hand over his.

Lucinda was thankful for the vote of confidence. She did know what accusing Geoffrey would mean. It was Robert who left her feeling uncertain — not about whether he could stop Geoffrey, but about whether he would vanish back into the shadows, back into himself, when he'd finished.

"Are you certain you don't want us to stay here with you?" Evie asked.

Blinking, Lucinda looked up. The carriage rolled to a stop in front of her home. "I'm certain."

"If the others find what they're looking for," Saint added, "they're likely to run them straight to the Horse Guards. Your father will be called there to see the evidence."

Lucinda nodded as she and Helena stepped to the ground. "Perhaps I can prepare him a little for it."

"Good luck, then. We'll head to Carroway House. The rest of the excitement's likely to happen there." With a cluck, Saint sent the team back down the drive.

Ballow opened the door as she reached it. "The general is in his office," he stated as she handed over her shawl. "Something seems to be . . . amiss."

Oh, dear. Nothing should have happened yet — it was too soon. Gathering her skirts, she hurried to his office, only to find his door locked. "Papa?" she called, knocking. "Papa, I need to speak to you."

His heavy tread approached, and the door rattled and opened. The expression on his face — hard, set, and angry — stopped her for a moment. "I need to speak to you, as well," he grated, stepping aside so she could enter.

"What's wrong?" she asked, and then her breath caught. Lord Geoffrey leaned in the window sill, gazing at her. "Geoffrey?" she asked, faltering for something to say. "Why did you abandon me at Tattersall's? And why are you here? Papa, what's going on?"

"I was just leaving," Geoffrey said, giving her a stiff nod as he passed her on the way to the door.

The first thing that occurred to her was that if he was here, then Robert would have a few more minutes to finish searching his home. "Did I say something to offend you?"

In the doorway he faced her. "I am disappointed," he murmured. "I had thought better of you."

Frowning, she watched him make his way down the hall and out the front door. When she turned back, her father's gaze was on her. "You went behind my back," he said quietly. "After you asked for my patience, you used that time to attempt to hurt someone else — someone I consider a friend. Someone I had hoped you would see as more than a friend."

"What in the world has he been telling you?"

Geoffrey couldn't know everything; if he did, he would have headed straight home instead of detouring to carry tales to her father. A thought turned her heart cold. He would have headed home unless he didn't have the papers there, or had them hidden so well that no one would ever find them — unless he had figured them out and had already taken steps to protect himself.

"What he told me," the general returned, raising his voice and not bothering to close the office door, "is that you've been conspiring with your so-called friends in an attempt to put the blame for the Horse Guards theft away from Robert Carroway. And that you and your friends have settled on him as your scapegoat."

"I —"

"Geoffrey even told me he's discovered that Carroway has made plans to plant the evidence, since by now he's realized that obviously he can't get rid of it without us knowing."

If there was one thing Geoffrey didn't lack, it was nerves. And his tale had enough of a flavor of the truth to make repudiating it extremely difficult. "Papa, there's more to this than you may realize."

"Than *I* may realize? Yes, I suppose thirty years serving in His Majesty's Army and three years as a senior member of the Horse Guards counts for nothing compared to the games of you and your cronies."

"That is not —"

"I beg your pardon, sir, but you may not enter this house!" Ballow's voice came, pitched high with distress.

Lucinda whipped around, just in time to see Robert shove the butler against the door and stride into the foyer. She could tell, just from the light glinting in his eyes, that he'd been successful. Her heart leapt. Less than a second later, though, tension and dread strangled through her again. If he'd found the papers, he should have gone straight to the Horse Guards. "Robert," she said shakily, "what are you doing here? You don't have —"

"Lucinda," he said, stopping at her side. His gaze, though, was on her father. "I require a word with General Barrett. In private."

"I want you out of my house, you damned rogue. Don't mistake my patience for leniency."

"Luce," Robert murmured, leaning closer, "please wait for us in the library."

She nodded. "Is everything all right?" she whispered, touching his sleeve.

"It will be."

Robert waited until she'd gone, then faced her father again. "Shall we do this in your office, or here in the hallway?"

"We won't do it at all," the general retorted. "Don't make me throw you bodily out of here, Carroway. Have the dignity to leave on your own."

"I will. In a few minutes." Robert gestured at the office, doing his best to conceal his own anger and frustration. "Inside, sir."

General Barrett gave him an assessing look, obviously calculating the three inches in height and twenty-five years in age difference between them. Looking as though he'd rather chew glass, Barrett nodded. "Two minutes," he snapped.

It would probably take longer than that. Robert followed him in, closing and locking the door behind him. "Sit, sir," he instructed.

"Nothing you say will convince me that you are anything but a traitor, Carroway. So unless you intend to kill me — which I don't suggest, given the number of witnesses in this house — you need to leave. Not just my home, but the country. That is the only favor I will do for you, and that is for Lucinda's sake."

"In April of 1814," Robert began, sitting in one of the desk's facing chairs and keeping his gaze on the cluttered desk surface, "you were in charge of one of the Army divisions surrounding Bayonne."

480

"I was there," the general snapped. "You don't need to tell me."

"Yes, I do. Bonaparte was finished; both sides had called a ceasefire."

"I know —"

"But you knew that General Thouvenot was still holding onto Bayonne, and that he wouldn't let go. And you also had word from French deserters that Thouvenot intended to attack you."

"That information was unreliable."

"Ah. So that's why you sent a patrol out in the middle of the night to take a survey of French entrenchments — because you knew no one was going to be changing positions."

"That is correct. What —"

"That was my patrol, General Barrett," Robert forced out, having to clench his fists to keep his voice low and steady. "A thousand French soldiers against fifteen English troops. Most of my men were dead before they could raise their weapons. Me they beat into unconsciousness, because their command wanted British officers for questioning."

The general's face had gone very still, gray tinging his usually ruddy countenance. "We had word," he said after a moment. "Everyone in the scouting patrol was killed."

"All but one. And then, twenty days after you beat him back into Bayonne, Thouvenot finally accepted that Bonaparte had abdicated, and the war ended." He leaned forward, lifting his gaze to meet the general's steel gray eyes. "But not for me. Chateau Pagnon never surrendered. The British Army never tried to take it. Their network stayed active, planning and plotting for Bonaparte's escape. They asked me about you, about your family, because you were my division commander and they were looking for ways to either assassinate British leaders or blackmail them."

"You —"

"I didn't say a word, General. And then finally, after seven months, when I realized I wasn't going to be able to hold out much longer, after I'd seen . . . things I won't ever be able to forget, I tricked them into killing me. Or into making a good try at it, anyway. Deciding I was dead, they tossed me over the wall. The Spanish resistance found me two days later and threw on enough bandages to hold me together." It had been worse than that, but telling it didn't serve any purpose. All he needed to do was convince General Barrett that he wasn't a traitor. The rest was for him, and he had no intention of sharing it.

"So . . . you blame me for what happened to you," the general said slowly, his voice rasping, as though his mouth had gone dry. "Is this why you —"

"Yes, I did blame you," Robert retorted. "But I don't want revenge. And I damned well don't want another war." He shuddered. "What happened to me, I would never wish on anyone else."

"Then —"

"Now, I need you to listen to me, very carefully. And not just for my sake or yours, but for Lucinda's. No interruptions, no contradictions, until I'm finished. Is that clear?"

The gruff look came into the general's face again. "If that's the only way to be rid of you," he growled, but his voice lacked conviction.

"It is. First, how long were those documents missing from the Horse Guards before the rumors about the theft started?"

Barrett narrowed his eyes. "One day," he finally said.

"And how long after you told Lord Geoffrey Newcombe that I'd been imprisoned at Chateau Pagnon did that news come out?"

"I don't —"

"Answer the bloody question."

The general thought about it; Robert could see the reluctant affirmation in his eyes. "Twelve hours. Perhaps less."

"I make a good scapegoat," Robert murmured, "but I didn't do it."

"And you think Geoffrey did."

"I *know* Geoffrey did." Taking a breath, Robert pulled the folded papers and blueprints from inside his coat and laid them on the general's desk. "I found them a few minutes ago, in Geoffrey's uniform trunk. The Duke of Wycliffe will attest to that fact, if it becomes necessary."

"You put them there. He told me you would attempt to put your theft onto his shoulders."

"Why? What would I have to gain from taking them in the first place?"

"I . . ." The general swore. "But what would Geoffrey have to gain?"

"Geoffrey wants a command in India. At the moment, he's a poor soldier with a good name. He can marry Lucinda and gain a promotion, but that's only if she agrees to it. In the meantime, he needs insurance. With those papers, he gains the money for selling them, and another war with Bonaparte, either or both of which would suffice to net him precisely what he wants."

"And what about your involvement?"

He shrugged. "I'm convenient, and not very popular, and a potential rival to Lucinda's affections. But the real question, General, is what about *your* involvement?"

The general lurched to his feet. "Are you accusing me of —"

"No, I'm not. But you're the reason Geoffrey had access to the Horse Guards, and he's made it clear to anyone who will listen that he considers you his mentor. This will probably have repercussions for you."

"He was just here," Barrett said, almost to himself. "Newcombe. Telling me that Lucinda and her friends had hatched a plot to save your reputation and discredit him. I was furious, but at the same time I remember thinking that Lucinda's friends had married an interesting assortment of rogues — Dare and St. Aubyn, to be exact — and I couldn't figure out why in the world they would have decided to dislike Geoffrey. Lucinda likes him, you know. Or she did."

"Yes, she did." Robert pushed to his feet. "So you have the recovered papers there in front of you, and my story to weigh against Geoffrey's. And your own reputation to think about. I'll be in the library when you come to a decision about what to do."

"And then you'll go ahead and discredit

Geoffrey and myself and go your merry way, laughing."

"No, I won't, because that would hurt Lucinda." He paused, wondering whether the general could hear in his voice how important that particular point was to him. "I will abide by whatever you decide," he continued. "The only thing I ask is that if you decide to blame me for all of this, you will make certain my family is cleared of any wrongdoing." What it would mean if soldiers came to his door to arrest him, he didn't know, but he did know that the choice rightfully needed to be left to General Augustus Barrett. And right and wrong, justice and iniquity, had come to be very important to him over the past few years.

He left the office, closing the door behind him. Lucinda sat on a couch in the library, her hands folded primly on her lap and her gaze out the window. Her knuckles showed white through her skin, and she practically vibrated with tension, but he supposed that anyone who didn't know her would think her the portrait of tranquil patience.

"Lucinda," he murmured, entering the room.

She swept to her feet. "What's happened?" she demanded, charging up and grabbing his sleeves in her fingers. "Did you find the papers? Geoffrey was here. I don't know everything that he told Papa, but he was trying to blame —"

Robert leaned down and covered her mouth with his. She felt so warm and alive — so different from the cold black story he'd just told her father. "I found the papers," he said quietly, tucking a straying lock of brown and copper hair behind her ear.

Lucinda wrapped her arms around him, holding him tightly. "Thank God," she breathed, her slender body shaking. "Thank God. I was so worried. When I saw Geoffrey here, I thought — I didn't know what to think."

He backed off a little to gaze at her face. It was becoming difficult for him to remember the grayness in his life before Lucinda — everything seemed colored by her compassion and her beauty. If these rumors had occurred a year ago, he would simply have left. Nothing had mattered, nothing felt . . . real — until he'd spoken with Lucinda and her hopefulness had touched him. Even with his arms around her now, it wasn't enough. She felt so fragile, as though she might vanish into smoke if he closed his eyes. And yet he knew how strong she was, how caring and honest.

He wanted to tell her. Wanted to tell her how much he loved her. That, though, wouldn't be fair. She wanted to marry someone simple and amiable, someone of whom her father would approve, someone other than him.

"Robert," she whispered, her brow furrowing, "what is it?"

He forced a smile. "Nothing. I've left everything with your father. I suppose the next step is up to him."

"What did you tell him?"

"That was between two soldiers, Lucinda. I can't tell you."

General Barrett cleared his throat. They both turned to see him eyeing them and the way Robert had his arms around her waist, and she had hers around his shoulders. He would have pulled away, but Lucinda locked her fingers behind his neck, keeping him there.

In his own hands, the general held the stack of stolen papers. "Lucinda, Robert and I need to go somewhere."

Her heart froze. Robert's muscles stiffened beneath her fingers, but he didn't move otherwise. What had they talked about? What had her father decided? She was afraid to let Robert go; she had the terrifying feeling that she would never be able to hold him again. "Go where?" she asked.

"To the Horse Guards, an—"

"No, Papa! Robert didn't do it!"

Her father stretched out one hand. "I know that. Now." He glanced at Robert, and then back to her. "Will you do me a favor, Lucinda?"

For the first time, she wanted to ask what the favor might be before she agreed to anything. She took a deep breath, reminding herself that she had always been able to trust him before. "Of course."

"I assume that the rest of your conspirators are at Carroway House?"

Robert nodded. "That's the designated meeting place."

"Good. Lucinda, I need you to go to Carroway House and ask the gentlemen there to locate Lord Geoffrey Newcombe. They're not to do anything but locate him, and send word back to Carroway House. Robert and I will be there shortly."

"You promise?"

"I promise." He cleared his throat again. "I may be a bit tardy, but I intend to do the right thing."

"I'll get my bonnet," Lucinda said, and hurried upstairs.

" 'The right thing,' " Robert repeated. "You know what that could do to you."

"If this is deemed to be my fault, I will face the consequences," the general answered. "At any rate, I will not let Geoffrey get away with this merely so I can save face."

Robert hadn't expected that. He'd thought at best that perhaps Geoffrey would make an unexpected trip to Australia or the Americas, and that the papers would magically turn up somewhere at the Horse Guards. He'd observed General Barrett over the years, looking for anything that would illustrate his boorishness and cowardice, or whatever it was that had caused him to send a patrol straight into an ambush. Perhaps he'd judged too harshly.

Lucinda reappeared in the doorway, out of breath and still practically shaking with tension. "I'll take Helena and the curricle. We'll get the search started."

"Be careful, Lucinda," Robert said.

To his surprise, she stopped halfway out the door and turned back. Striding straight up to him, she tugged on his hair to lower his face, and then kissed him soundly. "You be careful," she murmured, and was gone.

"Ahem."

The general stared at Robert, who gazed coolly back at him. He could draw whatever conclusions he chose; as far as he was concerned, Lucinda could tell whatever tale she chose about the two of them. Whatever *lay* between them, belonged to them — and no one else.

General Barrett had his gelding saddled, and the two of them rode in the direction of the Horse Guards. Neither spoke; Robert didn't want to, and Barrett obviously had a great deal on his mind.

"We had contradictory information," Barrett said abruptly, his eyes on the road ahead. "We were told that Thouvenot might make a run through St. Etienne the next morning. That's why I wanted information on any troop movement and cannon placement. If I'd known, I never would have sent out a lone patrol."

It wasn't an apology, but Robert wouldn't have accepted one, anyway. Instead he nodded. "What I told you about how I left Chateau Pagnon — that goes no further than the two of us."

"Agreed. I — It might be best if you waited in the foyer. You're not very popular here at the moment."

"It was never my aim to be popular at the Horse Guards." Swinging down from Tolley, Robert noted the suspicious looks from the sentries and otherwise ignored them. "I'll wait here."

The papers gripped in one hand, General Barrett strode into the building. Only to himself would Robert admit that he felt more comfortable staying close by Tolley, just in case he needed to make a quick escape. With its enclosed parade grounds, the Horse Guards looked far too like a prison for his taste. Hopefully the general would be quick and persuasive, and then they could figure out what they wanted to do with Geoffrey. And then he could figure out how to prevent Lucinda from setting her sights and aiming her lessons at someone else.

Chapter 25

I would die to make her happy.

— Victor Frankenstein, *Frankenstein*

"Bit went to the Horse Guards?" Tristan demanded. "Voluntarily?"

Lucinda tried to catch her breath. She didn't think she'd ever driven so fast, but even with wings it would have felt too slow. Robert and her father needed help, and they'd put her in charge of arranging it. "My father promised they would be here as soon as possible. Please. We need to locate Geoffrey."

Evelyn and Saint had joined the group as well, and Wycliffe remained, along with all of the Carroway brothers and Georgie. Everyone had jammed into the frilly morning room, which was beginning to look a bit overcrowded.

"I suggest we fan out in teams of two,"

Bradshaw contributed. "That way if we find him, one of us can return here with word, and the other can keep an eye on him."

Dare nodded. "That sounds good. Wycliffe and me, Shaw and Andrew, Saint and —"

"You're not leaving me out," Lucinda stated, folding her arms. "There are places I can look, as well."

"*We* can look," Evie amended.

"I'm going, too!" Edward yelled.

Dawkins scratched at the door. "Begging your pardon, my lord," the butler said, squaring his shoulders, "but if there's anything I can do to help, I should like to volunteer, as well. And I believe most of the household and stable staff agrees with me."

"Whatever we do, we need to do it fast," Wycliffe said. "Once Geoffrey reaches home, he'll know we found the papers. He could be halfway to Bristol by now."

"I don't think so," Lucinda returned. "He seemed fairly confident that he'd managed to turn the suspicion back on Robert. If he were to run, he'd definitely look guilty. It's more likely he's out trying to do more damage." She blanched. "Or trying to convince Bow Street that Robert's a traitor and needs to be killed."

"Let's not jump to conclusions," Tristan said, though his already serious expression became even grimmer. "All right. Dawkins, you stay here, to collect any information that comes back. We'll use grooms and footmen as our runners, but I think Georgie should remain."

"I'm going with Evie and Lucinda," the viscountess stated.

"I want Edward with me," Saint said, ruffling the boy's hair.

"But where are we going?" Edward wanted to know.

"I'll take White's," Wycliffe volunteered, "since half the Carroways are banned from the club. And the Society."

"We'll take the rest," Dare said, clapping Andrew on the arm. "And his house, in case he's still there."

"Bond Street," Evie suggested, and Lucinda nodded. It would be very like Geoffrey to go and purchase her a trinket to apologize to her once this mess had all been blamed on Robert. In addition, half the female population of Mayfair would be there at this time of morning; dozens of sympathetic ears for handsome Geoffrey's rumors.

"Piccadilly," Saint suggested.

"And I'll take Covent Garden." Bradshaw pulled on his riding gloves.

They headed out to the stables. While Dare helped Georgiana into Lucinda's curricle, she glanced at Robert's rose garden. One of the cuttings had actually sprouted buds. She smiled. Since she'd become involved with Robert she felt as though she'd bloomed, herself.

Dare handed her up. "The three of you be careful," he warned. "Geoffrey was ready to betray his country. I don't think he would hesitate to hurt one of you."

"Ha," Lucinda returned. "He'll wish he had the chance."

Taking up the reins, she clucked to her pair of grays, and they trotted down the drive. "I'm glad we're doing something," she said, after a few minutes of tense silence. "I don't think I could tolerate just sitting about, waiting to hear."

Seated in the back, Evie leaned forward between them. "Georgiana, guess what I saw at Tattersall's."

Lucinda blushed. "Evie, we're on a mission."

"What did you see?" Georgiana asked.

"I saw two people kissing. And not just kissing. Throwing their arms around each other and practically swooning to the ground."

"We were not swooning," Lucinda snapped, her face warming further.

Georgie looked at her, surprise and then comprehension dawning in her green eyes.

"You and Bit," she said slowly.

"I — I don't know how it happened. He's just . . . he's remarkable," she stumbled. "So much more than he realizes."

"You might have told me," Georgiana returned. "How serious are you?"

So serious she couldn't sleep without dreaming of him, or go through a day without thinking about him every two minutes. So serious that if he had to flee the country, she would go with him, or follow. "I think that's between Robert and me."

"Luce, you can't —"

"Look, we're here," she said gratefully. "Geoffrey left Barrett House on his chestnut gelding."

"Let's drive up the street first, and then work our way back on foot."

On first glance she didn't see Geoffrey's chestnut, Hercules, but there were numerous alleys and side streets where a gentleman could leave a horse. At the far end of the street they stopped, hopping — and in Georgiana's case, carefully creeping — to the ground.

Every sense felt alert as Lucinda led the way through the shopping district. She wanted to be the one to find Geoffrey. He'd tried to destroy Robert. He'd courted her, and kissed her, and proposed to her, all the while plotting to sell classified information to France and begin another war. Another war where someone else might be hurt as Robert had been.

"Luce, slow down," Evie called from behind, where she walked arm in arm with Georgie.

"I don't want him to get away," she returned, glancing over her shoulder at her friends. When she faced forward again she stopped so abruptly they nearly ran into her. "There," she hissed.

The tail end of Geoffrey's gray coat vanished into a sweet shop. Backing up, the three friends ducked into the nearest alley.

"Are you certain that was him?" Georgie asked.

"Oh, yes."

Evie nodded. "All right. We can't race back with Georgie, so the two of you wait here, and I'll go tell Dawkins. I'll be back as soon as I can." With that the marchioness hurried up the alley.

"We need to keep an eye on him," Georgiana said, edging back toward the street. "If he leaves before anyone else gets here, we'll have to start the search all over again."

Lucinda took a deep breath, trying to still the nervous fluttering of her heart. It wasn't just she who was involved here. Georgiana was only a few weeks from giving birth, and the excitement couldn't be at all good for her. "Why don't you wait here, and I'll follow him?"

"We'll go together."

"Why don't we all take a walk?" Geoffrey's voice came from the alley entrance.

Oh, no. Lucinda's first concern was for Georgiana, but when she glanced at the viscountess, her friend's expression was more angry than frightened. She shouldn't have been surprised. Robert had a special place in Georgie's heart, and Geoffrey had threatened him.

"Geoffrey," she said, thankful her voice sounded steady. "Thank goodness. Georgie was feeling a little faint. I do hope you're not so angry with me that you won't render us assistance."

With a nod, he strolled closer. "Of course I'll assist you," he returned. "Where did your friend Lady St. Aubyn go?"

"She went to fetch Dare," Lucinda answered. "We thought it would be easier to get Georgie home in their coach."

"Good thinking. Why don't we make for the Dulcé Café? We'll be able to have a seat there while you wait for reinforcements."

Lucinda didn't like the way he worded

that, but as long as they were in public he wasn't likely to attempt anything dastardly. He took Georgiana's arm and led the way back to the main thoroughfare.

She didn't think for a moment that he believed her, but as long as he went along with the deception they had time, and time was all they needed. At least seven gentlemen would be on their way in just a few minutes — unless, of course, something went wrong at the Horse Guards. Her throat tightened at the thought of Robert being arrested and dragged into a dark cell in one of the building's ample lower levels.

Whatever he'd told her father, the general had seemed to believe him. Her father, though, wasn't the only authority at the Horse Guards. *Please let Robert be all right,* she said to herself, even as she kept a close eye on Geoffrey. They all needed to get out of this in one piece — all of them except, perhaps, for Lord Geoffrey Newcombe.

Whatever Geoffrey had planned, he walked them to the café and sat between the two of them at one of the outdoor tables. To anyone else they must look just as he intended — a courting couple with their highly respectable chaperone. When he scooted his chair a little closer to her, however, she had to make herself stay where she was, keeping up the pretense of being pleased by his timely rescue. And then something hard touched her side, and she glanced down to see the distinctive outline of a pistol through his jacket pocket.

"Stay still, Luce," he murmured. "We're all friendly here."

"What are you doing?" she whispered back, noting from Georgie's widened eyes that she had seen the movement.

"Just waiting to see who comes to retrieve the two of you. A man has to protect his assets."

"With a pistol?"

He signaled a footman with his free hand. "Might we have some tea and biscuits?" he asked.

"Right away, my lord."

"Geoffrey, this is ridiculous. Yesterday we were discussing marriage."

"*I* was discussing marriage. You were apparently having a bit of fun at my expense. My home was broken into while we were at Tattersall's, you know."

"It was? My goodness! Did you inform the authorities?"

"I did. Thankfully, my servants were able to give a very good description of one of the participants." He turned his gaze on Georgie. "I'm sorry to tell you that it was your brother-in-law, Robert. Obviously he's completely lost his mind. I only hope he can be brought in peacefully for questioning. I would hate to see him shot and killed like a rabid dog."

Lucinda's fear evaporated. Abruptly she wanted to punch Lord Geoffrey very hard, and wipe the smug, confident smile off his handsome face. "If you harm him, you won't live to see prison," she said very quietly.

"My dear, people like me don't go to prison. We get thanked by the Prince Regent for our duty to the Crown, and we get our promotion and make our fortune, precisely as we planned."

Her father galloped around the corner, Dare and Bradshaw on either side. *Where was Robert? What had happened to Robert?*

"Well, this is interesting. No coach for our dear Lady Dare."

"They must have misunderstood."

"Newcombe!" her father bellowed. "Move away from the table."

"General Barrett? What in the world is wrong?" Geoffrey said, lifting an eyebrow. "Try to calm yourself, sir. Your daughter and I are merely having a chat. Perfectly respectable, I assure you."

The diners at the surrounding tables

began muttering to one another, but Lucinda kept her eyes on her father, willing him to realize that Geoffrey held a weapon. Dare looked angry but not alarmed, his own attention on his pale-cheeked wife.

Lucinda forced a smile. "Good heavens, Papa. You look as though you expect a flurry of weapons fire or something. As Geoffrey said, we're just chatting."

Dare's face went white, and her father's jaw clenched. They understood, thank goodness. "Geoffrey, this is gaining you nothing," the general said, his voice controlled and compelling. "Why don't you come along with us? We only want to talk."

"I'm quite comfortable here, thank you. Where might your blackguard of a brother be, Dare? He's been saying some nasty things about me."

"He's under arrest at the Horse Guards because of you," Tristan returned. "Apparently now someone is accusing him of breaking into your house. I would like you to come with us to refute that."

"He *did* break into my house, no doubt in an attempt to plant the papers he stole from the Horse Guards."

"Geoffrey, put away your pistol, and we'll talk." General Barrett held out both hands, as though to show that he wasn't armed.

All around them, diners began evacuating the tables. In a moment the street was lined with people and they sat alone in the café, just the three of them and Geoffrey's pistol. At least he'd pointed it at *her*, Lucinda reflected, and not at Georgiana. Apparently murdering a pregnant viscountess was too much, even for a traitor.

"Let Georgiana go," she whispered. "I'll stay here."

"I like sitting between two lovely ladies. You're comfortable here, aren't you, Lady Dare?"

"I'm afraid all the hot air coming from you is making me a bit lightheaded," Georgie snapped. "Put your damned gun away. If you hurt either of us you'll be grateful you can only die once."

"Ah, so we're not being polite any longer? What a shame. This afternoon has been so pleasant."

"And getting more so by the minute," Robert's hard voice came from directly behind them. Geoffrey's head went forward, as though he was bowing. As Lucinda turned to look, though, she realized his sudden contrition was because Robert was pushing the muzzle of a pistol hard against the back of Geoffrey's skull.

"I'll shoot her, Carroway," Geoffrey

snarled, all the amiable attitude gone from his voice.

"You can go to prison, or you can go to hell, Newcombe," Robert's cold, deadly voice came again. "You always have a chance of getting out of one of them, but the decision's yours."

Slowly the hard jab of the pistol left her side. "Georgiana, come with me," Lucinda said, keeping her voice low and quiet so she wouldn't rattle either man.

Swinging around the table she took Georgie's hand to pull her to her feet, and they backed away. In a moment Dare shoved his body in front of the two of them, and her father gripped her shoulder hard.

"Lucinda, are you hurt?" he rumbled.

She kept her gaze on Robert and Geoffrey, both as unmoving as statues. "I'm fine. Robert, we're fine," she repeated in a louder voice.

"Throw your damned pistol away," Robert growled through clenched teeth.

Geoffrey complied. "All right, Carroway. You've won," he snapped. "We can be gentlemen about this."

"I don't think we can." Robert didn't look as though he was finished with anything. He didn't even seem to be breathing, he stood so still, all of his attention on the man seated in front of him.

"Don't do it, Bit," Dare breathed, and abruptly Lucinda realized just how much trouble Geoffrey was in. He'd committed the cardinal sin; he'd threatened the lives of people Robert cared about.

Oh, no. Oh, no. Lucinda took a step forward, only to have her father's hand clamp down harder on her shoulder.

"Stay here," he said.

Shrugging free of her father's grip, she took another slow step forward. Robert hadn't moved; he still had the pistol shoved against the back of Geoffrey's head, the weapon gripped so hard in his hand that his knuckles showed white.

"Robert," she said quietly, moving to the far side of the table and laying her hands flat on its surface. "He's going to prison, just as you said. You did it."

His jaw worked. "He turned a pistol on you," he rasped.

"I'm not hurt."

"She's not hurt, Carroway. For Christ's sake."

"Geoffrey, shut up," she ordered, keeping her voice calm. "He hasn't gotten away with anything, Robert. Bit." Keeping her hands in front of her, she walked around the side of the table. "If you kill him, you'll have to go to prison. I don't want you to go to prison, Bit. I want you here, with me."

Geoffrey made a whimpering sound, but apparently he believed the threat to be real enough that he kept his mouth shut as she'd told him to. A muscle in Robert's jaw jumped, and abruptly she was aware of how quiet everything had become.

"It's just us, Robert." She put a hand on his shoulder, running it slowly down his outstretched arm until her hand covered his.

"I know. I know." With a deep, shuddering breath he relaxed, lifting his hand and turning it so she could take the pistol.

Just as she did, Geoffrey slammed back in his chair. The three of them tumbled to the ground in a writhing heap, and the pistol went flying. Panicked, Lucinda scrambled backward. Snarling, Geoffrey rolled onto his hands and knees and lunged at Robert. She screamed.

Robert ducked sideways, keeping himself between Geoffrey and her. With a quick, hard jab he sent Geoffrey reeling again. Without pause he threw himself onto Geoffrey, slamming him into the ground and smashing his fist again and again into Newcombe's stomach, his ribs, and his face.

"You don't know what it is to fight for

your life, do you?" he hissed, yanking Geoffrey up by his lapels. "You're about to find out." He shoved hard, and Geoffrey went backward through the café table.

"Robert, stop!"

Dare and Shaw swarmed up on either side of them, dragging Geoffrey backward, away from Robert. As soon as they had him in hand, Lucinda scrambled to her feet and wrapped her arms around Robert. People would talk, people would gossip, and she didn't care. His body shook, and after a moment his arms came up around her back, pulling her to him.

"I would die again for you, Lucinda," he murmured.

"I don't want you to die for me. I want you to live." Pulling his face down, she kissed him. Again and again, until he kissed her back with growing passion and until his body stopped shuddering. "I love you," she whispered against his mouth, knowing he wouldn't — couldn't — say it, himself.

And then he surprised her. "I love you, Lucinda," he whispered back. "I wish I could be what you want."

She lifted her head to look him in his deep blue eyes. "You *are* what I want, Robert. Even before I knew."

"I can't . . . be like other men," he returned, heat coming into his gaze, filling her heart with its fire. "I can try, but I —"

"Lesson number three was to have interests outside your physical appearance," she said, swiping hair from his left eye. "Lesson number four was to be able to show the same regard to my father's back as you show to his face. I know you don't like him, but you've shown him more respect than Geoffrey could ever dream of. You're him, Robert. You're the one I've been looking for. I don't want simple. I want you."

"You want me," he repeated, the tension slowly leaving his face. The soft, hesitant smile curved his lips. "You're very foolish."

"No, I'm finally not being foolish."

He leaned down again and kissed her, soft and light as a feather. "Are you certain about that?"

"Yes, I'm certain."

He took a breath, his eyes lighting to azure. "Will you marry me, Lucinda? Will you stay with me?"

She nodded. "I will marry you, and I will stay with you, Robert. I wouldn't be happy anywhere else."

"I couldn't breathe without you, I don't think."

Dare appeared at his brother's shoulder. "And he'd definitely kill the roses without your help," he said, the glint in his eyes far more meaningful than the light smile on his face.

"Yes, there is that," Robert agreed, tightening his grip around her waist and lifting her off the ground. "You brought me back to life."

She wiped an abrupt tear from her cheek. How odd that she was crying, when she was so happy, and relieved, and hopeful in his arms. "I think you taught me what being alive is. So we're even."

The rest of their army had arrived, Saint holding onto Edward's arm to keep the boy from kicking the kneeling Geoffrey in the head. They stood with varying degrees of surprise and approval on their faces. Even her father didn't look terribly upset. Whatever they'd spoken about in his office, the general had obviously been supremely impressed.

Robert's smile deepened. "What?" she asked, grinning in return.

"My knee doesn't hurt. You're a miracle worker."

"I'll remind you of that when I make you dance at our wedding."

He laughed. It was the first time she'd heard him do so, and it was definitely a sound she could get used to. It was a sound she intended to get used to. He'd said he couldn't be like other men, but she didn't consider that a detriment. He would have his bad moments, his dark memories, she knew, but they would deal with them together. She wanted to help him, and she wanted to be with him when he finally felt able to emerge fully into the sunlight. She glanced over to see Evie and Georgiana holding hands, both of them crying and laughing.

They'd done it. They'd delivered their lessons, and found their loves. For an idea spawned out of frustration on a rainy day, it had turned out rather well. Lucinda looked up at Robert again, and with a smile he kissed her softly on the lips. Their idea had turned out exceedingly well, if she said so herself.

About the Author

❦

A lifelong lover of books, SUZANNE ENOCH has been writing them since she learned to read. Born and raised in Southern California, she lives a few scant miles from Disneyland with her collection of *Star Wars* action figures and a Cairn terrier named Katie (after the heroine of her first Regency). She's still looking for her own hero, and hopes he will be handsome, titled, and just a little wicked. Meanwhile, she's currently at work inventing him in her next historical romance. Suzanne loves to hear from her readers, and may be reached at:

c/o Lowenstein Associates
121 W. 27th Street, Suite 601
New York, New York 10001
Or send her an e-mail at
suziee@earthlink.net
Visit her website at
www.suzanneenoch.com

512

M Smith
EP Fielders
Mary O.

ME
B B
SLM